SYNOPSIS

It was Frank's destiny to become a boss. Having been raised by a kingpin, Frank was groomed to follow in his footsteps. Stanley had begun to teach Frank the game when he was only ten years old, but love was never part of the curriculum.

When CeCe met Frank, she was drawn to him like a moth to a flame. She thought their love would last forever. Even though her mother hated him, CeCe fell in love with Frank Disciple. He showered her with any and everything her heart desired, but the one thing she needed from him, money couldn't buy.

Buck, Frank's long-time right hand, had his own unconventional ways he inherited from Stanley. As a pimp, Buck prefers the triad he's made a home with, but his unconventional lifestyle clashes combatively with Queen. For years, they constantly bumped heads. But one fateful moment forces Queen to have his back, leading them both to see each other in a new light. But they can't react to their feelings for one another because they both belong to someone else.

As Frank fights for a second chance with CeCe, he finds himself entangled in the struggle to maintain the empire he has inherited. Despite his efforts to keep things running smoothly, his distro is determined to push him into increasingly difficult situations, forcing him to navigate treacherous territory where every decision could have dire consequences.

As the lines between love and loyalty blur, this standalone unfolds into a gripping tale of second chances and enemies to lovers. Will Frank and CeCe find their way back to each other, and can Buck and Queen overcome their differences to feed the fire burning between them?

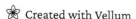 Created with Vellum

ABOUT THE AUTHOR

National Best Selling Author, Jessica N. Watkins, was born on April 1st in Chicago, Illinois. She obtained a Bachelor of Arts with Focus in Psychology from DePaul University and a Masters of Applied Professional Studies with a focus in Business Administration from the like institution. Working in Hospital Administration for most of her career, Watkins has also been an author of fiction literature since the young age of nine. Eventually, she used writing as an outlet during her freshmen year of high school as a single parent: "In the third grade, I entered a short story contest with a fiction tale of an apple tree that refused to grow despite the efforts of the darling main character. My writing evolved from apple trees to my seventh and eighth-grade classmates paying me to read novels I wrote about kids our age living the lives our parents wouldn't dare let us".

In September 2013, Jessica's novel, Secrets of a Side Bitch reached #1 on multiple charts, which catapulted her successful career in the Urban Fiction book industry and labeled her a national best-selling author. Since, Watkins' novels have matured into steamy, humorous, and realistic tales of African American Romance and Urban Fiction.

Jessica N. Watkins is available for talks, workshops, or book signings. Email her at authorjwatkins@gmail.com.

FOLLOW JESSICA ON SOCIAL MEDIA:
Instagram - @authorjwatkins
TikTok- @authorjwatkins
Twitter - @authorjwatkins
Facebook - @jwpresents
Facebook Group -
https://www.facebook.com/groups/femistryfans

CAPO
FRANK "CAPO" DISCIPLE

JESSICA N. WATKINS

WARNING:

Capo is a standalone that can be followed without reading anything prior. However, Frank, CeCe, Buck, and Queen were introduced to readers in the Property of a Rich Nigga series, **where the ending of this book was already written**.

PROLOGUE
YEAR 1996

1

FRANK "CAPO" DISCIPLE

The somber melody of a lone violin played softly in the background, draping a solemn veil over the funeral procession. I stood on the outskirts of the gathering, light-brown eyes hidden behind a pair of dark sunglasses, face a stoic mask. My boss, Stanley Barnes, lay in a polished mahogany casket adorned with lilies, surrounded by wreaths of white roses, which was a symbol of respect among the criminal elite.

The funeral was held in a big old church with towering arched ceilings that resembled a huge vault of hidden mysteries. Stained-glass windows filtered the afternoon sunlight, casting an assortment of colors on the mourners who had come to pay their respects. The pews were filled beyond capacity, proving Stanley's popularity in both the drug game and the community. Men and women in dark formal attire sat in quiet reverence. I recognized many faces from my years in the business. Both allies and opps had gathered, united in their shared grief.

The unmistakable police presence was evident, as the cobalt hue of their uniforms blatantly contrasted with the dark clothing worn by others. Officers watched with a careful eye. They weren't convinced that the gangsters from far and wide had agreed to put all beef aside that day. But the church, for this brief moment, was a sanctuary of unity where feuds had been put on hold and grievances set aside.

Grief pressed down on me like a heavy, unbearable weight that crushed my soul. Stanley had filled the role of a father in my life. He had been the only resemblance of family that had ever extended a caring hand. He'd been the one to teach me, to shield me when the streets threatened to devour me. I clenched and unclenched my fists inside my coat pockets. I couldn't allow my emotions to get the better of me, not when my mentor had been such a master of control.

As the procession moved along, I observed my fellow mourners. My eyes caught a glimpse of Stanley's widow, Eleanor, her tear-stained face etched with sorrow. She sat in the front row, her trembling hands clutching a handkerchief.

The priest's voice resonated throughout the church, offering words of comfort and hope, although they fell like distant echoes on my ears. I couldn't help but think of all the times me and Stanley had sat in his office, plotting, conspiring, and sometimes even laughing. I felt the weight of the legacy Stanley had left me and the burden of keeping it alive. The memories threatened to overwhelm me, but I remained persistent in my silence, controlling my emotions, not letting a nigga see me weak just like Stanley had taught me.

As I approached the casket, a lump formed in my throat. I could hardly look at Stanley. The sight of him lying there so still and lifeless stirred a storm of emotions within me. The sadness was overpowering, but beneath that sorrow was smoldering anger. Anger at the fact that he'd left us so soon, anger that his own bad habits had taken him away.

Most gangsters met their end through violence in the heart of the brutal hoods we often occupied. It was an expected occupational hazard. But Stanley had defied the odds, succumbing to the silent menace of his own vices. Despite the countless warnings from his doctors, the warnings to eat right and take care of his health, he'd refused to listen. He had always been stubborn, a trait that had served him well in our line of work. But eventually, it had been his downfall. Stanley had died of a heart attack, a fate none of us had anticipated. The man who had stared death in the face countless times had been demolished by something as mundane as his own negligence. It was a bitter irony and it left me with a bitter taste in my mouth.

As I gazed down at his lifeless form, I mentally gave my own eulogy.

I owe you everything, Stanley. You taught me the ropes, showed me the way, and now, you've left me to navigate this game without you. But I won't let your legacy fade. I'll carry it forward to make sure your name lives on, that it rings bells in these streets. Rest in peace, old man.

As I stood there, my emotions churning, my right hand, Buck, was right beside me. We were as close as brothers, and Stanley had been a father figure to us. Buck's eyes were misted with unshed tears. His face bore the same combination of grief and anger that I felt. He, too, had lost a father figure, and the pain was etched on his features.

Buck put a comforting arm around my shoulder. The gesture spoke to our shared grief. Together, we stared down at Stanley, each offering silent farewells to the man who had meant so much to us.

As Buck and I said our goodbyes, I felt renewed determination to honor Stanley's memory. It wasn't just for me anymore. It was for Buck and for the legacy that had bound us together as a family.

After a moment that felt like an eternity, I finally mustered the strength to walk away from Stanley's casket. Buck walked beside me as we approached Eleanor who sat there with her tear-soaked eyes fixated on the casket. Her body gently swayed back and forth.

"Eleanor," my deep voice called out gently. "I'm so sorry for your loss. I can't imagine how you must be feeling right now."

Being like a son to Stanley, I had been right by her side since his death. So, I had said these words to her many times since he'd passed away a week ago. But it felt as if I couldn't say them enough.

Buck nodded in agreement. His reply was just as sincere. "You know you can count on us just like you always have. Anything you need, anything at all, we're here for you."

Eleanor looked up at us. Though her eyes were tired and sad, they were also filled with gratitude. She had known us for years. She understood the depth of our loyalty to her and Stanley so she knew there was sincerity in our promise. "Thank you, both of you," her quivering voice replied. "You know you two are like sons to me too. So, I will appreciate it."

As Eleanor wiped away a tear, I placed a hand on her shoulder. "Of course."

Buck offered her a reassuring nod. "We'll be here for you, no matter what."

Eleanor mustered a weak smile. I knelt down, encircling her fragile frame in a warm and tight embrace.

Her feeble sobs tugged at my heartstrings as I held her close. Reluctantly, I released her and turned my gaze to Jovian, her and Stanley's only child. As Buck comforted Eleanor, Jovian rose and extended his hand for a handshake. We greeted one another with sharp nods.

As our hands met in a firm grip, he said, "Although my father is gone, know that you and Buck still hold the same positions in this organization. I wouldn't want anybody else by my side as I take over for my father."

I concealed my disapproval behind a brief nod and replied, "No doubt."

———

"Now that my father is buried, we need to get back to business. I need you to call a meeting with the crew within the next few days. There are some changes I'll be implementing."

Buck tilted his head, casting a scrutinizing gaze down on Jovian's shorter stature. "Changes like what?"

Jovian's smug grin irritated my nerves, causing a jolt of annoyance in my gut. "Most importantly, distribution. It's too many connects with their hands on our product. We need to be more exclusive."

A scowl contorted my face as I watched Jovian casually gnaw on the toothpick wedged between his teeth, idly spinning it with his fingers.

"So, you're trying to get rid of some of the crew?"

He nodded confidently. "Absolutely. My father was too fucking friendly."

Buck slid his hands into his pockets, something that I knew was an attempt to restrain the urge to unleash his fists on Jovian's smug expression. "Your father showed gratitude to those who were loyal to him," he told Jovian.

Jovian cockily waved him off. "Our product is pure, uncut. If less connects have their hands on it, we can make niggas pay top dollar for this shit."

Buck's bushy brows met together. But before he could say anything, I gave him a telling glare.

He remained quiet as Jovian grabbed my shoulder. "Set that meeting up and let me know when it is." He walked away without requiring any agreement from me.

Buck growled as he allowed his frustrations to surface. "He didn't even wait for Stanley's body to get cold before he started fucking up the business."

I slowly shook my head. "There is going to be a fucking war if he does this."

Buck's nostrils flared. "And you know this is only the beginning. Jovian's head has gotten big already. He's going to ruin everything his father built."

Amidst the subdued chatter and clinking glasses at the repast, Buck and I stood by the bar. Our eyes remained fixed on Jovian who stood with an air of cockiness that irked us to no end. Stanley had always known that Jovian needed grooming. Because of that, Stanley had leaned heavily on me and Buck. With Stanley's untimely passing, the looming dread of Jovian assuming control and potentially tarnishing the legacy we had collectively built was becoming a reality.

As the whispers of the mourners surrounded us, I leaned in closer to Buck while glaring at Jovian. "You're right. And Stanley knew that. This square is nowhere near ready to take the reins. This goofy motherfucka ain't equip to run shit."

Buck tapped my shoulder. "You know as well as I do that Stanley would've wanted you to take over."

It was evident to everyone in the game that even though Jovian was Stanley's blood, Buck and I were his left and right hands, his most trusted soldiers. We were the ones he could truly depend on as he tried to mold Jovian into a suitable heir to the Barnes Family throne. Yet, time and time again, Jovian had proved himself to be immature, overly confident, and too ornery to accept his father's knowledge.

But Buck and I had been his protégés since we were children. We were always by his side, thirsty to learn. Buck had embodied Stanley's solid sense of security, muscle, and loyalty. I had absorbed Stanley's sharp intelligence and calculation, fueled by my unquenchable thirst for the role of a boss.

After taking a sip of my drink, I told Buck, "Stanley never had a chance to make his wishes clear, but we know what he would've wanted. We can't let Jovian ruin everything we've worked for. We gotta handle this situation."

We exchanged a knowing look. It was a daunting task, one that meant going against the very blood that flowed through Stanley's veins. But we understood what needed to be done, even if it meant plotting Jovian's demise to preserve the empire Stanley had built.

We knew Stanley well. So, we also knew that he would rather us do this than to allow his entire empire to crumble. We owed this to Stanley, the man who had stepped in to raise two fatherless sons, born of women who had worked for him as prostitutes. Stanley's life was very complex. Besides being one of the biggest narcotics distributors in the Midwest, he'd also been a pimp.

My mother had been favored by Stanley, and it was this favor that had allowed her to move into his crowded house with me when I was five years old. Stanley had lived there with many of his hoes. As a young child, my innocent mind couldn't quite grasp what was happening in that house. All the women, including my mother, had catered to and shared intimate moments with Stanley. It had been a chaotic, bewildering world to me.

Eventually, Buck's mother had moved in as well, bringing him with her. Since Buck and I were the same age at the time, we'd instantly become glued to each other.

At just ten years old, Stanley had fully enveloped us in his world. He saw potential in our young, eager minds, recognizing that our age afforded us a certain level of immunity from the law. Thus, he'd taken us on as his prized protégés, molding us into the role of his corner boys. He taught us how to cook crack and bag heroin. He often used us to transport work as well.

Stanley became our guide in this treacherous game, instilling in us the necessary knowledge and skills to navigate the streets. We used to congregate in the kitchen where the stench of money mingled with the aroma of crystalized cocaine. There, in that makeshift lab, Buck and I honed our craft of cooking the purest heroin under Stanley's guidance.

Stanley had always wished that he could have the same relationship with his biological son. Eleanor had been a sophisticated woman who Stanley had kept separate from his hustle and pimping. She had been fully aware that he was a street nigga, but she'd never wanted any parts of it. Jovian didn't start to come around until we were teenagers. But being a few years younger than us and sheltered, Jovian had been far behind in Stanley's education and he had never truly caught up.

Eventually, Buck's mother and mine had become addicted to heroin. It had only taken a few years for the addiction to make them so unattractive that they weren't making Stanley money anymore. He'd ended up putting them out but allowed me and Buck to stay. I'd never had any ill feelings toward him for that because I had fully blamed my mother. Stanley had taught her better than allowing herself to get so addicted that she wasn't worth money anymore. Buck and I would often see our mothers on the corners that we wreaked havoc on. They were often begging or trying to sell their bodies for much less than Stanley would have gotten them.

We hadn't seen them in a few years, though. We both assumed they were dead.

2

CYNTHIA "CECE" DEBOIS

"I can't believe we're going to Freaknik. I'm so excited!" Tiffany's perfect white teeth glowed as the corners of her lips touched her ears.

"Me too, girl," I gushed as I scanned the racks at Legends, a neighborhood clothing store that sold all the latest fashion.

The smell of fresh cotton and leather wafted through the air as we put outfits together. Tiffany and I eagerly searched the racks of clothes to find the perfect outfits for our upcoming birthday trip in a week. The pulsating beat of rap music filled the air, setting the vibe. Stands of oversized graphic tees and baggy jeans lined the walls. The latest sneakers were displayed like prized gems in glass cases. It was a fashion paradise for anyone with an urban edge, and that's exactly what we were looking for.

"I can't wait to get there! It's going to be so many men there." Tiffany's eyes devilishly rolled as she held up a DKNY mini skirt. "Hopefully, I'll meet a few niggas with some bread."

"Girl, Freaknik is legendary. The news said there were over

a hundred thousand people there last year. You are going to meet way more than *a few* niggas."

Freaknik was a legendary and iconic annual event that took place in Atlanta, Georgia. It was a massive spring break party that attracted people from all over the United States. Thousands of young adults flocked to the city during the event. The streets of Atlanta, particularly the area around the historically black colleges and universities, including the Atlanta University Center, were transformed into a massive party zone.

One of my homegirls from my block had gone with her boyfriend last year. He'd taken a video camera with him. When she returned, she showed us the footage of jam-packed streets with people on the hoods of cars blasting loud music. Women were dancing on cars or next to them. They were surrounded by ogling and touchy-feely men with video cameras. Her boyfriend had also captured women on camera that were nearly or completely naked in public. He had also caught a few sexual acts being performed in a car or on the hoods of them. She had also seen a lot of famous people because of the concert line-up.

I was so intrigued by the massive party atmosphere that I was insistent on going this year, especially since my birthday fell on the weekend of the event.

"Ooo, CeCe, that's cute! You gotta get that!"

My head tilted as I stared at the Phat Farm denim daisy dukes with a matching crop. "You think so?"

"Yes, your booty is going to look so good in that."

I frowned, looking down at my slim frame. I was far from skinny, but I wasn't as thick as the vixens in music videos. "My booty isn't big enough."

Sucking her teeth, Tiffany waved her hand dismissively.

"Whatever. You have just the right amount of curves for your size."

Just as the next song started to play over the store's surround sound, Tiffany gasped with a cheesy grin. "Ooo, this is my song!" When the beat dropped, she started to snap her fingers and dance in place. "*You're the one for meeeee. You can call on meeeee. Is all I want us to beeee. You're the one for meeee.*"

The beat was so infectious that I started to dance in place as well as I sang along with Tiffany to "You're The One For Me." "*I know that you're somebody else's guy. But these feelings that I have for you I can't deny. She doesn't treat you the way you want her to. So come on, stop running. I wanna get with you.*"

Soon, Tiffany and I had abandoned the racks of clothes and were singing and dancing in crazy anticipation of a trip that felt as if it was going to be life changing.

———

As Tiffany and I stepped off the CTA bus at 79th and Morgan, there was so much lively energy surrounding us. Saturday nights on the south side of Chicago were always vibrant and alive and tonight was no exception.

Navigating through the crowded corner, Tiffany and I carried our shopping bags and made our way down the sidewalk, heading towards our homes just a block south. The sounds of cars honking, loud conversation, and music blasting from nearby shops created a perfect picture of living in the hood. The streetlights illuminated the block, casting a warm glow on the ghetto weekend shenanigans.

"Aye, shawty!" a deep voice catcalled from a porch as we passed by.

The block was littered with other women, so Tiffany and I continued walking.

"Shawty! Chocolate with the long hair, I know you hear me!" He stepped out of the shadows and looked directly at me and Tiffany.

Since Tiffany had a lighter complexion, I assumed he was talking to me. Not losing my quick pace, I looked over my shoulder. Through the darkness, I could see baggy jeans and a Bulls jersey. A fitted cap with a huge clock on the front of it covered his eyes.

"No, thank you. I have a boyfriend," I lied.

"I didn't ask you that," he quickly shot back.

"Oh God," I groaned as I faced the direction that I was going.

"Aye, chill," I heard a familiar voice say from the curb to the catcaller. Then it addressed me, "What's up, CeCe?"

Looking towards the curb, I saw Pep, the neighborhood mechanic leaning against his Chevy.

I smiled, "Hey, Pep." I continued following Tiffany toward our homes.

Tiffany's house was closer, so she reached her doorstep first. We paused at her steps for a moment, catching our breaths after the brisk walk.

"Why are you always lying about having a boyfriend?" Tiffany asked, slight irritation causing her eyes to roll a bit.

I leaned against her banister, clicking my tongue. "I'm not about to waste my time with these men who wanna play games."

"You didn't even give him a chance to see if he played games or not. He was cute."

I shook my head, insisting, "I'm good."

"You haven't had a boyfriend since junior year, girl," she reminded me.

"All of these guys are full of shit."

Tiffany raised a brow, knowing the root of my distrust in men. "Every guy won't be like DeMarco."

"These guys aren't serious. If they were, their approach would be different. They're just trying to get some ass."

"Umph," she grunted with a sigh. "You better not be acting like that in Atlanta."

I looked at Tiffany, a smile spreading across my face. "If I meet a real nigga, I won't."

Tiffany tossed her head from side to side, wearing a mocking smirk. "Okay, girl. I'll talk to you later. Are you coming back outside after you put your stuff up?"

"After I eat, yeah."

"Cool. I'll be out here."

As we hugged tightly, our shopping bags squeezed between us. With that, we released each other and went our separate ways. The sights, sounds, and chaos of the block were so familiar and felt like home. It was the beginning of April. The snow had melted, and the temps were warming. The hood was defrosting and coming back to life.

Unfortunately, the warmer weather reminded me of summer nights that were supposed to be spent walking in the perfect weather hand in hand with a man. The usual heartbreak set in as I climbed the front steps of my home on the corner. Every thought of dating brought me the same grief. I had had my first relationship with DeMarco Pontiac freshman year of high school. I was so in love. We'd had plans of going to college down south together. I was so excited about our prom night that I would have dreams about it. But he suddenly broke up with me in our junior year. He never gave me a real explanation. So, I never knew why until I saw him at the mall holding hands with a pregnant girl.

I hadn't dated since.

I walked through the front door, greeted by the enticing scent of fried chicken and cornbread wafting through the air. Instantly, my stomach growled in response, reminding me just how hungry I was. I hastily placed my shopping bags in my room, my appetite taking priority over anything else.

Racing to the bathroom sink, I washed my hands quickly while listening to the sound of my parents' laughter and the clinking of utensils. With my hands now clean, I made my way down the hall. As I entered the kitchen, I greeted my parents, "Hey, Ma. Hey, Dad." Approaching the table, I bent down and kissed them both on the cheek.

"Hey, baby," my daddy replied.

My mama simply accepted my kiss because her mouth was full. But her eyes twinkled with affection.

"Mmm, it smells so good in here," I exclaimed.

"Your mama put her foot in this chicken," he said.

The flirtatious glances my mama exchanged with my daddy, filled with unspoken understanding, were a constant reminder of the love and commitment that defined their relationship. Witnessing their unwavering bond for almost two decades, I had learned not to settle for anything less than a genuine connection. Men who played games or lacked sincerity had no place in my life.

In the twenty-five years my parents had spent together, I had never once heard my father raise his voice in anger at my mother. His demeanor was always gentle strength as he confidently assumed his role as the head of our household. He had the remarkable ability to remain patient and composed no matter what the situation was. I had never seen him get physical with her and I had never heard her speak of him being with another woman.

My daddy's adoration for my mother was evident in his every action. From the tender way he held her hand to the thoughtful gestures he made, it was clear that she had held the key to his heart since they'd met. And my mother reciprocated his love wholeheartedly, embracing her role as a devoted wife with grace and steadfast loyalty. Their relationship was the textbook definition of a partnership built on trust, respect, loyalty, and unwavering support. Their love story had become the foundation I wished to build my own relationships on, knowing that anything less than a love that mirrored theirs would never be enough.

ANTHONY "BUCK" PATTERSON

As I crouched in the shadows of a stolen car, the darkness of the night hid me like a cloak. Beside me, Frank was as still as a statue. His eyes were fixed on the entrance of the venue where the repast was still in full swing. We were waiting for our chance to put an end to the short-lived rise of Jovian's power over us.

The music, murmurs, and laughter from inside the venue seeped through the closed doors. Tension gripped us in the cold, damp alley. I clenched my fists, feeling the weight of the responsibility that had fallen on our shoulders. Frank and I had always respected the way that Stanley had run our crew. He'd been genuine, loyal, and deeply committed to fairness. His actions had been what had shaped our organization's core values. Because of how he'd run our crew, we'd experienced minimal issues, and our soldiers remained consistently loyal. Because of his character, Frank and I knew that Jovian was going to be a significant deviant from the honorable way that his father had led the crew. He would bring in an era of deceit, disloyalty, and uncontrolled bias. His arrogance and reckless-ness would lead us down a dangerous and deadly path.

I had always felt a profound level of self-esteem for being a part of this organization because of its sense of honor and purpose. Now, it felt like everything we had worked for was hanging in the balance. We couldn't allow someone like Jovian to lead us into chaos, even though he was Stanley's one and only biological son.

The minutes stretched into what felt like hours. Frank's jaw clenched, his eyes never leaving the door. We had to be patient, bide our time, and strike when the moment was right.

By the time Frank and I made the decision to slip away from the repast, a substantial amount of attendees had already left. As we concealed ourselves in the shadows, we observed the last few stragglers teetering and swaying as they exited the double doors, their legs unsteady from the generosity of the open bar. Finally, Eleanor emerged from the dimly-lit venue, her arm interlinked with the arm of her eldest brother's. The sight drew an audible sigh of relief from Frank and me. We were grateful that her departure preceded the inevitable murderous blood-shed about to erupt.

"We can't hit nobody but him."

I looked towards Frank as he stared out of the passenger's window. He watched Eleanor and her brother pull off while he toyed with the Mag that sat on his lap.

"I know," I replied, though I knew that Frank had been talking to himself since he would be the shooter. "Because of his cockiness, he got a lot of enemies," I reassured my right hand.

"So, it's a long list of names that want his head."

Though Frank's eyes were still angled out of the window, I nodded sharply. "Right."

Once more, the grand double doors of the venue swung open and there, as if a portal of divine chance, Jovian stepped out. His steps were unsteady and his movements lacked their usual command. The abundant amount of liquor he had consumed left his guard in shambles. He wandered aimlessly as his hazy gaze fixated on his phone.

Frank grumbled, "Motherfucka is so cocky that he's out here without security."

Studying Jovian, I tsked. "Doesn't even have his hammer in his hand."

Frank scoffed. "Stupid nigga..."

I nudged Frank with my elbow, demanding that he give me his attention. He slowly peeled his menacing glare off of Jovian and glanced over his shoulder at me.

"Now?" I questioned.

"Let's do it."

I ignited the car's engine, parked discreetly in the alley. I cautiously maneuvered out of the alley and inched my way toward the venue. Some of the attendees lingered, engaged in casual conversations, scattered about near their cars or on the sidewalk.

Whenever I found myself in these tense, murderous situations, time had a peculiar habit of slowing to a crawl, sharpening my focus to a laser point. Just like now, Frank had been by my side each time. We may have been the dedicated, loyal right and left hands of Stanley, but we had each other's backs just the same.

As we came upon the venue, Frank slowly sat up. He took his hammer into his hand before covering his head with his hood. Then he pulled his ski mask down over his face. I quickly hid my appearance by doing the same.

Finally, the stolen ride approached the curb where Jovian

precariously swayed, engrossed in his phone conversation. He barely paid attention to Frank leaning out of the window, aiming the barrel of the hammer right on him. Frank's finger hugged the trigger so tight that violent explosions erupted inside of the ride. Finally, Jovian's attention snapped to us. But it was too late. As soon as his eyes laid on the menacing sight of the barrel, remorse burdened his shoulders. Regret crept into his gaze, and his guard went up. But it was pointless. Before he could take cover, bullets tore through his once-athletic frame, turning the night into a canvas painted with blood.

———

Jovian's death had been detrimental to Eleanor. The unexpected passing of her husband had been devastating. Yet, losing her son on the day that she buried her husband had been completely unbearable. She had been inconsolable. My heart had gone out to her since she had been the closest thing to a mother I had ever known. But Jovian's death was to no surprise to anyone in the organization or the hood. The assumption of his rise as our leader had only fueled the murderous intent of his opps. So, his death had been inevitable. Frank and I had just fast-forwarded the clock. Some rumors had gotten back to Frank and I that pinned Jovian's murder on us. It was well-known in the hood and our organization that Frank should have been Stanley's successor. Though I had been right by his side as well, I was more muscle while Frank had the intelligence and patience to lead us in the same manner that Stanley had, possibly even better. But those rumors were mixed in with so many others that no one knew what to believe.

Three days after Jovian's death, Frank and I called a meeting of all the dealers in the Barnes Family network. Spook,

Ice, Debo, Fetti, Lucci, Priest, Rico, Marquis, Ty, Kofi, Frank, and I sat around the living room of one of the main dope houses that we had been using as our headquarters for years.

As we gathered in the dimly-lit living room, it was an eerie sight to see the vacant chair at the head of the table. Frank hadn't been able to bring himself to sit in it.

"I called this meeting to announce that as a result of Jovian's death, I will be taking the reins of our organization," Frank announced.

Most of the crew agreed with nods and murmurs in consensus.

"You should have been the one in the first place," Rico grumbled under his breath as he ran his fingertips over his fade.

"You're the definition of loyalty and your vision aligns closely with what we all knew under Stanley's command," Debo said. "So, I'm glad to have you leading us. Salute." Debo raised his plastic cup of brown liquor in the air, nodded, and took a sip.

Frank acknowledged him with a quick nod.

"You think just because Stanley favored you, you can waltz in here and take over?" Ty's voice boomed through the room, challenging Frank. "You're a young nigga. You just turned twenty-one. You still got tittie milk on your breath."

Frank's head tilted as his glare anchored on Ty. "Everybody in this room knows that the only reason that Jovian was about to take over was because Stanley had died before he could voice his wishes."

Ty sat up, causing Frank's brow to rise. "Every gangster knows that death is unpredictable. Stanley was a smart man. If he wanted you to take over, he would have made his wishes known loud and fucking clear a long time ago."

Spook spoke up. "His wishes were obviously *well* known because everybody in this room knows but you."

Tension escalated in the room like a pressure cooker on the brink of exploding. The others watched as the heated exchange unfolded, eyes bouncing between Ty and Frank.

Ty scoffed, shrugging his shoulders. "I definitely wasn't aware of shit."

Holding my face, I groaned. "Ty, please shut the fuck up. I don't feel like cleaning blood up today."

Ty sucked his teeth, waving his hand dismissively. He didn't even give me his attention. His eyes were still glaring across the coffee table at Frank who stood leaning against the island that separated the kitchen from the living and dining rooms.

I couldn't help but clench my fists underneath the table, my loyalty to Frank pushing me toward the urge to intervene, to protect his developing legacy.

The room sizzled with tension.

Cockily, Ty sat back, his arms outstretched on the back of the couch. "Look, Frank, I know that you have been by Stanley's side since you were a little boy, but there are some older, more established soldiers in this room that can be the new connect for this crew."

Lucci started to ask, "Like who, nig—"

Cutting Lucci off, Frank suddenly took a step forward, interrupting Lucci. In the time it took to bat an eye, he had pulled his hammer from his waistband. An explosive gun blast burst through the air, deafening us. Many of us jumped out of our skin in response to the sudden blast. My instinct was to protect Frank. Yet, as I went towards him, I realized that he was standing over Ty. His hammer was now in his hand on his side as he stared at the gaping, bloody hole between Ty's eyes. My gaze followed a small sliver of smoke floating from the hole that was now leaking blood and brain matter.

"Ah shit!" Marquis groaned as he realized that blood was all over the side of his face. He lurched forward, spewing his insides onto the floor all over his Louis Vuitton sneakers.

"Fuck! I just said I didn't feel like cleaning up blood today!" I barked.

Yet, Frank knew that I wasn't protesting what he'd done. He was well aware of rule number one: If you make an example out of one, you don't have to worry about the next. He had done what he'd needed to do to ensure that no one else would ever question or protest his reign.

"This is no longer the Barnes Family," Frank announced, still glaring at Ty's lifeless body. "I love Stanley like the father to me that he was and I will *always* respect him even in death. His rules and prices will remain intact. His principles will continue to guide us. But this is the Disciple Family now and *I* am the capo."

3
ANTHONY "BUCK" PATTERSON

The crew dispersed quickly. Hours later, Frank and I stood on the porch of the headquarters. He and I had cleaned up the blood and dissolved Ty's body in Stanley's barrel of acid that remained in the basement.

"This feels unreal." Frank's gaze was fixed upon the block that had been the foundation of Stanley's territory for over two decades. With his loyal soldiers at his side, that territory had spread its roots far and wide, stretching across the state and venturing into the heartland of the Midwest. Now, it was Frank's to control and his expression was a blend of pride and awe.

"This is what Stanley would have wanted," I assured him.

"I know."

"You got this shit."

Frank took a deep breath. I watched as his posture grew taller and his shoulders straightened. "I know."

"Frank!" I instantly groaned when I looked up and saw Queen sprinting towards the porch. "What's up, Frank?"

I grumbled, "Not now, Queen."

"Ain't nobody talking to you!" she snapped with a frown.

My nostrils flared as I gnawed on my bottom lip. "Lil' girl—"

"Lil' girl, *what?*" she sassed, throwing her hands on her hips.

I walked down the steps, jabbing my finger toward her face. "You lucky I don't want to go to jail for child abuse."

She didn't flinch. She glared at me past my finger and into my eyes. "I'm grown."

She had the nerve to push my finger away and walk right past me. "Frank, I need to talk to you."

Frank immediately shook his head. "I already told you, you are way too young to be trappin' with me."

"You got corner boys that's younger than me," she persisted.

"Yeah, *boys.* You're a *girl.* I'm not trying to have you out here in these streets, man. Be like the other girls and get you a nigga with some bread that's gonna take care of you."

Clearly disgusted, she frowned. "Unt uh! I don't want to rely on any of these niggas to feed me. C'mon, Frank. I can help you. The cops would never suspect me, so I can do anything for you."

"No, Queen," he insisted with a stern glare.

But she continued begging, "C'mon, Frank, please. I need to make some money."

"Everybody in this hood do," I interjected, causing Queen to plant narrowed eyes on me.

"Ain't nobody talking to you!" she quipped.

I heard Frank chuckle as he asked her, "How old are you, Queen?"

"Fifteen."

Repulsed, I turned my back on her and shook my head as I walked back up the stairs. "See? She's way too fucking young to be out here trying to trap."

"Shut up!" she spit.

I grabbed my belt buckle as I closed the space between us. "You want a fucking whooping? I will take off this belt and beat yo' ass."

She straightened her shoulders. "Do it, nigga! I dare you!"

"Out here playing tough because you wanna roll with the gangsters. You gonna find yourself in some shit you can't pray your way out of, lil' girl."

"It'll be better than what I'm dealing with, I'm sure."

Her defiance made my eyes narrow as I took a step backward, up the stairs. Something in her eyes was telling me that she had meant every word she'd just said.

Frank dug into his pocket. When he pulled out a wad of money, Queen sucked her teeth, saying, "I don't want your money, Frank."

"Take it, girl." He pushed the wad into her hand. Though she was sassy, she knew better than to not be obedient to Frank.

Sucking her teeth, she began to pout, and she pushed the money into her pocket. "I just wanna make my own money. I don't want to have to be under any of these niggas to get it."

"I know you want to make your own money," Frank told her, his tone softening. "And until you're old enough to, I got you."

Her pout deepened. As she nodded, tears filled her eyes. She sulked down the porch steps without another word.

"You mad at me?" Frank called after her as she moped away from the house.

When she didn't answer, he got louder. "Queen?! You mad at me?"

In answer, she stabbed her middle finger into the air.

He laughed, but I shook my head.

"That little girl something else," I spewed with annoyance.

"Leave her alone," Frank urged with compassion laced in his words. "You and I would have had fucked up attitudes if we had to get it on our own. Lucky for us, we had Stanley. She ain't got nobody."

"Having a pimp as a father and mothers that were strung out don't make our positions much better than hers."

"At least we had somebody making money and showed us how to get money. She doesn't have anyone."

Frank and I had watched Queen grow up just like the rest of the hood had. When we were ten-year-old corner boys hustling Stanley's packs, Queen was the four-year-old little girl who was often playing alone in her yard or up and down the sidewalk while her sister, May, was in school. Queen and May had been raised by their grandparents, but their grandmother was the breadwinner. She worked while their alcoholic grandfather stayed home. He was always too drunk to maintain a job. Since he didn't work, Queen was supposed to be his responsibility during the day while May went to school and their grandmother was at work. But his dedication was to liquor, not looking after Queen. A few years ago, her grandmother passed away. Afterward, things only got worse for Queen. May's father took custody of her, leaving Queen alone with her grandfather. Neighbors could see the house deteriorating from the outside, so we could only imagine how it looked on the inside. As she grew older, we would catch Queen outside panhandling at the streetlights. Everyone in the hood would try to help her out.

But being that she was such a young girl, it wasn't much we could do legally as grown men.

As we stood on the porch watching our block, my flip phone started to ring in my pocket. Motorola had just released the small flip phone earlier that year. I was still getting used to its small size in my hand in comparison to the Nokia.

"What's the word?" I answered the unsaved number.

"Meet me tomorrow at our usual spot and time ." Though the number wasn't saved, I recognized our distributor's voice.

"Bet," I replied before the line went dead.

Looking at Frank, I told him, "We have a meeting with the distro tomorrow."

———

I stepped through the front door of my apartment taking in a deep breath. It had been a long day of hustling, murder, and dealing with the underbelly of the city. The scent of smoke, sweat, and money clung to my clothes. Although it felt like Frank and I had finally accomplished taking the reins, it was apparent that a new era had begun.

As I walked into the living room, I was met with the sight of Peaches, reclining on the couch, her long legs stretched out before her. Her sultry gaze met mine. Peaches was my main chick, the woman who stood by my side through thick and thin, my first hoe. She knew the game and she knew me better than anyone else.

"Hey, Daddy," she purred, her voice dripping with seduction. "Rough day?"

I gave her a weary smile, dropping down onto the couch beside her. "You have no idea. The streets were heavy today.

But it's all a part of the game." I shrugged off the mental visions of Ty's brain matter all over the walls and couch.

The sound of sizzling grease called to me from the kitchen and I knew April was putting in work. The aroma lured me there. Before standing, I kissed Peaches on the forehead and left the living room. I made my way to the kitchen, following the heavenly aroma of Southern fried chicken. April stood at the stove, her silky curls cascading over her shoulders.

"Hey, Daddy," she greeted me, her eyes sparkling. "You hungry?"

I smirked, leaning against the kitchen counter. "Hell yeah. Always hungry for your food. You know it."

She laughed. "Good. I got a feast fit for the king you are, baby."

I watched as she expertly flipped a piece of chicken, the golden crust crackling and sizzling in the pan. April had a way with food just like I had a way with the streets. Next to the stove was baked macaroni and cheese, sweet potatoes, and Cajun corn.

"You almost done?" Peaches appeared in the doorway, staring at the stove with expectation.

"Yeah. These last few pieces are almost done. It's enough to make Daddy's plate, though."

Peaches walked deeper into the kitchen towards the cabinet where the plates were. Before sitting at the table, I palmed April's ass, giving it a firm, tight squeeze. Smiling, she looked over her shoulder and pushed her lips out for a kiss. I gave her a quick peck before pulling away.

"Where's Sparkle and Diamond?" I asked, sitting at the table. "Working?"

"Yeah. They had dates," April answered.

As I sat down at the kitchen table surrounded by the scent

of fried chicken and the presence of these two beautiful women, I enjoyed the peace that ritually came over me once I was home.

Stanley had taken me under his wing, teaching me the art of being a gangster. But he had also shared his passion of the pimp game. Growing up, Frank and I were surrounded by Stanley's hoes, our mothers being two of them. We were right there when men would come and go, when they would leave out of the room with our mothers, shake Stanley's hand, and give him cash before leaving. We could hear him disciplining them when they would step out of line. As adults, Frank went the complete opposite direction. He was a monster with his hustle, but he would put the right woman on a pedestal and handle her with kid gloves. On the flip side, I had embraced the pimp game wholeheartedly.

Growing up, I had closely watched Stanley work his magic. He had hailed as a master at pimping. From an early age, I was drawn to the allure of that lifestyle. The way Stanley commanded respect, the way women flocked to him, willingly surrendering their lives to his guidance and protection. It fascinated me, enticed me, and I found myself idolizing him for that, yearning to follow in his footsteps.

Pimping wasn't just about exploiting women, as some would think. It was about building a family, a tight-knit circle of loyalty and dedication. It was about providing for those in the pimp's care and protecting them from the harsh realities of the streets. There was a twisted sense of honor in it, a code that only true players understood.

My hoes didn't work corners, though. They were high-priced, beautiful clean women who served as escorts to professional athletes, rappers, and other rich, established men I was connected to that didn't mind paying top dollar for good, obedient, and quiet pussy.

I reveled in the power that came with being a pimp. The way the women looked at me with admiration and reverence, willing to do anything to please me. They were my soldiers, my queens, and I was their king.

I had become the man I'd idolized as a kid. I reveled in the loyalty and dedication of my hoes. We all lived under one roof. We had formed our own twisted family, bound by a shared hunger for money.

———

I stepped into the master bathroom of my four-bedroom condo in the South Loop on Michigan Avenue, feeling the exhaustion of the day melt away. Dinner had been the comfort food I'd needed. As I undressed, my body ached for the soothing embrace of a warm shower. Hot water was already cascading from the showerhead.

Just as I was about to step through the glass shower doors, I heard a soft, delicate knock on the bathroom door.

"Who is it?"

"It's Diamond, Daddy."

"C'mon," I commanded.

The door slowly swung open and Diamond walked in, her dark skin glistening under the soft bathroom lighting. Her curvaceous figure was a work of art, and she moved with grace as she closed the door behind her. Her eyes met mine, filled with desire and submission.

"What's up, Diamond?" I asked, raising an eyebrow.

"Can I spend some time with you tonight?"

"I'm exhausted, baby. But I promise I got you tomorrow."

She pouted, leaning against the sink, her eyes fixed on me as I eased into the shower.

I made an effort to divide my time equally among my girls. Peaches was more than just a business arrangement. We had a connection, a friendship that went beyond the transactions. Because she had been my first hoe, we had grown up in this game together, going through trials and errors side by side. She understood me and her place in my world. She didn't have a thirst for my attention because she knew she had a permanent spot in my heart.

April and Sparkle played their cards wisely. They expertly played their positions. Because of mutual love and respect, they didn't have personal feelings or attachments to me. They only cared about the money. As long as they had a position on my team, they were good. But Diamond was infatuated with me. I had met her in the traditional world, but I refused to entertain any woman that wasn't working for me. So, she agreed to come on board despite the fact that I had made it clear that it would never be more than sex and money between us. Once she turned her first trick, she became addicted to making thousands of dollars in just a few hours. But she was also just as addicted to having access to my dick and living under my roof.

Batting her eyes slowly, Diamond took in the heavy meat that fell against my thigh. "Then can I bathe you?"

I smiled at her efforts. "Sure, baby."

She sauntered towards me, her hips swaying. My thoughts had been so consumed by more pressing matters that I hadn't even thought about fucking tonight. Frank, now the capo, had ushered in a new era and the stakes had been raised significantly. Stanley's relentless training had prepared us for this moment, but I never imagined it would have arrived so quickly. At just twenty-one, I found myself at the wheel, responsible for nearly every ounce of dope in this entire state. The excitement mingled with an intimidating amount of weight on my shoulders.

As I locked eyes with Diamond, my earlier concerns took a back seat. She gracefully slipped out of that maxi dress, unveiling a seductive charm that I couldn't ignore. Like a magnetic pull, her presence drew me in, diverting my attention from the heavy weight of responsibilities to the irresistible pull of the woman standing in front of me.

Diamond stepped into the roomy shower with me. The steam wrapped around us, creating a sensual atmosphere. Warm water cascaded down, its gentle patter sounding in the air. My broad, football-player physique loomed over her.

She took the loofah in her delicate hand and added body wash to it. Her touch was gentle, her movements deliberate as she ran the soapy sponge across my chest, tracing the contours of my broad shoulders and the curves of my beer belly. I wasn't ashamed of that belly. It was the symbol of a man who enjoyed the finer things in life, a man who savored every moment.

Her fingers glided across my skin, leaving behind a path of warmth and desire. The sensation sparked electricity, each stroke of the sponge an enticing invitation to surrender to her gentle touch. I closed my eyes, fully embracing the moment, letting the soothing water and her tender caresses envelop me.

Diamond's lips brushed against my neck, her breath a sweet, sultry whisper against my ear. "I want you so bad, baby."

The combination of her touch and the intimate shower made my dick rock up, despite where my head was at. I could feel her passion, her love, in every gesture as she washed away the worries of the world and replaced them with an overwhelming sense of desire.

I tilted my head slightly, a smile playing on my lips. "You're a greedy girl, ain't you?"

"Yes, sir." She nodded, her lips parting in a seductive pout. "You know I am. I can't get enough of you."

I stepped closer, the steam from the shower wrapping around us. "Well, then," I said, my voice a soft growl, "Eat this dick with your greedy ass."

As she eagerly fell to her knees, the hot water continued to fall around us. She hungrily took me down her throat with ease as if it were trained for such a massive size.

"Fuck, baby girl," I growled, succumbing to the tight, wet hug that her throat was giving my dick.

She began to slurp and slob with such intensity that she was providing more moisture than the hot water raining down on us. She held me with both hands, grinding so expertly with her suction at the tip that I could have sworn that I was inside of her.

"Yeah, that's it, baby. Just like Daddy taught you."

4

FRANK "CAPO" DISCIPLE

Buck and I met with our distributor, Alexander, in the lavish lobby of a downtown Chicago hotel. We huddled into a corner, seated in plush chairs facing each other with a huge picture window on the other side, revealing the city's hustle under the warm April sun. I gazed out the window, taking in the vivid display of downtown Chicago on a busy Saturday afternoon. All walks of life, from the suited professionals to the street hustlers, moved with a purpose.

The traffic on Michigan Avenue was a chaotic dance of honking horns and swerving cars. Pedestrians weaved through the urban maze, some lost in their own worlds while others were immersed in animated conversations. Street vendors had set up their stalls, selling everything from hot dogs to trinkets.

Alexander sat across from Buck and me, drinking from a cup of coffee. He was a clean-cut and nerdy-looking white guy who didn't fit the typical profile of our associates in the game. Buck, Stanley, and I had always had our suspicions that he might be CIA or something equivalent, but as long as we kept getting those low prices, we couldn't have cared less.

Buck and I had met with Alexander on many occasions since we were Stanley's right and left hand. So, we were well aware of the fact that his nerdy appearance wasn't to be taken lightly. He was just as violent as any leader of a cartel.

"So, Frank, you're the capo now. Congratulations," Alexander commented, his gaze holding a challenging glint.

I gave him a short nod. "Thanks."

"I'm glad, honestly." Alexander's expression turned into a scowl. "Jovian was a simpleton. He would have run this operation into the ground." Before taking a sip of his coffee, he let out a disgusted chuckle, shaking his head. "It's a shame he didn't get the chance to prove otherwise." As he drank from the paper cup, he looked over it at us with his blonde, unkempt brow raised.

I shrugged my shoulder. "Yeah, it's a shame."

"How is Eleanor holding up?" he asked.

"As well as she can under the circumstances," Buck replied. "We're taking care of her, though. Making sure that she keeps it together as much as possible."

Though he was silent as he nodded, I could see real compassion in Alexander's eyes as he digested that answer.

"Frank," he called in a warning. "I hope you're as good as Stanley was. We have a good thing going, and I'd hate for that to change."

I leaned back in my chair, maintaining my usual composed demeanor. "You don't have anything to worry about. We're gonna make sure this operation runs even smoother than before. Just keep those shipments coming at the prices we love, and we'll handle the rest."

Doubt still lingered in Alexander's eyes. "You boys are

young, and I'll give it to you, Stanley sure taught you the ropes. From our past dealings, it's clear you're all business and fiercely loyal. But I have concerns that this new position might throw you into a whirlwind of attention and money that you might struggle to manage." Alexander sat back, concern etched on his face like a scar. His eyes bore into ours, sizing us up as if he were searching for any trace of uncertainty or doubt.

I leaned forward, resting my arms on the table, meeting Alexander's gaze head-on. "Look, we get it. We may be young, but we've been through enough in this game to understand the ropes. Stanley taught us well, and we've got a legacy that I'm not about to play games with."

Usually quiet and focused, Buck nodded in agreement. "We've always been about business, Alexander. Money and attention, they don't mean much if you're not alive to enjoy them."

Alexander leaned back in his chair, no doubt still scrutinizing us. "I've seen many young men get caught up in the lifestyle, start making mistakes, and lose their heads. It's a dangerous game, and you're stepping into big shoes."

I shared a knowing glance with Buck before responding, "We've never been strangers to money and attention, Alexander. Stanley made sure of that. But what sets us apart is that we've always been focused. Now, with this new position, we have even more to lose, so our focus will only sharpen. You've got nothing to worry about."

Buck added with an unyielding tone, "We've got respect for what we do, for the game, and for the organization. We'll make sure nothing changes, except the numbers on our bank accounts increasing."

Alexander studied our faces for a moment longer, then sighed as if the weight on his shoulders had lightened. "You better be right about this, boys. The consequences for mistakes are harsh."

Buck and I nodded in acknowledgment.

Alexander leaned in, his eyes darting around the dimly-lit room as his tone hushed. "So, onto the other reason that I called you here. I've got a shipment of firepower that needs to hit the streets. We're talking about a variety of weapons, AR-15s, Glocks, and some heavy artillery. There's a good market for it right now."

Buck and I exchanged glances, our suspicions about Alexander's true affiliations lingering like a shadow. It was so apparent that Alexander was CIA. There had been rumors of government agencies using drug money to fund wars and purposely infusing black neighborhoods with guns and drugs to destroy our communities. Alexander fit that bill precisely.

"This isn't the usual stuff. It's high quality," Alexander continued. "It's not going to come cheap. I can get you a shipment of about a hundred pieces and I'm talking big money here. These weapons can get you twice the amount you're used to with the drugs."

In the back of my mind, I couldn't help but think about what this meant for our communities. With his shipments of drugs and now weapons, Alexander was making our streets a warzone. I had to wonder if he was having the same conversation with white boys, or if this was just another scheme to keep our people down and tear apart our neighborhoods. But I had witnessed the way that Alexander could make opps disappear. He did it like a magician. No bloodshed. People just vanished. So, we didn't have a choice.

———

After our meeting with the distributor, a heavy sense of finality hung between Buck and me as a reminder that I was now officially the new head of the organization. The streets of downtown Chicago buzzed with life as my 1996 luxury BMW glided through the busy traffic. As we cruised through the city, I felt the need to escape, to take a breather from the game. The stories of FreakNik in Atlanta had always intrigued us, and we'd often dreamt about experiencing the wildness of that event. It was a place where we could be someone else for a while, where we could let loose and forget about the pressures of our lives.

Turning to Buck, I grinned, the idea forming in my mind. "Man, we've been talking about FreakNik for years. Why don't we make it happen? It's next week. We can get away from the game for a minute, meet some bitches, and go crazy."

Buck's eyes lit up, and a wide grin spread across his face. "I'm with it. We could use a break, just chill and enjoy life for a change."

I nodded as I merged onto the highway. "Exactly. We need to let go of the game and live a little. FreakNik is the place to do it."

Grinning, Buck nodded. "We're going to Atl then."

My dick was getting hard just thinking about the amount of pussy I was going to get in the A. Freaknik was known for its wild and legendary shenanigans. Numerous rumors and urban legends had been circulating about the event. Freaknik was infamous for its massive parties that took over the city of Atlanta. Rumors suggested that the entire city would come to a standstill as people partied on the streets. I had seen videos of intense ass-shaking competitions and impromptu twerking battles in the middle of the street. Major celebrities made surprise appearances. Wild stories circulated about people sucking and fucking in public spaces. The partying went on for days with attendees hardly getting any sleep.

I was down for it. Although I was just twenty-one, I had been so focused on the hustle that I had hardly ever been a kid. I could hardly remember a time when I wasn't constantly on guard, watching my back, thinking about my next move. I was looking forward to being in spaces where I knew there weren't any opps, no one knew who I was, and taking bitches down that couldn't expect any obligations from me because I would never see them again.

A WEEK LATER

CYNTHIA "CECE" DEBOIS

Seated at the dinner table, uncontainable excitement coursed through me. That next morning, me and Tiffany were leaving for Atlanta. I couldn't wait to party and shake my ass. By the next day, I'd be miles away from the watchful eyes of my parents, free to party and act a fool without a soul around who knew us and could potentially tell on us. I couldn't help but grin from ear to ear, my anticipation manifesting as I danced in my seat. However, my parents weren't sharing in my enthusiasm. Instead, irritation and concern had overtaken their expressions.

"I don't know what you so happy about," my mother fussed. "I've heard some crazy, *nasty* stories about that FreakNik."

Before shoveling greens into my mouth, I told her, "Mama, I'll be fine."

"I don't know about this." My mother maintained a questionable and uncertain glare on me as I tried to ignore her inquisitions by putting all of my attention on the plate of food in front of me. "All that nakedness. Men everywhere. Gyrating all over each other in the middle of traffic."

I discreetly chuckled. My mother didn't realize that while trying to talk me *out* of going, she was actually *persuading* me to go.

"What you doin' going to an event called *Freak*nik anyway? What you know about being a freak?" my father interrogated with a disgusted, questionable glare.

"She bet' not know nothing," my mother snapped.

"It's not about being a freak. It was actually started by college students. It was a picnic for students at the historical black colleges down south who were stuck on campus during spring break. It got bigger over the years."

What I was purposely leaving out was that as word of Freaknik spread out of the college campuses and into the hood, non-students started attending the event, turning it into a much less collegiate, chaotic street party.

"I just want to do something different for my birthday. I've never gone to a real spring break trip. It's just a little vacation," I tried to convince them.

"We just had a family vacation," my mother argued.

My face contorted into disgust. "A road trip with my parents to visit my grandmother in Mississippi is *not* a vacation."

Their offended glares made me feel immediately sympathetic. Breathing deeply, I shook my head with a wry chuckle. "Mama, Daddy, I'm sure it's nothing like people have made it seem." My daddy sucked his teeth, rolling his eyes. I spoke over his interjections, "And even if it is, I promise, me and Tiffany won't be a part of any of that. We're just going for the parties."

"You need to *just* be going to college," my father grumbled.

I groaned, "Oh God."

My mama spit, "Don't be using the Lord's name in vain!"

My dad sighed deeply. "CeCe, you can't just dismiss the idea of college. We want the best for you, baby."

I nodded, tracing the patterns on the tablecloth with my finger. "I know you do, Dad. But it costs too much. You know we don't have that kind of money lying around, and I don't want all of those student loans."

My mother's eyes softened as she chimed in. "We understand your concerns, but there are scholarships, grants, and part-time work-study programs. We can figure it out."

I met her gaze and forced a weak smile. "Ma, I did good enough in school, but not good enough to get a full ride or enough scholarships that tuition won't be a burden on us."

My father leaned forward, his expression full of love and desperation. "CeCe, we don't want you out there in the streets struggling, nor do we want you to end up pregnant. You've got so much potential."

I couldn't help but roll my eyes. "Dad, you know I'm not even dating anyone so I'm not going to get pregnant."

My mama eyed me over her glasses with scrunched eyes. "You not one of those lesbians, are you?"

My jaw dropped cartoonishly. "No!"

My father chuckled. "Shit, if she was, we wouldn't have to worry about her getting pregnant."

As I looked at my parents, their concern for my future was undeniable, and I appreciated their love and support. But the path I wanted to take didn't necessarily align with their aspirations for me. College held no allure for me. I'd witnessed countless folks from our neighborhood venture off to college only to return with either no employment prospects or meager-paying jobs that barely scratched the surface of their student-loan debt. I felt content with my position at the post office that allowed me to stash away some savings, ample enough to even pay for my trip to Atlanta.

"We just want the best for you," my mother assured. "I don't want you to end up like these other girls, laid up with some drug dealer, having babies, and doing nothing with your life but being heartbroken by him. I want more for you, baby."

The legit concern in her orbs made my eyes lower in sympathy for the worry she felt for her only child. "Mama, I promise. That will never be me."

5

FRANK "CAPO" DISCIPLE

I lifted Chrishell's banana-coated legs, resting her ankles on my shoulders, giving me full access to her dripping wet center. I drove my rigid dick deep into her in one, deep stroke.

She hissed at the sudden impact of my size stretching her walls apart. "*Mmmm*, yes, Frank!" she immediately started to sing my praises.

I softly caressed her perky, twenty-year-old breasts while I pumped deep into her pussy.

I removed one hand from her breast and put it between her legs. Using my thumb, I gently put pressure against her clit.

"Oh my God," she cried out.

Her pussy began to swell around my dick as I drove it to the deepest corners of her interior while I massaged her clit. The sensation of my touch and the feeling of such a large dick pumping in and out of her drove her body to the edge quickly. I made sure she felt every stroke of my thumb across her clit, sending electricity through her curvaceous body.

I quickened my pace, moving my thumb around in a circle faster and faster as my hips rocked against her. Her body reacted with each movement, shivering, and squirting around my strokes. The wetness dripped down my dick and her ample ass.

Her orgasms were unending, crashing through her one after another. I ground my dick deep inside of her, causing the stir of my impending nut. I released her breast and abandoned her clit. I grabbed her hips, pounding into her pussy deep and fast. Her huge breasts bounced around wildly with every violent stroke.

"Oh shit!" she exclaimed, pressing her palms on my thighs where I was meeting her center.

"Unt uh," I growled. "Move those hands."

I watched her huge breasts as they bounced and moved with my every thrust. My climax was roaring within me. Then the dam broke, and I was pouring blast after hot blast into the condom.

Panting, I fell backwards onto the bed, allowing her legs to relax.

With a heavy sigh, she climbed out of the bed. Like a creep, my eyes lustfully lowered into slits as I watched her ass bounce out of the room as if I just hadn't been deep inside of her.

As I lay there catching my breath, she quickly returned. Within seconds, I felt her removing the condom and then the comfort of a warm, soapy cloth on my dick soothed me.

"Baby?" she purred as she cleaned me.

"Yeah?"

"Why can't I go with you to Atlanta?" she whined.

"Because I already told you this is a guy's trip."

Even in the darkness, I could see her plump bottom lip poking out in a pout.

I playfully nudged her, enjoying the slow, sensual massage of the towel on my length and balls. "Stop it."

"You're always so busy. I rarely get the chance to spend real time with you. You finally take some time to chill and you're spending it with Buck. I'm jealous."

"Don't be."

She sighed but didn't argue with me because she knew better. I was a young, filthy rich nigga. Every bitch in the hood would have paid me to be the one washing my dick off instead of her.

"I'll give you some time, sweetheart. I promise." But I wasn't a heartless man. Growing up in a whore house had turned me into the opposite of what Stanley had been to his women, and I would never do anything remotely similar to pimping. I was gentle, caring, and considerate when it came to the women who chose to give their bodies to me. Chrishell was one woman amongst a few in my rotation. Despite my efforts to treat them all with care, acknowledging their desire for more from me, none of them managed to evoke the deep feelings necessary for me to commit to a relationship.

As she removed the washcloth, allowing the cool air of her apartment to wash over me, the quietness was abruptly interrupted by the shrill sound of my pager. In a city where hustlers ruled the streets, trust was scarce, and the old-school ways reigned supreme. While cell phones were gaining popularity, the streets preferred the discretion of pagers and the secrecy of pay phones.

I recognized the number as the pay phone that Rico liked to use.

"Hand me my phone."

Chrishell reached over to her nightstand for it. After handing it to me, she took my length into her other hand. As she began to massage it, I opened the flip phone and returned the page.

Rico answered on the first ring. "What up?"

"What's the word?" I returned.

"Just trying to catch you before you hit the road in the morning."

My breath hitched as Chrishell spewed a glob of saliva all over my dick. "What's going on?" I managed to ask Rico. My eyes rolled to the ceiling in response to Chrishell slowly massaging the moisture into my growing length.

"I need some more birds before you leave."

"You free in a minute?"

"Yep."

"I got you. Meet me at the spot in an hour."

Immediately, I felt Chrishell's warm mouth suctioning every inch of me. Surprised, my head sprang up, looking down on her eating my dick with precision.

"That's what's up," I heard Rico say as I closed the phone.

My hand went to her head, my fingertips finding her roots. I gripped them, using the hold to slowly guide her oral love-making from the tip down to the base of my shaft. She gagged but took every wide inch like a big girl.

I tried to focus. But, like it had been for the last week or so, my mind was consumed with my duties. I had been soaking up every bit of knowledge Stanley had ever offered me while I'd eagerly studied under his wing. Deep down, I always knew he was molding me to take over one day. But I hadn't been prepared for it to happen so soon. I especially hadn't expected the untimely death that had robbed me of my mentor. There had been no time to mourn, no luxury of grieving for the father figure he had become. I'd had to push the pain aside and dive headfirst into the work, focused sharper than ever. Yet, in the depths of my mind, there was a void, an ache for his guidance that I needed now more than ever.

But I couldn't be weak. I couldn't mourn. So, I closed my eyes and forced myself to let go of the game to enjoy the rare moment of peaceful pleasure.

———

The moment Stanley's mansion's front door swung open, we were met with the heavy presence of Eleanor's grief. She made no effort to conceal her sorrow as she greeted us with a weak, "H-Hi, y'all."

Buck crossed the threshold and drew Eleanor into a warm embrace, planting a gentle kiss on her cheek. "Hey, Elle."

I observed as she clung to him, her grip on his black T-shirt so tight that it bunched up at her fingertips. Her eyes squeezed shut as tears welled, reflecting the profound anguish she was grappling with.

She finally released her hold, opening her eyes to notice Melissa standing beside me.

I answered Eleanor's inquisitive glance, motioning to the neighborhood chef who was holding a tray of covered dishes. "This is Melissa. She prepared some food for you, enough to last a few days since Buck and I are leaving town in the morning."

A wave of overwhelming appreciation washed over Eleanor, causing her shoulders to slump. "You boys didn't have to do that. You've been taking such good care of me since..." Her voice faltered, her unfinished sentence hanging in the air.

I reached out, resting my hand on her shoulder, urging her to stop. "Yes, we did, Elle. Now, let us inside."

Tears fell from her eyes as she stepped aside, granting us entry.

As Buck and I stepped into Eleanor's opulent mansion, the sheer magnitude of her grief suffocated us. The home was a testament to Stanley's wealth, adorned with lavish décor and fine art that only made the majesty of the house feel more imposing. But, Eleanor, usually the embodiment of elegance, was inconsolable. Her tears flowed freely and her usually immaculate makeup was missing. She looked as if her world had come crashing down, never to be put together again.

Buck, Melissa, and I shared a somber glance as we followed Eleanor through the foyer and into the den. She moped towards the couch where evidence of her depression lay. Pillows, a blanket, and tissues cluttered the space that she plopped down onto.

"Eleanor, I can't even imagine what you must be going through right now," I told her as I looked down on her with somber eyes. "I'm so sorry."

I hated that I was the cause of her anguish. Despite my actions, I carried no shame within, however. Killing Jovian had been done for the sake of safeguarding her husband's legacy and sparing her family name from disgrace. Buck's and my actions had merely expedited the inevitable. If I hadn't decided to off Jovian, someone he would have eventually wronged or crossed would have done it instead.

Yet, Eleanor had always welcomed me with open arms and a mother's love, so my heart ached for her.

She nodded, her voice trembling as she spoke. "Thank you, Frank. It's just... it's unbearable."

Melissa stepped forward, placing the tray on the coffee table. "Mrs. Barnes, I've made your favorite dishes. I didn't know your husband, but I am well aware of his legacy. He took care of many families in my neighborhood. This is the least I could do to show my appreciation for all that he's done."

Eleanor's eyes flooded with tears again with both sorrow and gratefulness. "Thank you, Melissa."

Buck and I exchanged glances, our silent understanding of the burden that now rested on our shoulders. We were heading to Atlanta, but ensuring that Eleanor had some support during our absence was essential. The air in her lavish home was heavy with sorrow, but we were determined to provide the help and comfort she needed during her darkest hours.

Melissa delicately uncovered the dishes, revealing a spread of savory, home-cooked meals that filled the room with a comforting aroma. It was evident that she had poured her heart into each dish, a gesture of kindness that did not go unnoticed by Eleanor.

With gratitude in her eyes, Eleanor looked at Melissa. "You're too kind, sweetie. Thank you so much. I just hope I have the appetite to eat it."

Melissa nodded and smiled warmly. "You're welcome. If there's anything else you need or any specific requests, please don't hesitate to ask. We're here for you."

Eleanor's eyes drifted towards the large window that over-looked her sprawling estate. With the sun setting on what looked like a picture-perfect evening, the world outside was a complete difference to the turmoil inside of the home.

Buck and I exchanged another glance, silently acknowl-edging our own sorrow for Stanley's death. Eleanor had always been a pillar of strength and grace, and seeing her in such agony was a reminder of the fragility of life. She was pouring out emotions that Buck and I had learned to conceal. The tears streaming down her cheeks were the very same ones I would only let flow in shadows when I was alone.

CYNTHIA "CECE" DEBOIS

After enduring a ten-hour drive in Tiffany's family's 1990 Acura, we'd finally arrived at the infamous Freaknik. The Acura was a birthday gift from Tiffany's mom, who'd received a brand-new car from her boyfriend. My birthday was the next day, and the anticipation of what lay ahead had us ready for the turn-up.

We'd checked into the hotel on Rainbow Drive near South Dekalb Mall and lugged our suitcases inside the room. The second we closed the door, we couldn't contain our enthusiasm. We let out excited screams as we jumped up and down dancing in place.

"Oh my God! Did you see that nigga with the cornrows?" Tiffany swooned.

"Shit, which one?!" I laughed. It was as if every man we saw had a fresh set of cornrows accompanied with a perfect lining.

"I know right, girl?! There are *soooo* many niggas here!"

"Girl!" I spat in agreement.

I had never seen so many attractive men in one place. They

were a kaleidoscope of all skin colors and builds from all walks of life. They littered the streets and hotel lobby. Catcalls seemed to follow our every step after we parked and entered the hotel. I had always had a fascination for light-skinned men. My current crush was Krazy Bone. I loved his long hair. So, light-skinned men had my attention at the moment. And it was as though all the captivating light-skinned men in the world had congregated in Atlanta that weekend, and there had been a plethora of beautiful ones who had made my jaw drop.

The sound of music and laughter from outside began to seduce our senses. It was the first day of Freaknik, but the party had already erupted in the streets.

"Hurry up, CeCe!" Tiffany exclaimed as she crouched down, unzipping her suitcase. "We gotta go!"

I nodded, my heart racing with anticipation. "You're right. Let's hurry up and change so we can get out of here."

The closer we'd gotten to the inner city, the traffic had thickened. Young, vibrant crowds of black people filled the streets, hanging out of cars that thumped with booming music. It was a scene of unadulterated joy with people dancing, laughing, and relishing every moment.

I had never seen anything like it.

We were in the heart of Freaknik, and the streets had already transformed into a vibrant party. We were about to dive headfirst into this unforgettable experience.

Music flowed through the closed window, vibrating the walls of our hotel room. Laughter, cheers, and the enticing aroma of street food wafted in from the streets below.

Tiffany pulled out a vibrant, skin-tight mini tube dress from her suitcase that perfectly captured the spirit of Freaknik. "Should I wear this?"

I nodded feverishly as I pulled Daisy Dukes from my suit-case. "Yeah, that's going to be cute."

As I pulled out the rest of my outfit and toiletries for a shower, Tiffany plugged up her cassette player.

While entering the bathroom, "I Wanna Rock" exploded through the room. I instantly dropped my things on the tile floor, anchored my hands on my knees, and started throwing my ass up and down.

"*Ayyyyyyyye!*" I screamed as I twerked.

"'*Don't stop! Pop that pussy! Let me see you Doo Doo Brown!*'" I heard Tiffany loudly rap along to the lyrics inside of the room.

I was ecstatic to finally be able to let my hair down. Back in Chicago, the shadow of danger always loomed over our heads when we ventured outside for a good time. In the hood, the constant threat of drive-by shootings kept us on edge, and we couldn't stay out too late without watching our backs. So far, down south had been nothing like that. The people we'd met at gas stations, convenience stores, and the hotel were warm and welcoming, always flashing a friendly smile, nothing like the stern and guarded individuals we encountered in Chicago.

Being down south felt like a breath of fresh air. Finally, we could have unabashed fun without any worries. As I continued to twerk with my tongue sticking out of a wide grin, goose bumps tingled across my dark chocolate skin. I was so excited about the fun we were about to have.

———

"It's too much traffic." Tiffany practically had to yell because of the loud noise of radios and people yelling everywhere. We stood on the busy sidewalk, irritably eyeing the gridlock traffic in front of us. "We should just walk."

I shrugged. "That's cool. The whole street is a party so we can walk."

"We should walk down to South Dekalb Mall."

My eyes ballooned excitedly. "Yeah! There were a bunch of people in the lot when we drove past earlier."

"Bet. Let's go."

We linked arms to navigate safely through the lively crowd. We joined the mass of partiers, moving to the beats thumping through the city as we walked.

We were awestruck as women walked by us dressed in little to nothing. We even saw a few women walking in thong biki-nis. I had thought that I was pushing the envelope by wearing shorts that rode so high that my cheeks hung out of the bottoms a bit. But some of the women's outfits on the street made my shorts look like a choir robe. "Dazzey Duks" was still a popular song, so nearly every chick had them on, but unlike mine, theirs were so short that they looked like panties.

The scent of meat grilling wafted through the air. Vendors peddled everything from Freaknik '96 paraphernalia to street food. The streets had turned into a lively festival filled with a mix of vibrant outfits and energetic dance-offs.

Tiffany and I waded into the heart of the festivities, our excitement building with every step. We gawked at a woman riding on the window seal of a car with her skirt up and ass out while men fondled her cheeks as they walked by.

"Oh my God," I mumbled under my breath.

Freaknik was living up to its legendary reputation.

"This shit is wild!" Tiffany exclaimed with an excited grin.

She and I strolled through the bustling street, our excite-ment matching the vibrant energy all around us. Watching the mesmerizing spectacle, we looked like first timers. It felt like we were meandering through a car show, with flashy rides lined up along the road, each boasting booming sound systems that thumped so hard it reverberated through our chests.

The music surrounded us in disharmony, a mixture of different beats colliding and merging. Hip-hop, trap, and R&B all competed for supremacy in the air. It felt as though Martin Luther King Drive had become an enormous open-air club. The standstill traffic meant the cars were at a halt, but their blaring music persisted, forming a lively audible backdrop.

Amidst the chaos, we couldn't help but gawk at the scene. Women, dressed in outfits that left little to the imagination, danced with abandon on car hoods or leapt out of the car doors, their bodies swaying to the rhythm. It was provocative, an unapologetic display of sexuality. The air was thick with the scent of vulgarity.

Men couldn't resist the seductive allure of the women. They pursued them like moths to a flame, grinding with a level of provocation that left little to the imagination. It was a spectacle of freedom and unapologetic expression, a celebration of life in its most unfiltered form.

Suddenly, Tiffany was being pulled in the opposite direction.

"Aye, Red Bone."

We spun around, facing a group of three guys who were behind us.

"Excuse me!" Tiffany spit in response as she freed her arm from the grasp of one of them.

The devilish, lewd look on his face was scary.

He raised his hands in surrender, his flirtatious gaze meeting Tiffany's irritable one. "I'm sorry, Miss Lady. I was just trying to get your attention."

"Well, that's not how you do it," she fussed.

I avoided the lustful expressions on his homeboys' faces. Every last one of them was Flavor-Flav type ugly.

The one pursuing Tiffany, licked his lips lewdly as he stared down on her tight, mini skirt. "I like yo' attitude. Where you from?"

I rolled my eyes. This guy was so vulgar and ignorant with his jeans nearly falling to his knees and overly baggy T-shirt. Sweat poured from his brown skin excessively.

"Chicago," Tiffany answered with a disgusted frown blanketing her face.

He stepped closer, closing the space between them. "Where you staying at?"

She stepped back, frown deepening. "Why?"

"I'm trying to hang out with you later."

Repulsed, Tiffany shook her head. "I'm good."

As his friends laughed mockingly, his expression contoured to offense. "Well, fuck you then."

"Fuck you too!" Tiffany spat as she hurriedly pulled me along.

To get away from them, we pushed our way quickly through the crowd.

"Excuse us!" Tiffany said as we brushed past bodies. "Sorry!"

As I bumped into a large, broad body, I immediately apologized, "I'm so–" Looking up into his mesmerizing light-brown eyes, his beauty captured my tongue and held my words hostage. He was the most captivating light-skinned man I had ever seen. He possessed the commanding presence and exquisite allure of a god.

"You're so what, sweetheart?"

I swallowed hard, unable to gather my thoughts. "I-I–"

"She's sorry," Tiffany cut in. "And she can show her apologies further by giving you her number."

The dark-skinned, thick guy standing to his left chuckled. Catching her attention, Tiffany batted her eyes at him. "Hi. I'm Tiffany."

He greeted her with a quick raise of his chin. "What's up, shorty? I'm Buck."

"And you are?" was asked of me in a seducing baritone over a foot above me that made me melt.

"I'm..." I had suddenly forgotten my name. "I'm CeCe."

"Frank, baby." His large hand encompassed mine. "Nice to bump into you."

"Y-you too." He was so rough, so intimidating that I felt the need to flee. Taking Tiffany's hand, I pulled my eyes away from his seductive orbs. "C'mon, Tiffany."

I pulled her in the opposite direction so hard that she hardly had time to resist.

Catching up to me, she looped her arm through mine again. "Why did you walk away from him?! He was eye fucking you and he was fine as hell, girl! Did you see that ice on his neck? He has money!"

My heart was still racing from the impact his beauty had on me. "Unt uh. He was *too* fine. He looks like tears and heartbreak. I'm good."

6

FRANK "CAPO" DISCIPLE

"Damn, you gon' keep looking at her until she's two blocks away?" I heard Buck mock with a taunting chuckle.

I hadn't realized that I was still staring at the chocolate beauty. Blinking, I took note that she'd traveled quite a distance down the bustling street. The thick crowd between us seemed like an impossible barrier between me and what I prematurely wanted to conquer. If I were to try to get to her through the thick crowd, I would never be able to catch up with her.

CeCe's beauty was extraordinary. She was completely different from the women that flooded Martin Luther King Drive. Her beauty and curves were naturally stunning. Her appearance was humble. She looked home grown. Her presence felt like a familiar warmth that I hadn't known I longed for until she bumped into me.

"C'mon." Buck tapped me on the arm, pulling my attention away from my mesmerizing target. "We gotta hurry up before we miss the party, Cap."

I let out a low, raspy chuckle, still not fully accustomed to the nickname that Buck had given me since I'd taken charge of our crew. He'd started referring to me as "Cap" and "Capo," which was short for capo régime, a rank in the mafia that signified "the boss of all bosses."

"It's a lot of hoes out here," Buck crudely commented, his eyes fixed on a scantily clad woman passing by us in only a thong bikini. "I could make a lot of money off of a bunch of these bitches."

Buck and I had finally reached Atlanta two hours after the day party we were anticipating. Fully aware that Freaknik was essentially a car exhibition, we had decided to drive down in my 1994 Bentley Continental. It was a masterpiece of custom craftsmanship. The Bentley had been meticulously upgraded with lavish rims that gleamed with extravagance, a sound system so powerful it could shake the ground beneath it, and interiors adorned with tailored luxury.

But once we got into the heart of where Freaknik was and saw how people were dancing on cars, I decided to park my ride and walk. I would shoot a motherfucker for standing on my shit.

When I'd seen Luke's "Work It Out" video, which had been shot at Freaknik '93, I knew I wanted to go one day. Now that I was finally in the thick of the festivities, it was living up to everything I'd seen on videos that my homies had captured on their camcorders and the rumors I'd heard. I had never seen so much free ass in my life. There were naked women everywhere.

Because Buck and I had been successful in the game for many years, we'd experienced our share of thirsty women ready to take their clothes off for us. So, we weren't overly eager like the lame niggas that were hounding the women. I had seen it all in strip clubs. My right hand was a pimp who could get me any top-notch woman I wanted for free off of the strength that I was his partner. Therefore, it had been hard for me to be impressed by the excessive ass shaking that we walked by as we headed to the club two blocks away. Not many women had garnered my attention like CeCe had.

"Gawd damn, it's hot," Buck barked as he wiped his brow with the hem of his T-shirt. Letting it go, he let it rest on top of his protruding beer belly.

I chuckled in agreement. Chicago was just warming up while Atlanta was already over eighty degrees in April.

"This the spot right here," I told Buck as we approached a long line outside of a club. The line reached the opposite end of the block with people wearing pained expressions of waiting in it too long.

Yet, Buck led us to the front of it.

"You on the list?" the bouncer asked smugly without even giving us eye contact.

"Yeah. Frank Disciple."

The bouncer scanned the white sheet on the clipboard in his hand. Finding my name, he nodded and moved aside, granting us immediate entry.

"Let me come in with you, baby," I heard a woman purr nearby.

"You fine as hell, Big Daddy." Another one threw herself at Buck. "I got something special for you if you let me come with you."

Buck and I ignored the flirtatious begging as we entered the dark, smoky club. Weed smoke filled the air, leaving a cloud above the sweaty, dancing partiers that we maneuvered our way past.

As we inched through the crowd, Buck leaned over,

speaking into my ear. "Lucci bet not had played us on this hook up."

"I doubt it. He serves the promoter so I'm sure we good."

As we strolled towards the VIP section, seductive eyes from the ladies hungrily scanned the opulent chains hanging around our necks and the high-end brands that draped our bodies. Their gazes locked onto our obvious expensive style, and their arched eyebrows conveyed their admiration. It was clear that we weren't rocking the usual urban streetwear brands like Tommy Hilfiger, Guess, or Moschino. Instead, the brands that adorned our bodies whispered of extravagance and wealth, statements of our high-end taste and the unmistakable aura of affluence that clung to us.

After climbing the steps into the VIP section, I immediately spotted an empty couch with my name on the sign on top of the table in front of it. I tapped Buck's arm and nodded towards it. As he followed me over, I noticed many black celebrities and athletes in the sections surrounding it. We were surrounded by fame.

We perched on the back of those plush couches, our vantage point over the railing granting us a good view of the chaotic partying below. I was captivated by the frenetic energy of the party. I hadn't indulged in parties often. Stanley had drilled into us the need to prioritize stacking our paper, to stay focused and relentless. Moments of enjoyment were rare, and when we did indulge, it was always in the company of our inner circle—those few we could trust with our lives.

Because of that, the atmosphere in that party was intimidating. I had to constantly remind myself that there were no lurking enemies to watch for, no imminent danger to prepare for. I shifted my focus to the women in attendance, their bodies on shameless display, each one a tantalizing prospect. Yet, in the back of my mind, there was a persistent image of CeCe that kept resurfacing. My gaze roamed the crowd, searching for that daunting beauty, and I was surprised to find myself hoping to catch another glimpse of her.

CYNTHIA "CECE" DEBOIS

As the night fell, the street parties started to take a drastic turn. Things that were only seen in BET uncut videos were unfolding right in front of me. Men were fondling women with and *without* permission. Women were flashing their breasts, lifting their skirts and dresses to showcase their asses and even performing sexual acts in public.

Being raised on the south side of Chicago, Tiffany and I were able to take care of ourselves. However, when we watched in horror a woman get violated by twenty-plus men who ripped her clothes off, we hurried back to the hotel.

"That was crazy," I said with a sigh of relief as we entered the hotel lobby.

"I can't believe that." Tiffany's eyes were still enlarged with horror from what we'd just seen.

Thankfully, three men had come to the woman's aid. They pulled her out of the crazed melee of assaulters and covered her with a T-shirt one of them had taken off.

Even the walk back to the hotel was intense. Liquor had

seduced the minds of many. Tiffany and I held each other close as we pushed past men who were intoxicated with uncontrollable sexual desire. They were trying to open the car doors of the women who were inside of vehicles stuck in gridlock traffic. Some of them were successful and tried to pull the women out of their cars. Many people were still having innocent fun. They were still simply drunkenly dancing in the middle of the streets and on cars, congregating with friends, rapping along to concerts given by the booming sound systems of the rides that littered the streets. However, the unruly aggression and perversion of most of the men was too much to handle.

"Damn, this sucks." Tiffany pouted as we walked through the crowded lobby.

The hotel lobby was a wild, pulsating party in itself. We had to push our way through a sea of people. A mixture of lyrics filled the air with different cassette players blaring an assortment of songs, creating an audible array that added to the mayhem. Surprisingly, it felt like a sanctuary compared to what we had just escaped.

"It's okay," I assured Tiffany's disappointment. "I had a good time. We can go back out tomorrow. Maybe things will be calmer during the day."

"But your birthday is at midnight. We can't be in the room being boring."

I looked over at the bar in the lobby with hopeful eyes. But was let down when I saw that it was closed.

"We have liquor in our room," I told her. Fortunately, Pep had bought us some liquor for the trip before we'd left Chicago since we were underage. "And the hotel is a party too."

If the lobby was this lively, I could only imagine how bustling the floors were.

Tiffany forced a smile. "Okay."

We started to weave our way through the pulsating crowd, determined to reach the elevators. Hand-in-hand, we pushed forward, taking in the surrounding chaos. Suddenly, I felt a gentle tug on the belt loop of my shorts. My initial reaction was anger, my eyes narrowing with a hint of menace as my head whipped backward. But in an instant, my demeanor turned as soft and delicate as putty as I locked eyes with a figure possessing the essence of a gangster and the raw appeal of a model.

"Hey you." Only those two simple words had left Frank's lips, but two words had never been spoken to me in such exquisite poetry.

"Hi." I exhaled.

"Hey, what's up." Tiffany's mood had completely reversed. Her disappointment was now perky anticipation.

He coolly looked past me and greeted her with a lift of his chin. Then he anchored his hazel spheres back on me. "I was praying to God that I would bump into you again."

"Yeah?" I breathed. His intimidating presence had me so flustered that I could only manage one and two-word responses.

As I locked eyes with him, an inexplicably overwhelming attraction surged through me. It was as though we'd met in another lifetime, an instant connection that defied logic. I felt an immediate sense of security in his presence, an unspoken assurance that left me yearning for more.

He was so tall that his head was completely bowed in order to lock those bedroom eyes on me. "Where you goin'?"

"To my room."

He actually looked disappointed. "You're done partying already?"

"It got too crazy out there for us."

He chuckled with agreement. "Yeah, it is complete mayhem out there. I don't really want you out there either."

The way that he instantly took ownership of me was the complete opposite of the offensive aggression that I had been met with earlier in the day. Frank's was welcoming and a breath of fresh air.

I finally felt safe.

"So, you're going to your room?" he asked.

I nodded.

A playful smirked swayed on his chiseled face. "So, your room is here?"

His smirk was so devilishly playful that my eyes squinted with questions. "Yes."

"But we don't want to because her birthday is at midnight," Tiffany energetically interjected.

Frank's powerful eyes softened, and a boyish smile graced his kissable lips. That smile made me swoon. "Word?"

I blushed. "Yeah."

"Then we're partying in my room."

I inhaled, finally understanding the look on his face. "So, your room is in this hotel too."

He nodded slowly with his bottom lip caught gently between his teeth. I found it impossible to resist the magnetic pull of those commanding orbs as they remained fixed firmly on me.

"It's a party," he cooly told me,

His dominance was intoxicating, drawing me in like a magnet. The gangster persona he exuded only added to his magnetism, raw charisma that sent shivers through my slim-thick frame. His lightly tanned skin was a canvas for the vivid tapestry of tattoos that adorned him, each one a story written in ink, weaving a narrative across his body, even reaching up to his neck. I couldn't help but be captivated by the intense colors and intricate designs that painted his skin.

His mature, refined style spoke volumes. The expensive brands he wore hinted at a man who knew his worth. The way he carried himself, the confidence that oozed from every pore, and the depth of his character suffocated me with desire and curiosity. My attraction to him was a fierce, undeniable force, a connection that transcended mere physical appeal, pulling me into a world I never knew I needed.

"Bet!" Tiffany agreed before I could.

Frank looked back at his homeboy, Buck, who was standing behind him comfortably as if that had always been his position in their friendship. Buck agreed with a shrug of one shoulder.

"Bet. Let's ride then," Frank gently demanded.

When Frank took my hand, I expected my body to become rigid. Yet, I felt as if I were at home, like I was where I was supposed to be.

———

There had been very little conversation during the chaotic journey to his hotel room. The halls and elevator were filled to the brim with partiers that weren't against being completely obnoxious and obscene. Thankfully, Frank and Buck served as shields for us as they guided us through the melee. Frank had guided me by my hips, silently staking his claim for the men who eyed me with sexual longing, but undoubtedly making it hard for me to stand on my own two legs.

Every time the elevator door opened, we were met with the chaos of the party on that floor. Women were dancing nearly naked and provocatively against men who stood behind them with yearning dancing in their intoxicated eyes. Weed smoke filled the air. People had attempted to get on, crowding the already packed elevator, but Buck secured the doors effortlessly, forcing them to wait for the next one.

Once we arrived at the thirteenth floor, Frank led me off the elevator. Buck was right behind Tiffany, guiding her by the small of her back. The excited and anticipating glances that Tiffany and I shared told a story that one another completely understood.

Drill music threatened to damage our eardrums. We were pushed by people and couples dancing wildly. Frank and Buck ushered us through the gridlock body traffic of dancing and partying characters that cluttered his room door.

Frank used his hotel room key to open it. Then he hurriedly ushered me and Tiffany inside.

Once out of the mayhem, I let out a sigh of relief.

Hearing me, Frank chuckled. "You good?"

"Yeah." I looked forward, realizing that I was in a very large suite. It even had a nice sized kitchen. Trying to act oblivious to its luxuriousness, I continued, "I heard that Freaknik was crazy, but I never expected all of this."

"I feel you on that," Frank replied as he moved about the kitchen as if he was looking for something.

Since Buck traveled further into the suite, their attention was off of us. Tiffany and I took a moment to share dramatically impressed expressions.

As Buck plopped down on one end of the sectional, Frank bent down, disappearing behind the island. I then could hear what I assumed was a plastic bag shuffling.

"Y'all can have a seat," Buck told us as he waved towards the other end of the couch. "Get comfortable."

Buck exuded an effortless, cool demeanor that naturally drew women in. His rich, dark skin stood in striking contrast to

Frank's complexion, yet there was a rugged sexiness about him that was equally enticing. Though slightly shorter than Frank, he possessed a broad, thick frame that gave him a commanding presence with a hint of a well-earned beer belly. He, too, was dressed in the finest labels and was draped with impressive jewelry, radiating the same unshakable confidence that Frank wore like a second skin.

"I need to use the bathroom," Tiffany blurted out as she turned towards me. "Come to the bathroom with me."

I read her expression and agreed by nodding just as Frank stood upright on the other side of the island holding two bottles of alcohol.

"Where is it?" Tiffany asked as she looked around the living room.

"There is one right there by the front door. The other one is in the bedroom."

Finding the one by the entrance, Tiffany grabbed my hand and pulled me towards it. She nearly flung me inside, before hurrying in behind me and shutting the door.

We both let out silent, excited screams, waving our hands wildly. I leaned against the cool tile of the bathroom wall, holding my chest as I tried to catch the breath that Frank had taken away.

"I'm fucking that nigga," Tiffany said as she perfected her large swoop bang. "He's acting all cool, but I know he's down."

I giggled as I stood next to her, smoothing the edges of my crimped ponytail.

"Frank is so on you, girl," she softly said, swooning and smiling at me through the mirror.

The mere thought of his focused attention on me made me blush.

"I swear to God, you better fuck him," Tiffany threatened in a whisper through gritted teeth. "This nigga is rich! Do you see this suite?! *Fuck him.*"

But she didn't have to persuade me. If any man during this trip was going to get this pussy, it was going to be Frank. With his simple presence and effortless ability to make me feel so safe, he'd earned it. I had to, just to be able to say that I had done so, a story to tell others about my trip to the infamous Freaknik.

7
FRANK "CAPO" DISCIPLE

CeCe's friend had unmistakably claimed Buck as her own. The moment they came back from the bathroom, she zeroed in on him like a heat-seeking missile. She'd planted herself right next to him on the couch and hadn't budged for the entire two hours we'd been lounging and sipping drinks in the suite.

CeCe, with her captivating charm, sat perched on the kitchen island. Her slender yet curvaceous legs were open as my large, towering presence stood between them, gazing down at the tempting figure before me. That night, there was an unspoken determination to stake my claim on that pussy, even if it was only for the night.

"What is CeCe short for?" I asked her as she pulled her eyes away from my strong gaze.

"Cynthia."

"That's a pretty name."

"Thank you." She blushed, lowering her head.

"Unt uh." I gently grabbed her chin and lifted her head.

"Never bow your head, not even when I'm the one paying you compliments. You're deserving of admiration and praise, baby. Accept it proudly."

Since my large hand was gripping her thigh, I felt her body quiver.

It seemed she needed a break from the impact of my control, so I smoothly shifted gears to a different topic. "How old will you turn at midnight?"

She tilted her head, dropping her gentle smile as if she were ashamed to say. "Nineteen."

My brow rose. "Why did it look like you didn't want to tell me that?"

"I know I'm a lot younger than you."

I shrugged my shoulder. "I'm only twenty-one, baby."

Her eyes bucked a bit.

A chuckle rumbled deeply in my throat. "Damn, I look older?"

"Not so much that you *look* older. You act much more mature. So, I assumed you were older."

I flashed a wink, my grin laced with a hint of mischief. "I'll take that as a compliment."

Her captivating, playful gaze fixed upon me, and she sensually ran her tongue across her inviting lips. "You should."

We exchanged playful, lingering gazes, and as our conversation continued, a revelation struck me like a bolt of lightning. My attraction to her transcended past purely physical. There was an inexplicable magnetism, a pull she had on me that defied logic. Throughout my life, I had been in the company of many beautiful women, but CeCe's beauty was unlike anything I'd encountered before. It was an irresistible and intoxicating force, and I found myself yearning to be enveloped by it, to become lost in it.

Suddenly, CeCe yawned. "I hope I make it to midnight. What time is it?"

I understood her exhaustion. All of us had been drinking all day. In addition to the hot Georgia sun wearing us out, it hadn't taken long for the drinks we had consumed since we'd arrived at the suite to start making our eyes ride low.

I looked down at my diamond encrusted watch. Gently squeezing her thighs, I answered, "Eleven-fifteen." She looked disappointed, so I leaned in, asking, "Stay awake for me, okay?"

Her eyes conveyed an intensity that had her rich chocolate skin been capable of blushing, it would have turned a deep crimson.

"Okay," she replied, her voice a whisper.

"When you first got here, you looked so relieved to be away from the party. You're not having a good time?"

Her lips met in a hesitant, pressed line. "I was having fun earlier today. It seems like as more people got here, things became more tense and chaotic. I saw this girl get her clothes ripped off."

My expression contorted with rage. "Are you serious?"

She nodded, eyes widening with lingering disbelief. "*Yes*. It was like twenty men surrounding her, ripping all of her clothes off until she was naked."

"I've seen so many women out here flashing their titties and ass. I even saw a few chicks giving head out in the open."

"This girl wasn't doing any of that, though. She was just walking through the crowd with her friend. A couple of guys surrounded her, separating her from her friend. It looked like a guy tried to talk to her and she refused. He pulled on her arm, and she pushed him off. That's when he started to pull off her clothes. Then his friends joined. Then other guys who they didn't even know saw what they were doing and joined in too.

It was a mob of horny, aggressive men. She was screaming for help, but people could hardly hear her with all of the music and car engines. Because of the crowd around her, a lot of other men started to mob. I think they thought that something consensual was happening. Me and Tiffany were sitting on the top of the roof of a car, so we saw everything. Luckily, a few men in the mob helped her out. One man gave her his shirt. I couldn't believe what I had just seen. So, me and Tiffany decided to head back to the hotel. On the way, we saw so many men outright grabbing women sexually without consent. It was scary."

"One of my boy's homeboys was the promoter at the party we went to today," I told her. "He told us that Freaknik just started getting like this. At first, it was just a big-ass party for college students. It was wild but never like the ignorant shit that we've been seeing today. As word started to spread about Freaknik, more and more niggas started hearing about it, niggas that didn't have the morals and values that most students of historical black colleges and universities have. It turned into some other shit after that. City officials have been talking about shutting it down. Things will most definitely change next year."

CeCe and I delved into a conversation about the other wild things we'd seen that day. The once carefree, vibrant party atmosphere we had heard stories about and seen in old footage had given way to a tense, sexually-charged environment that was no longer safe for women who didn't get down like that.

Though she felt like she was so much younger, CeCe's conversation had a level of maturity I hadn't encountered in other women. It was far from the superficial or materialistic discussions I'd had with chicks. Not once did she inquire about my wealth or financial status. She wasn't throwing herself at me because she could tell that I was rich. Instead, her conversation delved into understanding me, getting to know the man beyond the labels and diamonds. It was a refreshing change, and I could sense that her interest in me ran deeper than the material possessions that I could buy for her.

Before I knew it, Tiffany was springing to her feet, excitedly exclaiming, "It's one minute until your birthday!" With a wide grin on her face, she ran around the sofa towards us, with Buck slowly following her.

I could tell by his slow gait that he was feeling his liquor. Tiffany's eyes ran low, and a playful, loose grin played on her lips, so she was obviously feeling her liquor too.

CeCe grinned at her friend as Tiffany ordered Buck, "We need some shots. Hurry up."

It was obvious that Tiffany was the stronger personality of the two.

Buck went behind the island, assumingly to find the disposable shot glasses we had brought with us.

"Hurry up!" Tiffany exclaimed as she hopped onto the island next to CeCe. She then threw her arm around her friend, pulling her into her as she looked at her watch. "We got ten seconds!"

Finding the shot cups, Buck hurriedly filled four of them and passed them out.

"To the sweetest, most loyal, ride-or-die bitch that I know!" Tiffany shrieked, looking at her watch as we all held our shot glasses in the air. "I love you, girl! Happy *Birthdaaaay!*"

———

I sensually traced the contours of her slick folds, each lingering stroke burying my tongue deeper into her essence. With every motion, CeCe's hips responded in rhythm, pressing against the caress of my eager tongue.

"Oh God!" she panted. "What the fuck are you doing to me, Frank?"

I was reluctant to leave my sweet meal, but I did, looking up into her eyes. The aroma of her juices in my mustache made my dick rock hard.

"What you mean what am I doing to you?" I rumbled into her wet folds, causing her body to quake.

Since I'd abruptly stopped her immeasurable pleasure, her head darted up and she looked at me.

Her chest heaved with each ragged breath, a futile attempt to regain control of her racing heartbeat. Beads of perspiration glistened on her skin, tracing the contours of her trembling body as the aftermath of our passionate encounter left her breathless and yearning for more. "Why are you eating my pussy like this?"

My gaze navigated the gentle curve of her elevated, silken hips, lingering on the captivating allure of her exquisite mounds before finally meeting her seductive, longing eyes. "It's your birthday, ain't it?" Her brows curled together, showing her confusion. I winked at her. "Happy Birthday."

My head dipped down again, my mouth hungrily searching for its sweet meal.

After we'd taken a few more shots for her birthday, Buck announced he and Tiffany's exit. It was pure elation on Tiffany's face when she realized that Buck had his own room. No sooner than the door closed behind him, I pulled CeCe into the bedroom.

I felt a sense of satisfaction as I noticed her lack of hesitation, though, in truth, I shouldn't have been surprised. Her struggle to conceal the impact I'd had on her all night had been apparent. It was Freaknik, after all, and while she might not have been among the women twerking on cars or baring it all, she was undeniably eager to let loose and have a good time.

And I was here to give it to her.

I lavished her moist folds with my eager tongue, each lick a calculated move to heighten her longing. Her desire surged higher with every flick. Just as it seemed she teetered on the edge of a breathtaking climax, I shifted my focus, zeroing in on her sensitive bud. With my mouth and tongue, I began to suck and tease her clitoris, the intensity building as I did. Simultaneously, my middle finger plunged deep into her welcoming warmth, seeking out her G-spot with expert precision, stroking it to drive her wild with pleasure.

"God!" she cried out.

CeCe bucked and screamed as she was engulfed with a massive orgasm. I continued to suck and lick on her clit and stroke her G-spot. Her orgasm reverberated through her again and again. I continued this until she had nearly reached her limit.

"Okay, okay," she panted with whimpers. I felt her hand pushing my head away. "Stop, Frank."

I left her center, my mouth watery with disappointment. As I looked up into her weary eyes, I asked, "What's wrong?"

"I can't cum anymore." She gasped for air, her breath escaping her in ragged, needy pants. "I can't."

"Yes, you can," I encouraged her.

"I can't," she whined.

I began to make small circles on her wet clit, and she convulsed, whimpering loudly with pleasure and regret. "I think you got one mo' in you."

"Oh God," she cried.

"*Please* cum for me, baby."

CYNTHIA "CECE" DEBOIS

My eyelids slowly fluttered open, my head throbbing with the aftermath of all the liquor I had consumed the day before. As I stirred, I realized that Frank's strong arm encircled my waist, and my back and ass was molded against his pelvis. I could feel the steady rise and fall of his chest as he slept beside me, an intimate reminder of the unforgettable sex we'd shared between the sheets.

Memories of our passionate encounter flooded back, and I marveled at the man spooning with me. Frank was so much more than the beautiful exterior he wore. He had a captivating magic in the bedroom, a talent that left me in awe. I'd had few sexual encounters since DeMarco, so comparisons were limited. However, Frank had undoubtedly set the bar high, and my throbbing headache was indeed a testament to the hours we'd passionately spent in each other's company.

It had nothing to do with the liquor. I had a *dick* hangover.

Feeling the strain of my full bladder, I reluctantly pulled myself from the comforting embrace of his sculpted, well-defined arms. I carefully peeled myself free in an effort not to wake him. As I slowly stood, I could feel the fatigue in my legs and the throbbing in my center. I giggled, silently, realizing the inerasable mark that Frank had left on my body.

I padded into the bathroom and then slowly closed the door so that it latched quietly. Once in the bathroom, I allowed my cheeks to break in a grin that spread from ear to ear. I swooned, falling back against the bathroom door, putting all of my weight against it as I hid my blushing in my hands.

I knew that I probably would never see Frank again. I had never been on a trip like this, but I had common sense. Men came to these events to do just what Frank had done to me, but with as many different women as they could before going home. No sooner than I left, I knew that he would be searching for his next victim to take down with that perfect, big dick.

After emptying my bladder, I washed my hands and finally looked in the mirror. I laughed at the disarray of my bangs and ponytail. Frank's large frame had been able to toss me around that bedroom like a ragdoll. Memories of him picking me up and pressing my body against the picture window as he drove a plethora of wide inches into me from the back made me quake and goose bumps sprouted all over my brown skin.

I sighed deeply, collecting myself. "Get it together, girl."

I had been uncontrollable, willing putty in that man's hands the night before, but now that it was the next day, I had to accept that it was over. I had to prepare myself for possibly seeing him in the hotel with his next conquest this evening.

I left the bathroom just as quietly as I had entered it. To my surprise, Frank was awake. He was sitting up, his large, colorful, muscular chest proudly on full display as he leaned against the headboard, a television remote control in his hand.

A devilish grin graced his lips as his eyes traveled towards me. "Good morning."

"Good morning," I replied sheepishly as I rounded the bed.

My mind started to race. I wanted to get back into bed to enjoy a few more minutes of his embrace before we parted for forever. We had spent so much time talking the night before, but he'd never asked for my number, not even where I was from.

Just as I eyed my clothes and shoes in a chaotic pile on the floor, I heard his deep baritone softly order, "Come here, mama."

My heart did a secret little dance, and I could feel the heat rush to my cheeks, a telltale sign of the intense flattery I felt as I submitted to his wishes.

After I climbed into bed, he gently turned my back towards him. He then brought all of my weight under him with such ease, as if I were as light as a feather. He secured me against him with his arm around my waist and his face pressed up against my back.

Though his room was then enveloped in silence, the chaos had already begun outside and in the hallway. Thunderous bass throbbed through the windows and doors, vibrating the air around us. Laughter, animated conversations, and jubilant screams were an unceasing soundtrack to the lively party atmosphere.

The quiet sanctuary of his room felt worlds apart from the raucous celebration beyond its walls.

"These niggas already starting," Frank scoffed humorously.

I groaned in reply.

As if Frank already felt my reluctance, he assured me, "You're gonna be good out there."

"Honestly, I'm scared," I revealed, seeing flashbacks of the assaults I'd seen the day before.

"Nothing is going to happen to y'all. As long as y'all stick with me and Buck, no other man is laying a finger on y'all, unless he's prepared to lose that motherfucker."

My body tensed up instinctively in response to the sudden, ominous edge in his voice. Even though I was aware his anger wasn't directed at me, there was no doubt that he wasn't to be played with. He'd meant every word, and he was ready to back them up with action.

"This is Freaknik. You're not going to be by my side all the time. You might not even want to see me after I leave in a few minutes."

His embrace intensified, drawing us even closer until our warm skin pressed together so snugly that our mingling perspiration became an intimate, shared connection. "I want you to be with me. So, if you're cool with it, then you never have to leave my side."

I shifted to lie on my back, my expression filled with doubt as I questioned the sincerity of his words. He gazed down at me with earnest eyes, a depth of sincerity that left me with no room to doubt his intentions.

"How do you know Buck is down with being stuck with Tiffany?"

Frank shrugged his shoulder. "He's down for whatever I'm down for."

I anchored my gaze on him for a few seconds before finally nodding. "Okay."

A slow, pleased grin spread on his chiseled face as his hand softly roamed my stomach then slipped between my legs. My head fell back as pleasure consumed me when he started to softly massage my nub.

His soft lips found my neck. He began to tenderly tongue kiss it while climbing on top of me. My eyes closed as I immersed myself in the pleasurable feeling of his weight on top of me. He took his time positioning himself at my entrance. As he gradually pushed inside, I couldn't help but release a low, sensuous moan. He slid in, filling me completely, beyond what I could take, and began a slow, tantalizing motion. My pussy responded obediently, moistening around him, and he moaned deeply in response to the gripping tightness of my walls.

With each passing moment, he increased his pace, transitioning into a powerful, unhurried rhythm that left me gasping with satisfaction. My moans intensified and my head thrashed from side to side, completely lost in the ecstasy of our instant connection.

8

CYNTHIA "CECE" DEBOIS

Tiffany and I had promised to page one another before leaving Frank or Buck's room so that we would know each other's whereabouts. So, as promised, I had received a page when Tiffany was leaving Buck's room. He'd escorted her to Frank's suite where we met and then she and I left to go to our room together. Frank was so protective that he insisted on walking us to the room.

"We'll be back here in an hour and a half to get y'all." He leaned against the doorframe with confidence, casting his gaze down upon me, his presence oozing with possession.

My eyes flirtatiously batted. "Okay."

When he began to close the space between us, I wondered what he was doing. Then he seized the back of my head. His lips claimed mine in a passionate kiss, only to pull away with a tormenting promise, leaving my heart racing.

He locked those beautiful brown eyes on me again, licking his lips slowly as he said, "I'll see you soon, shorty."

I replied with a breathy, "Okay."

We continued to give one another teasing, flirty gazes and grins as he walked away. I didn't step into the room to close the door until his sensual, cool gait became lost in the hallway.

I was weak as I shut the door. My smile was embarrassingly giddy.

"*Sooooo*, we're about to hang with them again?" Tiffany was annoyed, standing in front of her bed with her hand on her hip. "Girl, all these niggas down here and you wanna be all up under him?"

"I thought you wanted me to fuck him."

"Yes, *fuck* him, not be lame with him for the rest of the weekend." She slightly rolled her eyes.

I pouted as I walked towards her and sat at the foot of the bed. "I'm not really interested in finding another guy. Honestly, if he hadn't offered to be with us, I wouldn't have felt comfortable going back out there today. All of that crazy stuff didn't scare you yesterday?"

Tiffany thought for a few seconds before admittedly nodding. "Yeah, I was worried about it. But I didn't want to stay in the room. We only have one more day before we hit the road tomorrow."

Relieved, I smiled a bit. "So, at least now we get to go out there without being worried some crazy motherfuckers will attack us." Even though Tiffany had admitted being scared as well, she was still a bit reluctant. "What's wrong? You didn't have a good time with Buck?"

She shrugged her shoulder, wearing a nonchalant expression. "Yeah. He was cool, and the dick was great." Yet, she frowned disapprovingly. "I can just tell that he's a player. He's not on me the way that Frank is on you, and his phone was ringing all night."

"Well, if he's not all over you, then his attentions will be elsewhere. So, yours can be too, but at least you'll have some protection."

Finally, she nodded. "Okay."

"Cool. Let's get dressed."

Standing, I went over to the radio and turned on some music to get us ready to party. Then we took turns in the shower.

I washed my hair, choosing to allow my natural curls to come alive that day. As I got dressed, it air dried, forming into a voluminous, curly fro.

For my birthday outfit, I'd gotten a custom airbrushed short set made. The little dukes had my zodiac sign "Aries" spray-painted all over the back in vibrant shades of red, blue, and yellow. A cropped tank top perfectly matched the shorts, proudly displaying "CeCe" on the front in the same striking colors. To complete my birthday ensemble, I accessorized with big, shimmering gold hoops and a few chunky gold chains.

Even though Frank was just a temporary fantasy I was indulging in, I wanted to make an unforgettable impression. So, I applied some glowing moisturizer to my dark skin and added a hint of makeup.

"You look so cute." Tiffany's eyes glowed as she looked at me through the bathroom mirror.

Now dressed, we both stood in front of it, perfecting our hair and makeup as we awaited our bodyguards, Buck and Frank.

I arched my head to the side with a hint of drama, letting my lips curve into a suggestive smirk as my gaze lingered on her barely-there denim shorts and the revealing bikini top she was rocking with it. "I see you showing out today."

She raised a brow, wearing a cocky smirk on her glossed lips. "Shit, since we have security today, I might as well."

Playfully darting my tongue out through a grin, I sang, *"Owww!"* while giving her a hi-five.

Amid our uncontrollable giggles, a sudden, sharp knock on the door sliced through the music and the chaotic atmosphere on the other side. My cheeks instantly flushed, and an aroused shiver ran down my spine, knowing that Frank was waiting on the other side.

With a hidden grin, fueled by the perverted memories of me and Frank's morning and unforgettable night, I eagerly made my way to the door. As I pushed it open, I appreciated that Frank was just temporary in my life. His overwhelming sex appeal, his effortless charm, and his commanding presence were qualities that, while exciting in small doses, I knew would be a challenge to handle on a long-term basis. Such intensity might have brought out insecurities in me that weren't previously there.

"Damn," he softly growled, taking in my appearance with a slow lick of his lips.

Being under his intense gaze was an honor. The way he looked at me boosted my ego.

He slowly nodded. "Yeah, you were definitely going to get harassed out there with that on if you were by yourself. Ain't no way you should have been out there alone."

"I'm guessing that's a compliment."

"Hell yeah. It's definitely your birthday, baby."

Grinning, I moved out of the way to let them into the room. "Hey, Buck," I spoke as they walked by, their mixture of different colognes swimming in my nose.

"What's up, shorty?" he coolly said to me as he walked by the bathroom. He discreetly looked Tiffany up and down. "What's up, lil' mama?"

"Hey," Tiffany returned softly, still perfecting her big bang.

"Y'all ready to ride?" Frank asked as he sat at the foot of Tiffany's bed, careful not to sit on the clothes that she had pulled out of her suitcase. Buck stood, leaning back against the wall. I noticed that he was carrying a bag full of bottles of liquor.

"Yeah, we're ready," I replied as I sat next to him.

"I just need two minutes," Tiffany corrected me.

"Cool. We'll be on time then."

"Even with the traffic, Cap?" Buck asked.

My brows curled together, watching and listening to their interaction.

"It's in a few hours, so we should be good, especially since we're going in the opposite direction of all the events."

"Wait, where are we going?" I interjected.

A sneaky grin slowly spread across Frank's chiseled jaw line. "To the harbor, sweetheart."

"The harbor? For what?"

He gave me a comforting smile. "I know that you aren't really comfortable being in the streets around all that shit."

"But I'm cool as long as you are with me," I insisted, leaning into him.

"I got you something better, though." He placed a soothing hand on my inner thigh, causing my core to heat at his touch. "It's your birthday. So, I got a deejay, a bunch of bottles, some weed... I rented a yacht."

My mouth dropped cartoonishly. "A w-what... what? Why? Huh?"

He wore a confident expression as he stood. He was pleased that he had taken my breath away. Closing the space between us, he gently grabbed my hips and brought my body so close to his that our bodies pressed together. "I know you don't want to be out there. It's your birthday. I want to give you a gift anyway."

Swooning, I replied, "Okay." I gulped, forcing down the embarrassing amount of glee that wanted to erupt on my cheeks. "Thank you," I purred.

He slowly kissed my forehead. "You're welcome, Mama." Then he smacked my ass before giving me permission to leave his shadow. "With those lil' ass shorts on."

I blushed so hard that my chin kissed my shoulder.

I stood and switched into the bathroom. I could hear Frank and Buck behind me conversing about the boat. When I scooted into the bathroom, Tiffany's bucked eyes met mine, which were just as wide. We let out silent screams, so excited that we were jumping up and down quietly.

"Bitch, you still don't want to go with them?" I whispered with a teasing smirk.

She could only guiltily roll her eyes.

Deepening my smirk, I teased, "I thought so."

———

When we approached Frank's car, my breath caught in my throat. Tiffany and I discreetly unfolded after laying eyes on the Bentley. In that moment, it became clear that Frank belonged to a different echelon of society. He was rich. His undeniable wealth magnified the realization that our time together was only for that weekend. Men of his stature had countless options when it came to women. Yet, despite this realization, I couldn't resist being captivated by the lavish lifestyle he projected.

But as we boarded the yacht, I was left in complete awe of

Frank's efforts and the sheer extravagance that I was experiencing. My parents weren't what the government would classify as "poor." As my father worked his way up the ladder at the plant, we no longer relied on food stamps. In our neighborhood, having both parents at home was a rarity, but our income only stretched from one paycheck to the next. So, I had never really experienced such luxury.

Frank's surprise had made my heart swell with gratitude and in awe of him. I had only ever seen such luxurious yachts in rap videos and now, being on one, I couldn't help but feel like a glamorous video vixen from those very scenes. Adding to that fantasy becoming even more of my reality, the beat of rap music already reverberated through the air from the speaker next to the deejay that was already on board.

Touring the small yacht, we entered the spacious kitchenette and dining area.

My mouth fell open, tears coming to my eyes as I spotted a small gift bag, beautifully decorated cake and two clusters of pink birthday balloons. I spun around. My eyes were brimming with tears as they landed on Frank, who now appeared like a majestic, hood angel draped in tattoos, swagger, and Enyce as he stood between Buck and Tiffany with the proudest grin on his face.

"Why did you do this for me?" I let the tears flow.

Back at the hotel, before leaving out of the bathroom, Tiffany and I had told each other to be cool, to act as if this gesture was something we were used to. But I could no longer pretend.

He came towards me, taking me into his arms. "It's your birthday. You're on vacation. You deserve it. So, why the hell not?"

I began to sob as I rested my head on his shoulder.

In that tender moment, Tiffany softly sang, "*Awww.*" Her voice was now right next to my ear and her delicate hand caressed my back in a comforting motion. "But stop crying before you mess up your makeup," she whispered.

We all laughed. Thankfully, that made me get myself together. I raised my head, wiping away the tears that had fallen.

"Open your gift, girl," Tiffany urged.

Hurrying towards it, I opened the sparkly pink gift bag. Inside it were two bikinis.

"Just in case you and Tiffany want to change," Frank explained.

I couldn't control my blushing. "Thank you."

"Thank you, Frank. This is dope," Tiffany told him as she examined the bikinis.

"I'm here too," Buck spat with a gruff. "My big ass ain't invisible."

"You paid for this yacht?" she sassed.

"Believe me, I earned the money just as much as Cap did, lil' mama."

Tiffany's brow rose. Interest piqued all over her face as she looked back at him.

"Buck is my right hand," Frank explained. "Anything I have or buy is part of him."

"Well, thank you, Buck." I smiled.

"Thank you, Buck," Tiffany purred.

"You're welcome," he told me sincerely. Then his lip curled up as he glared at Tiffany. "Talkin' about did I pay for this yacht. I'm the one who figured out what size bikini you wore." Then he turned his back and marched out towards the deck.

Mouth falling agape, Tiffany took off after him. "I'm sorry, Buck!"

Frank and I shared a laugh as we followed them. Up ahead, Tiffany and Buck were engaged in a playful, mock wrestling match. Tiffany attempted to grasp Buck's arm, but he playfully pushed her away, their interaction resembling a pretend game of cat and mouse.

Taking in the surroundings, my heart raced with excitement. The deejay was stationed behind the driver's seat, spinning the latest rap songs. The spacious deck, an inviting space for lounging, basked in the warm sunlight. Their earlier efforts to purchase bikinis for us were much more apparent now.

As the boat's engine roared, Tiffany grabbed my hand. "Come on. Let's change into our bikinis."

Before I could answer, she took off, dragging me along with her, out of the deck and down the few stairs that led to the lower deck.

"Oh my God! I can't believe this!" Tiffany let her excitement flow freely, her enthusiasm evident as the thunderous roar of the engine and the pounding bass drowned out any chance of her joyful screams being heard.

"I know, girl!"

She began to strip off her clothes right in the dining area. I was surprised and hesitant at first, but then I remembered that Buck and Frank had already seen us naked or nearly naked and that we were having uninhibited fun.

We hurriedly changed into our bikinis as the boat glided away from the harbor. When we emerged on the deck, Buck and Frank had taken off their shirts. Frank had a camcorder in hand, capturing the scene. When he turned the camcorder toward me, I couldn't resist. Tiffany joined in, and we began to perform, throwing our asses, dancing for the camera, grinding against one another.

Usually, I would have been hesitant to allow a stranger to

get footage of me shaking my ass and popping my pussy, but Frank was different. He had left a profound mark on me in such a short time, and he'd made this birthday the most memorable of my life. He was a temporary savior, and in that moment, I was willing to give him whatever he desired.

9

FRANK "CAPO" DISCIPLE

"So, you're a drug dealer."

CeCe was staring off into the water. Her back was pressed against my chest as we sat on the deck, braced against the railing.

The fact that it had been a statement made me chuckle. "Are you the Feds?" I asked tauntingly.

Her face painted with humor and guilt. "I'm just being real."

"What if I was just a man who had figured out how to get rich legally?"

Her head shook, causing her curls to brush against my chin. "At your age, I doubt it. You're either a ball player or you sell drugs. Even though you are tall, I'm leaning towards selling drugs."

A low chuckle vibrated from my throat. "You're a smart girl."

"Why does Buck call you 'Cap'? What does that mean?"

"It means I'm a boss, baby."

Arousal and intrigue caused her eyes to whip back and up towards mine.

My brow rose. "Does that bother you?"

We locked eyes, exchanging needy glances filled with memories of the fucking we'd done earlier that day.

Finally, she broke our stare. "No."

I could tell she'd noticed my chest rising with approval. Her eyes searched my longing expression, one I couldn't conceal. Being out on that water had been a surreal experience I'd never imagined possible. It wasn't about the yacht or the company of a beautiful woman. I'd enjoyed those luxuries countless times before. But for the first time in my life, my guard was truly down.

"But why does it look like it bothers you?" CeCe asked.

"For the first time in my life, I'm living moments that I don't have to watch my back. There isn't a soul around me right now that I don't trust, that can rob me of anything, or who wants to kill me. Times like this, when I'm in a moment that I don't have to have my guard up or stay on my toes, I realize how free it feels and I wish I had turned out to be something different."

"As a kid, what did you want to be when you grew up?" she quizzed, truly interested.

"A superhero." I grinned, causing her to giggle. "But none of the heroes in the cartoons had money and they were always getting beat up."

Her eyes brightened with admiration and humor. "I like the name Frank better."

"Is that right?"

She nodded. "I met Frank. *That's* who I was with last night and this morning. That's who did all of this for me. That's who I'll always remember."

I was touched but was too macho to show it, so I just kissed her forehead.

"CeCe, let's take some pictures!" Tiffany's loud excitement interrupted yet another pure, intimate moment between us.

As CeCe sighed, I could feel her reluctance to leave this spot. I softly tapped her thigh, giving her permission. She slowly left her comfort zone against my chest and met Tiffany near the railing where she was holding a disposable camera.

Suddenly, a large shadow was over me. I didn't have to look up to know that it was Buck because as long as he was in my presence, nothing this large could make it this close to me other than him.

After sitting down next to me, he handed me a cup, which I knew was full of white liquor.

He lifted his own cup, and we toasted before taking sips.

"What you on with this chick?" he asked as he winced from the burn of the tequila. "You're romancing pussy you met on vacation."

"It's her birthday." I shrugged coolly. "I felt like doing something nice."

Buck frowned, obviously still unfazed.

"You would know nothing about this. I shower who I desire with the world, but you expect your woman to shower you. We're different."

Buck threw his head back, laughing in wholehearted agreement. I had a reputation as the toughest gangster in the hood. But when it came to a woman I wanted to claim as my own, I knew how to execute true finesse. Buck, on the other hand, lacked even a tiny fraction of a soft spot in his heart that would make him be this considerate. The only women he even thought to consider were those who made money for him.

"So, you're going to have some long-distance relationship with her?"

I shook my head, hating even the thought of being so far away from a woman like her.

"Where she from?" Buck asked.

"I don't even know. I'm assuming from down here some-where, especially since they are so young and drove alone. So, what's the point? Besides, it's Freaknik. We just here to have a good time."

"So, you did all of this..." He waved his hand around the boat. "... for a woman you don't plan on seeing again?"

I shrugged again, wearing a sly grin. "Yeah."

The in-depth answer was that she'd had a profound impact on me, reshaping my perception of the kind of woman I wanted. I felt a strong urge to show my appreciation, even though she most likely lived quite a distance from me. Her genuine wholesomeness, willingness to submit, and attentive-ness were unlike anything I'd experienced. With the charm of a Southern upbringing, she embodied traditional values. She felt like an unattainable dream, something I never knew I needed. I wanted to fully immerse myself, to experience everything as if she were truly mine before our inevitable return to the real world.

ANTHONY "BUCK" PATTERSON

Fortunately for Cap, back at home, I was always surrounded by willing pussy. Otherwise, I might not have been as agreeable about being on the yacht, missing out on the party back in the city. Cap was my brother, not by blood but through the unbreakable bond we'd forged in the streets, through all the blood, sweat, and tears we'd shed together in this game. I knew him inside out. I'd never witnessed him go to such lengths for a woman before, but I knew his potential to make a real effort when a woman made him feel at ease.

Feeling my stomach growl, I winced. "I'm going to get me something to eat."

As I moved to stand, he asked, "Aye, what's up with you and her friend?"

I scoffed with a chuckle. "Shorty cool. But, like you said, this vacation pussy, and I can tell she isn't interested in selling that tight, wet motherfucker for me. Besides, she has too much attitude. My bitches would kill her."

Frank's head fell back as he laughed.

Laughing as well, I told him, "I'll be back."

I stood and strolled off the deck. I passed by CeCe, who was snapping pictures of Tiffany as she struck some provocative poses on the railing of the boat. I mentally acknowledged Tiffany's beauty and the juicy, milky mounds on her chest that made my dick rise.

I had enjoyed her company the night before. But I was a seasoned player, a man with a mind sharpened by a legendary pimp who'd taught me the game. I knew how to read women like an open book. And as my eyes locked onto Tiffany, I knew she had too much sass, too much fire in her. That kind of woman was unable to be trained. It was in her nature.

Once on the lower deck, I grabbed some pizza slices and stacked them on a paper plate. I eagerly sat down at the small table, ready to feast when my phone rang.

Frustrated, I sighed as I took it from my pocket.

Since it was Diamond calling for the umpteenth time, I answered, "What's up, Diamond?"

"Hey, Daddy," she said with a relieved sigh.

"What's up?" I pressed.

"I was just calling to let you know that our dates went good this weekend."

"Oh yeah? How was the other night with those rapper niggas?"

"It was fun, to be honest. They had us backstage at the Jay Z concert."

My brows rose. "Word?"

"Yeah. It was crazy back there. Then we went to the hotel."

"They wanted some extra shit?" I grilled.

"They wanted to see me, Peaches, and April fuck each other."

"You charged them accordingly?"

"Of course. I just left the banks putting the money into your account."

I silently laughed at her exaggerated efforts, shaking my head. Diamond was so in love with me that she went over and beyond, trying to be my little personal assistant.

"Thank you," I told her.

"Are you having fun?"

"Yeah, it's a good time. I'm trying to eat right now, though."

"Okay." I could hear the sadness in her tone in response to me not giving her more.

But I couldn't be considerate or soft with her. She had always been a good girl, but she had the wrong type of feelings for me. "I gotta go."

"Okay, Daddy. I love you."

"I know you do."

I hung up. Before I could put the first piece of pizza in my mouth, however, I felt a presence. Looking up, I saw Tiffany saunter in, mischief gleaming in her eyes. She and I had been playing a game of back and forth, flirting one moment and irritating the hell out of each other the next. She had way too much mouth for my liking, and I sure as hell wasn't giving her the kind of attention she was used to.

Every time Frank whispered sweet, loving words to CeCe, Tiffany gave me attitude. But there was something about me that kept pulling her back in despite the irritation. We had a strange attraction to one another, though, that defied all the annoying moments between us.

Anchoring a frown on me, she stood in front of me. Her slanted eyes were even lower, so I knew the liquor was hitting her.

"What can I help you with, lil' mama?"

She wore a snarl on her face, attempting to come off as

offensive. But it only ignited a fire within me, stirring a need to turn that feistiness into submission.

She folded her arms and put all of her weight on her right hip. "You think you're all that, don't you?"

I deeply chuckled. "Humility ain't never looked good on me, sweetheart."

Clearly disgusted, she rolled her eyes. "I promise you're not all that."

I shrugged. "If you can't see that I am while looking at me, then you need your eyes checked."

She flung her head back, a defiant smirk dancing on her lips. "You think you're a player."

"Actually, I'mma pimp."

She laughed as if that notion was impossible.

I maintained a composed expression as I said, "Not all pimps rock flashy suits and strut around with canes, sweetheart. This ain't the '80s."

She finally grasped that I wasn't kidding, and her face showed a mix of offense and curiosity.

With deliberate slowness, I ran my tongue across my full lips, letting my gaze sweep her up and down. I allowed myself to appreciate her sensuality, letting my primal attraction flow through me, causing my nostrils to flare. "But trust me, pimping ain't dead, sweetheart. Niggas pay well for a good time with no headaches and commitment attached. I could turn you into a gold mine," I added. "I would make a killing off of how good that pussy is."

Now, she was fully offended, taking a step back.

"Don't worry. Like I said, these ain't the old days. I don't force a woman to sell pussy for me. All of my women are willingly working for Daddy."

My pride and unshakable dominance rekindled her curiosity and intensified it even more.

She slowly padded towards me on bare, pretty toes. "So, you liked this pussy?"

"It was superb, sweetheart."

It hadn't been the best I'd ever had, but it was exceptional. More importantly, her fiery sass ignited a desire to dominate her, to see that sassy attitude yield like a kitten under my command.

Blushing, she bit her lip while closing the small gap that was previously between us. Her small hand dug into my jeans, finding stiff inches. Swooning, her eyes lowered, and so did her body, onto her knees. She pulled it out, holding the mass in her small hand, gazing at it with savory orbs.

"This ain't a museum. If you pull it out, you gotta do something with it, baby."

The sass had vanished. Now, she was a pooling, willing servant.

She put me down her throat. The slick tightness of it made my eyes narrow. Her pretty pink lips looked marvelous around my dark, throbbing veins. I pushed her bang out of her face so that I could watch my size stretch her mouth to its capacity. I was impressed as she slowly made the stiff inches disappear.

I noticed a bottle of tequila on the table. I took it in to my free hand and was able to remove the top with my teeth. Guiding her throat up and down my shaft, I took a shot from the bottle.

It went down with a burn, but her tongue slurping at my head soothed me. I looked down, realizing that she was watching me. "You want some?" I asked. Before she could answer, using my grip on her roots, I pulled her away from my dick. "Open up," I ordered.

When she did, she made my dick concrete.

Grinning devilishly, I poured almost a double shot down her throat, causing some of it to spill out of the sides of her mouth.

I growled, then ordered, "Swallow."

CYNTHIA "CECE" DEBOIS

Riding shotgun in Frank's Bentley as we headed back towards the city, I couldn't help but marvel at the luxury surrounding me. The plush leather hugged me, and the smooth hum of the engine signaled a level of wealth I'd never experienced before. In just one day, Frank had whisked me away into a world of extravagance, leaving me wide-eyed and appreciative of the lavish lifestyle that had become my temporary reality. The city lights reflected off the polished exterior, and for the first time in my life, I was riding through the streets as if I belonged to this world of wealth and privilege.

While in Atlanta, Frank and Buck had mastered the back roads to avoid the usual gridlock. But as we neared the hotel, deep into the Freaknik festivities, chaos erupted on the streets. Men were leaping onto cars, some even attempting to flip them over.

Frank and Buck swiftly reached under their seats, pulling out guns. With their hands gripping them, they casually rested them out of the windows to ward off anyone eyeing his ride.

The rowdy figures on the streets naturally gravitated toward Frank's ride, ready to unleash their usual chaos. However, the moment they spotted the guns positioned on each side of the car, a sudden wave of fear seized them, forcing an abrupt pause in their wild antics.

As we maneuvered through the mayhem, people outside looked at Frank's Bentley with awe *and* envy. Women we rode by paid no mind to Tiffany and me. Instead, they focused their attention on Frank and Buck. Feminine catcalls filled the air, and some went as far as to bend over, lifting their skirts or even yanking down their shorts in an attempt to seduce them.

I looked back at Tiffany, and we shared the same stunned look. I imagined that Frank and Buck attracted this much attention effortlessly. I felt a twinge of sympathy for the women back home who dealt with this on a regular basis.

Once back at the hotel, Frank parked in the private lot. After the car came to a halt, Buck and Frank smoothly stepped out, ready to escort us through the tumultuous crowd of intoxicated partiers that had infiltrated every inch of the hotel—outside, the parking lot, halls, and lobby.

With Frank and Buck as our shield, we ventured through the unruly crowd, their strong presence warding off the advances of aggressive men. The air was thick with the scent of weed, and the sounds of laughter and music pierced through the chaos. Frank's hand, firmly nestled in the small of my back, guided me through the sea of partiers, ensuring we reached the elevator untouched. Buck, a silent force by our side, expertly navigated the wild scene, creating a path for us through the wild crowd. In the midst of such mayhem, I felt so safe.

"I'm going to Buck's room," Tiffany whispered as we rode the elevator.

I teasingly grinned as I rolled my eyes. "Duh."

Back on the boat, as the sultry sounds of intimate moans reached my ears from the lower deck, I initially brushed it off, thinking it was just a seamless blend with the sounds the deejay was spinning. However, Tiffany's songs of passion grew louder and more distinct. Jealousy stirred in my gut, and my own hormones started to ignite. I sat with my back pressed against Frank's chest on the upper deck, wishing that we had privacy to do the same.

"Whatever," Tiffany blushed.

"Mm humph..." I smirked just as the elevator doors opened.

A sea of unruly partiers greeted our vision. We pushed through the crowd, navigating through the haze of marijuana smoke, amidst the chaos of laughter and mayhem. Women, who were dressed in barely anything, string bikinis, or even naked, danced as if they were conjuring the attention of the many men surrounding them. A haze of intoxicated lust was in everyone's eyes.

As Frank took my hand, he looked back at Buck. "You good?"

He answered with a short nod and then asked, "You?"

Frank's gaze, dripping with sultry intensity, cascaded over me, engulfing me mercilessly to the point where each breath felt like a luxury. Locked in that magnetic stare, he uttered with smoothness, "I'm more than good."

Buck began to stroll away, further down the hall towards his room. Tiffany quickly followed, shouting over her shoulder, "I'll meet you at our room in the morning at nine so we can hit the road."

Her head spun around before I could answer. Giggling, I allowed Frank to continue guiding me down the cluttered hall towards his room.

"Are you sure you want to spend your last night inside?" I

asked Frank as we approached his room. "I know that I said that I didn't want to be out, but I know you want to party."

"We partied all day. I'm good."

I leaned into him as he searched his pockets for his keycard. "You sure?"

His sultry look devoured me as he assured me, "Baby girl, it's our last night. I want to spend the rest of my time with you deep in those guts."

———

Frank and I savored each other's company throughout the night. Moments of sleep occasionally claimed us, coaxing our eyes to close for an hour here or thirty minutes there. Yet, aware that this was our final night together, we resisted falling completely asleep.

Come morning, our limbs remained entwined. The heat lingered, beads of sweat covered our bodies, and the air was thick with the remnants of our heavy breaths. The room held the memories of long hours of Frank claiming my body with no mercy, etching himself into the fabric of the mark he'd left on my heart and body.

"Fuck, I'm cumming," Frank growled as he tangled his fingers through my curly fro. He secured a grip on my shoulder with his other hand. He slammed me onto his big dick, plunging his length as deep into me as our bodies would allow. Intensity built in my core so explosive that my body started to violently quake around each stroke. My knuckles whitened as I clutched the bed sheets in an effort to take all of him along with the fiery orgasm that was brewing.

The intensity of his strokes was conjuring my own orgasm. "Oh God!"

"You cummin' too?"

"Mm humph!"

"That's it," he coaxed me with a slow, deep stroke. "Cum with me, baby."

We climaxed together, creating a powerful connection with this stranger that had forever altered my life. I would never be the same after experiencing Frank. He had raised the bar.

He collapsed next to me on his back as I fell onto my stomach, still panting from the vigorous strokes he'd been delivering for the past forty-five minutes. My body lay spent, and my legs quivered beneath me, robbed of their strength.

With a smack on my moist ass cheek, he got my attention. I opened my heavy lids, meeting his curious gaze.

"Where do you live?"

I chuckled. "*Now* you wanna ask me that?"

Frank rolled over onto his side and rested his hand on his head, giving me his undivided attention. "Listen, sweetheart, I'll be straight with you. Initially, this was just a weekend fling for me. But you're more than just a pretty face. You're cool as hell. I can hop on a flight and reach you wherever you call home. I've never done the long-distance thing, but for you, I'll give it a shot." As I blushed, he asked again, "So, what city do you live in?"

My cheeks flushed with heat. I felt such honor that he was even interested in me beyond this weekend. "Chicago."

Suddenly, Frank's head fell back as he began to laugh so loud that his deep roars bounced off the wall.

"What?" I asked, watching his laughter curiously. "What's so funny?"

It took him a while to gather himself.

"What's funny?" I pressed.

Finally, he collected himself, but he was barely able to hold back a laugh. "Me too."

My brow rose, interest pushing me up onto my elbows. "You too *what?*"

"I live in Chicago too."

As my grin unfolded, stretching from ear to ear, a mischievous smirk crept across his face. The air between us sizzled with passionate, sneaky tension. His devilish expression told of the playful dance of enticement and attraction that sparked between us.

CAPO
FRANK "CAPO" DISCIPLE

Capo, *short for Caporegime, a rank in the Mafia. Capo dei capi, or capo di tutti capi, Italian for "boss of bosses", a phrase used to indicate a powerful individual in organized crime.*

FOUR YEARS LATER

10

CYNTHIA "CECE" DEBOIS

A chilly February breeze nipped at my exposed cheeks as I waddled towards the clinic door, struggling to maintain my balance. My hand clutched Jah's tiny fingers, his little feet dragging a bit as he tried to keep up with me. The weight of this second pregnancy pressed on me differently than the first, making each step difficult.

"Come on, Jah, baby," I coaxed, shivering as the oppressive cold encased us.

"Mommy, why are we here?"

"We're here to see the doctor, baby. Remember your little brother in Mommy's tummy?" I managed to smile through my discomfort as we stepped into the clinic's warmth.

I had been told that pregnancy was supposed to get easier with each one. With Jah, it was a breeze – minimal weight gain, barely any symptoms. Now, it felt like I was carrying a load, and every step was a chore.

The clinic's interior greeted us with a comforting blend of warmth and muted colors. A hushed murmur of conversations between patients and staff and the gentle buzz of the fluorescent lights filled the air. The magazines on the worn-out coffee table told stories that offered a glimpse into the year 2000.

As I took my coat off, the scent of antiseptic made me nauseous, mixing with the anxiety that accompanied any prenatal visit. Jah tugged at my hand, eager to explore the space as I checked in at the receptionist desk.

"Mommy, when is the baby coming out?" Jah's innocent voice piped up again, drawing a few adoring smiles from the other waiting mothers.

"Soon, baby. We just gotta make sure everything's okay in there," I reassured him.

Done checking in, I guided Jah to a row of well-worn chairs, easing myself into one as he fidgeted beside me. The plastic of the chair offered some comfort against my swollen body. I sighed deeply, finally relaxing, but I knew that the relief would only last for a moment. Being eight months pregnant while looking after a four-year-old, every day felt like a marathon.

As I sat there, catching my breath, irritation flashed across my face when Frank appeared through the entrance. I envied how he so casually strolled in after the struggle I'd had. I despised the breathtaking beauty he'd been blessed with. The winter air's bite kissed his light skin, casting a delicate pink hue. Diamonds adorned his neck, ears, and wrists, shimmering in the harsh glow of the clinic's fluorescent lights. Wrapped in a leather coat with lavish fur framing the hood, it screamed opulence. His tall, imposing figure cast a shadow over every woman he strolled past.

I despised it.

Jah, however, lit up at the sight of his daddy. He grinned excitedly as he quickly abandoned his chair and dashed towards Frank.

"Daddy!" Jah exclaimed, his tiny arms outstretched as he collided with Frank. The scene unfolded in a heartwarming display of father-son joy that many in the waiting room admired, while my blood boiled over as I stared at Frank.

Frank, with charming demeanor, naturally drew attention from the women in the waiting room. Their stolen looks were a backdrop to the father-son reunion.

"Hey, little man! Missed you, buddy," Frank's deep voice resonated as he lifted Jah into his arms. He threw him into the air repeatedly, making Jah explode with laughter. They played together like no one else was in the room.

Frank's eyes locked onto mine as he finally stopped playing with Jah and approached me with Jah nestled in his arms as his tiny arms encircled his father's neck. As he sat in the seat Jah had just vacated, I took a soothing breath. I refused to let Frank get to me. He had done enough of that over the years.

"What are you doing here?" I asked, trying desperately to mask the irritation in my tone.

His gaze, per usual, delved deep into the recesses of my soul. "You may be a single woman, but you aren't a single parent, CeCe."

I fell silent amidst the tension that had lingered between us for the past four years.

Frank and I had driven from Freaknik to Chicago together while Buck and Tiffany rode together in her car. In those initial months, Frank and I were inseparable. But the excitement of Freaknik soon gave way to the reality of our lives.

Just a few months after Freaknik, I found myself pregnant with Jah. Stanley may have taught Frank the ropes of being a boss, but when it came to relationships, they were uncharted territory for him. Frank mishandled the delicate threads that wove our connection, and we found ourselves plunged into parenthood before truly getting to know each other.

Suddenly, being parents hindered the nurturing of our relationship. A surge of responsibilities left little space for dating or understanding each other. The intricate details of our personalities were unexplored, and our lack of familiarity with each other was so apparent as we continued to butt heads.

Frank was a great father, but we never reached the shores of true commitment. Instead, a turbulent sea of continuous arguments pulled us further and further apart. Frank, having grown up in the stormy environment he had, considered our clashes normal while it felt nothing short of torturous for me. The constant bickering cast a shadow on the hopes of a stable family life for me and Frank.

Frank wanted to be a family man, but he didn't know how to love me. Stanley had taught him how to be a boss, but no one had taught him how to keep his woman happy. He only knew how to show love with big expensive gestures when all I wanted was him to be respectful, take me on dates, get to know me, and be present. He didn't know how to give me that and he was unapologetic about it because he didn't understand. He retaliated with frustration.

He had been raised on survival, so he thought as long as we had money, everything should be okay. And he reacted to every challenge with anger and hostility.

For Frank, other women became an escape from our tumultuous relationship. Despite his infidelity, he respected me enough to keep it hidden. But the life of a young, wealthy gangster occasionally allowed hints of indiscretions to slip through the cracks. Each instance added to the pain of our constant quarrels, deepening the wounds of our fractured connection.

Because I'd never seen my parents in such intense discord, I knew that Frank wasn't the example of a real man. He may have been great at being a boss, but he had failed at keeping me happy. I refused to subject myself and my child to the ongoing turbulence of a relationship that had lost its way. So, after Jah's birth, I'd made the difficult decision to sever ties with Frank for good.

However, Frank remained Frank with all of his imperfections that strangely felt like perfection to me. Numerous times, my body succumbed to his appeal and swag. It was a consistent weakness that granted him a sense of ownership over my body. The last instance was after Jah's fourth birthday party, when we'd conceived the child I was currently carrying. Realizing the consequences of having another baby by him, I understood the urgency to distance myself from Frank permanently.

The undeniable chemistry between us still lingered. It was an invisible force that continuously tugged at us. Yet, it was toxicity I had to escape. The cycle needed to break for the sake of my own well-being and the well-being of the lives we were bringing into this toxic dance.

FRANK "CAPO" DISCIPLE

After the prenatal appointment, I couldn't help but silently admire CeCe's beauty. There was something magical about seeing her carrying my child, the evidence of our love growing within her. It stirred the beast that was my obsession with her. Watching her embrace motherhood, being so attentive and caring, only intensified my love for her. It was such a big difference from what I'd seen growing up, especially from my own mother.

I'd always been in love with her since I was too young and too caught up in the chaos of being a boss to handle it properly. But as time passed, and I matured, the revelation of her carrying our second child shifted something in me. I really wanted to make it work this time, to build something meaningful together.

When we first met, it had been my first time being in love while navigating being a boss and having too much pride to truly mourn the loss of my father figure. I didn't handle her well back then. But now, I felt a burning desire to reclaim what would always be mine.

With her strength and the way she cared for our son, CeCe had a hold on me that I could no longer ignore.

After securing a peacefully sleeping Jah in his car seat, I slipped into the passenger's seat of CeCe's brand-new Lexus. Irritation painted all over her beautiful face, but I knew she wouldn't put up a fight. Not when she was behind the wheel of the car I had bought for her.

She shot me a glance that could cut through steel, but I leaned back, unfazed. I was well aware of the power dynamic at play, the silent acknowledgment that the car was a reminder of my presence in her life. I knew she resented it, my constant influence seeping into every aspect of her world. But as I settled into the passenger's seat, I couldn't help but revel in the fact that whether she liked it or not, my mark was all over her.

"Can we talk?" I ventured, breaking the uneasy silence that lingered in the car.

CeCe's eyes briefly met mine, guarded and skeptical. "About what?"

"Us." I cringed, hearing the desperate sincerity in my voice.

A furrow appeared between her brows as she questioned, "What about us?"

"You're having my baby... *again*," I stated. "Let's make this work."

She sighed with frustration and exhaustion. "It's been four years. If it hasn't worked now, it won't."

My gaze pleaded with her, searching for a crack in her defenses. "You don't want me?"

Her eyes softened briefly before she averted her gaze. "I *can't* want you, Frank. We don't get along, the other women—"

"I was young back then. I've changed."

Her dry laugh was eerily scary because of its lack of emotion. "Back when? Eight months ago? What about LaMonica and LuLu?"

My lips tightened. She had named the women currently in my life. Blowing out a heavy breath filled with defeat, I told her, "You know they mean nothing to me when it comes to you. You know I'll never let another woman come between us now."

Anger covered her expression. "And what about *us* coming between us? The constant fighting over anything and every-thing, it's exhausting, Frank."

"I've apologized for all of that."

Frustrated, she sucked her teeth. "When you mess up with someone you care about, own up to it and actually deal with the problem by putting in the work. Waiting around, hoping time will fix things is not saying you're sorry. Pretending like nothing went down when you call them up? Yeah, that's not an apology either. Acting all sweet, thinking they'll forget the mess you caused? Nope, that's not how you make things right. Hoping that new cars and furs will make me fuck you again is not showing me that you've changed. Until you actually put in the work, the hurt won't disappear. If you want solid relation-ships, you've got to know how to fix things the right way. You've never done that. I don't think you even have that in you."

"Then why are you having my baby again?" I pressed, genuine confusion in my voice.

Her eyes met mine. "You don't want him?"

I leaned forward, genuinely answering, "Of course, I do. But why are you having another baby by a man you want nothing to do with?" She didn't have to answer. I saw it in her eyes. No matter how frustrated she was with me, it was always there, from the moment we met. "Because you still love me."

"No, I don't." Her denial was swift, almost rehearsed.

"Yes, you do," I insisted. "And I know that I mishandled you before. But I finally know you more than intimately. I know every part of you, every thread, and every fiber. I can steer our relationship in the right direction I was supposed to."

I wanted to put the past behind us, to let the love that had always been there guide us towards a future we both deserved. I'd always been in love with her, and now, it was time to prove it.

But she refused. "No."

Frustrated, I pulled my bottom lip in between my teeth and nodded slowly. "Okay," I mumbled a little above a defeated whisper.

CeCe held a unique power over me, capable of making me feel defeated and unsuccessful in a way no one else could. Fleeing from that overwhelming emotion, I briskly opened the car door and climbed out in silence. The door closed with a low thud, and as our eyes locked, tension lingered in the air.

She wanted to wear a mask of disdain, to act like she hated me, but I could see the love and yearning in her eyes concealed behind the veil of frustration. As I watched her drive away, the distance between us stretched, leaving a void that only she could fill.

I had started off in the game as a corner boy for Stanley on a block on the south side that we called "The Wild." It was a block not even the police would come down. My first big job Stanley had asked me to do was to cut up a body. Buck was right by my side. It was hard, and we threw up a few times, but we got it done. Since then, my life had been full of violence that had only increased since becoming the head of the Disciple Family.

Navigating the game as a capo came with challenges. Opps

constantly sought to challenge my authority. Controlling every high in the Midwest brought wealth beyond my wildest dreams, but it also meant watching my back around the clock.

I rarely trusted anyone. Suspicion overshadowed every interaction I had with anyone. Only a select few earned my trust. But while enjoying unprecedented riches, I felt a void, as if I owned nothing of true value. Success failed to fill the emotional vacuum that Stanley's death and my mother left behind.

Jah's conception and birth happened amidst the whirlwind of significant change, catching me off guard. In that chaotic time, the importance of having him and CeCe in my life got lost. I'd become the father I had wished for during my youth; caring and attentive, the opposite of Stanley. Yet, I'd fumbled CeCe. I couldn't seamlessly integrate loving her into my life as a boss.

Now, as she was about to bless me with another child, it dawned on me that she was giving me purpose. With each birth, she was delivering the love and peace I needed to fuel my hustle. CeCe was the missing piece, the desired serenity essential for me to breathe.

11

ANTHONY "BUCK" PATTERSON

Peaches' clit grew hard and firm, calling me in. With a smooth rhythm, I traced the journey of her pussy from the bottom to the top with my tongue, hitting all the right notes. Each lap upward sent shivers through her. Her breathing escalated in sync with the sweet melody of her moans.

When the moment felt right, my forefinger and middle finger slipped into play, stroking that rough patch where her orgasm hid. My tongue quickened its dance, and in no time, Peaches was riding waves of pleasure. Her hips arched, fingertips unsuccessfully gripping my fade, and a primal growl erupted as she let out a long, deep moan.

"Oh my God," she said on a breath when the storm settled.

In the dimly lit room, me and Peaches were sharing one of our many moments that wasn't about business. My tongue, still playing a slow tune on her clit, refused to show her mercy.

Her grip on me tightened. "I need you inside me," she declared.

Climbing up her body, my pulsating dick pressed against her entrance.

I put her ankles on my shoulders. I stroked my dick against her southern lips, lubricating it with her own juices.

"Don't tease me," she mumbled, panting. "Fuck me, Daddy."

My brow rose cockily. I fixated my dark glare on her as I eased my dick into her haven. With a slight thrust, I breached her walls. Peaches let out a gasp of surprise and pleasure, her arms looping around my waist like she was holding on for dear life. Inside was a tight, moist embrace, and with each thrust, I delved deeper into what felt like the most divine vortex I'd ever known.

Her entrance had a snug grip. It wrapped around the base of my manhood, hugging it so tight that it set my senses ablaze. Further in, her inner sanctum was a heated, slippery haven, practically beckoning me to explore its depths even more.

"Fuck, that feels so good," she whispered on a breath. "You stretch this pussy open. I love feeling you deep inside me."

I growled as I succumbed to what she knew would make me cum. She knew I loved when she talked that shit to me.

Hours later, Peaches lay beside me, her breaths slowing, the rise and fall of her chest in sync with the rhythm of my own. Her body molded against mine with her head on my chest, a comforting warmth against the night's cold temps just on the other side of the picture window.

Tonight was hers, but she'd received a lot of my time as our bond had deepened over the years. I always had my guard up because everyone saw me as a pimp, a drug dealer, and a killer. But with Peaches, I was able to let my guard down. Behind closed doors, we had a bond that went deeper than the scars that our hustle had left behind on us.

Her curves told tales of nights we'd spent together. We knew each other's bodies like a well-worn book, every page turned, every story shared in the silent language only we understood. It wasn't just about the cash or the transactions. It was about *trust*, loyalty, and a connection forged in the fires of the city. She was my homie, my best friend, my bottom bitch. We laughed together in the face of danger, and when the world turned its back on us, we stood back-to-back, ready for whatever came our way.

The streets were unforgiving, and love wasn't a word I threw around at all. We weren't in love with each other. We just found peace and safety in each other's arms. So, when the city slept and the only sounds were distant sirens and the hum of car engines, me and Peaches often shared something rare—a connection that bloomed in the cracks of our hardened exteriors.

Hoes came and went, but Peaches, April, and Diamond were my constants. Sparkle had left about two years back. One of her rich clients had fallen for her, throwing bills like confetti at her just to have her around. He continuously booked her. So, as time went on, they got cozy. Love crept in and when Sparkle decided she'd rather be a kept woman instead of a hoe, I didn't put up a fight. I wasn't the kind of pimp that forced my hoes to stay with me. If they were offered better opportunities with a man who I knew would treat them as good as I did, I tipped my hat and let her walk.

Diamond was low-key thrilled that there was one less woman in the house to occupy my time. She would never let go and was hoping she'd be the last hoe standing.

Me and Peaches were locked in that post-fucking haze when my phone lit up, breaking the calm silence. I glanced at it on the nightstand. It was Frank on the line. Sighing, I answered, knowing if he was calling at this hour, it wasn't just to shoot the shit.

"Yeah, Cap?" I answered, Peaches shifting slightly beside me.

"We gotta meet up tomorrow with Alexander."

When I rolled my eyes, Peaches shot me a concerned look. "Is the motherfucker gonna show up?"

Lately, Alexander had been a damn headache. He was all over the place, causing shipments to be delayed, prices to flip-flop like a fish outta water, and meetings to turn into no-shows. It was a circus, and getting hold of him was like trying to catch smoke with your bare hands. On top of that, he was strutting around like he was some god, making it clear that the power had gone straight to his head.

Frank and I were itching to cut ties and find a distributor whose head was screwed on right. The problem was finding someone who could handle the workload.

"Sounds like it. He's talking about making some changes. We gotta sort this out."

I grunted in annoyance. Alexander was a loose cannon, a time bomb in a nice suit. He obviously had power, but he was riding the wave a little too high. His erratic behavior made it clear he was getting high on his own shit, and that was a recipe for disaster in our line of work.

"Ah'ight," I scoffed. "I'm tired of this motherfucka. He's all over the place."

Peaches propped herself up on an elbow, deepening her questioning look.

"I know, but it's distro. All we gotta do is move the weight for him, anything else ain't our problem," Cap assured me.

"We don't have to keep dealing with this shit, though. We

move major weight. Any distro would love to do business with us. I told you Hector wants to work with us bad."

"And I told you I'm not stepping on Keyes' toes like that."

Respectfully, I let it go. "Ah'ight, man."

"Holla," Frank returned before he ended the call.

I tossed the phone on the nightstand and sighed, Peaches still eyeing me.

"I'm sick of this white motherfucka," I muttered.

Peaches smirked, running her fingers over my fade. "What did Alexander do now?"

"I don't know. All Frank said was that Alexander wants to make some changes."

Peaches clicked her tongue. "Y'all need to find another connect."

I chuckled, pulling her close. "With that amount of work we get, it ain't that easy. But you're right, me and Cap gotta do something about him. We can't keep letting chaos run the show."

QUEEN ARIA BENSON

The next day, the moment I stepped into the Disciple Family headquarters, I could feel the tension in the air. Buck and Diamond were in the living room, and it was clear that my presence was about to turn it into a battleground.

Diamond shot me a look, sizing me up like I was a problem she needed to solve. Buck had that cocky, arrogant smirk on his face that irked me to no end. Since I was old enough to remember, Buck had paraded through the hood with an air of self-importance and entitlement that was way too high in my opinion. It was as if his hoes bore the weight of an invisible throne, parading him through the streets like a misplaced king. He thought he was so superior to everyone else, and the stupid women who followed him like misguided puppies were to blame.

I never had any words for Buck and his hoes. Instead, I let my disgusted gaze do the greeting. My disdain for Buck's whole operation was etched on my face. I didn't get how these women could let him play puppet master with their lives, stringing them along like some sick game.

"Queen," Buck greeted with a cocky tone. "Speak when you're walking into my shit."

I didn't bother responding.

Diamond piped up, "You hear him talking to you! Watch your attitude, Queen. Act like you got some sense. This ain't the street corner."

I let out a scoff, breaking into laughter so loud that their expressions twisted into confusion and irritation. "You'd be the expert on that, wouldn't you?" I managed to ask between fits of laughter.

Buck unhooked his arm from around Diamond and sat up. "Watch your mouth, lil' girl."

I met his gaze, not backing down. "Your little empire of broken dreams disgusts me, Buck. You think you're a king, but all you are is a low-life pimp. And these women..." I glanced at Diamond and then back at him. "They're fools for letting you control them like puppets."

Diamond's eyes blazed with anger as Buck chuckled, the sound grating my nerves. "Your mouth gon' get you in trouble one day, Queen. Get one thing straight: My business and my hoes ain't none of your fucking concern."

Snarling, I replied, "Your business becomes everyone's concern when you drag these women down with you. They deserve better than being pimped out like commodities."

Diamond scoffed, her loyalty to Buck evident in every eye roll. "You don't know shit about us, Queen. He's not dragging me anywhere. I do this by choice."

My gaze narrowed on her, and my words dripped with disdain. "*Choice?* More like you're all too blind to see the chains he's got you shackled with. It's pathetic."

Buck clenched his jaw, capturing his bottom lip between his teeth. From where I stood just a few feet away, I could practically see the fury flickering in his eyes.

Diamond growled, "Let me rock this bitch, *please.*"

She bolted off the couch, her eyes seething with hunger to strike me, the intensity amplified by her piercing gray contacts. Her fingers, transformed into wicked claws, extended towards me. I maintained my composure, secretly longing for her to touch me because I was eager to put my hands on her. I despised what Buck represented for these women. But at least Peaches and April weren't simple bitches. Diamond was a puppet.

Yet, before she could pounce, Buck sprang into action. With lightning speed, he encircled his lengthy, hefty arm around her waist, locking her tightly against his large physique, effectively halting her in her tracks.

"Let me go, Daddy!"

I cackled at the pet name, shaking my head. I stood calmly, arms crossed, giving her a taunting smile.

The reputation of Frank's crew rested on a foundation of respect, particularly for each other. That unspoken rule protected me in this volatile moment. Buck knew the boundaries. If I were any other woman, he'd have one of his loyal puppets carry out the retaliation he'd been wanting to for years. However, Frank didn't allow violence against each other amongst the crew.

"Get the fuck on before I have Diamond do something I'll regret," Buck gritted through clenched jaws as he continued clinging to her silly ass.

I smiled. "I love reminding you that not every woman bows down to your twisted version of power."

I shot them one last taunting look before turning on my

heels, heading down the hall. Buck's profanity and disdain sounded behind me.

"Stupid-ass bitch. She better be lucky Frank is protecting her."

"Why is he, though? She's so fucking disrespectful."

"He has a soft spot for her young ass because of how she grew up."

The mention of my past made my neck roll, but I held my composure.

My past was a haunting nightmare, a constant struggle growing up with my alcoholic grandfather. My mother had abandoned my sister, May, and I, leaving us in the care of her parents. It was a chaotic hell living with an alcoholic. The nightmare worsened, however, when my grandmother passed away. She left a void that seemed to consume everything. With her gone, my grandfather might as well have perished alongside her. He was useless, and I was then completely neglected.

Making matters worse, my sister's father took custody of her after my grandmother's death, leaving me completely abandoned.

My grandfather, reduced to a mere shell of his former self, only did the bare minimum necessary. But it wasn't out of love or responsibility. It was a calculated effort to maintain the appearance required to keep custody of me so that he could continue receiving government assistance. My well-being was collateral damage to fuel his addiction.

I missed my grandmother and sister so much for so long that I had become sick with longing. Eventually, that sickness became bitterness and strength to survive no matter what.

Now, everyone was gone. Me and my sister eventually reconnected when I got older. She had moved with her father to Georgia and still lived there. We talked every now and then.

But it was so evident how differently we had grown up that we weren't as close as we used to be.

"I keep telling you to stop fucking with Buck before he has one of his hoes unleash on you one day." Frank slowly looked up from the money counter that sat in front of him at the kitchen table. The corner of his mouth was turned up as a taunting smirk danced in his light-brown eyes. "Stop fucking with him because you know he won't do anything because of me. One day, he's going to get sick of that. He can't keep letting you get away with disrespecting him, especially in front of his hoes."

The mention of hoes made my eyes roll with disgust. But, out of respect for Frank, I simply replied, "I guess. Where the work at?"

As he reached into the massive pile of money on the table, Frank's head angled towards the chair at the head of it. In it sat the usual large duffle bag that I transported bricks in.

"Where is it going?" I asked as I took hold of it.

Frank continued feeding bills into the money counter. "To Spook's spot."

I threw the bag over my shoulder. "Okay. You need anything else?"

"Fetti got some bread for me, but he's out west. You feel like driving out there?"

I nodded sharply. "I got you."

"Bet."

"I'll be back in a minute."

Frank nodded in acknowledgment as I pivoted to depart from the kitchen. Swallowing hard, I made my way up the hall, battling the inner temptation to shoot Buck and his blindly devoted lackey disdainful glares. I managed to refrain from doing so, maintaining my composure as I exited.

When my grandfather passed away two years ago, Frank finally relented and allowed me to start working for him. Because of my youth, he believed I could handle making deliveries without attracting unwanted attention. It was a turning point for me. I was finally earning some money. While I still resided in my grandparents' house, the dynamic had shifted. I could now afford the rent. I found myself enjoying a better quality of life, no longer plagued by the constant worry of where the next meal would come from.

At nineteen, I yearned for a simpler life. I wished to have been in college, mingling with boys and engaging in idle gossip with friends about trivial things. Instead, I was immersed in the game.

———

As I entered my dimly lit house, a knot of anxiety twisted in my stomach. I knew tonight would be one of those nights, the ones where the shadows harbored more than just darkness. The air was thick with tension, and I braced myself for the storm I was about to face because I was so late getting home.

The door creaked shut behind me, and before I could even fathom the distance to the living room, Reggie's attack struck like a viper in the night. The element of surprise was his weapon, and he wielded it with vicious efficiency that made my heart pound in my chest.

"I told you to be home by midnight!" he barked as a sharp blow caught me off guard, the force of it sending me stumbling backward. The taste of iron filled my mouth as I bit down on my lip to stifle the pain. My hands instinctively shot up, a feeble attempt to shield myself from the rain of aggression he'd unleashed.

His fists were brutal, each strike extracted painful cries from me that surged through the silence of the house. Though I knew that it was useless, I fought back. My limbs moved on autopilot, fueled by resilience that had been imbedded into my bones by my trauma. Despite how much he tried to get it out of me with his cold words and brutality, I refused to let him see any weakness in me.

My house had once again turned into a vicious fight club, where the only goal was to stay alive. I dodged and weaved, but still my body became an unwilling target for his rage. But every time he hit me, it felt like the toughness I'd learned growing up was there, refusing to let me give up.

The scuffle intensified, and grunts and thuds sounded through the walls. The familiar sting of pain mixed with the metallic taste of blood and yet, I kept fighting back. The way I'd been raised taught me to keep going no matter how much it hurt, to always get back up after I'd been knocked down.

I felt the tension thickening every time I walked through that door, knowing Reggie was intimidated by the men I worked with. His pride took a hit because he wasn't rolling in bread like Buck and Frank. It fueled jealousy, especially when it came to the tight bond I shared with Frank. What made it worse was that Reggie was a dope boy too. He purchased his weight from Spook, a member of the Disciple Family. Reggie was so low on the totem pole of street niggas that neither Frank nor Buck even knew who he was. I'd first met Reggie when I was still fighting for the opportunity to work with Frank. I had taken Frank's advice and got with a man who would take care of me. But since Reggie wasn't selling much weight, he wasn't providing all that I needed to keep my grandmother's house. Then, Frank finally offered to give me a chance. At first, Reggie wasn't fazed because he just knew that his come-up was coming and he was unaware of how much Frank loved me. The longer it took for Reggie to get on even Spook's level, the more frustrated he became with my connection with that organization, despite how much I loved him. The arguing began to boil over into brutal physical fights. It was as if because he felt so low, he wanted to ensure that I did as well.

Yet, amidst the storm of his abuse, I clung to Reggie because, besides Frank, he was the only man who had ever shown me love in this unforgiving life.

I was a beast in the streets. No man or woman could lay a hand on me, but in my own home, I endured the abuse because I was accustomed to it being a place where I received both love and pain.

12

FRANK "CAPO" DISCIPLE

"Where you been, baby?" LuLu's soft voice swam through my headset as I eased into a parking space.

"In these streets. You know what it is."

"I miss you."

A deep chuckled replied. "Yeah?"

"Yeah. This pussy misses you even more," she purred. "What are you doing tonight?"

I inwardly cringed. There was nothing wrong with LuLu. She was a beautiful, curvaceous chocolate drop that sucked my dick with graceful expertise every time I was in her presence. I just wasn't feeling her. She was the wrong woman.

"You, if you answer the phone in a little while." I had to focus on something else before CeCe's rejection made me feel like less than the nigga I knew I was.

"You know I will," she drawled out seductively.

"Ah'ight, baby girl."

"Talk to you later." Her voice was so much chipper as she hung up.

"Who was that?" Buck asked.

"LuLu." I turned off the ignition, sitting back in the driver's seat. "She's trying to get put on the schedule. I haven't been fucking with her too tough."

"Why not?"

"Honestly?" As Buck nodded, I continued, "I've been too focused on trying to get my family back to even want these hoes."

Buck's head fell back as he chuckled at me mockingly. "I don't get you, nigga."

I lowered my head, shaking it, getting ready for one of Buck's animalistic rants.

"I know you love my sis and all, but you can't be out here butt hurt about that shit. You're a rich nigga. Sis is supposed to be chasing you, not the other way around."

"I'm not even about to explain this shit to you, my nigga. It's like explaining a giraffe's height to a turtle."

Buck scoffed, waving a dismissive hand at me.

Looking at the restaurant ahead, I shook my head at Buck. "Whatever, nigga. Let's ride."

I opened the door and hopped out just as Buck did. As I strolled through the frigid February evening, the snow fell gracefully from the charcoal sky. With Buck on my side, our figures cut through the snowy scene like shadows in the night. The city of Chicago wore its winter coat proudly, the streets beneath me blanketed in a thick layer of white. I pulled the hood of my quilted leather coat over my head. The fur-lined the hood, shielding me from the biting cold as I made my way towards the restaurant where we were meeting Alexander.

"I'mma end up getting my hoes to fuck Queen up," Buck griped with irritation.

"No, you ain't," I dismissed his threat calmly.

"Why you let her get away with so much?"

"Not so much, only when she talks shit to you." I laughed.

"Exactly!" he barked. "And she talks shit to me *a lot*, but you keep asking me to let it ride. I'm looking like a sucka out here."

I cut my eyes at him, wearing a humored smirk that peered through the black fur. "A nineteen-year-old can't make your grown ass look like a sucka."

"She can when she disrespects me in front of my hoes. She gets away with shit that I don't even let them get away with, shit they would never even try to pull. Just let me put one of my hoes on her. Peaches a killa, so it won't be her. I'll let Diamond do it. She can hardly fight, but she can't stand Queen as much as I do."

I chuckled. "You know Diamond will fight a bear for yo' ass."

He shrugged. "April then."

"How 'bout don't do shit because that lil' girl just likes you. That's why she talks so much shit. If you paid attention to bitches for more than them just making money for you, you would see that."

"Whatever, my nigga."

"And you go back and forth with her because you like her."

Buck's face folded in repulsion as we approached the restaurant. "Now, you trippin', dawg."

I laughed as I pushed the heavy wooden doors of the steak house open, revealing a dimly lit interior. It was instantly a warm escape from the winter chill. The scent of sizzling steaks and the murmur of low conversations greeted us as we stepped inside, leaving the snowy city behind, as well as our casual, playful conversation. We were now on business.

The hostess greeted us with a polished smile that hardly concealed her curiosity. "Good evening. Do you have a reservation?" she inquired, cynically.

I'd grown accustomed to this prejudice. I was well aware that our statistical appearances and ghetto personas were sending ripples of discomfort through the air. She assessed us as if our presence defied the very essence of the place.

Buck leaned in with his brash demeanor. "Of course. Otherwise, we wouldn't be at a *reservation-only* establishment."

Her thin brows rose as she turned pink.

"We're here to meet Alexander Pinsel," Buck told her.

The hostess brushed off his attitude with an ornery, professional air. Her fingers typed on the computer as a judgmental smirk continued to paint her face. However, in a sudden moment, she was visibly taken aback, recovering quickly with a tight-lipped response. "Right this way," she directed.

She led us through a maze of tables adorned with immaculate white linen.

Buck shot me a sly grin, clearly enjoying the perplexed glances thrown our way from many patrons. We navigated through the sea of affluent clienteles who eyed us as if we were a pair of misfit puzzle pieces in this refined establishment. But we cockily strolled through as if we belonged, unapologetic for being out of place.

The hostess eventually stopped at a table where Alexander sat. The contrast between us and the nerdy-looking Alexander only heightened the stares from nearby tables. I could practically hear the whispers, the unspoken judgment about what we were doing in a place like this.

"Mr. Pinsel, your guests have arrived," the hostess announced.

Alexander's eyes flitted up from his menu as Buck and I settled into our seats.

The jittery presence of Alexander didn't escape my notice. His usual composure was absent yet again. Once more, his appearance was unusually disheveled. I had been around addicts long enough to recognize the telltale signs, and it was clear Alexander was riding a high.

As soon as the hostess walked away, a waitress appeared. She took our drink orders before hurrying away to retrieve them. Then Alexander got straight to the point.

His speech stumbled as he began to ramble. "Um, guys, prices... Kilos going up. Ten percent." He gestured dramatically, his hands punctuating each word with points and snaps, creating an awkward dance as he continually fidgeted in his seat.

Buck shot a look at me, eyebrows raised. I responded with a subtle shake of my head, signaling him to hold back.

"Why the increase, Alexander?" Buck asked, leaning back with a hint of irritation covering his features.

Alexander's eyes darted nervously between us, his hands fiddling. "It's universal, man." He shrugged with his hands outstretched. "Prices are going up everywhere."

Buck scoffed, "Yeah, but you're not just some regular distributor with regular prices. You're getting this shit from some foreign motherfucka that's taking it right out of the ground. Let's not play games."

I remained composed as Alexander's movements became more erratic. He shrugged dramatically while chewing on air. "Look, it's just the way things are. Gotta roll with it."

I nodded slowly. "If I agree to this, it can't be a recurring theme."

Seemingly, Alexander either ignored the warning or he was too high to realize one had been issued. "So, we have a deal?" he blurted out, eyes darting nervously between Buck and me.

Buck darted a questioning glance towards me, but I dismissed it with another discreet, short shake of my head.

Alexander's gaze flitted around, his jittery movements betraying his cover.

I leaned back, keeping my expression unreadable. "We'll roll with it," I said, the words concealing the chess moves turning in my mind.

CYNTHIA "CECE" DEBOIS

I stood in the living room of my parents' home, watching as Jah beamed with excitement. It was Valentine's Day, and he had insisted on giving his grandmother a special gift. In his tiny hands, he held a bouquet of vibrant flowers and a small box of chocolates. I had bought the gifts earlier along with a cute card and had allowed Jah to scribble his name on it with his crayons.

With a prideful smile, he handed the carefully wrapped presents to my mom, who stood there, her eyes twinkling.

"Oh my goodness!" she gushed. "Jah, you're so sweet!"

"Happy Valentine's Day, GG!"

Her heartfelt chuckle was full of emotion. "Thank you, baby!" She hugged Jah tightly, showering him with kisses.

Letting him go, she looked up at me, eyes scanning my fitted black dress underneath one of the many floor-length chinchilla coats Frank had purchased me over the years.

"You look nice. Where are you going?"

I discreetly blew out a heavy breath in response to my mom's smart mouth. She knew exactly where I was going.

I tilted my head, fighting to keep an annoyed smirk from forming. "I'm going to Frank's Valentine's Day dinner."

Frank organized a Valentine's Day dinner for single mothers and widows in our neighborhood every year. It was one of the many charitable donations he made in his hood and the city. He was a real-life Robin Hood. For as much havoc he wreaked, he gave back that and then some in toys, money, food, and more to those in need.

Visibly annoyed, my mother asked, "Why do you have to go? You all aren't together anymore. You don't have to keep following him."

"I'm not following him. It's a nice dinner. If I don't have a Valentine, why would I miss it?"

"You don't have to let Frank know that you don't have a Valentine." She rolled her eyes as she mumbled, "You're going to be stuck with that nigga forever."

My parents had always been a significant influence in my life. I looked up to my mother and aspired to be like her, hoping to make her and my father proud. Above all, I longed for a relationship as strong and enduring as theirs. However, I couldn't escape the fact that I had disappointed them when I'd become pregnant with Jah. It was as if I had fulfilled their worst fears about the type of man I would end up with.

Growing up, I was the obedient daughter, trying to follow the path they had envisioned for me. They constantly instilled in me education, career, and stability. And for a while, I played the part, conforming to their hopes and dreams.

When I discovered I was pregnant, I braced myself for their disappointment. I could already hear their disapproval. I had let them down, shattered their hopes for my future. It was as if my actions were a direct reflection of their greatest fears.

Yet, my father set aside his reservations and embraced Jah

CAPO   155

with open arms. He saw beyond his disappointment in me and appreciated the joy and innocence Jah brought into our lives. My mother loved her grandchild as well, but she never hid her disdain for Frank. Since the beginning, she had looked down on him. She judged him by his rough, criminal cover. And when Frank and I broke up, that had only proved her right. She didn't miss a moment to remind me that Frank had ended up being the exact man she never wanted me involved with.

Deep down, I yearned for a perfect relationship like my parents, a love that endured through the trials and tribulations life threw its way. I wanted to prove to them that I could find happiness and fulfillment, even if my path wasn't what they had envisioned. But the man I'd fallen in love with was the complete opposite of the type my parents had had in mind. I knew that Frank wasn't the conventional choice, but love had a way of blurring your judgment and leading you into uncharted territories. Unfortunately, I couldn't love him enough to turn him into perfection.

"CeCe, I just don't understand why you're still so close to him," my mother said, her voice covered in concern. As she sat on the couch, Jah sat comfortably on the floor, watching cartoons on the television. "You deserve someone who treats you right, someone who values and respects you. Frank didn't do any of those things when you were together."

I sighed with my gaze fixed on the swirling patterns of her wallpaper. It wasn't the first time we had discussed this, and I knew my mother's intentions were rooted in love and a desire to protect me. But it wasn't that simple. Frank and I had history, a connection that went beyond the pain he had caused. And he was the father of my children. I couldn't completely cut him off.

"I know, Mom," I replied. "But he's my kids' father. It's not easy to just cut him out of my life."

She scoffed with a raised brow. "That's how you ended up pregnant again." When guilt and shame caused me to pout, my mother's eyes softened. "I understand what you're saying, CeCe. But I worry that as long as Frank is still in the picture, he'll always have one foot in the door. It's hard for you to truly move on and find the right man if you're holding on to him so tightly."

There was sadness in her eyes, a reflection of the pain she had witnessed me endure. She had seen the tears, the sleepless nights, and the broken trust.

"I get what you're saying, Mom. But it's not just about him. It's about our shared history, the friendship we built over the years. I can't just erase all of that."

My mother's expression tightened, a flash of frustration crossing her features. "But is it worth it, CeCe? Is it worth holding on to someone who hurt you so deeply? Who cheated on you?"

Pain washed over me, memories of heartbreak and betrayal resurfacing. I took a moment to compose myself, my voice steady but filled with emotion. "No, Mom, it's not worth it," I admitted. "But it's not about him deserving my support or friendship. It's about my kids. He hurt me, but he's a great father."

My mother's features softened. "I just want what's best for you, CeCe," her gentle voice told me. "I want you to find someone who will treat you the way you deserve, someone who will love and cherish you without reservation."

Tears of longing welled up in my eyes. I wanted the same for myself. For years, up until my second pregnancy, I wished it could have been Frank.

"I know, Mom," I admitted. "I'm working on it. I'm learning to let go and open my heart to new possibilities. But please understand that Frank will always be a part of my life, even if it's in a different capacity."

She nodded slowly, giving up. Sighing, I rounded the cocktail table. Bending down, I told Jah, "I'm going to leave you with Grandma for a little while, okay? I'll be back soon, baby." He nodded as I kissed his forehead and squeezed his tiny hand before turning to my mom.

As I turned to leave, she stopped me with a question. "You still aren't going to come with us to Mississippi?"

Every year, my family traveled down to Starkville, Mississippi in February to celebrate my maternal grandmother's birthday. She was now in her late seventies. My mother had been trying to convince her to move to Chicago to be closer to us for years. But she was old, stubborn, and refused to leave her roots.

"I really don't think I should since I'm so close to my due date."

My mother's lips spread with regret, but she nodded with understanding. "Okay."

Glancing down at Jah, I told her, "Thank you for watching him. I'll see you in a few hours."

I stepped out of my mother's house, the bitter winter air biting at my skin. I pulled the hood of my fur coat over my hip-length box braids, which were a temporary relief from the daily struggle of styling my hair. I had always taken pride in my appearance, especially once I was permanently connected to Frank. But as the months went by in this pregnancy, exhaustion seeped into every fiber of my being, and I longed for comfort and simplicity.

Though the hood had given me relief from the cold, my

heart still felt so heavy. Embarrassment and sadness washed over me, a heavy cloak I couldn't shake off. I couldn't help but feel like I had failed, failed to have my children with the perfect man. Frank was a constant reminder of my imperfections, my inability to find the kind of love my mother had with my father.

Cheating and fights were the norm in most relationships. It was a twisted cycle of pain and heartache. But my mother, shielded from the harsh realities of that world, knew nothing of it. My father embodied perfection, and my mother wanted the same for me.

———

Frank's generosity knew no bounds. As I stepped into the enchanted space, my eyes widened with awe. Entering the restaurant, the air pulsed with the thumping bass of rap music spun by the deejay. Conversations intertwined with the rhythm of the music. As I navigated through the sea of tables, the beats wrapped around me like a cloak. Frank had rented out an exquisite Italian restaurant in the heart of downtown Chicago. The space was elegant and sophisticated, every detail meticulously designed. Soft, ambient lighting bathed the room in a warm glow.

As I walked through the maze of tables, my eyes were immediately drawn to the grand gold centerpieces gracing each table that stood tall and magnificent. Delicate vines of gold branches pronged out in graceful arcs adorned with shimmering crystals that caught the light and scattered it across the room like a gathering of stars. Nestled within this golden cluster were lush bouquets of roses. The velvety petals were in various shades of crimson, blush, and ivory. Long-stemmed roses stood tall and proud, their heads reaching towards the ceiling, while clusters of shorter blooms nestled together, creating pockets of vibrant color and texture.

The abundance of roses was awe-inspiring, as if an entire garden had been transplanted into the heart of the restaurant. They cascaded from the centerpieces, spilling over the edges in a lavish display of floral abundance. Petals kissed the tabletops, creating a soft carpet of velvety beauty that beckoned guests to run their fingers through the delicate sea of petals. Soft candle-light flickered, forming a warm glow that danced across the faces of the guests.

The decor infused the room with an air of romance and celebration, as if every guest had stepped into a fairy tale. It was clear that Frank had carefully orchestrated every detail to create an unforgettable experience for these women.

"I hate him," I mumbled as I took off my coat. I draped it on the back of the chair next to Queen. She wasn't single, but she would never miss a Disciple Family event.

"What did you say?" she asked as I sat.

Pouting, I dropped my elbow onto the table right into a heap of rose petals. Resting my chin in my palm, I let out a sigh. "I said I hate Frank."

Queen tossed her head back, cracking up.

"It's not funny," I whined. "It's hard resisting him when he does these grand gestures. Look at his place!" I insisted as I waved my hand around.

"Just remember all the arguments and hoes," Queen said, anchoring a raised brow on me.

Being the sole woman in the crew, Queen and I had developed a tight bond. Despite her being four years younger than me, she had street smarts beyond her years. She understood the game better than I did. So, when I made the decision to cut ties with Frank once and for all, she was one of the few who understood and supported me. She had witnessed many of our relentless battles, whether it was Frank neglecting our plans for the Disciple Family or the harsh truth of him cheating on me. Queen had witnessed it all.

"You know I love Frank to death, but I know that your experience with him is much different than mine," Queen told me, leaning in. "So, I can be real with you: Don't let his money and grand gestures make you feel like you made a mistake. Some of these niggas let the money convince them that women can be treated any kind of way." As she spoke, her gaze left mine and a snarl formed on her face.

Following her icy orbs, I laughed when I realized that she was snarling at Buck as he walked into the restaurant with his harem in tow. Diamond, April, and Peaches were dressed beautifully and scantily clad in leather and lace and draped in diamonds.

Laughing, I told Queen, "Stop staring."

"Now, *that's* a nigga to hate...*out loud.*"

I began cracking up. Each time Queen expressed her disdain for Buck, I was reminded of Tiffany's feistiness. She and Queen were a lot alike, which was most likely why I had gotten so close to Queen so easily.

After Freaknik, Buck and Tiffany had attempted to continue their sexual relationship. No matter the way they bickered, they liked having sex with each other. But Tiffany couldn't handle Buck's harem and the fact that he was a pimp. So, their booty calls quickly fizzled into nothing.

As I continued to laugh, so did Queen, causing her head to slightly tilt backward. My eyes narrowed when I noticed a mark on her neck.

Reaching towards it, I asked, "What's that?"

She backed away, swatting at my hands. "What's what?"

"On your neck. There is a mark."

Her face turned into a guilty smirk. "I like it a little rough."

I frowned playfully. "You and Reggie are so nasty! Where is he anyway? Why didn't he come with you?"

"He let me come for a little while. He and I are going to celebrate Valentine's Day later tonight."

Just then the melody of "Sweet Lady" by Tyrese began to fill the air. The familiar tune wrapped around me like a bittersweet embrace, evoking memories of moments with Frank that I could never leave behind.

"*Ooo!* This is my song!" Queen exclaimed, her eyes closed as her head swayed to the beat.

As the melody played, Frank appeared before me. He was rocking a stylish Sean John sweater and matching jeans. The diamonds around his neck caught the light, briefly blinding me as he leaned in.

His voice was low and enticing in my ear, "Can I dance with the most beautiful woman in the room?" His erotic, woody scent sprinkled with hints of cedar and cinnamon, overwhelmed all five of my senses.

Despite how much he'd hurt me, I couldn't deny the magnetic pull he still had on me. With a hesitant nod, I followed him to the dance floor. As he extended his hand to me, I melted, yearning for the dominance and security that came with being under his command.

The music swirled around us, its lyrics mirroring the conflict within my heart. As we moved together in a slow dance, the rhythm seemed to synchronize with the beats of my emotions. Frank's arms enveloped me, his touch familiar yet foreign, igniting a cascade of feelings that were too stubborn to fade.

The lyrics echoed the whispers of my heart, the yearning for a love that once was.

"Sweet lady, would you be mine? Sweet love for a lifetime." I felt his breath against my ear as he whispered the lyrics, and for a moment, it was as if time had rewound.

His strong arms held me close, reminding me of the ease we once had before the bickering and the other women. Our locked gazes spoke volumes in a heart-to-heart silent conversation of longing and regret. As we swayed, the party faded into the background. It felt like it was just Frank and me in a dance that surpassed our fractured past.

But our reality still lingered, and the pain was still there.

13

FRANK "CAPO" DISCIPLE

As I held CeCe in my arms on the dance floor, the distance she'd forced between us was so obvious. She was no longer soft with me. Her guard was still up. The woman who would have given me any and everything four years ago was gone. She wasn't the same starry-eyed girl blindly in love with me.

I despised the immaturity of the past version of myself for not cherishing what we had then. CeCe possessed an unearthly beauty that left everyone in awe. Every time I looked at her, it amazed me how unrealistically beautiful she was. Her smile was my favorite view. She was impossible to resist.

But I had chosen to see all of that when it was too late. Now, there was a barrier she'd put between us that frustrated me. I knew I couldn't penetrate the fortress of walls around her heart as easily as I once had. Back then, she was putty in my hands, but now she had toughened, grown resilient.

Regret gnawed at me as I recalled my own stupidity. The pressures of suddenly being a boss, boyfriend, and father had become too much for me to handle. The weight of it all had bore down on me, and in my frustration, she had taken the brunt of it. It had all been an immature response to the overwhelming chaos of my life.

Now, as I swayed with her, enjoying a rare moment of feeling her curves in my arms, I feared that I might never break through the emotional armor she'd put on. I missed the simplicity of us. The realization that I might have lost her forever weighed on me. It gave me an uncomfortable feeling of defeat that a boss like me never had to deal with because I always got whatever I wanted.

Like a chameleon, the deejay switched gears, seamlessly transitioning from Tyrese to Jay Z. I felt the faint shift in CeCe as she nervously peeled herself out of my arms. Her eyes evaded mine, and with a quick excuse, "I'm hungry," she scurried away, leaving me feeling like a stranger, someone she wanted nothing to do with instead of the man she used to love so much that every beat of her heart whispered my name.

She left me standing there, looking pitiful and alone. Tucking my tail, I draped myself in my swag and cockily strolled off the dance floor in the opposite direction. I proudly walked through the sea of round tables, nodding at smiles that were appreciative and most that were filled with flirtation.

I wanted the single and widowed women in my hood to feel cherished and celebrated on Valentine's Day, so I'd made sure they didn't have to be alone. All the food and drinks were on me. With each entrance, I presented every woman with a stunning bouquet of roses. They were also given gift cards to Macy's that were filled generously.

I slid back into my chair at the table with Buck and the girls. Keyes had appeared since I'd left to dance with CeCe. Keyes, Buck, and I used to run the streets together when we were kids. Keyes was always the epitome of cool. Stanley used to try to rope him into working for him, but Keyes was his own man, always wanting to carve his own path.

Now, Keyes was our only competition. He had the same quality of heroin and cocaine as the Disciple Family, but even he couldn't match our prices. Despite that, Keyes never crossed the line. He never stepped on the toes of the Disciple Family. There was always silent but known respect between us.

As Keyes stood up, we shared a firm grip and exchanged nods.

"Frank, my nigga. What up?"

"Same shit, different day. You know how it is," I replied with a cool grin.

The vibration of my phone interrupted our conversation. I excused myself, glancing at the screen to see the mayor's name flashing.

With an irritable sigh, I answered, "I'm not doing business today. I'm busy."

Ignoring me, Mayor Rossi's voice cut through the line. "Frank, we got a problem." As I groaned, he rushed on to say, "There have been a lot of shootings in the last few days. I need you to handle it."

I walked away from the table and leaned against the wall, keeping my cool. "Rossi, that ain't my crew. My people know better. This ain't on me."

Two crews were at war in Pocket Town. There had been a string of shootings and murders for the last two weeks. Though my crew was spread all over the city, we didn't get involved in petty- ass wars. Our focus was on getting to the bag. The way we moved didn't cause beef. And when we crossed paths with a hater or opp, we dealt with it quietly so that it didn't interfere with our bread.

"Frank, your reign and respect are city-wide. No matter whose crew it is, they will look up to you. You need to go talk to these motherfuckers. I can't keep my position if I can't control this city. Re-elections are coming up."

I scowled as my head rested back against the wall. "Look, this has nothing to do with me."

Rossi's tone grew more insistent and desperate. "Frank, we need these streets quiet. You know how it works. Handle this with the same energy that I use to keep your business protected from state charges. This is the arrangement we made. You have my influence with the police department as long as I have yours in the streets."

My jaws clenched. "Fine. I got you," I spit.

Rossi's gratitude seeped through the phone. "Appreciate it. You keep the peace, and we'll keep things running smooth."

I ended the call, frustration lingering in the air. After becoming the capo, I was called into the mayor's office. When I left, I had agreed to give sizeable donations to the mayor's campaign fund to protect the Disciple Family from any future state charges. However, I still had to maintain a low profile because he couldn't protect us from federal charges.

The streets were a chessboard, and I was always a pawn, making moves to keep my kingdom intact. But as my eyes drifted to CeCe's perfection, I realized that keeping my kingdom intact had cost me leaving my family in shambles.

CYNTHIA "CECE" DEBOIS

After the Valentine's Day party, Frank was a bit tipsy from the drinks that had flowed freely. He had insisted on riding home with me, and although I might have suspected an ulterior motive in the past, I knew better. We were more than exes. We were good friends, co-parenting in a way that worked well for all of us.

Jah giggled uncontrollably as Frank tossed him playfully into the air in Jah's bedroom. Their laughter filled the room, and I couldn't help but admire the sight. Frank was known for a tough and unyielding presence in the streets, but he easily transformed into a gentle giant when it came to our son.

"Again, Daddy!" Jah squealed.

As Frank chuckled, his rough exterior softened by the love he showered on our son. "One more time, little man," he declared, tossing Jah high in the air before catching him with ease.

As I watched from the sidelines, my heart swelled with gratitude. Despite the complications of our past, moments like this reassured me that we had been doing something right when we created our kids together. As Frank continued to play with Jah, I couldn't help but appreciate his beauty.

The difference between his usual tough, gangster exterior and the vulnerability that surfaced whenever he was with Jah was so overwhelming. The tattoos that covered his arms, the hard persona—it all seemed to fade into the background and for a moment, he wasn't the hardened boss the streets knew him to be. Instead, he was just a father wrapped up in the pure joy of making our son happy. There was something enchanting about the way his eyes softened when our son looked up at him with admiration. The street-hardened gaze turned into one of genuine affection and a tender smile played on his lips. It was a side of him that few were privileged to see. I couldn't help but feel a sense of intimacy knowing that he so effortlessly let me see it, however. The tough exterior melted away like a mask, revealing the depth of his love for our family. It was in these moments that I found him even more irresistible. The vulnerability he displayed, the raw emotion that surfaced when he let his guard down—it all added layers to the complex man I had fallen for.

Each time I witnessed this softer side of him, it became increasingly difficult to resist the magnetic pull he had on my heart.

"Alright, lil' man, it's time for bed," Frank announced with a gentle but firm voice that even I wanted to obey.

Jah's bottom lip protruded, displaying his disappointment. "But Daddy, I don't wanna go to bed. I wanna play more!"

I exchanged a knowing glance with Frank, silently acknowledging the typical bedtime resistance. "Come on, Jah, we'll play more tomorrow. Daddy's right. It's way past your bedtime," I chimed in.

With a reluctant sigh, Jah allowed us to tuck him into bed. Frank and I each planted a kiss on his forehead, promising him more play time in the morning.

As we left Jah's room, Frank's hand found its way to my pregnant belly.

"Make me a drink." He grinned; his signature charm evident even in the simplicity of the request.

I obliged, easily slipping into my past role of serving him. I guided him to the sleek bar in the living room's corner. Walking through, I admired the beautiful home Frank had purchased for us when I was pregnant with Jah. Situated near the University of Chicago campus, it served as a two-story symbol of the future I had longed for. The cozy living room boasted large windows, welcoming the moonlight while the hardwood floors beneath us murmured stories of laughter, love, tumultuous fights, and tears. Family photos adorned the walls, chronicling our short-lived romance.

"You really outdid yourself today," I told him with admiration in my eyes. "It gets better and better each year."

His smile was so charming that it made my center ache. "Thank you. I'm glad you came out."

I playfully rolled my eyes, knowing that he was teasing me. Frank knew that I wouldn't have been anywhere else since it was impossible for me to date while carrying his very large eight-month-old fetus.

Once at the bar, Frank settled onto one of the plush barstools. The soft light from the chandelier cast a warm spotlight on his perfect features. I tore my gaze away from his captivating details. Instead, I focused on preparing his drink. As I did, he let his gaze wander all over my body, making it impossible for me to breathe. The air between us was comfortable, familiar, and sparked with history only the two of us understood.

"You looked beautiful tonight."

His eyes were locked on mine. A faint blush crept onto my cheeks, and I found myself momentarily speechless. In the past, Frank hadn't been the soft and romantic type. Besides saying "I love you," he made his feelings known with grand gestures, which was easily ignored or forgotten about when his usual disrespect resurfaced. But now, he was doing things he never had before: holding me tenderly while dancing with me, giving me compliments, and gazing at me with admiration in those cognac orbs.

Yet, I fought the urge to let him see the impact of his words, determined not to appear vulnerable.

"Thanks, Frank," I softly replied with a genuine smile on my lips.

"Frank?" he mocked with a laugh.

My playful orbs teasingly rolled. "I am *not* calling you *Cap*."

He chuckled lightly. "You never have."

His intense gaze anchored on my face, filled with admiration that made my breath catch. I had to look away to steady myself. "And I never will."

His eyes lowered to my protruding belly. "You're carrying this baby so beautifully. It suits you. I love seeing you pregnant."

The compliment, smooth and sincere, caught me off guard. I was grateful for the dim lighting concealing the warmth rising in my face. Frank had always been suave, a trait I had found attractive and despised equally since the day we'd met.

"Well, you know, trying to stay fly even with a baby on the way," I quipped, attempting to playfully break up the tension.

Frank sexily chuckled, allowing deep arousal to pour from his lips.

I took a seat beside him at the bar, appreciating this rare moment of familiarity. Even though Frank had driven me crazy back then, he was still the only man who made me feel safe besides my father.

"CeCe," he began, the seriousness of his gaze meeting mine, "I wouldn't want any other woman to be the mother of my children."

The corners of my lips slowly spread to my ears. "Really? Why is that?"

"You're strong, you're caring, and your heart is so pure." His words held vulnerability I hadn't often seen in him. I appreciated the rare moment of raw honesty. But I couldn't handle such humility, maturity, and acknowledgement from him. That was what I'd wanted and needed from him forever. Finally hearing it suddenly stirred up all kinds of emotions inside of me. "Frank—"

He raised a hand, gently silencing me. "Let me finish. I need you to know that I understand I wasn't what you needed in the past. I was immature and caught up in the streets. When things shifted, and I had to suddenly be a boss, a boyfriend, *and* a father all at once..." His eyes lowered shamefully and then he finally continued, "I couldn't handle it."

There was visible sincerity in his eyes that exhibited the depth of his confession. His admission told of the struggles I'd already known, but for the first time, he had finally acknowledged it.

"But I'm trying to be better. I'm trying to be the man you and Jah deserve," he continued.

My breath hitched when I recognized the regret and determination in his tone. At a loss for words, I simply nodded.

A small smile tugged at the corners of his lips. "Better late than never, right?"

Our eyes met, and for the first time, it felt like we were not just co-parents, but individuals who were finally growing and understanding each other.

We had definitely reached a milestone.

Looking at Frank, I could see the sincerity and the vulnerability in his soul. This wasn't just manipulation to get me back. At last, he realized just how deeply he'd hurt me back then.

To hear him finally acknowledge my hurt and his faults gave me such relief. So, I listened, my heart basking in the authenticity of his words.

14

FRANK "CAPO" DISCIPLE

As I stirred on the couch, the familiar scent of sausage and French toast invaded my nostrils. Jah's playful laughter sounded in the background, a sweet soundtrack to wake up to. For a moment, everything seemed normal. But then, reality hit me like a ton of bricks.

As I shifted, a dull ache in my back reminded me that I was on the couch instead of in CeCe's warm bed where I used to be. It was a blinding reminder that my life had changed, that I had ruined things.

I had put my heart on the line last night. The words I had spoken weren't some slick game. They were the emotions I hadn't been mature enough to express when CeCe was truly mine. Despite the appreciation in her eyes, my heartfelt words seemed to have fallen on deaf ears. I had to understand that CeCe wasn't an ordinary woman. So, years of taking her for granted and shattering her heart couldn't be healed with a handful of sweet sentiments and definitely not in one night.

The noises coming from the kitchen were once comforting

sounds that reminded me of home. Now, they reminded me of my failures. CeCe was busy cooking, creating a heartfelt sensation that felt gratifying and distant at the same time. The sounds of Jah's laughter filled the air like a bittersweet reminder of what I yearned to reclaim. I craved these mornings when I had once taken them for granted. But now, if given the chance, I swore I would cherish them like never before. The absence of CeCe had left my world cold. No other woman provided the same sense of security, love, and belonging that she did. That pussy knew me better than I knew myself. I had been blind to the rarity of that feeling, stumbling and mistreating it in my immaturity. So, I had fumbled it. Now, I would pay any price to have it back.

Even in her distance, I sensed that she still belonged to me.

I prayed that it wasn't too late.

As I lay there, my phone vibrated as it lay on the floor. I rolled over, peering at it over the edge of the couch. Lamonica's name flashed on the screen, and I hesitated before answering, not wanting CeCe to overhear. I answered quietly, "Yo."

"'Yo'?" she mocked with irritation. "What the fuck, Cap?! Where have you been all night?"

I groaned and sucked my teeth. "You knew where I was."

"I mean *after* your event. Why didn't you spend Valentine's Day with me?" she snapped.

"I was busy."

"Busy doing what?!"

I frowned, running a hand over my face. "Lamonica, we're not official. We don't go on dates. You know how it is between us."

She huffed. "Were you busy with *CeCe* again?"

I rolled my eyes, irritated by the jealousy. "Don't speak of the mother of my children."

"Were you with her?!" she defiantly pressed anyway.

"It doesn't matter who I was with because you ain't my woman. We never go out. I don't date you." I sighed, growing irritable of the conversation. "Look, this is how it is. If you're not okay with it, you know where the door is."

She huffed again, muttering, "Any other night, you're with me. So, I thought maybe we would've spent Valentine's Day together."

I shook my head, even though she couldn't see it. "We're not there, Lamonica. And honestly, I don't know if we ever will be. If you can't handle that, I respect it."

The other end of the line fell silent.

"Think about it," I added before ending the call. Then I rose from the couch and made my way to the kitchen.

When I stepped into the kitchen, CeCe was standing with her back to me as she stood at the stove. I took a moment, absorbing the beauty that always left me breathless. My addiction to her chocolate skin was undeniable, and those curves of hers, each pregnancy only enhancing them, transformed my dick into steel every time I had the pleasure of being in their presence. Since the day we met, her body had matured into that of a grown woman, and I couldn't get enough of it.

She was wearing a pair of pajama shorts that left little to the imagination, and a matching crop top that showcased her protruding pregnant belly. As she turned towards me, that belly met my gaze before her eyes did, and in that moment, I realized that I was infatuated with the incredible woman standing before me.

A smile curved her lips as CeCe greeted me. "Morning, Frank."

Jah ran up, wrapping his small arms around my legs. "Good morning, son," I told him just as he took off out of the kitchen.

CeCe turned back to the sizzling sausage in the pan. I seized the moment, hoping the words I poured out to her the night before had melted the icy barrier around her heart. Quietly, I approached, slipping my arms around her waist and resting my chin on her shoulder.

I felt her body tense for a brief moment. I held my breath, waiting for her to push me away as she usually did. But I was prepared to take advantage of each second that she allowed to be close to her.

Then, a deep sigh escaped her, and slowly, she relaxed into my embrace. The silent exchange spoke volumes, and in that moment, I held on to the hope that my words had started to thaw the coldness between us.

"You make enough for me?" As I spoke, my breath against her skin made her body shiver in my embrace.

Thankfully, I felt her relax even more. "Of course, I did."

ANTHONY "BUCK" PATTERSON

I leaned back in the Durango, eyes scanning the busy block as we watched the corner boys handle our business. Jah, sitting in my lap, was playing, mimicking driving.

"Man, I finally laid it all out for CeCe," Cap said, his voice low and gravelly. "Told her what's been on my mind."

I nodded, keeping my eyes on the corner boys. "And?"

"And it feels like she's starting to thaw, you know?" Cap's gaze lingered on the scene before us. "We had breakfast together."

My head whipped towards him, my brow arched high. "Word?" I could swear this nigga was blushing.

"Yeah. But I didn't press on anything physical."

"Smart move," I replied. "She needs time, especially after all that's gone down."

Jah made car sounds, steering the wheel with his tiny hands.

The steady hustle and bustle of the street played behind

Cap's words, "I know. She's been through a lot with me. My past mistakes, the streets... it ain't easy for her to let it go. I can feel it."

I grunted in agreement, my eyes narrowing as I watched the corner boys. "Yeah, it takes time for wounds to heal. But she'll come around. Y'all have been through too much not to get it together eventually."

Cap's gaze shifted to Jah playing in my lap. A small smile pulled at his lips. "I'm just trying to be there for my kids too. They deserve better than what I had growing up."

I nodded. "Family's everything. And you're doin' right by them. It may have taken you a minute to get it right, but I believe she loves you so much that you still got a chance."

My focus shifted from Cap's goofy, hopeful grin to the corner. The chill in the air was apparent. I watched as people walking in it attempted to hide from it behind the collars of their coats. The faint glow of the streetlights reflected off the snow-covered ground, casting a light against the dimly lit storefronts.

On the corner, the 63rd Street bus stop hummed with activity. Commuters hurriedly shuffled to catch the approaching bus, their breaths visible in the cold air. The bitter wind cut through the layers of clothing, but the rhythm of the hood continued to flow in spite of it.

Crack heads stumbled along the sidewalks like aimless ghosts. Hollow eyes and gaunt faces told the toll of their choices had taken.

Despite the harshness and ugliness of what I was seeing, it still felt like home.

"You see that shit?" I asked, eyes narrowing on the corner boys.

Cap sat straight up. "Yeah, I saw that shit."

"Here." I lifted Jah from my lap and handed him to his pops. "I'm fucking him up."

I climbed out of my ride, eyes narrowed with irritation. Me and Cap made enough money selling bricks that we didn't have to employ anybody to work the corners. However, to keep the little guys in the neighborhood from robbing houses and our small businesses, we allowed them to make money by selling smaller bags of weight. We knew the boys who had potential to do better. Those who did, we encouraged them to focus on school and helped them get jobs within the community. But those like me and Cap, who were destined for a life of crime, were put to work and taught the game, in hopes to keep them out of trouble. But one of the corner boys, Joc, had just broken one of the first rules we had taught him. He had made a hand-to-hand sell, physically exchanging drugs with a crack head when he should have taken the bread and then sent him to the next station to collect.

The bitter cold gnawed at my skin as I approached the corner.

Joc eyed me with surprise. "Oh shit! What's up, Buck? What—"

His attempt at a greeting was cut short as I snatched his ass up by the collar. Eazy, his partner, quickly stepped back, aware of the storm about to hit. The cold air was thick with tension as I drug Joc towards the steel gate, his eyes widening in a desperate plea for understanding.

"What did I do?!" Joc protested as I slammed him against the cold metal surface of the gate, eliciting a pained grunt. His confusion fueled my irritation. "Argh! Buck, c'mon, man, what did I do?"

"You tell me, motherfucker!" I barked, my grip tightening around his collar.

"I don't know!" Joc's voice weakened under the pressure.

"Think about it!"

His face contorted with pain as I applied more pressure, his mind racing to unravel the mystery of his transgression. The frigid air seemed to thicken as he struggled for an answer.

"Okay, okay, okay!" he finally gasped. "I did a hand-to-hand sell!"

"Exactly, *stupid*." With a calculated release, I let him go, the chill in the air mirroring the cold reality settling over him. He crumpled to his knees, gasping for air. "I'm sorry. I was moving too quick."

"Then slow the fuck down! You're playing with your freedom. You never touch the packs. Never!"

"I'm sorry, Buck!"

"Do it again, and I'm going to do more than take the air from your lungs. I'd rather kill you before I let you mess up this operation."

"Okay!" he pleaded with his eyes wide with fear.

My gaze, still fiery with anger, shifted toward Eazy. He instinctively jumped back, his hands raised in a defensive stance.

"You should have checked him before I got here," I scolded him.

"I didn't see him do it!" Eazy protested, his defense barely holding up against my furious scrutiny.

"I told you, you watch everything, every moment!"

"Okay!" Eazy quickly exclaimed, still keeping his hands up as a sign of surrender.

With anger still pouring through my veins, I turned my attention back to Joc who was still catching his breath. Before he could fully recover, I swung my Timberland-clad foot into his side, sending his frail frame flying a few inches as he bellowed in pain.

My barbaric command echoed off the brick homes around us, "Don't do it again!"

CYNTHIA "CECE" DEBOIS

As I drove through the city towards my parents' house, I poured my heart out to Tiffany over the phone.

"Tiff, I really think Frank has changed. He seems different, more mature."

Tiffany sucked her teeth. "He's *been* trying to show you that he's changed."

"I thought it was just a ploy to get me back, but I don't think so anymore. I think he really gets it now. But I'm scared to give him another chance. I can't experience that hurt again. I don't know if I can survive it. It nearly broke me the first time."

I passed by the familiar streets and buildings that held memories of my childhood. Seventy-ninth Street was so nostalgic for me, the laundromat, the corner stores, the bus stops.

"He says the right things, and I want to believe him. But what if it's just a temporary change? What if he reverts back to his old self?"

"CeCe, girl, you've been through a lot with him. It's natural to be scared. But you also deserve happiness, and if he's truly changed, maybe it's worth considering. If he's serious about change, he'll understand your reservations and work to earn your trust."

I sighed, contemplating Tiff's words. "I just don't want to be naïve, you know? I've got Jah to think about too. Thankfully, he was too young to remember the arguments and fights. But now he can pick up on all of that."

As I parked outside my parents' home, Tiffany replied, "CeCe, listen. Relationships aren't always a smooth ride. Even if Frank has changed, you're still going to face challenges. It's not about expecting everything to be rosy. It's about navigating those ups and downs together."

I sighed, taking in her wisdom. Tiffany had moved to Houston when she met a third-string defensive lineman that played for the Houston Texans in a club one night. They had been together for three years. Having a professional athlete as a significant other, Tiffany most definitely knew how to work through the complexities of being with an attractive man with status and money.

I blew out a heavy breath. "You're right, Tiff. I can't expect perfection. But you know it's hard not to be cautious after everything we've been through."

As I climbed out of my car, Tiffany's tone softened, understanding seeping through. "Absolutely. Take your time, but don't let fear alone decide your path. Love is a risk and sometimes it's worth taking that leap."

I climbed the steps to my parents' porch, still tingling from Frank's touch earlier that morning. It had been so long since I had been comfortably in his arms. I wanted to lock Jah in his room and allow Frank to take me on the kitchen table. But thankfully I was strong, and Frank didn't push. We simply enjoyed breakfast together.

As I stepped into the warmth of my parents' home, Tiffany said, "Remember when I went through it all with my man? I endured cheating, knock-down drag-outs, and betrayal that hurt so bad that I could feel the pain in my chest. But you know what I tell myself? The bad times don't outweigh the good ones. You need to think about whether the good times with Frank outweigh the bad and if the bad is really worth not having him in your life."

I silently acknowledged my mother, who sat on the couch watching the conversation unfold. Tiffany's words resonated with truth that went beyond mere advice. I mouthed, "hello," to my mother, who smiled in return.

"Does it?" Tiffany pressed.

Sighing, I slipped into the bathroom to finish my call. "We went through some things, but you're right," I said, after closing the bathroom door. "It doesn't feel worth not having him in my life. It's just hard to forget the pain sometimes."

Moments of thoughtful silence passed before Tiffany responded, "I get it, CeCe. But don't let fear steal your joy. Give yourself the chance to be happy. You deserve it."

"You're right. But let me get off of this phone. I've made it to my mother's house."

"Okay, girl. Call me back when you leave if you still need to talk."

"Thanks, Tiff."

No sooner than I hung up and opened the door, my mother offered her two cents. "Don't you listen to that bullshit."

My mouth fell open. "Were you listening to me?!"

She shrugged, rolling her eyes. "This is my house. I can do what I want."

I groaned. "How can you tell me not to listen to her when you couldn't hear what she was saying??"

"I can gather what was said from your responses. Don't let her corrupt you," my mother fussed as I plopped down beside her. "You deserve perfection, a man who doesn't cheat and puts you on a pedestal. If you give Frank another chance, he'll only hurt you again and ruin everything. Look at your father. He's never wavered, and he's always been here."

I couldn't help but glance at the photo of my parents on the wall above the loveseat. I'd always seen my father as perfect, but that seemed so unrealistic, especially in their marriage. But he'd never shown me anything but perfection, something that Frank had failed at time and time again.

My mother turned towards me, placing a comforting hand on my knee. "Your father has been my rock, CeCe. He's never given me a reason to doubt him. You should aim for the same kind of love. And you can have that. Don't give up because you think that another man won't want you with two kids. You can find the right man, CeCe."

Listening to her, I wrestled with if such perfection truly existed. The sounds of Tiffany's encouragement collided with my mother's caution, creating a storm of conflicting thoughts.

As I sat there, absorbing what my mother had said, her dislike for Frank echoed in every word. He embodied everything she had warned me about—the roughneck, the street guy, the man who would get me pregnant but leave me unmarried, the exact opposite of what she had envisioned for me. I remembered the disappointment in her eyes when I didn't go to college and got pregnant. I felt like I had let her down, and now, the prospect of giving Frank another chance seemed like another step in the wrong direction.

A part of me wanted to prove to my mother that I could do better, that I could have the stable, perfect life she always wished for me. The desire for her approval clashed with the complicated feelings I had for Frank. It was a battle between my own yearning for a better life and the undeniable connection I still felt with a man who had been both a source of joy and pain.

15

CYNTHIA "CECE" DEBOIS

The biting cold of February stung my skin as I stepped out of the car. The snowflakes fell around me like soft crystals. The winter air cut through my coat, and I shivered, hugging myself to preserve any warmth I could. Being eight months pregnant added an extra layer of discomfort to the cold, making every step feel heavier.

My tired body ached, and the soreness seemed to intensify with each passing day. The weight of carrying another life inside of me took its toll, especially in the winter chill. I took slow, deliberate steps toward Frank's headquarters, the porch steps feeling like a mountain to climb.

I paused outside the door, a small smile playing on my lips as I heard the familiar sounds of Frank and Jah engaged in conversation. The excited cadence of Jah's four-year-old voice reached my ears, creating a comforting melody. Despite the cold seeping through my coat, I lingered for a moment, relishing the warmth of the relationship he had with his father.

The bond between Frank and Jah was undeniable, and witnessing the love and joy exchanged between them warmed my heart. Despite the rocky path Frank and I had walked, I couldn't deny the deep affection I still held for him. Much of the love that I still harbored for him was a result of watching how he was such a loving father to our son.

After finally knocking on the door, the lively conversation between Frank and Jah abruptly ceased, leaving only the whispers of hushed tones. Moments later, faint sounds of shuffling signaled Frank's approach to the door. My palms grew clammy, and my breath caught in my throat. I shook my head in disbelief that after all of these years, after so many fights and so much heartbreak, Frank still had this effect on me.

The sounds of the latches unlocking got my attention. Then he stood before me, leaning against the doorway with an aura of striking swag. He effortlessly seized my focus, exuding an air of sensual dominance that never failed to captivate me. My eyes were instantly drawn to him, as they always were, completely absorbed by his presence.

Frank's light complexion accentuated the vibrant, colorful tattoos adorning his arms and torso. Each intricate design told a story, a medley of emotions etched on his skin. With light-brown eyes that shimmered with mystery, every glance from him was an invitation to explore a world filled with long nights of good dick and addictive satisfaction.

His curly hair, seemingly defying any attempts at taming, added a touch of wildness to his otherwise menacing look. Every curl had a mind of its own, dancing in harmony with his every movement.

But it wasn't just his striking appearance that held me captive. Frank's presence alone had the ability to make me weak at the knees. It was the way he carried himself, with quiet strength that spoke volumes. He was a man of power. His mere presence demanded respect. And yet, there was gentleness in his smile, a warmth that melted away any reservations I had, leaving only the desire to know him more intimately.

Grinning, he grabbed my round belly, rubbing it as if it were the Tree of Hope stump on the stage of the Apollo Theater.

"What's up?" he greeted me, but he was smiling at my belly as he continued to rub it.

"Don't wake him up," I warned softly.

"He's been acting up in there?"

"All day..." I sighed. "Doing summersaults and shit."

Frank's smile met my expression. Our eyes locked in an unspoken connection. I couldn't help but feel the familiar surge of attraction flowing through my veins. Though four years had passed, the magnetic pull between us remained as potent as ever. Frank was an enigma, a captivating force that I couldn't resist.

But my mother's warnings and expectations kept ringing in my head. Even if Frank had changed, he was still in the game and the game came with its own recipe of disaster for any relationship. I wanted so badly to prove to my mother that I could make better choices in life and in men, so I buried my attraction to Frank. I buried it away and brushed past him and rushed inside of the house.

I entered the headquarters, my mind swirling with conflicting thoughts and emotions. But I was snatched off of my usual emotional rollercoaster when I saw Jah sitting at the money counter, feeding it bills. "Frank!" I exclaimed. "What the hell?! Jah should not be playing with money like that!"

Frank was completely oblivious as he rounded the cocktail

table and sat behind Jah. "I'm teaching him how to count," he explained with a nonchalant shrug. "He needs to understand the value of money and make sure not a dollar is missing."

I sighed, torn between knowing that Frank was only mimicking how he'd grown up and my deep-seated fears about my boys ending up in the game. Even though Frank and Buck were respected and hadn't been in any real danger because of their reputation, Frank couldn't ensure that for our sons. I didn't want my boys to follow in their father's footsteps, but I knew that Frank wouldn't have it any other way. My mother's constant reminders of the downsides that came with being involved with someone from the streets replayed in my mind. But seeing Frank's genuine care for Jah made it harder to dismiss him completely.

"Frank, I appreciate your desire to educate Jah," I replied carefully. "But I'm worried about the risks and influences associated with this lifestyle. We need to find another way to teach Jah without exposing him to all of this."

"It's just money, CeCe."

"But it's more money than any normal person will ever see. If he sees this growing up, he's going to expect it."

"Exactly." Seeing my lingering frustration, his eyes filled with sincerity. "I understand your concerns," he said gently. "I don't want our sons to inherit this game. I'd prefer if I can create generational wealth for them, so they'll never have to touch drugs. But being in this game, it's no guarantee that I will live long enough to do that." The reminder of that possibility made my heart cry out in agony as he continued. "And just in case that happens, and they are forced to hustle, I have to educate him on this shit. Please trust me on this."

I took a deep breath, willing myself to trust him. No matter how he'd mishandled me, he had never fumbled Jah, his money, or the game. "Okay," I finally conceded reluctantly, though. "But we need to find safer ways for Jah to learn and grow up. Let's work together to provide him with the best opportunities, so that following in your footsteps isn't the only option."

FRANK "CAPO" DISCIPLE

My gaze hardened as I looked at Alexander who seemed more disheveled and desperate than ever. A few days later, Buck and I were in a meeting with him in our usual spot, the dimly lit Drake hotel lobby in downtown Chicago. But something wasn't right. Every time I laid eyes on Alexander, he seemed to have fallen deeper into the abyss of addiction.

"Goddamn junky," I grumbled under my breath as I took a seat.

Buck chuckled, letting me know that he'd heard me.

Alexander shifted uncomfortably in his seat, his eyes darting nervously. First, we went over the usual stuff like shipments, delivery, and numbers.

But then he hit me with some bullshit.

"This Keyes character is in the way. He's blocking me from expanding my business into new territories. You gotta take care of him."

My eyes narrowed at the way he'd said that shit so casually. I leaned back in my chair, trying to keep my anger in check.

Keyes was a friend of mine and had never wronged me. Loyalty was a prized virtue in my world, and Keyes had always respected that boundary. "Keyes ain't never crossed me. You know I don't move against my own unless they do first. I ain't takin' a hit out on him just 'cause *you* want to spread your wings."

Alexander's eyes narrowed, obvious frustration blending with his desperation. "This ain't about your personal feelings. This is *business*, and Keyes is standing in my way. You think loyalty matters in this game? It's eat or be eaten. I need his network to depend on me for their supply. They won't come over to your team until we get rid of him."

In 1994, President Bill Clinton signed the Violent Crime Control and Law Enforcement Act, which provided incentives for states to adopt their own "Three Strikes" laws. This legislation contributed to the nationwide adoption and expansion of such laws in various states across the country. Six years later, a lot of hustlers were going to prison for longer sentences, some even life, for simply selling cocaine. There weren't as many hustlers as before. The Disciple Family and Keyes' crew were currently two of the biggest connects in the Midwest. If Keyes was exterminated, that would leave his network without a supplier.

The room fell silent for a moment as I stared at Alexander, contemplating my next move. This was a critical moment. Losing Alexander as an ally could mean losing my own life. But at the same time, turning against my homie was something I wasn't down for.

"Buck..." I broke the silence, turning to my right hand. "You think I should entertain this shit?" My voice was dripping with disbelief and sarcasm.

Buck looked at me with his eyes reflecting the unwavering

loyalty he had for me. "Cap, you know I ride or die with you. Whatever you decide, I got your back," he responded, his words as solid as granite.

I turned my attention back to Alexander, my eyes narrowing to slits. "I ain't doin' this. Keyes is off-limits. Find another solution or another stooge to do your dirty work," I hissed.

Alexander's face fell with clear disappointment mixed with desperation and determination. "All right, Frank. I'll find another way. But I promise you won't like it." Alexander gave me a menacing glare before he rose to his feet. Without uttering another word, he strutted away.

Buck let out a weary sigh and sat up, his eyes filled with dread. "You know he's going to kill us, right?"

At this point, Buck and I were fully convinced that Alexander was no ordinary white man. It had been talks amongst the hood that the CIA was behind the flood of drugs and guns that had infiltrated the streets in the 80's and 90's, that the white man was filling our ghettos with heroin and crack, causing a plague of mayhem and death. Buck and I were proof of that. So, Alexander most definitely possessed the means to eliminate us without batting an eye and swiftly replace us with someone far more obedient.

"Yeah..." I replied, my voice laced with resignation. "I know."

———

Back at the headquarters, Buck and I came up with the daunting plan of getting rid of Alexander before he had a chance to take us out.

"You sure about this?" Buck asked, a puff of weed smoke floating from his large lips.

"I don't see any other way. I'm not putting a hit on Keyes. He's never stepped on our toes. He always stays in his lane. Killing him would be foul as fuck. Besides, if I do and it's connected back to us, that will start a war. I'm not putting CeCe at risk like that."

When it came to war in this game, revenge was cutthroat. I wouldn't be a target; my loved ones would be. And CeCe, my son, and Buck were the only people on this earth that I loved.

"We can try to get him on our team. Give him a lower price so that he can still make money off of his network."

I shook my head at Buck's offer. "And have him work for us? He'd never go for that."

"He'd go for it if we tell him what Alexander wants us to do."

"Then he'd always look at us as a threat. He'd never trust us."

Buck cringed. "*Shit.*"

"We gotta do this."

He scoffed, knowing it was true. "I know. I was just hoping there was another way. I'm no pussy, but killing the CIA? *Maaan...*" He paused, allowing the weight of that to linger in the air as he hit the blunt again. Then frustration blew loudly from my throat. "That motherfucker is out here bad. It's obvious. So, we can't be the only people he's creating bad blood with."

"True."

"If we do it right and make sure we don't leave a trace, we should be okay."

"Right. It has to be done. The crew was tired of the constant changes. It was time for us to get a new connect, but Alexander was never going to let that happen. We're killing two birds with one stone—*literally*."

"We'll need a new connect that can provide us with the quantity we need at the same prices. That shit is going to be difficult."

"Hopefully, our reputation will grant us access to the right distro or—"

There was a sudden creak as the front door swung open. We were expecting Queen, so our guards weren't up.

She barged in like a hurricane.

"Hey, Frank," she blurted out, rushing into the living room. She slammed a duffle bag onto the table and then hurried over to me, leaning down to give me a quick embrace.

"What's up, Queen? Everything go smooth?" I asked.

"Yeah," she said, shrugging it off like a pro. "I didn't have any issues. Made the delivery, got the cash, and that was it."

"Good," I replied, my gaze locked on her.

She playfully rolled her eyes. "And, yeah, I counted it."

"Thanks. Where you rushing off to?" I inquired.

"I promised Reggie I'd be home early tonight," she urgently explained.

I nodded, noticing her eyes drift unintentionally towards Buck. She quickly rolled them back, her pretty face contorted into a scowl.

Buck scoffed, "Don't start, lil' girl."

"I'm a *grown woman*," she spat.

Buck tauntingly chuckled. "I wish you'd act like it then."

"When you stop actin' like a lil' boy, I will."

"Aye—"

"Aye, nothing!" Queen spat, jabbing her hand into the air. "You ain't gotta say shit else to me because I'm out!" Queen spun around, bolting out as quickly as she'd come in.

I chuckled, shaking my head as she closed the door behind her, leaving Buck stewing in frustration.

"Y'all funny as hell," I said.

"I don't see shit funny. Why she even work for us? She is disrespectful as hell."

"Just go ahead and take her down."

Buck frowned. "What?"

"All of this tension between y'all is *sexual*."

Buck frowned and convulsed as if he were repulsed. "Whatever, man."

ANTHONY "BUCK" PATTERSON

I sat back in my leather armchair with the tension of the day weighing heavily on me. The decision me and Frank had come to had been a hard one, but I had felt for some time now that it was coming. Though killing was easy for us, it was never an easy decision to come to, especially when it came to a man of Alexander's stature. We would have to be precise without leaving any trace of evidence behind. We would also now have to find a new connect.

Peaches sat on my lap, rubbing my head. April was in the kitchen, whipping up some dinner. Diamond was on the floor, gently massaging my tired feet while lost in her own world with her CD player and headphones, humming Aaliyah tunes.

"You get so much more respect from me for choosing not to kill Keyes," Peaches poured into me. "I know that this was a hard decision, though."

"I hate this part of the game," I growled, my fingers gripping the armrest. "He's been causing problems for far too long. Now, he wants us to pop Keyes? Hell nah."

Peaches sat back, her eyes scanning the room before locking onto mine. "You sure about this, Buck? This kind of shit can bring a lot of trouble."

My gaze darkened, enraged that Alexander had even put us in this situation. The way that Frank and I ran this tight ship, we rarely had issues so grave. "I know. But this is business, and in our line of work, you gotta take care of problems like Alexander. It's either him or us."

Peaches nodded, her lips pursed. "You're right. If you don't, Alexander is only going to get worse. And if there's anyone who can do it, it's you and Frank."

Pride welled up inside me as I looked at Peaches. She understood me, she understood what needed to be done.

I leaned back in my chair, my gaze sweeping over the room. Frank had me at his right hand and he had CeCe and his children to go home to receive love that the streets didn't have for gangsters like us. I had my hoes for support.

Locking eyes with me, Peaches flashed a coy smile that woke my dick right up. Slowly, she leaned in, and her velvety lips met mine in a sloppy, wet dance. The warmth of her tongue met mine, dissolving the lingering tension of the day.

As Peaches deepened the kiss, her fingers traced gentle patterns on my bare chest. The touch of her dainty hands felt like a loving caress, soothing the nerves that had been erupting with frustrations all day.

I sensed Diamond's grip fading from my feet. The subtle sound of headphones hitting the floor sounded in the room. Suddenly, her hands found their way into my basketball shorts. She gripped my dick tightly with both hands. The sound of her spitting on it caused me to exhale deeply into Peaches' kiss. As she cupped my face, Diamond's touch added another layer, turning a simple kiss into a sexual explosion that we often shared together.

As Diamond began to jag my dick expertly, Peaches' lips left mine. She then climbed off of me and joined Diamond on the floor. They both began to tongue kiss my dick while Diamond's hands hugged it, Peaches on the head and Diamond on my shaft balls.

They had been sucking my dick for years. So, I had taught them how to get me off with expertise. Soon, I was unloading into Peaches' mouth. She eagerly swallowed every ounce. But she continued to jag my dick as she wiped me clean with her tongue while Diamond massaged my balls.

"Fuck!" I barked, my head falling back. "Gawd damn," I gritted.

"You're still so hard, Daddy," Diamond panted.

I looked down, though I could feel my dick painfully still aiming towards the ceiling.

Diamond sat back on her knees, eagerly awaiting instruction while Peaches continued sucking my cum off of my length.

"Yo', April!" I called out.

Soon, her voice came out of the kitchen, into the living and dining room area. "Yes, Daddy?"

"Come sit on this dick."

She smiled devilishly as she hurried towards me on bare feet. She padded into the living room, pulling her boy shorts down to her ankles. She kicked them off as Diamond and Peaches gave her room to straddle me in the reverse-cowgirl position. As she did, I saw disappoint flash in Diamond's eyes.

April's tight pussy started to bounce up and down on my dick, her slick walls pulling on every inch. I could feel Peaches now orally massaging my balls as I watched Diamond pout as she stood up. Our eyes met, and I motioned for her to come to me. She readily did, and I gently grabbed her by the throat, bringing her ear to my mouth.

April's wet ride brought low grunts from me as I whispered into Diamond's ear. "You gotta stop being so jealous."

She gently held the wrist of the hand that was holding her neck in place. "I just love you so much, Daddy."

I pushed back against her throat, making her look at me. My eyes squinted as April's center hugged my dick. "Too much?" I whispered to April. "You can't do this no more?"

"I can do it," she eagerly told me. "I'm good. I promise."

Though I knew that she was lying, I told her, "Then get down there and help Peaches."

16

QUEEN ARIA BENSON

As I sat down at the dinner table, surrounded by the scent of fried catfish, Southern-style green beans, macaroni and cheese, and rolls, I felt so many mixed emotions. This meal was filled with flavors of my grandmother's upbringing in Jackson, Mississippi, and it brought back cherished memories of her. She was the one who had taught me how to cook, passing down her wisdom and recipes with love before she died.

That was how Reggie had fallen for me. He was attracted to the way that I could prepare home cooked meals at such a young age. My grandmother had taught me to cook and clean the way no other nineteen-year-old ever could. One of the easiest ways that I could soothe Reggie was to feed him. Watching the satisfaction on his face made me so proud.

But there was another side to Reggie that I feared, that broke my heart. I hated his unpredictable temper, his outbursts, and the way he could change from kind and loving to someone I barely recognized. Deep down, I knew he was a ticking time bomb waiting to explode with anger and fury. It was disheartening to see the man I loved turn into someone so different, someone who frightened me.

Even with these fears, I tried to stay calm. But nervousness still seeped in because I was never sure of Reggie's mood. Eating dinner with him had been like walking on eggshells, hoping each bite of food would turn his rage into peace.

I smiled when I saw Reggie's eyes close as he chewed a bite of catfish. "It's good, baby?" I asked with my grin widening teasingly.

When his eyes opened, I wished to see warmth and love, but I only saw irritation. "Yeah, it's cool. I saw you in here rushing. You wouldn't have had to rush home if you stopped running behind Frank like he's your man."

Anxiety clenched at my chest. Each bite of food that I took became an act of survival, an attempt to muffle the defiant words that I wanted to spew in response.

"It's about time you stopped working for him."

Defiance and fear welled up in me as I mustered my response, "I need the money. We need the money." I tried to keep my voice steady, searching for a shred of understanding in Reggie's eyes.

Reggie's anger surged, his fist slamming down on the table with force that vibrated through the room.

Startled, I flinched, my heart racing as he bellowed, "I don't need them niggas!"

"Calm down, baby," I pleaded, my voice barely a whisper. I reached out, my hand trembling, hoping to suppress the storm brewing inside him. But my effort was in vain.

"If you want me to be calm, don't tell me that I need those

motherfuckas!" Reggie's roar sent shivers down my spine. As he shouted, pieces of catfish flew from his tightly clenched lips.

Defeated and disappointed, my voice lowered along with my spirits. "*Okay*, Reggie. I'm sorry."

CYNTHIA "CECE" DEBOIS

My father and I sat together in the cozy mom-and-pop Mexican restaurant on the east side of Chicago. The vibrant colors of the walls adorned with beautiful hand-painted murals made me feel like I was in Mexico. The sound of cheerful Mexican music filled the air and set the tone even more. The aroma of freshly made tortillas and sizzling meats wafted from the kitchen. The plates in front of us were Mexican culinary masterpieces.

Between mouthfuls of the flavorful food, my father got in my business, which I knew was the purpose of this one-on-one dinner. "How's the pregnancy going, CeCe? Are you ready for another baby?"

I glanced down at my growing belly and smiled. "Honestly, I'm feeling a little overwhelmed. But I know deep down that things will go smoothly because I have such an amazing support system."

My father's eyes sparkled with pride as he reached across

the table, placing a gentle hand on mine. "You're right, sweetheart. Me and your mother are always here for you. We love helping with Jah and we'll continue to do so with the new baby. We always kind of regretted not having a bigger family. I guess you're fixing that for us." He let out a hearty laugh that I joined in on.

"I don't know, Dad. I think this is my last one."

Because I was an only child, I had initially looked forward to me and Frank having as many kids as God allowed. But, now that I was a single mother, I was too overwhelmed to ever consider having more kids with anyone else.

My father rolled his eyes, smirking at me jokingly as if he didn't believe me. When his laughter subsided, he said, "No matter what your mother thinks of him, Frank is an incredible father."

Thinking of him made my smile reach my ears. "I'm glad you know that, Dad. I'm so thankful for Frank," I replied. "He may not have been the perfect boyfriend, but he's an awesome father."

My father clearly admired the affectionate expression on my face. Feeling a pang of guilt, I lowered my head, blushing bashfully. My father reached across the table again and gently patted my hand.

"It's okay," he reassured me.

Confused, my eyes fluttered, seeking an explanation.

"He's not perfect, and that's totally fine. No one is flawless, especially a young man suddenly thrust into fatherhood. I, too, have made mistakes. Mistakes that I'm grateful your mother forgave me for," my father admitted with a chuckle, shaking his head slightly.

I was stunned. I had always seen my father as the epitome of perfection, a man who could do no wrong.

He chuckled at my shock. Then he gave me a quick shrug with a guilty glare in his eyes. "Your mother is a Taurus, baby. She likes to put up a facade of perfection that isn't realistic. But we shielded you from our shortcomings."

I couldn't help but ask, "Shortcomings? What do you mean?"

A shameful smirk painted his face. "Everyone makes mistakes."

I pressed on, my eyes wildly searching for answers, "Mistakes like what? What did you do, Daddy?"

He looked at me, his expression turning serious. He leaned forward, clasping my hand tightly. "Things you don't need to know. Just understand that every man falls short, that not every man is ready for a committed relationship and sadly, many men cheat."

I gasped and sat back, shocked by his admission.

Seeing my reaction, my father leaned in further, gripping my hand tightly. "I'm telling you this because I can see how much you love Frank, and I can see how much he loves you. When I first married your mother, before we had you, I too made mistakes. But thanks to her forgiveness, I had the opportunity to grow into the man you think is perfect. While your mother wants to shield you from pain, she doesn't realize that you can't always avoid it because we're all human. If it's not Frank, it will be the next man because every relationship is a flawed yet beautiful journey of love and sacrifice, leading to a connection that can be perfect in its own imperfect way."

I sat back, shock covering me. But as I wrestled with the vague confessions my father had made, I was reminded of the things Tiffany had said during our last conversation. I had been so confused with how to move forward with Frank. The hurt wouldn't allow me to be vulnerable with him again, but I couldn't deny the love that still lingered in my heart for him, love that was getting encouragement from a lot of sources to give him a second chance.

FRANK "CAPO" DISCIPLE

"Yes, baby! Oh my God," Lamonica's voice quivered as she threw her ass back on my dick. "*Fuck!*"

Lamonica was being tortured because I felt like I was. In a few hours, Buck and I would have to carry out one of the biggest hits of our careers in the game. And killing Alexander would only fix one of our problems and give us an even bigger one, which was finding a new connect.

On top of that, lately, CeCe had been more receptive to me and more open. I wanted to pounce and reclaim her, but I knew she wasn't ready. Something was still keeping her at arm's length. I was so frustrated. I wanted that woman so bad. In my world, I was surrounded my visions of ugliness and death. But her beauty made me grateful for the ability to see, but she was still torturing me with her distance, so I was torturing Lamonica with dick deep in her guts.

I drove every inch in deep, holding her ass cheeks wide open. Her ass fell back against my pelvis, causing a clapping sound to erupt around the room. Thoughts of CeCe frustrated me, driving me to take Lamonica's long ponytail into my hand. I used it as leverage. Her pleas for mercy and moans of pleasure muffled into the pillow that her face was buried in.

"*Ooooh!*"

"Hold that ass open for me." I positioned her perfectly, back arched so that her ass was high in the air with her chest and face pressed into the pillow. I took her hands and put them on her ass cheeks, and she spread them open.

"Yeah, just like that."

With one hand planted on her headboard and the other gripping her ponytail, I erupted into a quick, steady rhythm of deep strokes that made her body convulse on my dick.

"Fuck me just like that," she panted.

Even though she asked for it, the deeper I got, she tensed up.

"Don't move," I roared gently. "Just take it."

"Shit!" she whimpered.

The creamy sound of me milking her sloppy center had me hard as a rock. I felt her cumming.

"That's it. Take it," I encouraged her.

"*Uuuh!*"

Her walls clenched, sucking me in. Just then, a burst of liquid exploded around my dick, and I continued to drive in and out of her. "C'mon. That's it. Give it to me."

"*Arrrrgh!*" she cried out as she squirted her juices all over me.

Giving her no mercy, I continued delivering punishable strokes. "That ain't enough. Give me some more."

"Oh, Cap!"

Each stroke was conjuring her to cum more for me. "Give me some more."

"Oh my God, baby, stop," she pleaded as another explosion of juices burst all over me. "*Pleeeease* stop."

"Unt uh. Give me some more."

———

Later that evening, in the heart of downtown, Buck and I positioned ourselves discreetly outside the Drake hotel. We were masked in the shadows, our bodies concealed beneath dark motorcycle gear and helmets. The streets were alive with the hustle and bustle of passing pedestrians, the sound of their hurried footsteps echoed around us.

As we sat on our motorcycles, I peered across the street, keeping an attentive eye on the steady stream of people flowing in and out of the hotel. Couples in elegant attire, their laughter muffled by the biting wind, strolled arm in arm. They were completely oblivious to the danger lurking nearby. A group of rowdy college kids stumbled out of a nearby bar, their boisterous voices bouncing off of the buildings surrounding us.

I clenched my jaw as my focus sharpened with each passing minute. This was no ordinary hit. We were about to take down a man who very well may have been a member of the covert world of the CIA. By killing him, we risked attracting a heightened police presence that could suffocate the very essence of our operation. However, we were willing to take that risk to save the life of a man who was naively unaware of the jeopardy his life was in. In the aftermath, we hoped like hell to find a new connect before our supply ran out. Beneath Alexander's thirst for Keyes' life, it had been apparent for a while that he had been slowly unraveling.

He needed to die.

Just as the bite of the wintry wind threatened to make me

buckle, Buck's low voice broke the silence, jolting me from my thoughts. "Cap, there he is."

I followed Buck's gaze, directing mine towards the hotel's grand entrance. Alexander casually strolled across the lobby with misplaced confidence. Despite his expensive tailored suit that screamed affluence, his disheveled hair and jittery movements hinted at his downfall.

A dark twisted grin escaped my lips as I tightened my grip on the handlebars. Buck and I revved our engines, the roar cutting through the night like the predators we were. As I watched, a sleek black vehicle pulled up by the curb. My gut told me it was the usual private car arranged for Alexander's departure back to New York. Finally, he emerged from the lobby, and we watched him intently. The driver of the black car emerged, rounding the hood. The driver eagerly met Alexander on the curb. They shook hands before the driver opened the back passenger's door for Alexander who climbed in.

With precision, Buck and I kept a discreet distance behind the car as it rolled through downtown and onto the expressway.

As the traffic flow became more predictable, a moment presented itself. I pulled alongside the passenger's side of the black car. My hand reached into my waistband where my gun was concealed. With swift determination, I pulled the weapon and released the safety. Alexander sat in the back seat unaware of his impending demise. My finger found the trigger, and the tension built inside me before finally exploding into action.

The gun erupted in my hand, emptying the clip into the back seat. The sound of gunfire pierced the air, shattering the silence of the expressway. My gaze locked onto the chaos unfolding within the car, an image forever etched in my memory. The car swerved, its driver panicking as the black sedan careened towards the inevitable abyss.

It was done. The black car, now veering uncontrollably, swayed towards the road's edge, leaving only destruction in its wake. My hands trembled, the adrenaline coursing through my veins.

As the black car finally came to rest, Buck and I continued our journey, leaving behind a scene of chaos and death.

Buck and I swiftly took the first exit off the expressway. We raced towards the alley where we had stashed our trap car. Arriving at the dark confines, the glow of flames illuminated the night sky as we set our motorcycles ablaze. The crackling fire devoured the evidence, erasing any connection between us and Alexander's death. Satisfied, we drove to the onramp nearest to the spot where the black car had come to a stop. Concealed within the darkness of the night, we watched intently as many police and ambulances arrived. Eventually, they extracted Alexander's lifeless body from the twisted wreckage. It was only then that we allowed ourselves to breathe with satisfaction, knowing that Alexander was dead.

The next day, I sat in my crib, waiting for CeCe to drop Jah off. I couldn't focus, however, although I knew that there was no evidence to identify me and Buck as suspects in Alexander's murder. However, the pressure of finding a new connect was weighing on me. Luckily, we had a lot of product to hold us over for some time. But if I didn't want to look like I had taken over this organization in vain, I had to find a new connect quickly.

"Gawd damn." I frowned while looking at my phone ring. Lamonica was calling for the umpteenth time. I was now regretting giving her so many orgasms the day before. I usually rationed the dick and time out to women to keep them from getting too obsessed. I didn't get too emotional, and I kept them at arm's length. I had known that Lamonica was overstepping when she expected me to spend time with her on Valentine's Day. But being around CeCe's softening heart had my dick so hard that I'd had to let loose on something.

The doorbell rang, bringing me to my feet. With so much chaos unfolding the day before, I was looking forward to spending this day in the house alone with my son. I hurried to the door, in a rush to get my family out of the frigid cold air.

After opening it, CeCe rushed Jah in without saying hello. "Gawd damn, it's cold out there."

Her intoxicating scent enveloped my senses, a sweet and alluring fragrance that filled the room. With eagerness that seemed like an obsession, she hurried into the foyer, captivating me with each step. I struggled to catch a glimpse of her delicate features hidden beneath the plush fur hood that shielded her from the cold. But with a swift, graceful movement, she pulled back the hood, revealing a face that could launch a thousand ships. Her mere presence had the power to unravel me completely. She was the only woman who didn't need keys to drive me crazy.

"Hey, beautiful," I flirted, closing out the brick cold.

Caught off guard with the way that my gaze inhaled her, she stuttered. "H-hey, Frank."

She was beautiful to me, not because of her physical, but because of how she made me feel on the inside. When I looked at her, I was simply Frank, not the capo of an organization that made deadly decisions. I was simply a boy in love, not a man with blood on my hands. I was a father of two sons, not a boss.

"What are you going to do with your free day?"

Her eyes met mine, and a mischievous smile danced across her face. "Me and Queen are going to go shopping and go to the movies to see Scream 3." As she spoke, our gazes locked, and an electric charge passed between us, intensifying the attraction that simmered beneath the surface.

"We should take Jah to see The Tiger Movie," I suggested.

I was shocked when she so easily agreed. "That's cool."

"Both of us," I reiterated.

There was a moment of hesitation. I watched her struggle internally, gnawing on that plump bottom lip that I wanted to suck on. For a moment, I thought I had pushed too far. We had been co-parenting within the four walls of my house or hers, but she hadn't allowed me to take her out in public in a long time. But it seemed like something had gotten through to her overnight. We had only communicated via text, but she suddenly seemed even more open than she had been lately.

Then she did it.

In a moment that seemed to hang in time, she gave in, breathing out a soft, "Okay."

Her surrender stole the wind from my lungs, making me nearly lose my balance. I grinned, slowly walking towards her. "Yeah?"

She giggled at my excitement, nodding slowly, licking her lips. "Yes, Frank, we—"

"Cap!" The sound of Lamonica's shrieking filled the foyer followed by relentless banging on my front door. "Cap! Open the damn door!"

Instantly, the relief that had flooded through me vanished, leaving me in a state of defeat. CeCe's expression twisted with rage as I glanced at her, the happiness instantly wiped from her face.

The banging continued, shaking the foundation of the house and causing Jah to jump out of his skin. CeCe quickly bent down to Jah's level, her voice strained but gentle towards him. "Go into the den and take off your coat, baby."

"Okay, Mommy!" Jah, oblivious to the turmoil that had just engulfed his father's world, obeyed his mother without question.

I watched as CeCe kept her eyes on Jah until he disappeared into the safety of the den. Meanwhile, Lamonica's insistent banging served as a haunting backdrop to the end of me and CeCe's potential unfolding before my eyes.

As soon as CeCe's furious gaze landed on me, my heart sank. I desperately tried to find the right words, pleading with her through the haze of our crumbling relationship. "CeCe–"

"But you wanna be with me?" she hissed, her eyes burning with anger.

"She shouldn't even be here." Rage boiled under my defeat. I had purposely never brought a woman to my house. Where I lay my head was an intimate place that I reserved only for my loved ones.

"You want to make us work?" CeCe taunted me. "You want to prove that things will be better, but the moment that I finally feel comfortable enough to try, we're back dealing with the same shit!"

"Cap, open the door!" Lamonica's screaming cut into the house, ending me, burying me.

Defeat made my head lower.

"Gon' head and open the door, Frank!" CeCe snapped.

"You haven't been giving me the time of day. What do you expect me to do, CeCe?"

"I expect you to stop putting me in this position! I expect you to stop embarrassing me over and over again! And she obviously means something to you because she knows where you live!"

"I swear to God I don't know how she knows where I live! I don't play like that, and you know it!"

That she knew, so at least she gave me that, not arguing with me long enough for me to hear Lamonica explode. "She's in there?! You're with her when you was just fucking me last night?!"

Disgusted, CeCe groaned, holding her head.

Fueled by anger, I ripped the door open, paying no attention to the chilly winds that clawed at me. In nothing but a T-shirt, Nike shorts, and Nike slides, I stormed out onto the porch, the screen door swinging wide open. Lamonica foolishly attempted to force her way inside. I grabbed the leather of her coat by the shoulders and forcefully pushed her away. The icy porch caused her to lose her footing. With a painful thud, her butt crashed onto the unforgiving cement, sending her sliding down the short flight of porch steps, all while her shrill shrieks pierced the air.

CeCe's demented chuckle caused me to turn around with pleading eyes. The calm in her walk was frightening. The tranquility in her expression was even more terrifying. She looked like a woman who was more than done as she stepped out onto the porch.

As she descended the steps, I tried to reach for her. But she snatched away, eyes narrowing, "Don't fucking touch me!"

"I hate you, Cap!" Lamonica cried as she scrambled to her feet. The scarf around her neck got tangled in the dead branches, making it difficult for her to stand up. But she still screamed at me, "You ain't shit, nigga!"

Descending the stairs, CeCe started to laugh. "I agree."

"But you keep letting him knock you up!" Lamonica sneered as she finally stood up.

I jumped down the steps, lunging towards Lamonica. But

CeCe had already leaned over the banister, pulled her arm back, and sent a chinchilla cloaked arm flying towards Lamonica's nose. Lamonica's neck snapped back. Her body went flying into a dead hydrangea bush.

"CeCe!" I warned as softly as I could, grabbing her around the waist from the back. "The baby!"

"Fuck you, Frank! Let me go!" As she fought to get out of my arms, I allowed it, not wanting to put any stress on my son, but as she turned and focused such disappointed and hurtful orbs on me, I knew that it was useless. "I'm so tired of you letting me down."

"I'm fucking you up, bitch," we heard Lamonica strain. Out of the corner of my eyes, I could see her struggling to get out of the barrage of branches and dead leaves.

But my gaze remained on CeCe, watching tears pool in her eyes, dissolving my heart strings. "Please leave me alone," she begged as a tear fell. "*Please?*"

As another one dropped down her cheek, she turned and marched to her ride.

I had too much love for her to stop her.

A FEW WEEKS LATER...

17

FRANK "CAPO" DISCIPLE

"Meechie said he got a guy that's getting birds from some dude in India."

I sucked my teeth as I put Jah's pizza in the oven. "That motherfucka be lying."

Buck chuckled on the other end of the phone. "Yeah, he do. But it don't hurt to look into it."

"If you wanna waste your time, gon' 'head."

Just as I closed the oven door, I turned to find Jah standing on the kitchen island, his tiny feet planted firmly on the smooth surface. My heart skipped a beat at the sight. Then I chuckled, shaking my head. "Get down, lil' man."

"I wanna jump, Daddy!" he eagerly exclaimed.

I put a finger up to my lips to quiet him.

"Hector is still trying to meet with us," Buck reminded me.

I leaned against the island to prevent Jah from falling because his hard-headed butt was still standing up. "We can't go behind Keyes' back like that."

"He's willing to give us the prices we want."

"I know."

"You already saved the nigga's life. He would honor that."

Hector was the type of distributor that didn't want to work with too many connects, especially too many connects in the same region. Keyes' had the Midwest sowed up for Hector. However, the Disciple Family moved more weight and faster than Keyes' crew. Knowing that, Hector would prefer the Disciple Family to move his weight, moving Keyes' out of his position. Though Hector had never told me that, I knew he would because it was a boss move.

"We wouldn't appreciate having to transition from bosses to henchmen," I told Buck. "You know that Hector would replace Keyes with us as soon as we agree to work with him."

Buck blew out a frustrated breath. He wasn't frustrated with me, though. He was frustrated with our circumstance. "You're right."

As suspected, Buck and I had yet to be connected to Alexander's murder. However, we had yet to find a new distributor. It was hard to get a distributor to trust new hustlers. Luckily, some either knew us or had heard of our legendary work in the streets, but they either couldn't provide us with the prices we wanted or couldn't supply us with the amount we needed as quickly as we needed it.

"We'll figure it out," I told Buck. "I'm going to get up with you after I drop Jah off at CeCe's in a few hours."

"Bet."

As I hung up, Jah declared excitedly, "Daddy, I wanna jump!"

I turned around, smiling at his nerve. I spread my arms wide open, ready to catch him. "All right," I replied. "Jump. I'll catch you."

Jah's eyes widened, a glint of fear flashing across his face. "But Daddy, I'm scared. What if you don't catch me?"

"I got you. I *promise*. Daddy is always going to catch you."

He bent his knees as if he were about to leap, but he hesitated, giggling with bashful fear. "I can't do it. Pick me up."

I took a step closer, bending down so that we were eye to eye. "Living in fear is just another way of dying before your time."

Confusion caused his eyes to narrow as his head tilted.

Laughing, I tried again, "One day, you'll become a big boy who can't live in fear. Life is full of challenges, and you have to face them like a man. You can't let fear hold you back. You never have to be afraid of doing anything you want to do."

I could see the wheels turning in his little brain as he continued contemplating. This was something simple, jumping off the island and into my arms. But I wanted Jah to learn early that he couldn't be a scary nigga.

He looked down at the distance between us and then back up at me, his eyes searching for reassurance. Recognizing his fear crushed me. It was a simple task, but, as his father, I never wanted him to fear anything. I wanted to take the fear out of his heart and demolish it.

"Trust me, Jah. I will always be here for you, ready to catch you whenever you need me. Jump."

Trepidation danced in Jah's eyes, but a flicker of determination began to surface. He took a deep breath and then in one swift motion, he pushed off with all his might, propelling himself toward me. Jah's small body soared through the air, fear and excitement written across his face. As he descended into my waiting arms, a surge of pride and joy washed over me. It was like that simple leap of faith was his first step towards becoming the brave man I needed him to eventually become.

I held him tight against my chest. "You did it! I'm so proud of you."

Giggling uncontrollably, his hands pressed into my chest as he pushed back to look up at me. "I did it, Daddy!"

I was grinning from ear to ear. "Yeah, you did, lil' man."

Jah beamed up at me, his eyes shining with newfound confidence. "I wanna do it again!"

"Bet."

I stood him back up on the island and allowed him to jump off over and over again.

Moments like this with Jah always brought a smile to my face, a smile that felt so unfamiliar because, lately, it had been hard to smile. Ever since the altercation with Lamonica and CeCe a few weeks back, I hadn't been myself. That whole mess had just solidified that things were truly over between me and CeCe. The distance I'd been trying so hard to bridge between us was now like a football field, and it seemed permanent.

Now, CeCe barely talked to me, barely even looked at me. It was like I was a ghost, and the silence from her was so suffocating. I'd lost something I never knew I needed and now I couldn't shake the feeling of emptiness that had settled in.

"Wait a minute," I told Jah as my phone rang. I held an arm out, to stop him from jumping again. Looking at it, I saw that Richard, CeCe's father, was calling. Though CeCe's mother hated me, her father was more down to earth. He would reach out when he needed the strength of a younger man to help him around the house or when he was looking for CeCe. "Hello?"

"Frank!" he blurted out, making my brow furrow with concern. "CeCe went into labor!"

CYNTHIA "CECE" DEBOIS

The room was quiet as I lay in the hospital bed, exhaustion tugging at every muscle in my body. The soft glow of the night-light cast a warm hue across the room. Frank sat in a recliner next to the bed, cradling our newborn son, Shauka, against his bare chest.

Surprisingly, Shauka had been a quiet child, thus far. He only cried when he was hungry. Otherwise, he was such a chill baby. I prayed that he stayed that way. As I watched Frank with him, a swell of emotions surged through me. His eyes were fixed on Shauka with tenderness that melted my heart. The love in his touch, the way he whispered words of endearment to our son—I couldn't deny the beauty of it all. A part of me had always known that Frank would make an incredible father, but witnessing it over and over again was both a blessing and a curse. The walls I had built so carefully, the fortress I'd constructed to protect me from the pain and disappointment I had endured in the past from Frank, still crumbled in his presence.

But as much as I wanted to surrender all my doubts and fears, a voice of caution echoed in the depths of my soul. The scars that Frank had left on my heart were still healing, each one a reminder of the way he had hurt me. The wounds were still fresh from Lamonica's unexpected arrival at his house, a painful reminder that it was a possibility that Frank still hadn't changed. When she'd shown up at his house, it was as if the rug was being pulled right from under me. I felt as if the universe was playing a cruel joke.

"The back of his ears aren't dark. He might have my skin color," Frank whispered, his smile feeble but filled with hope and admiration.

I couldn't help but smile back, basking in the possibility. But as I gazed at him, I realized his eyes couldn't meet mine. "I think he will. He looks like you already."

Frank chuckled half-heartedly. "Yeah, he does."

I sighed, hating the lack of life that had been in Frank and between us lately. Ever since the altercation with Lamonica, something in Frank had changed. It was as though that incident had nudged him over the edge, pushing him further away from our relationship. He no longer seemed interested in reconciling or rekindling the connection we'd once had. The space between us had grown, fueled by my anger that rendered me nearly speechless. We had become nothing more than co-parents, and I despised how the warmth and closeness we once shared had dissipated. I longed for us to find our way back to each other, yearning to erase the sadness that clouded his eyes. I wanted nothing more than to be the one who could make it all vanish.

Desire and anxiety, conflicting emotions, danced within me. I yearned to trust Frank, to let go of my fear and embrace the love that could be ours, but I was terrified of being hurt again. The thought of opening my heart to him fully, only to have it shattered once more, felt like an unbearable risk.

As I watched Frank serenade our baby boy with soft whispers, my heart ached with the pain of indecision. I longed for a love that would stand the test of time, a love built on trust and mutual respect. But I questioned whether Frank was capable of giving me that, whether his promises of change were sincere or merely temporary.

With a tired sigh, I snuggled deeper into the hospital bed, my gaze fixed on the breathtaking sight before me. It was a vision of a family in its most vulnerable and beautiful state, and I couldn't help but wonder if just maybe we could find our way back to each other and build a love story that would stand the test of time.

QUEEN ARIA BENSON

The living room was filled with the energizing sounds of the NBA game as Reggie and I cozied up on the couch. My head was settled in his lap. His fingers were in my hair, softly scratching my scalp.

"Did you see that dunk, baby?" Reggie's excitement floated above the sounds of the television. "Mike is a beast!"

I chuckled softly. "Yeah, baby, he's the best in the league for a reason."

In this moment, everything felt perfect. I relished in the happiness and peace. Reggie's love and touch had the power to make me forget the bad times.

Suddenly, the familiar sound of Frank's ringtone pierced through the serenity of the moment. I glanced at my phone, seeing his name flashing on the screen. I hesitated, knowing that answering the call might shatter this peaceful bubble Reggie and I were in. I wanted to be present with Reggie, to cherish this rare, beautiful moment we were having. I swiped to reject the call, my eyes returning to Reggie's face, hoping he hadn't notice.

"Defense! Defense!" Reggie shouted. "Get that rebound!"

Lying there on the couch, my head nestled in Reggie's lap, the soft strokes of his fingers in my hair created a tranquil bubble amidst the intensity of the game. Reggie's scratches against my scalp felt like an unspoken language of love, a brief escape from the gritty reality of our relationship.

As the game unfolded, a familiar vibration sounded through the room, breaking the serene atmosphere. My phone, displaying Frank's name again, insisted on disrupting the peace. I hesitated, torn between the desire to preserve this perfect night with Reggie and the gnawing reality that Frank rarely called twice unless it was urgent.

Reggie's jealousy, a volatile force that could swiftly turn a loving evening into a thunderstorm, lingered in the back of my mind. I vividly recalled his ability to transform from affectionate to monstrous in the blink of an eye. The fear of triggering that transformation paralyzed me for a moment, but the incessant ringing of the phone pushed me to answer.

Just as my fingers reached for the phone, Reggie, in a sudden eruption of possessive rage, snatched it from my hand and hurled it across the room. "Why the fuck does he keep calling you?!"

The shattering sound pierced through the living room.

"Reggie, what the hell?" I exclaimed, attempting to sit up, but before I could fully rise, he yanked me back, his fingers intertwining in my hair like a vise.

"Ow! Reggie, stop! Let me go!"

His eyes, once warm and filled with love, now burned with intensity that sent a shiver down my spine. "Why is he blowing your phone up like that? Are you fucking him?!"

"No!" I exclaimed as tears came to my eyes. "Let me go, Reggie! Please?"

I winced as he tightened his grip.

As the shards of my shattered phone lay scattered across the room, Reggie's fingers finally released my hair. In an abrupt motion, he forcefully pushed my head, sending a wave of pain through my scalp. The unexpectedness of the gesture caught me off guard, and I struggled to regain my composure.

Attempting to sit up, my hands trembling, I felt Reggie's gaze piercing through me. Before I could fully rise, he threatened through gritted teeth, "You better not move."

Reluctantly, I obeyed. Slowly, I returned my head to his lap, the once serene vibe now tainted by the fear that lingered in the room. Reggie's fingers resumed their place in my hair, but the tenderness was replaced by an unspoken warning. I lay there with tears streaming down my face, staring at the broken pieces of the phone that mirrored Reggie's fragile ego.

"Come on, MJ!" Reggie bellowed excitedly as if nothing had just happened. "Show 'em how Chicago do it!"

———

The next day, I burst through the hospital room door, my heart pounding in my chest. The sterile smell hit me as I scanned the room, my eyes landing on CeCe, exhausted but beaming with joy, cradling their newborn. Frank stood nearby, his eyes leaving the tiny bundle in CeCe's arms and landing on me.

"Queen, where the hell you been?" Frank's tone cut through the air, and I cringed, knowing I was wrong.

I swallowed hard, guilt clawing at me. Reggie's temper had me dealing with one problem after another, and now I'd missed the birth of their baby.

"I... My phone broke last night," I stammered, avoiding eye contact. "I got a new one this morning. I swear I would've been here if I had known."

CeCe shot me a sympathetic look, understanding in her tired eyes, but Frank wasn't as understanding. "We've been trying to reach you all damn night. It's your job to be there when we need you. You can't be having issues with your phone."

I inwardly gritted, despising whatever part of me that couldn't let Reggie's problematic ass go.

I took a step closer, putting my gaze on the baby instead of Frank. "I'm sorry. I really am. It fell and cracked when I was on my way into the house. The stores were closed by then. As soon as I woke up, I went to get another one."

His eyes narrowed with disappointment. "Get a backup phone."

I swallowed hard, keeping the shameful tears at bay. Frank had always been there for me and so had CeCe. I owed him the same, and the fact that I hadn't been there because of Reggie made me feel so low. But I just nodded, trying to keep it together. "I will. I promise." I looked at CeCe, a weak smile on my lips. "Congratulations, girl. He's so cute."

CeCe managed a tired grin, but I could see the fatigue etched on her face. "Thanks. He's so yellow, isn't he? Frank is finally going to get a son that has his color." She laughed weakly as she dreamily looked at Frank.

As I watched them, my guilt bubbled up. I should've been here. I should've been by CeCe's side. Instead, I was catering to Reggie's bruised ego.

I lingered in the room, feeling like an intruder in their celebration. Guilt made me gnaw nervously on my bottom lip, and

I couldn't shake the feeling that Reggie's temper was a storm I would never be able to escape.

18

FRANK "CAPO" DISCIPLE

"Welcome, everyone!" the instructor, Daphne, greeted the crew with a warm smile. "Today, we're going to dive into the basic elements of real estate and how it can be a valuable asset for young entrepreneurs like yourselves."

Scanning the room, while sitting on top of a desk in the back of the classroom at the neighborhood Park District, I chuckled at the uninterested eye rolls and sighs of some of the younger hustlers.

I was always grateful for the knowledge and wisdom Stanley instilled in me and Buck. Because of how he'd groomed us, my right hand and I were the more mature hustlers, despite being younger than most of them. We were focused on elevating our hustle and investing our bread rather than the bullshit that got other hustlers locked up or killed. We had learned the game from the ground up, but more importantly, we'd learned about the value of life beyond the streets.

As Buck and I led our crew, we made it our mission to pass

on the same wisdom Stanley had given us. We organized regular classes for our crew, focusing on topics like money management, investing, and financial literacy. Our goal was to help our people get out of the game faster in order to keep their minds focused on elevating themselves, rather than getting caught up in more crime that could bring heat down on the organization or end their lives. The longer someone stayed in the game, the greater their chances of ending up in the grave or behind bars. We'd seen it happen too many times and we refused to let history repeat itself within our family.

Attendance at these classes was mandatory for the younger members of The Disciple Family. We wanted to ensure that everyone had the opportunity to learn these essential skills that could make a real difference in their lives. It would be up to the individual if they would actually put these skills to use, but we believed that it was our responsibility to plant the seeds.

Surprisingly, some of the older hustlers in our crew also took part in these classes at times. It was a powerful sight to see them sitting alongside the younger generation, eager to learn.

"Real estate offers great opportunities for generating income and building long-term wealth. It refers to property, including land and any structures on it. It can include residential, commercial, or industrial properties. In this course, we'll focus primarily on residential and commercial real estate. Real estate can provide multiple benefits. First, it offers a tangible asset that can appreciate in value over time, allowing you to build equity. Secondly—"

The jarring ringtone of my phone interrupted the lecturer. I hopped up and slipped out of the classroom. Having a two-day old infant, I was jumping to answer every phone call, even though Shauka was healthy. However, it was Mayor Rossi.

"What up?" I answered.

"Frank, we've got a situation," the mayor urgently announced. "The DEA got wind of a drug shipment coming into the docks this evening. They are preparing to raid."

For the first time in my life, I didn't have to be concerned. "I'm not involved in that. I'm sure you heard of Alexander's murder."

The mayor let out a sigh of relief. "Thank goodness. Apparently, you haven't found a replacement for Alexander yet."

"I haven't."

"Considering the amount of product the DEA was told it would be, I figured you had to be involved." He let out another relieved breath. "Well, at least you have nothing to worry about today. I'll be in touch."

"Wait a minute," I insisted. "How much are we talking about?"

"A couple hundred bricks."

"Thanks," I mumbled and hung up.

There was only one distributor in this city that could get his hands on that much work.

Before going back into the classroom, I sent Hector a text: *Abort.*

CYNTHIA "CECE" DEBOIS

I was sitting on the couch, feeling a wave of relief wash over me as the nanny took over for a few hours. "Thank you so much, Nicole." I sighed with relief as the Jamaican woman in her forties took Shauka from my arms.

She smiled warmly. "You're welcome. I'm going to put him down to sleep."

"Frank just went to the kitchen to warm a bottle for him."

Nicole's smile grew. "Great. Have him bring it to me when he's done."

I nodded and Nicole floated out of the room, gazing into Shauka's face and cooing along the way.

I blew out a heavy breath, leaning back in the rocking chair nestled in the corner of my bedroom.

Managing a toddler and a newborn had been more overwhelming than I could have ever imagined even with help. My mother was in the room with me folding laundry. Frank had rehired Nicole who had been the same nanny that had assisted me after I gave birth to Jah. Because of her help, I was able to get a few hours of peace here and there throughout the day.

Thankfully, Jah was already down for the night. So, I hoped that Shauka wouldn't wake up until midnight for his next feeding.

When Frank walked into the room carrying a warm bottle for the baby, I told him, "Nicole took Shauka to the nursery already."

He simply nodded, not saying a word. His ongoing silence was crushing. He was so defeated around me now. All hope was lost in his eyes.

As he turned to leave the room, my mother stopped him, "Wait," she spit. "Let me check to see if that bottle is too hot, boy."

I cringed at how condescending her tone was.

"It's fine, Ma," I interjected, trying to diffuse the tension. "He's made plenty of bottles before."

But my mother didn't listen. She went over to him anyway. I could tell that Frank was desperately trying to bite his tongue. My mother took the bottle from his hand, testing the temperature herself by shaking a few drops on her wrists. "You shouldn't trust him to do it right every time, CeCe."

Frank was taken aback, his brows furrowing and a subtle frown forming on his face, but he didn't say anything. Even I was floored. My mother had always distrusted Frank and his motives. But it was as if now that he had lived up to her expectations, her disdain for him was loud and in his face.

My mother thrust the bottle back into his hand without even acknowledging him with her eyesight. I could sense the frustration building inside Frank, but thankfully he left the room quietly.

"I trust Frank to take care of the babies, Ma. Stop treating him like he isn't good for anything. He takes very good care of the boys. Me too."

She scoffed as she returned to the pile of clothes she'd been folding. "With drug money."

I looked at my mother, trying to understand why she still harbored such negativity towards him, especially now.

"Mom, why are you still so nasty to Frank? We're not even together anymore."

My mother sighed heavily before speaking, "Because he ruined your life by getting you pregnant *twice* without being a good-enough man for you to want to be with."

As they had been since our dinner, my father's words rang in my head once again.

"Did Dad ever cheat on you?" I blurted out impulsively.

My mother's expression turned to one of shock and repulsion. "Absolutely not!" she snapped firmly. "Your father would *never* do such a thing."

I couldn't help but feel disappointed in my mother's response. It was disheartening to witness her dishonesty, especially when it came to something so significant.

"Why would you ask me that?"

I swallowed hard, biting my words. "You guys just seem so perfect. I wanted to know if it was really possible to have a man truly devoted to me."

My mother smiled. "It is. Of course, it is."

I didn't push the issue any further, but the weight of her words lingered in the air, leaving a bitter taste in my mouth.

ANTHONY "BUCK" PATTERSON

I strolled towards the trap house. The familiar chill of the winter wrapped around me like a second skin. The phone pressed against my ear as Peaches rambled on about the night's earnings. She, Diamond and April had been scheduled for a date with three local rappers, a setup I'd orchestrated. The anticipation of the cash rolling in tonight had a grin piercing through my beard.

"Make sure they know the drill," I told her. "These are new clients. Don't let them see the pussy before they pay you, and if they start actin' up, you know what to do."

"We got it, Daddy. Don't worry. We'll handle them," Peaches replied, her voice laced with the confidence born from years of navigating the streets under my guidance.

"Good girl. Make sure Diamond and April keep their eyes open too. No surprises, you hear me?" I emphasized as I climbed up the porch.

"Absolutely. We got this under control. You know we always do," she reassured me.

As I keyed into the trap house, unease suddenly settled in. Something didn't feel right, prompting me to cut the call short. "Hold up, Peaches. Let me hit you back."

I ended the call abruptly and the unnerving silence of the dark interior devoured me. With my Glock in hand, I carefully navigated through the shadows, my senses on high alert. As I delved into the pitch-black interior, my instincts started to explode. The darkness hit me like a brick wall. Not a single damn light was on. I never left it that way and neither did Frank.

A shiver ran down my spine, and the air grew thick with threatening silence that gnawed at my nerves.

"Frank, you in there?" I called out, my voice a low rumble that bounced off the walls.

No response.

Not a creak, not even a whisper. Just the unsettling void of blackness.

My hand tightened around the grip of my Glock as I inched forward. The floor creaked beneath my weight, but the silence persisted. As I carefully crept through the living room, the over-turned cocktail table caught my eye. My gut twisted. Someone had either been inside or was still lurking within the shadows.

Approaching the living room light switch, a bead of sweat rolled down my temple, revealing the unease erupting beneath my skin. Just as my fingers brushed against the switch, the cold steel of a gun pressed firmly against the back of my head.

A shaky, nervous male voice cut through the dark silence, commanding me with urgency. "Don't move."

I froze, the weight of the gun's barrel digging into my skull, the butt of the weapon trembling against my skin. I could sense the inexperience in his shuddering tone. The stench of filth wafted in the air, smelling of desperation and addiction.

Caution flooded my veins. Young robbers, particularly those addicted to drugs or forced by the hand of desperation, didn't give a fuck about taking a life. Knowing that my life hung in the balance of a jittery immature hand caused fear to blanket me.

He pressed the metal into my head deeper, forcing my head to lean forward. "Where is the stash, nigga?"

"Fuck you," I growled, remaining completely still. "I'm not giving you shit."

"Don't make me shoot you!"

"You're going to shoot me anyway."

That's how it went. These young motherfuckas were sloppy and frantic. They murdered unnecessarily and left a trail of disaster behind them.

Time reduced to a crawl as the cold metal of the gun remained pressed against my head. Images of a life unlived, the echoes of unborn laughter, and the distant dreams I'd never get to chase flashed before my eyes. The harsh reality of impending death became a suffocating weight on my chest.

The young robber's trembling grip tightened on the gun, just as an explosion rang in my ears. I braced myself for the inevitable pain that would follow the gunshot. But instead of searing agony, I felt thick liquid splatter against the back of my head.

Confusion clawed at my senses as I lunged toward the light switch. With a swift flick, the room was bathed in light just in time for me to see the young thief falling to his knees. His body slacked as my gaze shifted upward to the person responsible for the abrupt turn of my fate. Queen stood there, holding a gun with a steady hand, the barrel still pointed at the now life-less robber as his body collapsed onto the floor.

The room was submerged in silence. Only the distant hum of the city outside crept inside. When Queen's eyes met mine, a different kind of energy filled the room. I marveled at the sight of her holding that gun with determination in her eyes. It was the sexiest sight I'd ever seen. The line between fear and desire began to blur as I took her in. As the chaos settled, I felt a sudden connection simmering, making me wrestle with the unexpected attraction to a woman who had just saved my life.

QUEEN ARIA BENSON

I had never taken a life before. Considering the life I lived, I knew that eventually, death would face me. However, I had never expected to be the one to end a life.

"You good?"

He had asked me that so many times. As we put the body in the trunk of his trap car, as we dug a hole in the Dan Ryan Woods, and as we buried it, Buck kept asking me if I was okay when he had been the one facing death.

"I told you I'm fine." But as I grabbed the margarita glass and brought it to my lips, the Patrón mixture shook and swished as a result of my hands trembling.

Buck's brow rose as he stared intensely at my hand. He grabbed it and placed the glass down on the bar before I wasted it. "You ain't fine."

After cleaning up the trap house, we needed a drink. So, we'd come to the local hole in the wall to drown our nerves in tequila.

Buck chuckled, shaking his head. I stared at his laughter

with confusion as it grew until it bounced off of the walls around us.

"What?" I pressed in a high pitch.

"I never thought *you'd* save my life."

My head fell back as I laughed as well. "I'm surprised I did too." But then the vision of his large figure on the other side of that gun flashed before my eyes. My laughter faded and I was reminded of the anxiety I'd felt. He constantly rode my nerves. I despised him, but... "You're family," I softly told him.

Buck dramatically brought his hand to his chest.

"Whatever," I laughed. "I can't stand you, but in that moment when I thought you could get shot, I just didn't want to see you die. I didn't want to see Frank mourn you. I couldn't have lived with it."

He grinned teasingly. "So, you care about a nigga!"

I playfully rolled my eyes. "I still hate you."

"Why?" he asked, suddenly becoming serious. "Why do you hate me?"

Thinking for a moment, I took a sip of my drink. "I hate what you represent as a pimp."

His brow rose. "So, being a drug dealer is okay, but being a pimp is unacceptable."

"I hate what a pimp represents for women. The control, possession, using them, and the abuse—"

"Have you ever seen me abuse my women?"

"No."

His brow rose higher as intensity grew in his gaze. "You ever seen me control them?"

"No."

"Because I don't do either of those things. I make them feel comfortable enough to trust me to manage how they make money safely. I never made either of them be with me, and I don't own them. They can leave whenever they get ready."

"*Soooo*," I sang as I prepared to pry. "You really have sex with all of them?"

"Yeah."

My eyes grew with intrigue. "Altogether? Like a foursome?"

He coolly shrugged. "Sometimes."

My brows curled with curiosity. "And you don't care about them fucking other men?"

"Not when it's making me money. And those sexual acts are work for them. It's for pleasure with me."

I frowned. "What about STD's?"

"They know to use protection with clients. They respect and love me too much to bring me any diseases."

I could feel my nerves soothing. Finally much calmer, I picked up my drink from the bar and leaned back. "What made you become a pimp?"

"You didn't know Stanley was a pimp?"

My mouth dropped. "He was?"

He chuckled at my naïveté. "Yeah, back in the day he was a well-known pimp. I guess you were too young to realize it back then. He stopped when he got older. But, yes, Stanley was a pimp. Frank's mother and mine were two of his hoes." When my mouth dropped animatedly, he laughed. "Frank and I were raised in his house. He taught us the game. Hell, he taught us everything. Frank only inherited the drug game from Stanley, but I inherited his pimp game too. It's not about greed. It's not about wanting to control women. I saw the intimacy in the household between him and his women. I saw how they leaned on one another. I liked how he always had support when he came home at the end of the day." A smile slowly spread across his chocolate face. "I guess I wanted that too."

I had never seen him so vulnerable. It was refreshing and adorable. I was seeing Buck in a whole new light, and I got lost in it. When I caught myself gazing at him, I gulped, pulling my eyes away from his.

"I-I..." He was making me stutter. "I guess you're cool."

He reached over, tapping my wrist. "I guess you're cool too."

As his fingertip grazed my wrist, an electrifying sensation traveled throughout my body, causing me to tremble with desire. I had never been this close to him. I had never had his skin brush against mine until this night. But as he'd brought me close to calm me down, took the gun from my hand, and held my hand to support my weak knees as we walked out of the woods, I felt intoxicating and addictive allure. He had confident dominance that I wanted to drink.

"What's that?"

I blinked rapidly, bringing myself back to reality. "What's *what*?"

His eyes were on the wrist he had just tapped. His contact had caused my jacket to move, revealing one of the most recent bruises Reggie had given me during one of his violent outbursts.

I sheepishly pulled my sleeve down. "I have to stop wearing costume jewelry."

His dark eyes twinkled when he smiled. "We pay you too much for you to be wearing that shit."

I blushed with embarrassment. "You're right."

Suddenly, he turned his whole body toward me, grabbing my hand softly. "For real, though, Queen, thank you. You bossed up and it saved my life. I'm forever in your debt, baby girl."

I swallowed hard, unable to find the words because they

were being suffocated by the sudden realization of who Buck truly was.

There was a magnetic force in the air drawing me toward him despite the bitterness that colored our past. It was as if the universe had orchestrated a shift in our dynamic, leading my heart to a rhythm I had not anticipated. The disdain that I once had for Buck now gave way to a mesmerizing attraction, leaving me both bewildered and enchanted.

TWO MONTHS LATER

19

CYNTHIA "CECE" DEBOIS

By June, it was beyond apparent that Frank and I were over. He had suddenly come into my life and changed it for the better. I had two beautiful boys who had an amazing father. We had had our passionate, hood love story and, now, it was over.

"You don't have to go." My head tilted as I watched Frank move about Shauka's room, packing his baby bag. He was looking for specific outfits. He loved to dress the boys. Jah and Shauka were draped in as many high-end brands and jewelry as Frank was.

"Grandma already called me." He shrugged as he dug through one of Shauka's drawers. "She's expecting me."

I laughed as I shook my head, leaning in the doorway. "She's not *your* grandmother."

Frank cut his eyes at me. "Yes, she is." His expression dared me to argue, and I knew not to. My mother may not have ever accepted Frank, but my grandmother had. He'd ridden down to Starkville, Mississippi with me the first year we were together.

As soon as my grandmother met him, she adopted Frank as her own grandson. Considering the way Frank had grown up, he hadn't had the nurturing love of a grandmother, so he'd accepted it with open arms. Since then, he'd taken the trek yearly for my grandmother's birthday in February and in the summers for our family reunions.

"Besides, I'm not letting y'all get on that road without me."

I sighed, knowing that it was useless to argue with him. No matter the state of our relationship, he still considered us family. So, he was going to protect us. He had even offered to buy the family plane tickets so that we wouldn't have to make the long, ten-hour drive. But my father had refused to allow him to waste that amount of money.

I discreetly took a deep breath, preparing myself for the tension between Frank and my mother for ten hours. I was used to it because it had been going on for four years. No matter how much my mother exclaimed her dislike for Frank, it never stopped him from being involved in our family. That was one of the things that I loved so much about him. He was still so willing to be around and play his part despite how dismissive my mother treated him.

As I watched Frank diligently search for the best outfits for a two-month-old to wear, my heart was filled with longing, missing the long conversations, the times that he would spend the night after being here so late with Jah. The space between us was daunting. I had only known him for four years, but now, I didn't like how life felt without him. He no longer spent the night. Our friendship was fading.

Thankfully, I could hear my cell ringing in the distance, so I could no longer dwell. I jogged up the hallway towards the sound, quickly, to keep the incessant ringing from waking Shauka, who was asleep in his swing.

I found the phone in the kitchen, and hurriedly answered, "Hello?"

"Hey girl."

"Hey, Queen."

"I'll be there in fifteen minutes."

"Okay, cool."

"I need a favor."

"What?" I asked, leaning against the island.

"Reggie was only cool with me riding down there with you guys because I told him that Frank and Buck wouldn't be there. So, if he ever asks, they weren't there."

I chuckled, shaking my head as I went into the living room to check on Shauka. "Okay, but if you gotta do all of this lying, why are you going?"

Queen sucked her teeth. "Because I need a break from Chicago," she whined. "Reggie never wants to do anything out of the ordinary, and I am going to be bored as hell without you all for three days. So, I wanna go."

"Okay, boo. But you'll be fine. Buck and Frank don't tell the crew their comings and goings. So, no one but us know where they will be."

My eyes narrowed inquisitively when she sighed with relief. "Cool."

"I'll see you in a few minutes."

"Okay. Bye," Queen rushed.

Hanging up, my brows curled in confusion. It was normal for Buck to ride down to Mississippi with Frank. He rarely left Frank's side for too long. But Queen's urgency was sketchy. She'd gone from not wanting to be in the same room as Buck to willingly taking trips that he would be on. They were now getting along much better since the situation at the trap house two months ago. But something about this felt suspect.

QUEEN ARIA BENSON

I had slept on Buck. I had been in a coma, but now I was wide awake. I had completely underestimated him. I had judged him and seen him as a cocky, arrogant, womanizer when for the past two months, I had been learning that he was the complete opposite.

Buck's good looks had always been undeniable, but without the false cloak of my judgment, I had become obsessed. For the last two months, we had finally become friends. We'd gotten to know each other. We'd hung out late, drinking, laughing, and dancing. And now I was crushing. I was his fan. And I had to laugh at myself every time I found myself fantasizing about a man I had previously despised.

So, I had done what I had to do to be on this trip. It had taken a lot of lying to Reggie to get him on board with letting me come. And I was taking a huge risk if Reggie ever found out that Frank and Buck were there. But it was a risk I was eager to take because I needed to see if my attraction to Buck was real.

"What are you laughing at?" CeCe's inquisition cut into my

fantasy as I stared at Buck while he stood at the bar.

I quickly shook my head, lying, "Nothing."

CeCe's eyes narrowed. "You drunk already?"

I rolled my eyes playfully. "No."

After arriving in Starkville, we checked into our hotel rooms. I was sharing a room with CeCe and the boys. After unpacking, Frank, Buck, CeCe, and I had decided to hit up a bar since it was too late to do anything else. The hole in the wall was on a back country road. It had no air. My skin was sticky with perspiration. Every curl in my hair was gone. But the drinks were cheap and strong.

"Ladies and gentlemen, get ready to unleash your hidden star power because tonight, we're taking you on a musical journey like no other!" the deejay's voice belted over the mic. "The stage is set, the microphones are live, and the spotlight eagerly awaits your moment to shine. Karaoke night is in full swing. So, gather your courage, loosen those vocal cords, and prepare to take the mic!"

With wide eyes, CeCe turned towards me. "You gotta sing, Queen!"

I smiled bashfully, shaking my head. "I'm good."

"What you good on?" Buck asked, suddenly appearing at the table.

Looking up at him, I lost all train of thought. It was blowing my mind how I had gone from rudely checking this man to being unable to think clearly when in his presence.

"I'm trying to get her to do a song for karaoke," CeCe answered.

Buck sat my drink in front of me as Frank gave CeCe hers. He then slid into the stool next to me, his massive build brushing against my tiny frame. His cologne molested my senses, turning them into chaotic fireworks.

Frowning, Frank said, "Karaoke is supposed to be for people who *can't* sing."

"Exactly!" I finally found my voice.

"You can sing like that?" Buck asked with a messy, bushy brow raised like he was challenging me.

I shrugged. "I do all right."

"She is being humble as fuck right now," CeCe blurted.

I didn't sing in front of many people. I would sing along to songs in the car or in the shower. But CeCe had heard me truly sing when I was drunk and singing my heart out to Xscape after a really bad fight I'd had with Reggie.

"Okay, who's going to be the first to take the mic?!" the deejay asked.

"She is!" CeCe spat excitedly. She leaned against the table, bracing herself as she stood up with her feet on the anchors of the stool, pointing at me. "She's going first!"

"CeCe!" I exclaimed, feeling my skin flush.

Before I knew it, the deejay took my hand and pulled me off of the stool. With Buck's anticipating eyes on me, I couldn't resist. He had a gentle dominance about him that made a woman want to give him whatever he desired.

Once at the deejay booth, the deejay asked, "What song do you want to sing?"

With Buck's eyes on me, I could feel his influence. He only treated me like a friend. I doubted that he saw me as anything more than the little, dirty girl on the block that used to beg for work, the one who Frank would show pity on by giving money to, like a charity. In Buck's eyes, I was still the young girl who had been rude to him for years. But I had weaseled my way on this trip, hoping the time away from Chicago and the crew would change that.

Finally, I answered, "'As We Lay' by Kelly Price."

The deejay's eyes widened, clearly impressed with my selection. His eyes grazed me questionably as if I couldn't deliver such a challenging vocal performance.

Smirking with a raised brow, he handed me the mic. The large projector screen began to show the lyrics as the beat dropped. As I took hold of the microphone, the dimly lit bar buzzed with the doubtful chatter of patrons. Yet, amongst the sea of uncertainty, CeCe stood out. Her beaming smile reassured me, giving me courage.

With a deep breath, I began to sing along with the beat. The atmosphere shifted, silence gripping the room as I embraced the lyrics, pouring my soul into each word. The runs, rifts, and high notes of the second verse challenged me, but I executed them fearlessly, surprising even myself. In an instant, the doubters transformed into an explosive chorus of praise and applause, their hesitation replaced by hoots and hollers of admiration.

As I continued singing, a fantasy unfolded in my mind. I imagined Buck and I forgetting our relationships back home. I imagined him taking me passionately. The lyrics resonated deeply, as if they were words I had yearned to express but never found the voice for. With every line, the passionate connection I felt with Buck grew stronger, and it fueled my performance.

I scanned the room, courageously locking eyes with Buck. His expression held amazement and admiration. Those eyes fixed on me with unwavering attention, provided the encouragement I didn't know I needed. With newfound confidence, I sang each note with more intensity, hoping that I was leaving an impression on his heart and that he was finally seeing me... the *real* me.

FRANK "CAPO" DISCIPLE

"Frank."

I grinned at the way CeCe slurred my name. She had taken advantage of having a night out without the boys. Her mother was keeping an eye on them. Since getting to the bar, she had allowed herself to be completely free. So free, that she had destroyed the space that had been between us.

She was my friend again. So, taking Linda's slick comments and disregard during the long drive had been worth it. Even though it was obvious to CeCe and me now that we were over, her mother couldn't let go of her prejudices and preconceived notions about me. I would forever be a ghetto loser in that woman's eyes.

CeCe's sneaky smirk was so infectious that it made me grin. "Yes?"

"What's been up with you?"

My eyes narrowed. "What do you mean?"

"It seems like something has been on your mind. You were so quiet during the drive down here."

Taking a minute, my eyes grazed the small bar. They landed on Buck and Queen dancing to "Danger." I was so relieved that they had finally squashed their beef.

"There has been a lot going on with the crew," I finally revealed to CeCe.

She leaned in. "Like what?"

"I need a new connect."

Her face blanketed with confusion. "Where is Alexander?"

"Alexander is dead."

Her mouth fell open. "Huh? Wait! What? What happened to him?"

I raised a brow. "Honestly?"

"Yes," she insisted.

"I killed him."

"You what?!" she harshly whispered, scooting closer to me.

Her sudden closeness after so long made it hard to focus. The floral hints in her aroma made my dick hard.

"W—why... why did you kill him?"

"He wanted me to kill Keyes. He felt like Keyes was too much competition, a threat to the expansion of his distribution. I refused because Keyes has never done me wrong, but more importantly, I couldn't start a war that would put you and the boys in danger."

She blinked slowly, taking it all in. "So, you don't have a distributor right now?"

"Nah."

"What are you going to do?"

I shrugged, allowing myself to be vulnerable in front of the only person I was willing to. "I don't know. Either the connect can't front us as much work as we need, or he can't give it to us at the prices we want. Others don't want to fuck with us because they haven't heard of us. Hector really wants to work with us, especially after I looked out for him with that raid. But I don't want to cross Keyes like that."

With each word, she discreetly unraveled. She noticed the distress in my eyes and pouted. "Why didn't you tell me any of this?"

"This all happened around the time that bullshit happened at my house with Lamonica, so..." Leaving it at that, I shrugged.

Pouting, CeCe asked, "So, you feel like you can't talk to me anymore?"

"I feel like I need to let you go."

Her expression became completely still and stoic. She sat there, blinking owlishly.

"We've been going back and forth for four years and all I've been doing is hurting you. I wanted to make things right, but I know that the altercation with Lamonica was the last straw. I know you're tired of me embarrassing you and hurting you. Obviously, no matter how hard I try, I can't get it right. So, I have to truly separate myself from you so that you can move on, so that you can find that nigga that can get it right." With her elbow on the old, wooden table, CeCe rested her head in her hand, staring up at me. I could see the sorrow in her eyes and that's what fueled the confidence in my words. I was tired of hurting her, tired of not getting it right. "I'm sorry."

She breathed out so slowly, as if she had been waiting to hear those words sincerely so that she could finally exhale.

"I'm really sorry for everything. We never got the chance to really get to know each other, to be boyfriend and girlfriend before we were forced to handle real life issues. We never got to form the bond that was needed to handle those issues with love. I should have made sure that we did before I started making a family with you that I couldn't emotionally handle or take care of. I'm truly sorry that I fumbled you before I could really show you what you meant to me and what you deserve."

She sat up, deeply exhaling. Finally, she sighed. "I really needed to hear that. Thank you, Frank."

20

ANTHONY "BUCK" PATTERSON

After a grueling, long drive to Mississippi, CeCe and Frank didn't last but a few hours at the bar before they were tired from the road and drinks at karaoke. After arriving at the Hilton, Frank and CeCe headed to the fourth floor to retrieve their sons, leaving me and Queen roaming the quiet halls on the third floor where our rooms were.

Walking down the dimly lit corridor, tiredness from the journey weighed on my bones, but watching Queen's ass switch gave me energy. Her curves swayed with each step, demanding my gaze like a hypnotist. Her beautiful brown skin, kissed by the sun, glowed under the hallway lights. She was a breathtaking sight.

"You have a really beautiful singing voice," I told her.

She tried to discreetly blush, but I caught the subtle hue that colored her cheeks. Over the past two months, I'd noticed her attempts to conceal her attraction to me. As someone who had been raised in the pimp game, reading a woman was second nature to me.

Queen saving my life was an eye-opener. Her defiance, strength, and feistiness now intrigued me. The layers of her personality unfolded as we hung out more over the last two months, showing me that she was so much more than the irritating, begging little girl I previously thought she was. She'd blossomed into a confident and brave woman, unafraid to face mortality for me. To me, she embodied the beauty and strength of an attractive, fearless super woman.

She beamed. "Thanks, Buck."

"You should be a professional singer," I sincerely told her. "Your voice is like a gift. You'd be real competition for female artists."

I watched as a flicker of surprise crossed her features, the depth and sincerity of my words taking hers. The corridor may have been quiet, but the air sizzled with the spark of our attraction to one another. I admired the strength and beauty that Queen possessed. It was a rare combination that left me captivated and yearning for more.

I had been feeling her for a few weeks. But I had never been involved with a woman who didn't make me money. I was willing to shoot the dice, but I knew that would cause chaos in my household. The girls wouldn't be able to handle it, especially not Diamond. They had been loyal to me, so I would forever be loyal to being careful with their feelings.

As we reached her room, Queen spun around, sheepishly biting on her bottom lip. She looked up at me with entrancing, submissive eyes that seemed to be begging me "I'm not tired yet." She blinked slowly. "Are you?"

The fatigue lingered in the lines of her face, but there was a rebellious spark that told me she wasn't quite ready to call it a night. A playful glint in her eyes danced as we stood outside of her room, wrapping itself around my dick and hugging it.

My eyes were burning. I was anticipating diving headfirst into the bed as soon as I made sure that she was secure in her room.

"Nah." But I couldn't tell her no.

She smiled bashfully. "Then let's kick it in your room. I'm not ready for the night to be over." The mischief in her tone made my brow rise.

A sly grin crept onto my face. "Bet."

As we walked a few feet down the hallway, the atmosphere shifted. The thought of Queen in my room, away from the usual shared spaces we were in with the crew, stirred the beast in me.

Being in close proximity of a bed with Queen made my dick harden with fantasies and anticipation. Her presence, the subtle sway of her hips as she walked, began to fuel a different kind of desire. We had always been together in a crowd, amidst the laughter and noise, or working the streets, but this was different. Now, it was just the two of us alone in a room.

The click of the keycard resonated through the hallway as I unlocked the door to my room. As we stepped inside, the air exploded with longing. I couldn't wait any longer. The magnetism of Queen's presence had ignited a fire that begged to be smoldered.

Guiding her with a gentle hand on the small of her back, I ushered her into the room. The door closed and the latch clicked into place behind us, but my focus was solely on Queen.

My dick begged to be inside of her immediately. Turning her to face me, I took her by the waist, feeling the warmth of her skin beneath my fingertips. With our bodies now intimately close, she gasped as our lips met in a kiss that felt like more than the simplicity of lust. It was a kiss that whispered the connection between us. It was different, a dance of tongues and intertwining breaths. It wasn't rushed, but deliberate and unhurried. There was acute intimacy in the way our lips moved, a slow exploration of uncharted territory we were finally navigating.

As our kiss deepened, I could feel its difference. It wasn't like any other encounter I'd had with a woman before. With Queen, there was tenderness, a desire to savor each second. It wasn't just about dicking her down. It was about connection, an agreement that this night held significance beyond my dick yearning to find the furthest corners of her pussy.

QUEEN ARIA BENSON

Breaking the kiss, Buck's eyes searched my face as if anticipating resistance that he would never experience from me. He could have me whenever he wanted. He was softer with me than I'd imagined he would be. He gently lowered me on the bed by gripping my waist. As I lay down, he positioned himself over me, his lips placing a soft kiss on mine. Then he pulled down my jean shorts. I kicked them off eagerly along with my flip flops. I swooned at the way he marveled at my center.

"You're not wearing any panties," he growled, salivating.

He was no longer gentle then. He positioned himself between my legs. He then dug into his pocket and pulled out a Magnum before pulling his pants down to his knees. A beast revealed himself, dark, evenly chocolate, big, and beautiful. His eyes buried into mine as he slid on the protection. His large chest rose and fell rhythmically with anticipation.

He then took the back of my knees into his grip and pushed them back until they rested next to my ears. My pussy was wide open for him. His large hand was able to hold both of my ankles in position as he used the other to guide his mass into my leaking center. He slammed his pelvis into mine, and I was so happy to take it all.

I hissed, determined to take all of him.

"*Fuuuck*," he growled. "This pussy tight."

Moments earlier when strolling down the hotel corridor with Buck, I had realized why I was becoming obsessed with him. He gave me an unfamiliar sense of security and gentle dominance that cloaked me like a comforting embrace. With Reggie, every step I took was cautious. My femininity was held captive by the constant need to watch my back, be on guard, and navigate a world where danger lurked in every shadow. Walking on eggshells had become the norm, leaving me little room to truly be a woman.

But as I followed Buck, a quiet reassurance had covered me. It wasn't just the safety of the moment it was the unspoken understanding that I could let my guard down, if only for a brief moment. In his presence, I felt dainty, a word that had long been absent from my vocabulary. The weight of constant caution lifted, and for the first time, I could breathe without the heavy burden of anxiety. It was as if, in those few steps down the hall, I could reclaim a part of myself that had been suppressed for far too long.

Reggie's world demanded strength and resilience, traits I had learned to exert like armor. But the armor came at a cost, the sacrifice of my own femininity, the softness that had been tucked away beneath layers of survival instincts. The streets demanded a different kind of toughness, leaving little room for the delicacy of being a woman.

But with Buck, an unfamiliar sense of safety whispered promises of liberation. It reclaimed my femininity in the presence of a man who wouldn't dare let me be masculine. I felt freedom I hadn't known with Reggie, the freedom to be a woman, unguarded.

So, when he kissed me, I felt so honored that I forgot that we both belonged to someone else.

Now his strokes were so hypnotizing. Each one plunged into the depths of my ecstasy, making my head spin with each careful thrust. His fixated, sensual gaze was locked on mine, daring me to look away, daring me to take all of him. Though his strokes were deep, they were so passionate and purposeful. My toes curled each time the tip of his dick kissed my cervix.

"This pussy so wet that it's loud, baby."

Our bodies moved in a silent dialogue, expressing desires too strong for words. Each deep thrust created a masterpiece of sensations that left me breathless and completely consumed by him.

CYNTHIA "CECE" DEBOIS

As I sat amidst my aunts and older female cousins at the family picnic, the scorching June sun beat down on us relentlessly, making the air thick that lingered over the park. Their conversation was filled with stories of family gossip and throw-back memories. I smiled watching Frank effortlessly juggle Shauka in one arm while tossing a football to Jah and some of my little cousins. Buck stood by his side, watching as he squinted angrily at the heat. Beads of sweat dripped down his brow. Queen was at the spread of food making plates for us.

Everyone around me was so happy when I was miserable. Restless tears welled up, threatening to spill over at any given moment. Profound sadness cloaked me. Frank and I may have been over for quite some time, but the words he'd said the night before at the bar felt like the final nail in the coffin of our relationship. It truly felt like we were over and that any possibility of us getting back together had shattered. The thought of seeing him move on, living a lifetime of happiness with another woman, pierced me with indescribable pain. I wondered if I had given up too easily. I was overwhelmed with the confusion of who was right, my mother or father.

Leaning over to my great-aunt Dot, I whispered. "Auntie, can I ask you something?"

Dot nodded kindly. "Sure, baby."

"Did you go through a lot with your husband? Did you all fight a lot? Did he ever......er... um... *cheat?*"

Dot's eyes crinkled at the corners as she let out a hearty laugh. "Oh, child, of course. I experienced all of that and then some with that man."

My eyes narrowed, shocked at how easily she had admitted it. "Really?"

She laughed at my innocence. "Yes. Trials and tribulations in a relationship are the oldest dance in the book. Love ain't always smooth, but it's the bumps that teach you how to two-step."

Surprisingly, my other great-aunt, Wanda, had overheard us and chimed in. "Mm-hmm, CeCe, your Uncle Earl and I had our fair share of shit. It took years for him to figure it all out."

I looked over at my mother, who was tight-lipped with a stern-faced expression. She sat amongst the women, listening intently but revealing nothing.

Tammy, one of my older cousins, sat up. "My husband ain't cheated that I know of," she confessed. "But I won't put it past him. What matters is that if he has, he's been careful enough not to let me find out. We've had our troubles, though. We came real close to a divorce."

Grandma's sarcastic laugh sounded like she was recalling decades of memories. "Child, I can't even count how many times I had to fight them side chicks back in the day," she said, her frown still carrying decades of resentment. "They'd show up on the farm, demanding to talk to your granddaddy." I widened my eyes at the revelation. "Had me out there fighting Tootie in the cornfields!" she laughed heartedly.

"Mama, hush now!" my mother snapped. "That's not everybody's business."

With a scoff, Grandma waved away her warning. "Child, it ain't no secret down here in Starkville that John was a slut. But that slut loved me to the day he died."

We all hushed, admiring the love that danced in her eyes as she thought of Granddaddy.

"CeCe," she said leaning forward with a sincere gaze anchored on me. "I ain't saying it's okay for a man to cheat and I ain't saying you should always be fighting with your man. But what you gotta understand is it's up to *you* what you'll accept from a man. You set your boundaries. No relationship is perfect. Every one of us is flawed. It's about finding the person you can be flawed together with, the one you can weather the storm with. Because, baby, let me tell you, storms *will* come." Her eyes floated over to my mother, holding a telling glare before putting her eyes back on me. "But once you've weathered that storm together, you'll see the rainbow, and you'll feel the warmth of the sunshine. That's when you'll know you've built something unbreakable, a bond formed through blood, sweat, and tears."

———

As I returned to the hotel, I was still in my head. After a long shower washed away the dirt and sweat, I slipped into a flowing maxi dress that grazed the floor. Looking in the floor-length mirror, I admired a body that was bouncing back from giving birth. I had a small kangaroo pouch, but it was over-looked because of the voluptuousness of my curves and slimness of my waist.

Moisturizing my skin, I caught Queen's curious gaze from across the room as she lay on the bed, tickling Jah.

"Could you watch the boys for a few hours?" My heart was beating so hard with excitement and nervousness that my breath was shaky as I spoke.

Queen's eyebrow arched in curiosity, but she nodded. "Yeah. Everything okay?"

I managed to smile. "Yeah, I just need to talk to Frank about something."

Her gaze was still curious, but she simply answered, "Okay," and continued making Jah giggle uncontrollably while cartoons played on the television.

Done moisturizing, I sprayed my body with my usual scent. I then fingered combed the bone straight, Yaky bundles that I had recently gotten sewn in after finally taking down the braids I'd worn during my pregnancy.

Finally leaving the room, I walked down the hall, the anticipation and desire for Frank building with each step. My heart pounded, and my palms grew clammy as I approached his door. Nervously, I knocked, interrupting the silence in the quiet hallway.

When the door swung open, revealing Frank's puzzled expression, my mind went blank. The words I had rehearsed during my shower vanished into thin air, leaving me standing there, speechless.

Frank's eyes searched mine, confusion etched across his breathtaking face. "What's wrong?"

Unable to find the right words, I felt a lump forming in my throat. Instead of explaining, tears welled up in my eyes and one by one, they spilled down my cheeks. Emotions that had been building up all day overwhelmed me, and all I could do was stand there in the doorway of Frank's room, tears streaming down my face, unspoken longing and turmoil spilling from my heart.

Frank's confusion shifted to concern as he gently grabbed my wrists and led me into the room. The door closed behind us. The space was filled with the lingering scent of him—his cologne, his body wash—intoxicating and familiar. He guided me to the queen-sized bed and sat me down.

As I struggled to find the right words, tears continued to stream down my face. His eyes held worry and care.

He softly asked, "CeCe, what's wrong? Talk to me."

I was about to take such a big risk. I didn't know if he had completely given up on us or not or if he had truly changed. But I was so tired of ignoring my feelings for him. Being hurt with him felt better than being without him.

I took a shaky breath, attempting to compose myself. It took a few moments, but the words spilled out like rain after a drought. "I... I want to weather the storms with you."

Frank's brow furrowed in initial confusion before realization dawned in his eyes. He was silent for a moment, processing the meaning of my words. The room seemed to stand still and the air around us felt like it ceased to rotate. Then a humble warmth in the form of a smile spread across his features.

His gaze softened and he gently wiped away the tears on my cheeks with his thumb. "CeCe," he whispered, "I'd love that more than anything, but..."

I held my breath, bracing myself for rejection.

"But I promise, baby, the only storms you'll weather with me from now on will be because of mother nature and I'll be sure to protect you from those too."

His words made me weak with desire. Relieved, I climbed onto his lap, grinning as I straddled him.

Longing erupted from his throat in a low, deep groan. His hands glided sensuously up my spine, threading through my hair. A sudden pull had my hair wrapped around his hand, drawing me closer until our lips met in a feverish kiss. Our tongues entwined, engaging in a passionate dance.

Yet, the kiss was a mere prelude, a taste of the forbidden fruit that left me craving for more. The ache of desire intensified, lighting a relentless fire that surged through my veins. I yearned to feel him inside me, aching for the fullness of him.

The inferno of yearning and want inside me grew unbearable. A desperate whimper escaped my lips as I pressed my center against his jeans where his dick caused a long hump. Frustration fueled my desire, knowing that the only obstacles between me and the ecstasy I sought were the denim and a thin layer of cotton. I pulled my dress up around my waist as he dug into his jeans, pulling out what else had been missing in my life for almost a year. He eagerly brought it to my center. I anchored my tip toes on the bed, hovering above the oozing head of his masterpiece of a dick.

Sliding down on it, fresh tears came to my eyes. I looped my arms tightly around his neck, holding on. Then I began my ride, bringing his head all the way to my entrance before slowly driving it so far that it felt like it was in my stomach.

"Fuck, I missed this pussy." Frank's breathy moan was against my ear as his large hands gripped my ass cheeks. "CeCe, shit."

Hearing him say my name made my juice pour out in love. My pussy clenched, hugging him to say hello, and that it missed him too.

"Shit, baby." His breath was choppy as he used his hands on

my ass to assist in the ride, to drive himself to depths that were impossible.

"Mmph!" I whimpered, my body convulsing as it pressed against his. "Oh God."

"I love you, baby. I love you so much."

Pushing back, I looked into his eyes. I had missed those words so much that I wanted to see them come from his mouth. Slowly bouncing, my breasts brushing against his chest slowly, I told him, "Say it again."

His eyes lowered into lustful slits as he bit his bottom lip, hips moving along with our rhythmic dance. "I love you more than I did yesterday."

My eyes watered, haven't had heard our ritualistic sentiment in so long. "...and less than I will tomorrow," I finished for him. "I love you so much, Frank," I confessed before pressing my mouth against his, eliciting a low growl of pleasure from the back of his throat that made my pussy clench. My tongue traced the seam of his lips before he opened for me, allowing me to explore his mouth and ride him so slowly that I felt every vein in his dick.

A primal groan flowed from his throat into my mouth. "Anyone who says Disneyland is the happiest place on earth has clearly never been in this pussy."

21

ANTHONY "BUCK" PATTERSON

The next day, CeCe and her family were having their yearly church service at their grandmother's home church. Queen had gone along with them. Me and Frank stayed behind. We were having drinks at the bar in the lobby when Diamond called.

"Hello?"

"Baby," Diamond purred into the phone.

"Hey, you, what's going on?"

"I miss you, Daddy."

"I know you do, baby. Everything okay?"

"Yeah. Peaches and I are getting ready for our dates with the 'old men'."

I deeply chuckled, picking up my glass of cognac and taking a sip. The "Old Men" were two, white men in their sixties. They were best friends who loved the taste of young pussy. I'd met them when serving them an ounce of cocaine that they used as party favors. Diamond and Peaches happened to be with me. When I saw the twinkle in their eyes as they looked at my hoes,

I offered them to the "old men" for five thousand each for the night. Since then, they had been loyal clients.

"Cool. Be careful."

"I made a deposit into your account today," she offered eagerly.

"Oh, word? I haven't checked my emails."

"Yes. It's the money from all our dates this week."

"Thank you, baby."

"When are you coming home?"

"We head back in the morning."

Obviously relieved, she sighed. "Okay."

As I hung up, Frank looked at me with an exaggerated arched brow.

I chuckled as I smirked, knowing that face meant he was about to bring up some bullshit. "What, dawg?" I asked reluctantly before taking another sip of the Hennessy.

"Diamond is never going anywhere." He laughed, shaking his head.

"She never has to as long as she keeps playing her part as well as she does."

However, as I sat back glancing at the television screen above the bar, I wondered if that in fact was true. After spending the night between Queen's legs, I wondered how long I could live this lifestyle. It was all good as long as the woman I was fucking and spending my time with was a hoe. But if I ever found myself with a woman like Queen, I wondered if I could have both. I had never been attracted to a woman who wasn't giving me something in return. And I had hoped that my attraction to Queen was a physical obsession that would go away once I finally got her. But as she woke up in my arms that morning, I thanked God that our lifestyles were so different. I appreciated that she had a man at home and that she despised the lifestyle that I lived. That left no opportunity for there to be anything more between us beyond the hours she'd spent draining my dick last night. But now I knew that it was possible for me to be attracted to a normal woman.

"Guess what?"

Looking over at Cap, I cracked up. It was so easy to forget how young we were because of the mature roles we had been in since we were teenagers. But looking at him with this corny grin on his face, he looked every bit like a little boy who had finally gotten the toy he'd always wanted.

"You finally got CeCe," I revealed with a knowing chuckle.

His grin grew even wider as he nodded slowly. "How'd you know?"

"C'mon, dawg. It's my job to know you."

Honored, Cap simply nodded.

I had known that he was different when we met up that morning. His steps were effortless, lighter. He had an air about him that had only been there when he had CeCe in his life.

"So, y'all back together?" I asked with an excited raised brow.

"Yeah, we back."

We shared a grin as I reached for his hand and shook up with him.

"That's what's up," I told him.

I was truly happy for Cap. Even though I knew nothing about monogamy, it was something that he seemed to yearn and from one woman in particular. So, I was happy that he'd finally gotten what he wanted so he could have some peace and happiness to go home to after leaving the streets behind at night.

"What about LuLu?"

Cap shrugged. "I haven't been fucking with her like that.

So, it's nothing she can say. She is way more levelheaded than Lamonica was. Won't be no issues out of her. I told her this morning that I was back with my baby mama. She was cool."

"Long as she gets to say she fucked with Cap, she's all right."

As we laughed boisterously, I noticed the bartender tensing up, his eyes darting towards the entrance. I followed his line of vision. My surprise matched Frank's as we laid eyes on Hector walking in. The tension in the room grew, and I could practically feel the unease radiating from the bartender.

We were in the Deep South, and the bartender was already uncomfortable with the presence of two niggas that were obvious gangsters, tatted from head to toe with jewelry on worth more than his yearly salary. But with Hector, a Mexican gangster, stepping in, the bartender blushed even more with discomfort.

As Hector strolled toward into the bar, Frank and I continued to share shocked glances, confused to see him all the way down in Mississippi. It was a surprise that threw us completely off guard, but despite our surprise, Frank and I maintained our composed dispositions.

"Gentlemen!" Hector approached with outstretched arms and a mischievous grin on his face. "The things that I have to do to get your attention."

Smirking, Frank stood. The mischief exploded from Hector's throat in a hearty laugh as he shook hands with Frank. I spun around in the barstool and shook his hand as well.

"What the hell are you doing down here?" Frank asked.

Looking at the curious bartender behind us, Hector motioned for us to follow him. "Come. Let's talk."

Frank and I stood and followed Hector over to a more secluded area of the bar where no listening ears could pry. We got comfortable in lounge chairs that sat in a circle around a small, elegant cocktail table.

"You came all this way to talk?" Frank asked.

"I came all of this way to get your attention." Leaning in, Hector flashed a sly grin, letting his elbows find a comfortable perch on his knees. "You have to be running out of product by now. And I've been told that you haven't found a new distributor yet–"

"Hector—" Frank tried to interrupt him.

"Hear me out, Frank. Your operation runs smooth and low-key. You are the type of man that I can trust to expand my distribution. I like the way that you run your organization. You're respectful and respected. You fly under the radar. I need that type of man to be the connect to my product. I'm getting old and tired. I no longer want to be in the forefront. I need to give this position to someone I can trust to handle it properly."

Frank's expression was stoic as he shook his head. "Let Keyes do it."

"You know that Keyes doesn't have the connections that you have, Frank."

"I'm not stepping on Keyes' toes."

"*Fraaank*," Hector sang lowly as he tilted his head. "Keyes is a boss. We know this. But *you*, you're a *leader*."

My eyes bounced back and forth between them.

"I'm willing to offer 18.5 a key," Hector said with a challenging smirk.

I fought to keep an unimpressed expression. Eighteen and a half for a brick was a steal when a brick of high-quality cocaine was going for thirty-five thousand on the street. Alexander's prices hadn't been this low.

"Why are you willing to go so low?" Frank asked, suspicion narrowing his eyes.

Hector nonchalantly shrugged, sporting a self-assured smile. "Because, considering the volume you move, I'll make up the difference. Plus, it gives you room to toss Keyes whatever bone you want, a figure that'll soften the blow of getting undercut."

Frank looked over at me. His eyes sought my advice.

"If we give Keyes a price he can't be mad at, then he can't be mad at us," I suggested.

Sighing, Frank interlocked his hands together, bringing them to his mouth as he pondered for a few seconds. Slowly, he brought them down to his lap and fixed his gaze on Hector. "You got a deal."

Hector's smile widened, excitement evident as he stood, extending his hand for a shake. Reluctantly, Frank rose. Concern etched across his face as he clasped Hector's hand.

"This will be a great partnership, gentlemen," Hector boasted. "Let's drink to the occasion."

Hector strolled away, heading toward the bar. Frank and I exchanged a reluctant glance before trailing him. In that shared look, I knew what he was thinking. He knew that this deal was too good to pass up, but now he was faced with undermining a friend.

"Give these two gentlemen the finest liquor that you have," Hector told the bartender.

As Frank and I returned to our barstools, tension lingered like the quiet before a storm. The clinking of glasses rang through the room as we toasted to the beginning of a new alliance, but dark shadows danced in Frank's eyes. I could almost hear the unspoken words in his mind, questioning the cost of this newfound partnership for the loyalty he owed to Keyes.

QUEEN ARIA BENSON

I stood in the mirror of the hotel bathroom doing my hair. Reggie's voice barked through my headset, drowning out Shauka's cries.

"When are you coming back?"

"We're driving back tomorrow morning."

"You probably down there in niggas' faces and shit," Reggie grumbled.

I sighed as I worked the curlers. "Reggie, don't start."

Unfortunately, his insecurity clung stubbornly. He sucked his teeth. "Whatever, man. Ain't no other reason you wanted to go to somebody else's family reunion."

"CeCe is like family to me. You know that. And she needed some help traveling with the boys."

As I continued to style my hair, I could hear the distant sounds of CeCe getting herself and the boys dressed for our trip to the mall.

"When you comin' back?" he asked.

"Tomorrow morning, Reggie. I just told you that."

"I'm just making sure you ain't lying."

I rolled my eyes as I perfected my bang.

"It's time for you to come home," he fussed. "I know how these trips go. Women always act different when they away from their men."

I sighed, feeling my frustration building. "Reggie, I love you. Ain't nobody else on my mind."

His insecurity spilled into accusations. "You think I'm stupid, don't you?"

"No," I pressed, irritated.

"You promise you'll be back tomorrow? I don't want you stayin' longer."

"I promise," I reassured him as my head ached from the burden of constantly catering to his insecurities.

As I listened to Reggie's persistent nagging, disgust crept over me. The difference between Buck's confidence and Reggie's insecurity was so obvious.

Buck's lingering scent was still all over my skin. No matter how much I had showered since he'd taken me, I could still smell him on me. Memories of Buck fucking me gently but mercilessly until tears came to my eyes danced in my mind as Reggie's insecurity continued to gnaw at me through the phone.

Buck's secure, calm, and confident presence made Reggie seem like a mere shadow. It was an embarrassing realization that made me suddenly ashamed to even be with Reggie. His insecurities felt like chains, and I yearned for the liberation that Buck had introduced me to.

Though Buck and I were just friends, the appeal of his beauty, swag, and good dick had ignited something deeper. I was obsessed with how he made me feel. I was counting the minutes until I felt him inside of me again, even though I didn't have an exact time because I knew I couldn't cross that line. Buck had his relationships, and I had my commitment to Reggie, as flawed as it was.

ANTHONY "BUCK" PATTERSON

When the girls returned from church, we all went our separate ways to get dressed. As I finished lacing up my Gucci sneakers, there was a knock on the door. When I opened it, the look in her eyes was begging me to take her. I hadn't known if that night with Queen was a one-time thing or not. Since then, we hadn't been alone. We had been constantly surrounded by our friends and CeCe's family. But she would sneak flirtatious glances at me here and there. When she'd left my hotel room the morning after, I had no idea when or if I would feel that amazing pussy again. I wanted to desperately, but I knew that because of our situations at home, I shouldn't push.

"Y'all ready?" I asked.

A flirtatious flutter of her lashes accompanied her response, "Yeah."

"Cool. I'm ready too."

But, instead of leading the way to the elevator, she walked into the room. Mischief danced in her eyes, drawing me in like a moth to a flame.

"What you doin'?" I pried gently, my eyes locking with hers.

She gracefully climbed onto the bed, teasingly lifting the hem of her maxi dress over her waist. With a tempting arch of her back, she revealed a delicate, pink center that held my gaze captive. Her lustful eyes devoured me as she pulled her bottom lip between her teeth.

Caught off guard, I stood there for a moment, my breath catching as desire coursed through me, causing my jeans to tighten. Our eyes locked, and I found myself relishing in her beauty. Licking my lips, I strolled towards the bed. Along the way, I grabbed a condom from the dresser.

As I stood behind her, I dropped my jeans to my ankles. I slid on the condom and positioned myself perfectly at her entrance. I pressed slowly forward. My dick slid in carefully, first the smooth mushroom head, then gradually the rest of my shaft. I could feel her pussy grip around my rock-hard member, and I knew she was already struggling to take my girth.

She began to whimper and moan. "*Ooooh*, fuck."

I kept pressing forward, carefully but firmly, pushing every inch of my dick inside until I was buried deep in her juicy canal. She was so tight around me.

"*Fuckkk*," I growled.

I began thrusting in and out of her as her pussy gripped and strained around me. I could feel and hear my balls slapping against her clit with each thrust. Her heavy breathing and aroused whimpers soon became louder moans and shouts.

"Yeah, give me all of it," she begged.

I was viciously pounding my dick all the way into her and all the way out again. Over and over, I rammed it deep into her as her pussy stretched to accept all of me.

"Oh, God!" she yelped. "You're fucking the shit out of me."

My eyes fell, landing on an amazing, arousing sight. As I pulled out of her, her thick, milky juices covered me.

"Look at you creaming all over this dick," I panted.

As I pumped my thick tool into her, I placed one hand on her waist to keep her in position and the other on the back of her neck. I then set to pound her into oblivion.

"Oh my God!" she began to grit on repeat, louder each time. "Oh my God! Oh my God! Oh my God!'

She arched her back even more, opening herself up for me, hungrily trying to accept every last millimeter of me into the depths of her core. I fucked her harder and harder, desperately trying to hold back from letting loose for as long as I possibly could.

"I'm going to cum all over this dick," she told me, panting with a hint of surprise.

"That's what I like to hear."

———

I wanted to spend the rest of the afternoon in that pussy, but I'd had to cut it short because Frank and CeCe were waiting in the lobby.

After cumming, I pulled out of her and waddled to the bathroom, jeans still at my ankles. I peeled off the rubber and flushed it. Then I turned towards the sink to wash off.

Staring in the mirror, I could see the satisfaction in my eyes. A grin pulled at the corner of my full lips that I was too bashful to set free.

"So, is this what it's going to be?"

I couldn't believe that I even wanted or cared to know. But I needed to know how and when I would get the blessing of her wrapped around my dick again because it couldn't stop when we got back home. I wouldn't be able to take the withdrawals.

"What do you mean?" Suddenly, her voice was right next to me. Shocked, I turned to see her standing in the doorway watching suds dance on my dick with desire in her eyes.

"Stop before it ends up back up in you again," I warned.

She brought her eyes up to me as she devilishly smirked.

I shook my head, still breathing hard. "Unt uh. We gotta go."

Pouting, she went around me for a towel. "What did you mean?"

"What's up? What's this?" I reiterated. "You got a man back at home, but I'm still going to want some of that good-good when we're in Chicago."

She flashed me a playful grin. Finished washing off, I stepped back. She slid between me and the sink, locking eyes with me. That mischievous grin of hers grew as she glanced up at me.

"This pussy is good to you?" She was stirring the beast.

Closing the small space between us, I gently grabbed her neck. "Stop playing. Don't it feel like it's real good to me when I'm knee deep in it?"

She shivered as I let her neck go. I had to leave the bathroom. Had I not, we wouldn't be able to make it out of the room.

"I'm not about to be one of your hoes," she warned.

I laughed as I entered the room. "You're too defiant to play that part, sweetheart."

"What about your girlfriends?" she asked as the water ran. "They won't be mad if you're fucking me?"

"They do what I tell them to."

"Umph," she grunted in a high pitch.

"What about your boyfriend?"

She quieted as the water shut off. My eyes watched the bathroom doorway. Soon, she appeared in it, guilt replacing her playful expression. "What about him?" She shrugged.

I nodded slowly.

"We're friends," she finally answered my questions. "Friends that fuck when time permits."

I chuckled. "When time permits. Huh?"

Her smile returned. "Yeah."

"So, fuck buddies?" I asked with playfulness in my tone.

Her eyes sparkled with a flirtatious glint. "Yeah. That's cool?"

I couldn't help but flash a warm smile, my gaze lingering on her. "That's perfect, sweetheart."

However, our exchanged glances hinted at something more.

CYNTHIA "CECE" DEBOIS

Walking through the cozy mall, Frank gripped my hand, our fingers weaving together, forming a link that symbolized our renewed love. His touch was soothing like medicine for my soul. Every step we took together felt like shedding the weight of the past.

With Frank's other hand, he was pushing the double stroller. Thankfully, the ride to the mall had put both of the boys to sleep. Buck and Queen strolled beside us.

Frank and I had been immersing ourselves in that love since we reconnected. Me and the boys had practically moved into his hotel room. Initially hesitant to revisit the past with Frank, now that I was his again, it felt like I'd found my rightful place no matter what lay ahead.

As we strolled through the mall, I noticed the elusive glances between Queen and Buck. Queen's flirtatious gaze met Buck's eyes, and there was a playful energy between them. It was like a secret language only the two of them understood.

What struck me even more was Buck's demeanor. Normally

reserved and distant, he wore a radiant smile that seemed reserved just for Queen. His usual hard core was now light, and he matched Queen's flirtatiousness with his own. It was a side of Buck I hadn't seen before.

As I watched them carefully, realization dawned on me.

"Ooo!" I squealed so loud that I got everyone's attention. I stopped dead in my tracks, aiming my pointer fingers, one at Buck and the other at Queen. They had stopped in their tracks as well, looking at me like I had three heads.

"What's wrong, baby?" Frank asked.

"They fucking!" I announced loud enough that other shoppers around us stared at our little group.

Frank's brow furrowed. But Buck only chuckled a bit while Queen's face washed with guilt.

"Oh my God!" I bellowed with laughter, jumping up and down.

Frank placed his hands in his pockets, staring at Buck and Queen with wide eyes and a smile. "Word?"

My loud, uncontrollably laughter made Queen cringe. "Would you shut up, CeCe?"

"*Wooooow!*" I exhaled.

She rushed towards me, grabbing me by the elbow. "Would you *shut up*?"

"You gon' be hoe number four?!" I cackled.

Frank burst into laughter. I held my stomach, unable to stop cracking up as Queen dragged me past the guys.

"It's not funny," she gritted.

I took deep breaths, trying to calm down. "Okay," I said, out of breath. "Okay, okay, I'm sorry."

"Thank you," she said through tight lips.

I leaned in, asking, "Was it good?"

When her eyes rolled to the back of her head, my mouth fell open.

"He got so much dick, girl," she gushed shamelessly. "That stomach didn't hide shit."

I screamed, causing her to cringe.

I figured that Buck had to have some good dick to have three women in control and selling pussy for him. But to see Queen's usually defiant, stubborn demeanor reduced to putty was blowing my mind.

22

FRANK "CAPO" DISCIPLE

Waking up back in Chicago with CeCe nestled against my chest in my bed, her arm draped across my stomach, was a sight I thanked God for. Her warm and familiar presence gave me a sense of completeness. I looked down at her, taking in the way she lay there, peacefully sleeping. She was finally mine again, and I wasn't letting her slip away.

As I lay there, I thought about the journey we'd been through. Seeing her lying there, wrapped up in the aftermath of a long drive, it felt like we'd weathered the storm and come out on the other side stronger.

I reached down, brushing a strand of hair from her face, staring at her with eyes full of love and devotion. CeCe was my anchor. Having her in my arms again was a reminder of what truly mattered. I wasn't the kind of nigga to lay my feelings bare, but in the moment, I couldn't deny the depths of what I felt for her.

She stirred and nestled even closer. It was simple, but to me, it meant everything.

Greedy, I gently slipped from underneath her, causing her to gently fall over on her stomach. As I straddled her, I admired how the sunlight danced on her beautifully sculpted back. The curves and lines of her body were a masterpiece, a work of art that left me in awe. There was a certain elegance in the way the light played on her skin, accentuating every tone. As I admired her, pride and possessiveness made my dick turn into steel. This living example of beauty and strength was mine.

I couldn't resist the temptation, drawn irresistibly to the canvas of her back. Leaning in, I pressed soft kisses on her neck, savoring the warmth of her skin beneath my lips. Each kiss trailed down slowly, as I gently explored the curves that had me captivated.

As my lips brushed against her back, she stirred in her sleep. I continued the tender descent, filling the room with the soft sounds of my lips and tongue tasting her.

A delicate, groggy moaned fueled my desire to explore every inch of her. I reached the arch of her back and spread her ass cheeks open. My tongue slid down her crack, making her back arch as she dazedly hissed.

I carefully opened her folds with my tongue. She brought the pussy to me by arching her back even more, as my tongue explored her delicate flower.

"Oh, Frank," she began to moan as I flicked and sucked her clit.

Her hips moved urgently, widening the space between her knees. I traced my tongue along the path below her clit, sliding toward the entrance of her drenched center. There the taste of her sweet essence met my tongue, and I delved inside. As I started to pleasure her with my tongue, her moans intensified, echoing in the room, confirming I'd found the sweet spot.

I pressed my face deeper, making it harder for me to breathe as my tongue explored the depths of her. She ground her pussy further into my face, while reaching one hand back and intertwining her fingers in my hair, anchoring my tongue in place. With each lick, her moans grew louder. I maintained my focus, keeping up the rhythmic penetration with my tongue.

"I'm cumming," she sang after a few moments.

My tongue remained deeply nestled inside of her, determined to drench itself in her cum. As her moans increased, I felt the rhythmic spasms of her insides embracing my tongue. I hungrily savored every drop of the juices released from her core. In the midst of her orgasm, she tightly clasped her legs together around my ears, an intimate embrace that I would gladly live in forever.

———

I left the first love of my life to be with the second. Being a boss had always made me the happiest I had ever been, even when deep in some pussy, until I met CeCe.

"He does not look happy," Buck mumbled as we strolled through the bar towards Keyes, who sat there waiting for us. A hardened expression covered his entire face as his gaze lingered on us for a moment. Then, he averted his eyes, shifting his focus back to the clear liquid swirling in the glass in front of him.

A chuckle escaped me as I prepared for this tough conversation. As a leader, I'd navigated the cutthroat world of undercutting the competition more times than I could count. However, this time felt different, somewhat remorseful. I'd never found myself in the position of doing it to a friend before.

"Cap!" I excitedly heard next to me.

I turned, searching the empty bar. A woman was sitting at a high-boy waving at me excitedly. She'd even gotten Keyes' attention as he sat at the bar. She jumped down off of the stool, shuffling towards me with the biggest smile on her face. I could tell that she was slightly older than us, maybe in her forties. As she jogged towards us, large breasts and hips jiggled along the way. My eyes narrowed, as I wondered what she could want. Considering my popularity, there was no guessing.

"You don't know me," she said with a giggle as she approached me and Buck. "I was at the Mother's Day event you had a few weeks ago. I just wanted to thank you for that beautiful dinner. I lost both of my sons last year to gun violence, so I was really regretting Mother's Day. But one of my friends knew about your event and encouraged me to go. I'm so glad that I did." Her eyes got glassy as she continued fighting to keep her composure. "It gave me something else to think about other than my grief. And I actually met other mothers there who have lost their children. We're friends now, and we support each other."

Smiling, I told her, "That's great. What's your name?"

She smiled sheepishly. "They call me Ms. Candy, sweetheart."

"Well, it's nice to meet you, Ms. Candy."

Glancing over at Buck, she told me, "I didn't mean to interrupt y'all. I just wanted to personally say thank you. I never thought I would get the chance to."

"Well, you're welcome. I appreciate that." I bent down and hugged her.

"Take care," she said giving me a tight, motherly squeeze.

"And God bless you." She released me and hurried back to her seat.

"That old lady thick as hell," Buck mumbled.

I scoffed with a chuckle, tossing my head from side to side as we approached Keyes.

"What up?" Buck greeted Keyes as we closed in on him, flanking him on each side.

He offered a curt head nod before taking a sip from his glass. His demeanor was already cold and against us.

I settled onto the barstool next to him, signaling the bartender. Her big, voluptuous breasts greeted me before she did.

A smirk teased her red lips as she stood in front of me. "What can I get you, Frank?"

"Give me a double shot of Clase Azul neat and a bottle of water."

She nodded, glancing at Buck. "What about you?"

"Same."

As she strolled away, Keyes let out a frustrated sigh.

"I take it by your demeanor that you know why we asked to meet with you," I said.

"Hector already told me that some changes were being made and that you would be reaching out to me. Since you've been looking for a connect, I can guess what this is about." The disgust and betrayal on Keyes' face was intense as he kept his eyes away from me and Buck. He stared blankly into his drink, avoiding our gaze. "I thought we were boys."

"We *are*," I insisted. "I didn't really have a choice so—"

"You did!" he interjected, finally stabbing his narrowed eyes through me. "You could have found another con—"

"It was taking too long. And Hector came to *me*. Over and over again, he kept coming to me. I told him no a lot of times.

But let's be real. He's trying to expand, and you don't have the network or connections that I have to help him do that."

"So, I'm supposed to go from being a boss to working under y'all?" he asked with a snarl.

"You're still a boss," I assured him. "To your team you're still a boss."

Gritting, he shook his head. "I don't like this shit. If I wanted to work under you, I could have started out that way. You know I've always wanted to be my own man."

"And you still can be. With the prices that I'm going to give you, you're going to make a bag and be able to make your team bigger. All the dope boys are going to want to fuck with you."

Keyes scoffed. "If they don't fuck with you first."

I nodded slowly. "Yeah, if they don't fuck with me first."

He grimaced. "And I'm making you richer."

"We're *all* getting richer."

Abruptly, he pushed his drink back and moved as if he were about to stand.

Buck stuck his hand out. "Chill, my nigga."

Keyes' head snapped back, obviously offended at Buck's audacity. Chuckling, he looked at me while aiming his thumb at Buck. "See? You niggas not about to be checking me."

"We won't have to if you be cool."

We quieted when the bartender returned, placing Buck's drink and mine in front of us. Then she disappeared to the other side of the empty bar.

"He saved your life," Buck informed him in an effort to reduce the tension.

Squinting, Keyes gave Buck his attention.

"Alexander wanted to kill you. He wanted to expand too and felt like you were competition. Cap wasn't down for that shit, so he killed Alexander. Hector has been trying to link with

Cap for a long time, but Cap has refused because of his loyalty to you. He's in this position because he saved your life. He could have his old connect, but then *you would be dead*. He was loyal to you as long as he could be."

Unfortunately, that only seemed to take the edge off a little. Keyes remained standing as he dug in his pocket. He pulled out a wad of cash and peeled a few tens off of it. He dropped them on the bar, nodding slowly. "So, I'm working for you niggas now." It wasn't a question. It was a defeated reality.

"Don't think of it like that," Buck replied.

A wry chuckle that was nearly demonic erupted from Keyes' throat. "Yeah, ah'ight."

He stood, and this time Buck didn't stop him.

With that, he strolled away, hands in his pocket, shoulders slumped with defeat.

"He's not going to be cool with this," Buck dejectedly revealed as he leaned onto the bar.

Shaking my head, I picked up my glass. "I know."

CYNTHIA "CECE" DEBOIS

Ever since I got back with Frank, there was this newfound happiness bubbling inside of me and it spilled over into everything I did, especially tending to my kids.

The next day, as I bustled around the living room, the sweet melody of Shauka's cooing in his bassinet filled the room. In the kitchen, Nicole was washing dishes. She had become a reliable support in my challenging task of raising two small kids.

"Here, Mommy!" I turned to see Jah passing my cell phone back to me.

"Is Grandma still on the phone?"

He nodded while hurrying away towards his bin of toys. I groaned, knowing that he was about to make the chore of cleaning up even harder.

"Hey, Mama," I said with a sigh.

"That boy is something else," she said with a peculiar laugh.

"What do you mean?"

"He told me about his daddy sleeping in his mommy's bed again."

My eyes closed with fear and regret for a second before I plopped down on the couch.

Finally, my mother's judgment filled the awkward silence. "So, you got back with him?"

There was so much disdain and hatred in her tone that I instantly regretted giving Frank a second chance. But then I recalled how confident I was in the changes he'd made.

"Yes," I said proudly. "Yes, we got back together, Mama."

She scoffed with disgust dripping from her throat. "Oh my God, CeCe."

"He's changed," I insisted.

"He's going to hurt you again."

"You sound like you want him to hurt me again."

"This is why I don't like him. Ever since you met him, it's like all of the common sense that your daddy and I taught you vanished!"

I cringed, lowering my head.

"Has he not ruined your life enough?! Has he not broken your heart enough?! It didn't hurt enough the first time, so you had to go back and let him finish?"

"Mama—"

"I don't want to hear it," she hissed. "I'm done. I have to go, CeCe."

When her end of the line went dead, my mouth dropped slightly. I swallowed hard, forcing back the emotions I felt knowing I'd let her down. I reminded myself that I had to live my love life for me and unapologetically to ensure that I'd have no regrets. I forced myself to recall the perfection that had convinced me to give him a second chance and continued cleaning.

As I straightened up the living room, the doorbell's chime sliced through the air. Nicole darted out of the kitchen and headed to answer it. I craned my neck, watching curiously. I wasn't expecting anyone. The revolving door of aid and assistance I had after Shauka's arrival had slowed down. Now, it was mainly Nicole and Frank, holding down the fort. My parents stepped in here and there, babysitting when they could, but the eager support I had was a distant memory.

As Nicole opened the door, a familiar voice floated in, and my eyes widened at the sight of Frank stepping into the room. My pulse quickened and I salivated over how good he looked. The expensive diamonds glinted in his ears, around his wrists, and draped around his neck, were a lavish display that made my heart skip a beat. His outfit, dressier than usual, was a pair of denim jeans and a Ralph Lauren polo.

"Daddy!" Jah exclaimed, taking off towards Frank.

Frank bent down to pick Jah up before he could collide with his legs.

A smile tugged on my lips as I asked, "What you doing here?"

He returned my smile, his eyes filled with a mischievous sparkle. "Get dressed," he softly commanded.

Confusion clouded my face. It was just a regular Tuesday evening, and we didn't have any plans. "Where are we going?" I inquired, trying to decode the mystery behind his teasing smile.

"I heard you, CeCe. You said we should have dated, to get to know each other, right?"

My shoulders slumped as I was overcome with emotion.

"So, I'm taking you on a date," he informed me with a twinkle in his eyes.

The setting sun bathed downtown Chicago in hues of warm orange as Frank and I entered the lavish seafood restaurant he had chosen for our surprise date. The atmosphere was a far cry from the usual bars and spots we frequented in the city. Soft music played in the background, and the low hum of conversation blended with the clinking of fine silverware against fine china. The restaurant radiated with an air of sophistication that felt unfamiliar to us. The well-dressed patrons, engaged in hushed conversations, cast curious glances our way as we walked to our table.

As we settled into our seats, the aroma of freshly cooked seafood filled our nostrils. Frank's eyes met mine in a moment of steamy flirtation, creating an intimate bubble even as we were surrounded by so many others in a public setting. Our conversation flowed, delving into topics we should have explored when we first met.

"Did you ever really want kids?"

Thinking of Jah and Shauka made me smile. "Yeah. Not this soon, though. But I always envisioned having a lot of kids, especially since I'm an only child."

Frank's brow rose drastically. "A lot?"

I giggled. "Four or five."

Frank nodded slowly.

"What about you?"

"I never really thought about it, but if it's with *you*, I could see us having a whole football team."

I blushed. "What about getting married?" I asked.

Licking his lips, he reached across the table for my hand and held it. "You wanna marry me?"

I playfully rolled my eyes. "We barely can get being in a relationship right."

Frank's gaze met mine, and he admitted, "We're going to get it right this time." His sincerity wrapped around me, making me blush. Then he went on, "But to answer your question, I never saw myself getting married, but once again, with *you*, I can see it. I can see us building something real."

The waiter approached, ready to take our orders, and Frank gestured for me to go first.

"I'll have the lobster tail and shrimp scampi please," I said, my eyes never leaving Frank's.

He grinned, giving his order, and when the waiter left, he leaned in with an intense gaze. "You look beautiful tonight, CeCe," he whispered, his words sending a shiver down my spine.

A blush crept over my cheeks. "You're not looking too bad yourself."

Frank's eyes softened. "I want a life with you, CeCe... a real life. No more immature, petty shit that's going to push us apart."

My blush deepened. "I want that too. I want a life where we can build something real and lasting."

He watched me so intently that I had to bashfully look away. My eyes swept over the restaurant.

Looking around, I felt so grateful. "Thank you for tonight. This was a good surprise. Thank you for listening to me."

He brought the back of my hand to his lips and kissed it so slowly that my lips got jealous. "Thank you for a second chance. This is just the beginning, baby."

QUEEN ARIA BENSON

I stood in my bedroom, folding laundry and lost in the memories of the time I had spent with Buck down in Mississippi. The heat of those moments still lingered in my heart and made my pussy throb. I had become addicted to the way he made me feel, the security and joy that wrapped around me like a protective cocoon. It was all that I could think about. In just a few days, Buck had managed to breathe life into my weary spirit.

As I heard Reggie arriving home, I pouted with disappointment. I wanted to stay in this happy bubble. But I knew that he could easily ruin it, depending on what mood he was in.

Reggie's entrance into the bedroom was dramatic. His attitude practically oozed from every pore. I chose to ignore it, hoping to preserve my peace.

"Where my plate at?" Reggie's gruff voice cut through my thoughts.

I glanced at him, offering a simple answer, "In the microwave."

"Warm it up for me," he ordered as he plopped down on the foot of the bed and kicked off his shoes.

I looked him in the eye, newfound courage stirring in me. "You can warm it up yourself. You see I'm busy." Irritation caused my eyes to roll. "You're always expecting housewife duties out of me when I pay bills too," I muttered.

He glared at the sudden departure from my usual obedience. It shocked even me, the way I stood up to him. I knew that my sudden rebellion had everything to do with the strength Buck had instilled in me during our time together.

As I turned away, preparing to resume my chores, Reggie's anger erupted like a volcano. His attack was sudden, catching me off guard. His hands became instruments of violence. He struck me with force that sent me stumbling backward, the laundry falling from my hands.

Suddenly, the bedroom was now a battleground. His blows landed like thunder. Pain radiated through me, both physical and emotional, as I tried to shield myself from the attack. I could feel the weight of his anger in every blow.

I begged him to stop, each plea met with another wave of aggression. The room blurred, tears streaming down my face as I realized how extreme this beating was. The sound of his fists hitting flesh was all that I could hear, drowning out my pleas.

I zoned out, mentally going back to the previous weekend. I couldn't understand how both could be my reality, how I could have been in complete bliss just a few days ago and now here, experiencing devastating physical abuse. The image of Buck's face, filled with understanding and kindness, clashed with the anger contorting Reggie's. Buck's hands had traced patterns of comfort across my skin, while Reggie's became instruments of pain.

23

ANTHONY "BUCK" PATTERSON

Weed smoke hung heavy in Debo's dimly lit den. The scent of Lynette's tacos mingled with the pungent aroma of burning blunts. Tuesday night meant family time at Debo's crib. Sometimes, they extended the invite to the crew. Lynette had thrown down in the kitchen for Taco Tuesday.

Debo, Lynette, Cap, CeCe, Marquis, and Kofi were chilling in the room. Their kids were playing on the second floor, along with Jah. Shauka was sleeping in his car seat in the living room nearby. Spades cards slapped against the table as boisterous shouts mixed with the beats Kofi was spinning. He played around with deejay equipment from time to time.

I leaned back, sipping on my drink, watching the spades game unfold with Peaches sitting next to me. Debo, Cap, CeCe, and Marquis were deep in it, cards held close to their chests like prized possessions.

CeCe couldn't hide the excitement in her eyes as she slammed down the last card. "That's game! We won, baby!"

Reaching across the table, Cap dabbed her up with a wide grin.

Marquis slammed his hand on the table, a scowl creasing his face. "Nah, that ain't right. Y'all cheating or somethin'."

Cap leaned back in his chair, a smug grin on his face. "Ain't nobody cheating, Marq. We just better players, my nigga. It's cool."

Marquis leaned back in the folding chair, the veins in his neck bulging. "Debo, you cut, man! I need another partner!"

Debo leaned forward with his eyes locked on Marquis. "I ain't cut, bro. Check the cards."

CeCe chimed in with a taunting tone. "Marq, it was a fair game, baby. Stop cryin'."

Marquis pointed a finger at Debo. "You cut, and you know it. Ain't no way we lost like that."

I shook my head, laughing at the seriousness of the game. I leaned over to Peaches, whispering, "These motherfuckers take spades too serious, like it's life or death. That's why I never play."

Peaches laughed with her eyes glued to the game. "That's the only way to play. You know that."

CeCe started shuffling the cards for the next round, although the tension from the previous game still remained in the air. Just then, the den's door creaked open. Queen entered, a vision that made my heart skip a beat. Her legs were out and shiny as if they had been lathered in coconut oil. The stomach that I had traced kisses on was on display because of a cropped top. I hadn't seen her since we returned from Mississippi. The mere sight of her caused a tidal wave of longing to violently crash through me. Her presence had a magnetic pull, and my body stiffened with desire and need.

Trying to play it cool, I averted my gaze, not wanting to

stare too obviously. But it was hard not to. I had been thinking about her since we'd made it back home. Peaches, April, and Diamond had been getting punished with dick because it was longing for a feeling that they couldn't fulfill no matter how much I tried.

Queen moved gracefully around the room, exchanging hugs and greetings with everyone. When she got to me, I felt a rush of warmth that went straight to my core. She wrapped her arms around me, and for a moment, I lost myself in her embrace.

"Hey," she spoke softly against my ear.

My dick rocked up. But I cleared my throat, replying with a cool, "What's up?"

The sweet scent of her perfume engulfed me, and it took all my self-control to let her go. I knew others were watching, especially Peaches, so I forced myself to release her.

As Queen walked away, I could feel Peaches' eyes on me. I reluctantly gave her my attention, meeting her taunting, questionable orbs. Laughing guiltily, I asked, "What, man?"

"What's up with that?" she quietly asked while discreetly pointing at Queen.

It was so hard to hold back my grin. "What?"

She quietly gasped, smacking my bicep as her eyes ballooned with a smile. "Oh my God!"

My eyes bounced around, hoping that no one had heard her. Luckily, she was quiet enough that the loud music and conversations had drowned her out.

I sat back, still smiling, as I reminisced about that pussy.

"Are you blushing, nigga?!" she spat looking back at me.

I sat back up, resting my elbows on my knees. "We fucked in Mississippi."

When she shrugged nonchalantly, my brows narrowed.

"I knew it was going to happen," she whispered coolly, answering my silent question. "Once y'all got cool, I knew it was a matter of time."

"How?"

"I could tell by the way you looked at her that you were attracted to her. And she tries to hide it, but it was obvious to me that she was feeling something different about you."

I sighed, relieved that she was cool with this, though I had assumed that as my friend, she would. So, I told her everything, how we'd hooked up in Mississippi, how good it was. I had always told Peaches everything, but I rarely had to tell her something like this because I hardly dealt with women outside of my hoes.

"So, what does this mean?" she asked.

I shrugged, casually looking over at Queen, feeling my dick press against my jeans. She was wearing a tiny pair of Dazzey Dukes that I hoped she had put on in hopes of enticing me.

"It doesn't mean anything. She has a man, and I got y'all. She said we're fuck buddies, and I'm cool with that." But my dick was anxious, waiting on pins and needles for the moment we would be fuck buddies again.

"The way you're looking at her says otherwise," Peaches teasingly revealed.

"Nah, she's not like us," I said, shaking my head with sincere regret. "Even if she didn't have a man, I can't have her and my hoes too. It would never work."

FRANK "CAPO" DISCIPLE

Getting that first shipment from Hector a few days later was like tapping into a gold mine. The prices we had agreed to made it possible for me to make more bread than I had ever imagined. In a perfect world, this partnership would have been ideal. But Keyes had been running his mouth to the wrong people, letting his pride ruin what could have been a perfect union. The streets had brought back the news that Keyes still wasn't happy with the new game plan. He'd been talking recklessly, even going so far as threatening me and Buck's lives. He couldn't see the big picture. His pride had him by the throat, and he was too blinded by his own ego to see the fortune staring him in the face.

I would've preferred not to have had to step on Keyes' toes to make this happen, but it was one of those hiccups in the game that came with being a boss. Threatening our lives was a bold move that I didn't think Keyes had in him, though. I'd hoped that underneath his bruised ego, the respect that we had gained for one another over the years would remain intact.

Apparently, it hadn't.

So, when Buck and I arrived at Keyes' warehouse with the first shipment of product, we were prepared. We stepped inside his spot with multiple duffle bags filled with product slung over our shoulders. Instantly, the air was so thick with tension that it was suffocating. One could practically cut through it. Keyes was posted up at an old metal table, his eyes narrowing as they locked on us. His henchmen, strategically scattered throughout the warehouse, watched our every move like hawks. I could feel their glares and I knew they all had their hammers and trigger fingers on ready.

The silence was deafening as we approached the table. Keyes' icy glower dug into me. The atmosphere was drenched with animosity. Buck and I dropped the heavy duffle bags onto the old metal table, the impact sending dust particles dancing through the air like a grim celebration. One of Keyes' henchmen approached, hands moving to unzip the bags and reveal the bricks inside. The counting began. Rhythmic thuds of the product sounded throughout the warehouse as he dropped them on the table.

"Keyes..." My deep rumble sliced through the eerie silence as I sat on the table so close to Keyes that he sat back, snarling. "I hear you got a problem."

Buck was stoic as he stood by my side.

Keyes' eyes shot daggers at me with a smug grin on his lips. "You already know I do."

I leveled my gaze at him. "Don't lose your life over a partnership that could be smooth sailing if you get past your jealousy and insecurities."

Keyes scoffed, leaning forward. "*Jealousy?*"

I shot back, my words dripping with menace, "You feel like Hector should've put you in his position. Apparently, he had a reason why he didn't. But don't be stupid. This partnership could be a gold mine for all of us if you'd stop acting like a lil' bitch."

He chuckled, a cold sound that vibrated throughout the warehouse. "*A bitch?*"

I leaned in, our faces inches apart. "You heard what I said, nigga. This shit is happening whether you like it or not. Those hits you're putting on me and Buck's head are only making the one on yours even bigger. We're on the verge of being rich and living like fucking kings. You need to wise up or you're gonna find out the hard way that your pride ain't worth sacrificing a fortune and your life for."

As Keyes' temper flared, he jumped up from his chair, the screech of its legs pierced through the tense atmosphere. In a swift motion, he yanked his gun from his waistband, aiming it squarely at me. His henchmen followed his lead, pulling their weapons from their hiding places.

"See? This is your problem!" Keyes spat venomously, his eyes blazing with anger. "Stanley may have raised you, but you ain't him! You don't run this city!"

I remained calmly seated on the table with a sly grin on my lips. "Look around you, Keyes," I said coolly, gesturing with a nod.

His eyes, filled with curiosity and rage, scanned the room. What he saw made the blood drain from his face. Besides the two henchmen aiming guns at Buck and me, the others had turned against him. Their weapons were pointed squarely at Keyes. The balance of power had shifted, and his punk ass was on the losing end of the standoff he had initiated. The defeat and hurt in Keyes' eyes were unmistakable. Slowly, he lowered his Glock. The two goons that naïvely had his back did the same.

My grin slowly spread until it touched my ears and brightened my eyes. "I do, *in fact*, run this city, motherfucka. I keep giving you slack because of our history, but I don't like repeating myself. Fall the fuck in line."

Looking back, I found Ramon in position with his hammer pointed at Keyes. When we caught eyes, he lifted his head, acknowledging me. "Get my bread," I told him.

Ramon bent down and retrieved a bookbag from underneath the table. He then tossed it over his shoulder.

Looking around, I told those of his crew that had turned against him, "Let's ride."

As Buck and I calmly walked out of Keyes' warehouse, a steady recession formed behind us. The henchmen who had turned against Keyes fell in line. These were the same henchmen who had expressed their desire to become a part of something more significant than Keyes' crew for years. They'd kept me informed of everything he had been saying since the moment I took over for Hector. Loyalty in these streets was fickle, and with my reputation preceding me, people were quick to align themselves with The Disciple Family.

ANTHONY "BUCK" PATTERSON

After we left the warehouse, I needed to relax. The headquarters offered a quiet space where I could clear my head. The smell of money lingered in the air as I counted the cash Keyes had paid us.

Once the bread was counted and stashed, I rolled a blunt. As I reclined in the chair, the smoke curling around me, I couldn't shake the weight of the decision looming over us.

Keyes had to go. The look in his eyes back at the warehouse told me he wasn't bowing out gracefully. As Frank's muscle, I was no stranger to the dirty work, but this one was different. Keyes and I went way back, a friendship that had weathered the storms of the hood. The burden of having to turn on a life-long friend pressed heavily on my heart.

I took a drag, letting the smoke linger as I stared at the ceiling, lost in my thoughts. Loyalty in our world was a rare luxury, and betraying Keyes wasn't just a move that needed to be made, it was a personal betrayal. But he had made the first chess move. The streets had their own rules and sometimes, those rules demanded the hardest choices.

The quiet solitude of the headquarters was disrupted by the sound of the door being unlocked. I knew it couldn't be Frank because he had headed home to be with CeCe and the boys. The only person it could be was Queen. We hadn't spoken much in the past few days since our return from Mississippi, but since she'd saved my life, her presence never failed to ignite a longing in me that made my dick immediately hard.

As Queen walked in, I noticed the lingering desire that had been simmering beneath the surface erupt into a fiery intensity. Her mere presence had that effect on me.

She immediately noticed my solemn disposition. She dropped the paper bags she was carrying and came towards me. The paper bags tipped over, and a cascade of money spilled out. The green bills scattered across the floor.

"What's wrong?" Queen's sweet, concerned voice floated through the smoky air as she stood over me.

I offered no words. Instead, I set the blunt down in the ashtray. In that moment, the stress release that she could give me superseded words. I reached for her, pulling her close by the waist and settled her on my lap. Her immediate response, straddling me, told me she understood the unspoken language between us.

Gently, I cupped the back of her head, my fingers gripping her roots with tender firmness. Our lips met in a slow dance, a kiss that was both sloppy and passionate.

———

"Yes, Buck," Queen's pants encouraged my strokes. "Just like that..."

As soon as she moaned those words of desire, I could feel the tension building as my balls tightened. My nut was loading for an explosion.

I gently lifted one of her legs and then the other, resting them on my shoulders. Her flower was now fully open and exposed, and she welcomed every inch of me. I thrust into her, savoring the caress of her walls. I stroked her as long, deep, and intently as I could until I felt the unmistakable wave of ecstasy that preceded my release.

"*Fuckkk,*" I barked as I bucked wildly into her.

A warm release started to fill the protection between us. A low, beastly growl escaped my lips as I poured out every bit of ecstasy. Her body tightened around me, pulsating in response. Sensing her pleasure, I intensified my movements, thrusting more vigorously. She was cumming with me. So, I delved further into her.

In an instant, she responded by unleashing a loud, violent orgasm. "Oh fuck!" she began yelling at the top of her lungs as she lifted her head up off the carpet and then slammed it back down. "Don't stop!" she begged. "Please don't stop!"

I kept pounding her essence through the peak, firing off the last shots of my warm, sticky nut as I felt her own orgasm avalanching around me and then settling. With no more left to give, I carefully peeled her legs off my shoulders before collapsing into her arms. We struggled to catch our breath as her baggy T-shirt absorbed the perspiration dripping from my bare chest.

I turned my head, nestling my nose against her neck. "Sing for me, baby."

She weakly chuckled. "You like my voice that much?"

"I do. I need to hear it."

"Okay."

The way she obliged me had me ready to fuck her again.

As Queen and I lay there, wrapped up in the afterglow of hours of fucking, she cleared her throat.

"*'I found out what I've been missing. Always on the run'...*" She was singing Whitney Houston's "You Give Good Love to Me."

Her voice was a bit weak, breath choppy from the vigorous exercise, but it was beautiful, nonetheless. I closed my eyes, letting the melody wash over us. Her singing was soothing and captivating like a balm. The crooning that came from her tiny throat was so beautiful that it nearly brought a tear to my eye.

The room became my own private refuge. For a moment, all the stress and weight of the game dissolved. Her voice wrapped around me like a sweet serenade that lingered in the air. I marveled at the beauty of the difficult notes she delivered effortlessly. The way her voice weaved through the room was hypnotizing, carrying a vulnerability that made it even more enchanting. As she sang the lyrics, I found so much peace in the simplicity of the moment. Nestled against her, I became nothing but Anthony. There were no intricate games to navigate, no hustle to manage, and no delicate personalities to appease. It was just us.

CYNTHIA "CECE" DEBOIS

As we stumbled onto the front porch of the headquarters, a bit tipsy from the bar, I couldn't resist flirting with Frank. He was fumbling with the keys to unlock the door, so I took the opportunity to tease him. I pressed my body against his back and reached around him, attempting to slip my hands into his jogging pants.

"Why you playin'?" his deep, sexy rasp asked.

The rumble of his voice made me squirm, biting my lip, as I continued digging for gold. Finding it, I began to massage it.

"Ah'ight," he warned. "We gon' be fuckin' on this porch. Then everybody on Loomis is going to know how your ass looks."

Giggling, I withdrew my hand. He finally unlocked the door and followed him inside. Buck sat in the recliner, shirtless with a cloud of smoke surrounding him as he puffed on a blunt. Frank and I exchanged hesitant glances, unsure if we were intruding on something. Buck, however, seemed unfazed, a mischievous grin playing on his lips.

I caught sight of a familiar pair of shoes, and it dawned on me. "Oops," I whispered, unsure if we should make a swift exit or not.

But before I could decide, Buck laughed and waved us in. "Nah, y'all ain't gotta leave. We're finished," he cockily said as the smoke swirled around him.

Looking around the living room, I asked, "Where is Queen?"

"Back there washing off."

"Baby, can you go in the stash and get some bread? Twenty thousand," Frank said to me as he got comfortable on the couch.

"Sure, baby."

I headed down the hall to Frank's stash in the bedroom. A giggle escaped me as I contemplated the fact that Queen and Buck hadn't been just a weekend fling. The two people who once despised each other were actually fucking.

Hurrying into the bedroom, I was still lost in my own amusement when I stumbled upon Queen. Her back was to me as she was in the midst of putting on her shirt. My laughter froze as I took in the unexpected sight, concern quickly replacing amusement.

"What the hell happened to you?!"

The shock on her face as she spun around mirrored my own. She hurriedly threw her shirt over her head, pulling it down in a rush to cover herself. But it was too late. I had already seen the bruises on her back.

"Sshh!" she insisted with wide eyes.

Instantly, I saw her panic, her desperation to keep me quiet, but I was too tipsy to care.

"Who the fuck did that to you?" I gritted. "Queen, please?

Frank!" I shouted, making Queen cringe. My eyes ballooned. "Was it Buck?"

"No!" she immediately protested.

My eyes grew bigger. "So, it was Reggie?!"

"What's going on?" Frank's voice sounded behind me, resulting in Queen flopping down onto the bed, holding her face with both hands.

"Show him, Queen!" I demanded.

"It's not that serious," she whined.

"It *is* that fucking serious!" I snapped.

Frank's concerned eyes whipped towards my sudden rage. Curiosity flooded his light-brown eyes as Buck appeared behind him.

"What happened?" As soon as Queen heard his smooth baritone, she began to sob.

Buck's brows curled with curiosity. Seeing her in tears caused his chest to rise and fall with concern and anger.

Sucking my teeth, I marched towards her. I then turned her around and lifted her shirt.

As Buck's eyes fell on the bruises, old and new, scattered across Queen's back, a surge of rage twisted his expression. His features contorted, and a storm brewed in his eyes. Without uttering a word, Buck turned abruptly and thundered down the hall. The soles of his shoes caused loud hurried, rhythmic thuds towards the front door. Queen, now sobbing, buried her face in my chest as Frank rushed after Buck.

I held Queen, rocking her back and forth, allowing her to cry. Her tears sounded like those of relief from finally being able to unveil this secret.

Tears came to my eyes as I asked, "How long has he been doing this to you?"

I only received sobs in answer.

24

ANTHONY "BUCK" PATTERSON

In a blazing rage, I raced to Queen's house. My tires screeched as I sped through the streets. Headlights wildly followed me. Looking through the rearview mirror, I knew it was Frank on my tail.

Reggie had signed his own death certificate. That pussy had only been mine for a few days, but whether we hated each other or not, she had always been family, and I didn't play when it came to protecting and avenging my family. Arriving at Queen's house, I barely bothered to park before launching myself out of the car. The engine still revved. As I surveyed the scene, I spotted Reggie's LeSabre parked nearby, a few feet away from the house. Satisfaction mixed with my rage. Without hesitation, I stormed up the stairs, my heavy footsteps echoing through the neighborhood. I kicked down the door, the wood splintering and yielding to my rage. In the midst of the chaos, I spotted Frank approaching with his gun drawn as the door clattered to the ground.

Reggie, in the act of pulling his gun from his waistband,

froze as he locked eyes with me. Confusion wrinkling his face, he seemed less guarded but more bewildered by my sudden intrusion. But confusion would be the least of his worries.

Without a moment's hesitation, I launched into a vicious attack. The size difference between us was obvious and Reggie struggled to defend himself. My anger fueled each punishing blow, and the beating intensified with every strike as the thought of him putting his hands on Queen played in my mind.

Reggie's attempts to defend himself became feeble against the relentless assault. He was no match for the fury I unleashed, and the room roared with the brutal sounds of my rage. My anger was scorching.

"You wanna put your hands on her?" I yelled. "Put your hands on me, nigga!"

As Reggie stumbled backward from a blow, I unleashed a flood of deathly blows that caused every hole in his face to leak blood. When he crashed to the floor, I began stumping him. Each kick landed with a thunderous impact, the force behind them enough to send Reggie sprawling.

"Put your hands on me!" I barked. "Beat *me*, you bitch-ass nigga!"

The living room became a violent battlefield, furniture becoming collateral in the storm of my wrath. I swung whatever I could get my hands on—a chair, a lamp, anything that I could use to destroy him.

Reggie struggled to get back on his feet. But he was met with a relentless bombardment of furniture crashing against his body. With every strike, I channeled the fury that unfolded when I saw Queen's back and tears. Frank watched as he stood calmly behind me. Overwhelmed and beaten brutally, Reggie could only offer feeble attempts at defense before he eventually stopped moving.

Suddenly, I felt Frank's strong arm wrap around my chest, pulling me back.

His voice managed to cut through my rage. "It's over."

I couldn't wrap my head around what he was saying. I heaved, trying to escape his grasp, but he held me tighter until I was no longer seeing red.

"It's over," Frank repeated calmly. "He's gone." The words rang in my ears, gradually penetrating the red haze of anger that had clouded my vision.

I could still feel the adrenaline coursing through my veins. The living room was now a scene of disarray. Reggie, battered and beaten, lay sprawled on the floor lifeless.

QUEEN ARIA BENSON

"How long has he been putting his hands on you, Queen?" CeCe leaned forward, her knee propped against her elbow and her chin cradled in her hand. A genuine concern spilled from her eyes as she rubbed my back.

We were still in the bedroom at the headquarters seated at the foot of the bed. She had let me sit there, silently crying in shame. She had only offered me a drink. For an hour, we had been drinking in silence, but I knew she would want to pry eventually.

Hanging my head helplessly, I confessed, "A little while after I started working for Frank."

Though her question had been gentle, I was so embarrassed. The shock and concern in her expression left me feeling exposed and ashamed, proving why I had kept silent.

CeCe gasped. "Queen! Why didn't you tell anyone?!"

I knew why she was so shocked. Reggie was a peon compared to the men I was around on a regular basis. I was feisty and never let a man disrespect me. But I had allowed a bum like Reggie to leave me battered and bruised.

"Because he's not always mean and violent." I lowered my head, shaking it. "I know that that sounds stupid, but I felt like he loved me. You know how I grew up. My grandfather didn't give a fuck about me. Before I started working for the Disciple Family, Reggie was the only man who ever really showed me what felt like, love. He was jealous of my connection to Frank and me being constantly surrounded by men who were doing better than him. I hoped that the jealousy would finally subside, and we could get back to normal." Speaking those words aloud only intensified the shame I had been concealing. "I feel so stupid now."

"Don't," CeCe insisted, rubbing my back. "It's so many women in your situation."

"But I'm so strong in every other area in my life."

"Because you feel like you have to be. You've always had to look out for yourself, have your guard up, to take care of yourself. At the same time, you took the abuse because you were used to it. Your grandfather didn't abuse you, but he neglected you. You were used to living with trauma."

Though that made sense, it didn't make the shame go away. I wished that I had been smart enough to leave him before things had gotten this far.

"What do you think they are doing to him?" I asked reluctantly.

"You know what they're doing," CeCe muttered.

I sighed as I cringed.

CeCe's mouth opened and closed before she hesitantly asked, "You care?"

Thinking of the possibilities, relief flooded me. Suddenly, I felt truly safe. "No." Tears of freedom came to my eyes. "I hated what he was doing to me, but I couldn't let him go. I would wish him death or prison, anything to get him away from me without me having to actually do the work."

As CeCe opened her mouth to respond, the sound of heavy footsteps came down the hall, abruptly silencing her. My body tensed with embarrassment, knowing that it was either Buck or Frank or both. In the doorway, Buck's large frame emerged, his breathing uncontrollable and his demeanor anything but pleasant.

The tension in the room quieted us.

CeCe's lips pressed into a thin line. Sighing heavily, she stood. "I'll give you two some privacy."

Buck's eyes were planted on me. I avoided them as CeCe left the room. After closing the door behind her, the room suddenly felt smaller. Buck's stern expression told me everything he was thinking.

"Why didn't you tell us?" The regret in his calm, brooding voice made me shrink.

"I was embarrassed." I could hardly look at him.

His eyes narrowed. "Why? You aren't the only woman dealing with that."

His massive frame carefully inched towards me. His heavy weight sat closely next to me. My body was still stiff, fearing that he was disappointed in me. But then he laid a comforting hand on my thigh.

"At the time, I wasn't thinking about that. I felt alone. And I always have had to take care of myself... *always*. That's what I'm used to so that's what I did."

"You ain't that little girl all alone in that house with your grandfather anymore. You've got us." His eyes bore into mine as he promised, "You got me."

Swooning from his surprising display of affection and

emotion, I couldn't resist the impulse to seek comfort in Buck's shadow. Climbing onto his lap, I felt minuscule against his large frame. Straddling his enormous thighs, I felt safer than I ever had in my existence.

My lips met his in a steamy kiss. Our connection felt magnetic, a merging of two souls confessing their feelings for one another in a shared moment of pure understanding. As our lips danced in harmony, the weight of my burdens lifted, replaced by the warmth of mutual acceptance and a connection that surpassed the short time our attraction to one another had existed.

He pulled back, ending the kiss. My lips felt so abandoned. He stared at me with so much intensity in his eyes. "I made sure to clean up your house and got rid of his body before I left. I got somebody over there replacing the door right now."

I wanted to ask what all he had done, but I didn't care as long as I was free, able to be with him in that moment without fear of Reggie.

"But you can stay here tonight with me."

I nodded feverishly. "Okay." Then I linked my arms around his neck, straddling him closer, more intimately. "You know you're my man now, right?"

His big, mean self had the nerve to blush. "Oh yeah?"

"Is that okay?"

His gaze lingered on me. He took his time, seemingly savoring the sight of me. Finally, he nodded slowly. "Yeah, that's okay." The vulnerability in his eyes was daunting.

Smiling slowly, I leaned in closer. Right before kissing him, I told him, "I don't know what you're going to do about your hoes, but this dick belongs to only me now."

———

I hesitated at the doorstep, my heart hammering with anticipation and dread. Last night felt unreal, like it truly hadn't happened. But, facing the brand-new front door, holding the new keys in my hand, I knew it was real. I braced myself for the aftermath, expecting to see my home in shambles although Buck had told me that the clean up job had been thorough.

As the door swung open, I was met with the sight of the living room in perfect condition. There was no sign of the chaos I had anticipated. No shattered furniture, no lingering evidence of Buck's fury. It was as if the storm had passed, leaving behind eerie calmness.

I stepped further into the room, my eyes scanning every corner. Buck's clean-up job was precise, almost surgical. There wasn't even a trace of the door that he had knocked down in a fit of rage. Buck had erased the physical remnants of my tumultuous past with Reggie, leaving only the scars engraved into my memory.

I had refused Buck's offer to come home with me. In case I mourned a man who had made my life a living hell, I wanted to shed those shameful tears in peace. But standing in the living room where Reggie had taken his last breath, I actually felt an unexpected surge of relief. The weight that had chained me to Reggie's toxic presence had finally been lifted.

The air felt different. My home felt like a place of new beginnings. My vision lingered on the spot where Buck had told me Reggie took his last breath. Instead of sorrow, I felt a sense of liberation. Buck's actions put a small smile of appreciation on my face. He had rid my life of the shadows that haunted it.

I took a deep breath, inhaling the scent of a space no longer tainted by Reggie's toxicity. The silence echoed with the promise of a fresh start. There was a complexity of emotions in me, but one thing was clear. I was free from the chains that had once bound me to a man who only knew how to destroy.

CYNTHIA "CECE" DEBOIS

A few days later, the ambiance of the members-only bar shimmered with a dangerous kind of luxury. Diamonds sparkled from every corner of the room. The scent of expensive cigars, weed, and power lingered in the air. The room was filled with the elite of Chicago's drug lords, all decked out in high-end labels and dripping with diamond-studded arrogance for Amir's birthday. He was a hustler who had the pill game on lock.

Seeing Frank in this environment turned me on. The way everyone respected him and showed him love made me so proud. The love in his eyes as he watched me from across the room was as genuine as it was new. There was something different in the way he looked at me now that we were back together. It was proud, assuring, and confident.

I was seated with Queen in a secluded corner. Buck was at the bar with Frank and some of their crew.

"You look relaxed," Queen told me with a smile. "I'm happy for you."

I giggled bashfully, sipping on my Hennessy. "He's trying, Queen. He really is." Thinking of Frank's efforts, the dates, and the attentiveness made my blushing linger. The heat of the blush ran from my face to my core, causing my clit to thump.

Queen raised an eyebrow, her glossy lips curling into a grin. "You believe he's changed for good? It seems like he has. That man don't play about you."

I nodded, my gaze softening as I watched Frank, his posture relaxed yet commanding as he leaned on the bar. The old Frank would've been in the thick of the debauchery, but now, he seemed content to sit back, his focus continuously returning to me. "He's... *different*. He's not the same man I met. He's better."

Queen chuckled with her gaze still on me. "Better? The same Frank who was more focused on the crew than you? The one who argued with you over every little thing and took you for granted?"

I nodded, my fingers tracing the rim of my glass. "Yep. He's trying so hard to be a better man for me and our boys."

Thinking about our recent dates made me blush. Memories of the sweet nothings he'd whispered in my ear made my pussy leak. Recants of the way he'd held me close during our dance sessions at clubs or in the house made my heart palpitate with joy. "He's taking me out, treating me like a queen. He listens to me and respects my thoughts and feelings. He's patient with me, and we hardly ever fight anymore. He's really putting forth an effort. He's trying to do right by me, by *us*."

I watched as Queen's gaze floated over to Buck. Her eyes held a flash of vulnerability as she said, "I only asked because I wonder if Buck can really change for me too."

I laughed, still feeling the disbelief as I shook my head. "I still can't believe y'all are together."

Even as she blushed, it was unbelievable that Buck was the

source of it. He was charismatic, rich, powerful, and a beautiful chocolate man. Queen was equally beautiful. Yet, considering the way they had been at each other's throats for years made their sudden connection hard to grasp. But it was adorable how they were humbling one another.

"I know. It's crazy. I truly slept on that man," Queen admitted. "For years, I couldn't see who he truly was because I made assumptions about him. Now, I can't get enough of him." She had to laugh at herself. "I've never had a man be so protective, that made me feel so safe. When he showed me how far he would go to protect me, he didn't have a choice but to be my nigga."

"So, you just told him he couldn't fuck the triplets no more and he respected it?"

"Yeah." She smiled. "I'm just wondering how long it will last, if he can truly let them go. He's been sleeping at my house the last few nights."

Impressed, I raised a brow, nodding my head slowly. Queen may have only been nineteen, but trauma and fending for herself had made her wise beyond her years.

"He was living a whole different lifestyle, you know. He had three women. Now, he's with me, and I can see he wants it, but... I wonder if a man can truly change his ways because of his need to have a particular woman in his life."

"People can change, boo, especially when they find something worth changing for."

Queen sighed, her gaze drifting to where Buck was still conversing with the crew.

"How are you handling things as far as Reggie is concerned?"

She pouted slightly. "It's hard to grieve him when he put me through so much shit. I probably would miss the good times if Buck wasn't here to replace them with even better ones. I did love Reggie, so I am sad that he's no longer here, but I know he deserved to lose his life the way he did...Tragically."

"Has his people been asking about him?"

"His mother and most of his family live in Minnesota. I told everybody that he went out one night and never came back. Since everybody knows he was in the game, they figured he met some foul play. His mom did fill out a missing person's report, though."

As I nodded, the door of the club opened, allowing the humidity of the June night to sweep in. Keyes strolled in wearing a cocky and defiant expression with a few men alongside him.

A hush fell over the room, and there was a shift in the atmosphere. Keyes' presence caused the crew's guards to go on high alert, their eyes scanning the room with practiced caution. I felt my stomach tighten, and I exchanged a knowing look with Queen. However, Frank and Buck's expressions were unbothered as they remained cool.

Keyes acknowledged the other hustlers in the room with a nod or a brief exchange, but as he made his way around, he purposefully avoided Frank and Buck. It was a deliberate snub, a silent declaration of disdain that didn't go unnoticed by anyone in the room. Frank and Buck exchanged a look. Then, they shook their heads, their actions denouncing Keyes without a word.

I felt a flare of worry for what this beef would lead to. Keyes had no choice but to get his work from Frank, but he wasn't falling in line willingly.

ANTHONY "BUCK" PATTERSON

I leaned against the bar with Debo, Fetti, Lucci, Priest, and Rico surrounding me and Cap. Keyes' entrance had brought instant tension to the once laidback atmosphere of the party.

Priest nudged Fetti with a scowl on his face. "Fetti, you see this nigga coming in here like shit sweet?"

I followed his gaze towards Keyes.

"What's the deal?" I asked before taking a sip of my whiskey.

Debo shot me a look that could cut glass, so his frustration was evident. "That bitch-ass nigga, Keyes. He's been causin' trouble in the hood, tryna mess with our turf."

Fetti chimed in, his voice dripping with disdain. "Yeah, he's been tryna undercut us with our own customers."

Cap scoffed as he shook his head slowly, disdain darkening his eyes.

I took another sip. The burn of the whiskey matched the fire building inside me. Keyes was blatantly undermining our authority, playing in our faces.

"When this happen?" Cap asked.

"One of my customers told me about it today," Fetti said.

"I've been getting hollered at about it all week by my people," Rico added. "Luckily, all my customers loyal as fuck."

"We've been talking about it all day," Debo cut in. "We were going to holla at you about it tonight. We never thought he would have the nerve to show up here."

Lucci cracked his knuckles, a sinister grin spreading across his face. "We gotta show Keyes that we don't operate like bitch-ass niggas within the family. What's up? I'm on go."

Priest added his two cents. "On the real. That nigga acting real sheisty, and he's moving real grimy. He needs to know that shit don't slide in the Disciple Family."

Rico flexed his biceps, a silent agreement to whatever retaliation was on the table. "We can't let this slide. It's about respect."

I nodded, my jaw set. "All right. But ain't shit going down tonight. Y'all don't have to do shit. We'll deal with him. Let me holla at Cap."

They nodded, giving me and Cap privacy by walking away.

"Aye, enough is enough," I told him, rage causing my nostrils to flare.

"You're right," Cap seemed reluctant to admit.

"It's time for that nigga to go. I know that's our homie, but he ain't acting like family no more. We done gave this nigga too many chances off of the strength of our history. But he don't care, so we gotta let that shit go."

Cap raised his hand, stopping my rage from exploding. "*I know*. You ain't gotta convince me. I agree. He's done."

Yet, I still could see the conflict in his eyes. Cap was built different. When it came to loyalty and family, it was hard to get him to budge.

But that's what he had me for.

25

FRANK "CAPO" DISCIPLE

A week later, I was pacing back and forth in Linda's kitchen, the anticipation building in my chest like the climax before pulling a trigger. Outside, the night sky was ablaze with fireworks, a show I shelled out over ten grand for every year. It was a tradition that Richard had started when CeCe was a child. I had joined in when I came into her life.

The explosive bursts mirrored the anxiety in my chest as I grappled with thoughts of commitment, a concept foreign to a man who had been raised by a pimp. Though I had always done the opposite of Stanley when it came to women, I had never taken such a large step as I was about to. CeCe was the exception to every rule, however. She had burrowed her way into my chaotic world and made a peaceful home for me and my children in the midst of madness.

As the fireworks painted the night with spectacular lights, I wrestled with the truth. CeCe was the only woman I wanted by my side for the rest of my life. It was time to shed the reservations, embrace the commitment, and declare her as the queen of my empire.

As I continued my internal wrestling, Linda sauntered into the kitchen through the sliding patio door. Her disdain for my presence was evident in the icy glint of her eyes. She didn't bother saying a word to me. But, after four years, I was used to her attitude. I simply offered a curt nod, acknowledging her presence. The tension thickened as she maneuvered around me, attempting to grab a twenty-four-pack of water from the floor.

I cringed, hating that the gentlemen in me wouldn't let her struggle. "I got that for you."

"I don't need your help, Frank," she spat.

I took a step back, scoffing quietly. Fireworks crackled outside, emphasizing the tension in the kitchen.

As Linda approached the patio door, struggling with the water, Buck strolled in through the same entrance. Linda's disdain for both of us was always unmistakable. Buck, well acquainted with her cold demeanor, simply stepped back, allowing her to navigate through the door without offering any help.

With Linda finally outside, Buck told me, "It's time, Cap."

I acknowledged him nervously, my mind still swirling.

Buck quickly caught on to my unease. "You okay, man?"

I mustered a nod and admitted, "Just nervous. But I know I want to do this. I love CeCe."

"I get it," he reassured me. "You're supposed to be nervous. But you know she's who you want to be with, so let's make this happen."

Buck wasn't one for conventional relationships, so his understanding was appreciative and gave me the courage to walk through the patio door.

Buck followed me into the backyard. The night sky was adorned with bursts of illuminating color. Linda, Richard, the children, Queen, and neighbors reveled in the spectacle. As the crowded backyard exploded with celebration, I fought my way through the crowd, trying to find CeCe in the thick of the exciting holiday bustle. When I finally spotted her by the fence holding onto Jah's hand with one hand and cradling Shauka on her hip with the other arm, certainty was confirmed. CeCe was the only woman I wanted by my side.

Queen, standing nearby, noticed my approach and flashed a wide grin. I signaled her with a nod and a gesture, prompting her to step in. She gently took Shauka from CeCe's hip and Jah's hand.

CeCe looked puzzled as the children were taken away from her, but before she could question it, the backyard erupted in wild cheers and shouts. Everyone looked from the sky to her repeatedly as they screamed and jumped up and down with excitement. Confused, she glanced around and then followed the collective gaze toward the sky. Lit in the bursting fireworks were the words, *CeCe, will you marry me?*

As the crowd's cheers erupted, I dropped to one knee. I could feel my body quaking as I fumbled in my pocket for the ring.

CeCe, with a blank expression, pulled her attention away from the sky. However, instead of the joy I expected to see on her face, her reaction fueled anxiety and embarrassment in my chest.

"Get up," she urged, looking down on me with eyes that I couldn't read.

I was too ashamed to look around. I kept my eyes on hers as I stood. She held my wrist and pulled me close.

"So, we're just going to get married?" she whispered in my

ear so that I could hear her with the screams and fireworks exploding in the background. "I thought we agreed that we needed to date, to get to know each other."

My heart hammered against my chest as I responded, "You're right. We do. But can we do it while you're my wife?"

Still, anxiety painted her face. "Are you sure?"

Looking at her, the overwhelming flood of assurance made my shoulders sink. "I'm sand next to a sea type of sure about you, baby.

Though she was now blushing, her perplexed expression lingered. The cheers around us blended with the fireworks. Her indecisive silence felt like an eternity. It had been so long since I'd felt such fear.

"Outside of all those questions, do you want me? Do you love me?" I pressed.

The seconds torturously ticked by before CeCe broke the silence, "Get down on your knee."

She stepped back, giving me room.

As the fireworks continued to paint the night sky with brilliant light, I fell to my knee. With the ring in my hand, I looked deep into her eyes and uttered the words, "CeCe, will you marry me?"

CeCe's eyes widened at the elegance and size of the ring's center diamond. Then, with a radiant smile, she exclaimed, "Yes!" In a rush of emotions, she dropped down to her knees as well. Cupping my face in her hands, she leaned in and kissed me passionately as the cheers and applause of our friends and family filled the air.

"I love you more than I did yesterday," she spoke into our kiss.

A sheepish grin spread against my lips as I promised, "And less than I will tomorrow."

CYNTHIA "CECE" DEBOIS

My cheeks were wet with joyful tears as Frank tenderly concluded our kiss. My heart thrashed against my chest. He stood, holding my hands, and gently assisted me to my feet, my legs trembling with excitement. As I gazed into Frank's eyes, a wave of happy disbelief engulfed my entire being.

The cheers of our family and friends harmonized with the explosive bursts of fireworks, creating a celebration around us as Frank delicately slid a two-carat excellent cut round diamond engagement ring onto my quivering finger.

My eyes remained fixed on the dazzling brilliance of the ring, and my breath caught in my throat. An overwhelming sense of honor swept over me. This man wanted to spend his life with me. The realization that he had transformed for our happiness filled me with overwhelming gratitude that poured out of my body in tears. While a trace of fear lingered in the back of my mind that he would disappoint me, Frank's eyes beamed with pride, reassuring me that he was committed to our future. As I looked forward to a lifetime of submitting to his love, I trusted that he wouldn't let me down.

"Congratulations!!" Queen squealed in my ear as she hugged me from the side.

Her high-pitched shouting brought me back to reality. I tore my eyes off of Frank and looked around the backyard. Elijah, one of the neighbors, was taking photos with his professional camera. I looked back at Frank, grinning at his effort.

"You knew this was going to happen?" I asked Queen.

Cheesing from ear to ear, she nodded proudly.

I looked around at everyone's pleased expressions, but since no one looked as shocked as me, I figured everyone had known this moment was going to happen except me.

My father's pleased smirk parted through the crowd that was surrounding me and Frank. Breaking through, he wrapped one arm around my shoulders and the other around Frank's.

"Congratulations," he said, smiling at me before kissing my forehead. Then he looked at Frank. "You make me proud, son."

A flash of emotion washed over Frank. Pulling his bottom lip in between his teeth, he nodded sharply. "Thank you."

Tears continued to paint my face as my father made room for others to approach us with their congratulatory embraces. Frank and I were swarmed with hugs and kisses. My hand was no longer my own as everyone pulled on it as they gawked at my ring.

Yet, I realized that none of the congratulations surrounding me were from my mother. My eyes searched the crowd for her but couldn't find her. I then looked behind everyone, towards the house. I found her ascending the back porch steps with a disgusted look on her face. As if she felt me watching her, she looked over her shoulder. When our eyes met, I hoped for a smile, for some support. But all I got was a scowl of disappointment before she pulled her eyes away and opened the patio door. My heart sank as she disappeared into the house.

A tug on my fingers demanded my attention. I pulled my eyes away from the patio and saw my father giving me a loving, supportive stare.

"Unt uh," he grunted. "Don't pay that no mind. Stay in the moment. This is a day you'll remember forever."

Smiling, I pushed past the hurt. Still, painful tears mixed in with the joyful ones.

ANTHONY "BUCK" PETERSON

When Queen told me I was her man, something shifted inside me. It was like a flutter in my chest, a soft whisper that told me she held the power to mold me like putty in her hands. I wanted to give her everything she desired, to stand by her side and shield her from any pain. She didn't have to protect herself anymore as long as she had me.

As I watched Frank propose to CeCe earlier that evening, I realized how much Queen had changed me too. The ease with which I had let my guard down with her shocked me. I had always prided myself on keeping emotions at bay and never letting anyone get too close. I had love for Peaches, April, and Diamond, but what Queen brought out of me was different. She had this way about her, this quiet strength that drew me in and made me want to submit to her the way women had been submitting to me for years.

When I thought of her, warmth spread throughout my chest. I was ready to lay down my defenses for her. It was a new sensation that felt scary but right. I had been surrounded by women, but there was a haven in Queen that I craved. I wanted to be her rock, her anchor in the storm. I wanted to be the one she could always rely on, the one who would never let her down. And as I reached out to touch her hand, I knew that I was ready to take that leap, to open myself up to the vulnerability that came with loving someone so deeply.

"What you over there thinking about?" she asked from the passenger's seat. "Keyes?"

I scoffed with a grin. "Nah, I'm not thinking about that nigga. I've already made my mind up about how I need to handle him. Cap won't like it, but he'll get over it. I prefer to do it my way."

"What's on your mind then?"

"We need to go to my house."

Queen bucked her eyes. Since we had made it official, we had been avoiding the inevitable. We had been locked up in her house engulfed in one another as we helped Frank plan his engagement, but it was time for me to stop leaving the other girls hanging. They needed to know what was up. Although Queen hadn't given me an option, she knew how big of a deal this was, so she hadn't been forcing me to tell the girls.

"You sure?" she asked with a raised brow.

I had been living this lifestyle for years. I had always had the intimacy of multiple women. But when I was with a Queen, she gave me the energy of three women. I was fulfilled.

"Yeah. I want you to be able to be at my crib too. Plus, I don't want it to seem like I'm hiding you from them."

The ride to my house was quick since Linda lived close by. As I parked, I waited to feel some type of anxiety. I had never prepared myself to have this conversation because I assumed that this would be my lifestyle forever. Peaches would be fine because we would always be friends. April didn't have enough feelings for me to be that invested. But I knew that Diamond would be devastated.

Though it was late, Diamond, Peaches, and April were waiting for me in the living room as I had requested in my text. Diamond was only wearing a sports bra and the tiniest shorts in an effort to get my attention since I hadn't been home in days. The seduction in her eyes disappeared when she realized that Queen was with me. Rage turned her skin red.

Sitting beside Diamond, April looked puzzled. Peaches, trying to mask a pleased smirk, sat on the other side of Diamond grinning at me with pride and a bit of teasing.

Walking deeper into the living room, I sat on the loveseat. Queen perched on the arm of it.

Diamond's nostrils flared at the sight of Queen so close to me. "What is she doing here?" Fear coated her question as she glared at Queen.

"Chill out," I barked, making her scowl deepen.

"Queen is going to be around a lot. She's my lady." I blinked rapidly, realizing how easily and proudly I had made the announcement.

Peaches' brows rose as that teasing but proud smirk extended. April simply nodded.

Diamond scooted to the edge of the couch, hands on her knees as her leg bounced angrily. "Okay, and what that mean?" she hissed. "We're *all* yours."

"Not anymore," I told her softly but firmly.

Her head reared back as her chest started to rise and fall angrily. "What the fuck does that mean?"

"It means not anymore!" Queen snapped as she leaned forward.

I tried to stop her, calling out, "Queen–"

"It means the dick is *mine* and only mine so you can't fuck him no more!" Queen snapped.

Peaches was quietly laughing hysterically behind Diamond's back as she spewed, "I'm not talking to you, bitch!"

"Watch your mouth, Diamond." The way I checked her made the hurt intensify.

Tears came to her eyes. "Are you serious right now, Daddy?"

"He's very fucking serious!" Queen spewed. "You can still sell that pussy for him and make him his money, but don't fucking touch him."

I jolted to my feet and took Queen by the hand. I then pulled her into my bedroom, closed the door, and locked it.

Pulling her close, I told her, "Aye, you gotta chill."

She snatched away, pacing with a scowl. "I was cool until she acted like she didn't get the point. I know she's in love with you so I'm not about to play with her."

Sighing, I walked over to the foot of the bed and sat on it. As a man who had been involved with three different women, I had been used to juggling multiple personalities, jealousy, and feelings. But this was new territory. "You should have let me handle that, baby."

Seeing the stress in my eyes, she walked towards me. She then straddled me, wrapping her arms around my neck. I think being in my lap was her favorite place on earth. "Was I lying?" she asked softly.

"No, but you should have been more careful with their feelings. Like I told you, I'm not like other pimps that mishandle my women. I may not have the feelings for them that I have for you, but they are family. So, you let me handle them how I see fit, you hear me?"

She was a defiant young thing. I loved her strength and sass, but I was going to have to humble that mouth. She stubbornly remained silent, so I grabbed her chin gently, demanding her attention with a slow kiss.

"You hear me?" I repeated against her lips.

She pouted, sighing. "Yes."

"I should make yo' ass say "Yes, Daddy.""

Her head tilted back as she hollered, "Ha! I wish *the fuck* you would!"

———————

I figured the only way I could have the conversation with Diamond peacefully was if Queen wasn't around. So, I fucked her to sleep. By the time I emerged from the bedroom, Diamond was the only one still in the living room. I was struck by the sight of her, sobbing uncontrollably, sitting Indian-style on the couch in dim lighting. She was beyond heartbroken.

As she looked up at me with tear-soaked eyes, she begged, "Please don't do this to me, Daddy."

I felt a pang of guilt as I watched her anguish. I sat down next to her, wrapping an arm around her trembling shoulders. She leaned into me.

"Diamond, you know I care about you. But I have different feelings for Queen, and I have to be true to that."

Diamond's cries grew louder, and she clung to me desperately.

"I never wanted to hurt you," I insisted regretfully. "But I can't deny what I feel for Queen. And I have to honor what she wants."

"But what about *me*? I love you, Buck," Diamond cried, her words choked with emotion. "*Please*, don't do this."

"I care about you. I really do," I promised. "But I can't deny what's in my heart. I want to be with Queen."

Diamond buried her face in my shoulder. "I can't believe this," she sobbed. "She is so disrespectful. She can't handle your lifestyle. She doesn't deserve you."

Sighing, I gently rubbed her shoulder. "I know you're hurt, but you have to respect my woman, Diamond."

Blowing out a heavy breath, she lifted her head. Her face was close to mine that my beard absorbed a few of her tears. As she tried to kiss me, I pushed her back. "What did I just say, Diamond?"

Her breathing was erratic as she became more desperate. She reached for the waistband of my shorts, trying to reach inside for my dick.

I grabbed her wrist so hard that she cringed. I then threw her arm away and stood up. Standing over her looking at her sternly, I told her, "If you want to remain on the team, you have to respect my woman. If not, I'm choosing her over you."

Taken aback, she inhaled dramatically. But I turned away from her and went into the kitchen for a glass of water before returning to the bedroom.

On the way to the kitchen, I saw that April's bedroom door was closed. Even though I could hear that her TV was on, I knew that she was asleep because she couldn't sleep in complete silence.

Peaches was inside the kitchen, leaning against the island as she drank from a bottle of water. When our eyes met, she chuckled.

"What you laughing at?" I asked regretfully.

She gave me a taunting smile that spread from ear to ear. "I like Queen."

"Really?"

She nodded. "Really. I always have. She don't play. So, I know she's not going to play about you."

A smile threatened to break out.

Peaches planted an angled brow on me. "I heard her boyfriend is missing."

My guilty conscience made me grin devilishly as I opened the refrigerator.

Seeing it, Peaches' eyes bucked. "Wow."

"I didn't do it because I wanted her," I corrected her shocked tone. "I did it because he was beating the shit out of her."

Her eyes swelled, and then she nodded slowly.

Opening the water bottle, I leaned against the refrigerator.

As I took a sip, Peaches studied me. "I've never seen you like this."

"Like what?"

"She relaxes you. She humbles you." She grinned. "I like it."

My smile matched hers. "Thank you."

"But you know that Diamond isn't going to bow out gracefully."

"She better." I scoffed. "Otherwise, she's going to be losing more than just a man."

QUEEN ARIA BENSON

That next morning, I was pleasantly surprised by April and Peaches' friendliness. April had even cooked breakfast for everyone. However, Diamond's refusal to come out of her room let me know she was going to be a problem. But I refused to let her disrupt the beautiful connection that was blossoming between Buck and me. I was determined to stand by him, to embrace the loyalty and love that he had shown me. I was happy to navigate any obstacles that lay ahead as long as Buck remained mine.

After breakfast, Buck asked me to ride with him to see Keyes. I was game, determined to stand by him no matter what. I was ready to be his ride or die, to support him through thick and thin.

Riding shot gun next to Buck, I felt like I was where I belonged. He had become more to me in a short time than anyone else in my life besides my grandmother. His enduring loyalty was overwhelming, yet it filled me with a sense of security and warmth that I had never known before.

The bass thumped through the car speakers as Buck and I sped through the city. Jay Z's "I Just Want to Love You" mirrored my carefree mood. Buck effortlessly rapped along, and I joined in, feeling the rhythm and soaking up the serenity that being with him brought. I couldn't deny the peace that had settled in me, a big difference to the constant tension that used to cling to my every step when I was with Reggie.

As we pulled up to Keyes' barbershop on Jeffery, the morning sun painted the city in shades of gold. I felt alive, unburdened by the fear that used to grip my heart since I was a child.

Buck and I stepped out of the car. Keyes, in the process of unlocking the shop, visibly tensed up as he spotted us.

"What you doing here?" he grunted with defensiveness already in his tone.

Buck was calm and collected as he leaned against the car with a sly smile on his lips. "I need a lineup, nigga. I heard you're the best in the business."

Keyes scoffed, his defensive wall rising. "I don't cut hair. I'm a boss."

I stood by Buck's side, quietly watching the exchange.

Keyes' eyes were full of skepticism as he watched Buck. He hesitated with his hand frozen on the lock.

"Unlock the door, motherfucka," Buck urged. The deep tone in his authority made my pussy leak.

Keyes shot me a glance. His shoulders lowered and his stance softened as if he felt safer because I was there. Unlocking the door, he let out a reluctant sigh. We all entered the barbershop and were overcome by the smell of fresh-cut hair and barbering products.

Buck and Keyes settled into barber chairs side by side. I positioned myself near the door.

Buck scanned over Keyes' scowl. "G', you're acting like I'm here to take over your whole operation," he taunted him with a playful smirk on his face.

Keyes chuckled nervously. "Then what you here for?"

"You should've just fallen in line," Buck coolly replied.

Scoffing, Keyes shook his head defiantly. "I'm not a kid, nigga."

Buck's eyes narrowed. I knew that his patience was wearing thin. "You've been acting like one."

Keyes leaned back in his chair, crossing his arms in defiance. "So, this is how it is? We got history. We go all the way back to—"

Laughing, Buck interrupted him. "You haven't been acting like it."

"You know my wife, my kids," Keyes urged.

Buck's expression remained stoic. "You know I'll take care of them."

A heavy sigh escaped Keyes as he dropped his arms, running his hands slowly over his face.

The air in the shop thickened with deadly tension. I stood on the sidelines, my eyes darting between the two of them.

In an instant, Keyes made a sudden move, his hand darting towards his waistband. But, just as Buck had warned me, I was ready. My reflexes were faster than Keyes could comprehend. My finger was already on the trigger of the gun concealed in my purse. In one swift motion, I pulled it out and fired, the shots echoing throughout the confined space.

The bullets found their target, hitting Keyes multiple times and in different places on his body. The air filled with the pungent smell of gun smoke. As Keyes crumpled to the floor, Buck's gaze met mine, eyes admiring me with approval.

FRANK "CAPO" DISCIPLE

"You could have told me."

Buck's sly grin lowered as he pulled his eyes away from me. He looked around Duke's Lounge, focusing on everyone else in the bar, except me.

As soon as I'd heard that Keyes had been found dead in his barbershop that morning, I knew that it was Buck. Though the rest of the crew had beef with Keyes, they were too loyal to go against my orders to let me and Buck handle it.

"I didn't want you to have anything to do with it," Buck replied.

"Why not?"

"Because I knew that you were doing it because you had to, not because you wanted to. Keyes was your homie–"

"He was your homie too," I reminded him.

"But I could see that you were regretting having to take care of him. Now, his blood doesn't have to be on your hands; it's on mine."

I nodded slowly. Buck's loyalty was always so surreal to me.

Though we had been raised by the same man in the same house, we weren't brothers. Yet, he was devoted to having my back as if we had come from the same womb. I had never witnessed such loyalty in the streets.

I nudged him in the side, causing him to look over and witness my taunting grin. "Really it's on Queen's hands, though, right?"

I chuckled as he laughed aloud, attracting glances from patrons around us.

Once he'd met me at the bar about an hour ago, he told me every detail of Keyes' murder, including Queen's involvement.

"And she didn't have any issues pulling that trigger?" I asked.

Buck's grin deepened. Pride blanketed his eyes as he thought of her. "Hell nah. She took care of that shit like a G'."

The twinkle in his eyes was hilarious, but I loved my dawg too much to tease him about it.

"I can't believe you let that girl bag you that easily," I said instead.

As he shook his head, I could see the same disbelief in his eyes that was in my head. "I honestly can't believe it either."

I raised a brow. "The pussy that good?"

A diabolical grin slowly spread across his face. His eyes closed for a second before he answered, "It's superb, my nigga."

"You bag multiple bitches like its two of you. So, how are you going to be in a committed relationship with one woman?"

He shrugged with ease, as if he had been monogamous his entire life. "She makes it easy. I don't have the need for other women when I'm with her. I don't even think about it."

My eyes bucked as my teasing grin widened. "Wow."

"I'm not going to lie, though..." Buck sighed as he grabbed his drink and took a sip. He squinted as the burn flowed down his chest. "I wonder if I can do it long term. Right now, I'm motivated by the pussy and these new feelings for her. I honestly want to give her what she wants, what she needs. But I know me; I like having more than one woman. I just wonder how long it's going to last."

26

CYNTHIA "CECE" DEBOIS

A week later, I couldn't believe it when Frank told me he had planned a day on a yacht for us. The July sun was shining, the breeze was scorching, and memories of our first date invaded my mind. I was touched by his effort to re-enact the day that marked the beginning for us.

As we boarded the yacht at the 31st Pier, the sight of the private chef preparing brunch made my glossed lips curve into a smile. I narrowed my eyes when the sounds of a saxophone playing nearby caught my ears. The saxophonist was playing a beautiful rendition of "Giving Him Something He Can Feel." I craned my neck around the boat, my eyes trying to find where the sound was coming from. I found the young, Puerto Rican woman on the deck.

"Frank," I purred on a breath with a smile.

His chest swelled with pride as he took my hand, resting his chin on my shoulder from behind.

The aroma of the food, the sound of the saxophonist playing En Vogue, and the gentle sway of the boat on Lake

Michigan created such a dream-like day. It was like stepping into a fantasy, and I felt like the luckiest woman in the world.

"Frank, this is amazing," I said, looking out on the blue water. As the boat pulled away from the pier, I suddenly felt like I was on a getaway, like we were no longer in Chicago. We were leaving gunshots and the violence of the hood behind us for a moment.

Frank gave me that smooth, alluring smile that always made my heart skip a beat. "I told you that I was going to do things different this time and I'm a man of my word. I'm going to make up for every time I made you cry. I promise."

My face heated with a blush as I slowly smiled. I leaned back, wanting to be as close to him as possible. The chill of his chain pressing against my bare back was a temporary relief from the sun.

Frank had truly been showing me that I had made the right decision to give him a second chance. He was no longer buying my love with money and expensive gifts. He was still taking good care of me and the boys, and I could have anything I wanted. But, this time, he was actually focused on our relationship outside of the kids and sex. He was courting me.

After brunch, I changed into the Louis Vuitton swimsuit Frank had on board. He had swim trunks underneath his jeans. After changing, he took my hand and led me to the edge of the yacht.

"Let's jump in," he said with a mischievous flash in his eyes.

I laughed, but Frank's expression never changed. Realizing he wasn't joking, my eyes ballooned. "Oh, you're serious."

"Yeah, c'mon. You can swim."

"But I've never jumped from something this high."

He grabbed both of my hands and brought my body against his. Kissing me softly on my lips, he promised, "I got you."

My heart fluttered because I knew he did.

Frank's grip tightened on my hand as he led me to the edge of the yacht. Anxiety bubbled up in me as the slight breeze tousled my hair. The yacht gently swayed in the pulsing dance of the water. Frank's gaze locked onto mine, a playful sparkle in his eyes.

We leaped off the side of the yacht, plummeting through the air. The world blurred around us as the lake rapidly approached. The thrill of the fall sent shivers down my spine, and the rush of wind drowned out any other sound. I could feel Frank's firm presence beside me, his hand holding mine as if he'd never let go.

We hit the water with a splash, the cool embrace devouring us. The underwater world surrounded me for a brief moment before I kicked my legs, pushing myself back up to the surface. Frank emerged alongside me, his light, curly hair now slicked back by the water. As we broke through to the sunlight, I felt his hand still intertwined with mine.

Bobbing on the surface, Frank pulled me into him. He took my mouth with his, tasting my full lips before sucking the bottom one and guiding me into a passionate kiss. The taste of saltwater lingered on our lips as the sun warmed our skin as the waves gently rocked us.

As we splashed and laughed in the cool, refreshing water, I was so grateful for the change that was happening in Frank. As I looked at him, there was more peace and confidence in him than I ever had. And I was so proud of myself for making sure that my kids had a father as loving and attentive as mine was.

After our playful swim, we climbed back onto the yacht, the sun glistening on our skin. I made a beeline for the tray of fruit that the chef had set out.

Frank settled beside me on the bench on other side of the table.

"So, when can I move back in with you and the kids?"

I smirked as I picked up a strawberry.

Frank responded to my smirk with a guilty grin. "You knew it was coming."

"I have no issue living with you, baby. You know that. I just..." I swallowed hard, regretting bringing up any heartache on such a beautiful day.

He softly bumped my shoulder with his. "What's up, baby?" his deep, sexy voice sweetly asked.

"There are a lot of bad memories for us in my place. If we are starting fresh, can we do it in a new house?"

Frank's worry washed away and was replaced with relief.

I giggled. "You thought it was something worse?"

He laughed. "Hell yeah." He slid his arm around me, bringing me into his shadow. "You can have whatever you want, baby. Find the house and I'll buy it for you."

I smiled into his eyes. "Thank you."

Grabbing a plump, juicy strawberry, I turned to Frank with a mischievous twinkle in my eye.

"Here, try this," I said, holding the strawberry to his lips.

Frank chuckled and shook his head. "Nah, I'm good. I'm supposed to be feeding you the strawberry. I'm not a soft nigga, baby."

I pouted playfully, feigning disappointment. "It's not soft. Come on. Just one bite for me?"

He looked at me, and I could see the smile tugging at the corners of his mouth. "All right, baby. Only for you," he relented, leaning in to take a bite of the strawberry from my fingers.

As he savored the sweetness, I grinned, feeling a rush of

affection for this man who always knew how to make me laugh and feel cherished. Only now, he was finally learning how to love me.

———

A few days later, my dad called me over to confirm some of the wedding details. He was so happy for Frank and me. Even though Frank could afford to give me any wedding I wanted, my father had begged Frank to allow him to pay for the wedding. He had saved money all of his life to be able to give me a wedding and it was an honor to him. It had taken every-thing in Frank to allow him to pay for it, but when he thought of the little girl we may have one day, he most definitely understood.

My mother and I had become more and more distant since the engagement. She never talked about the proposal or wedding with me. She hadn't even looked at the ring or congratulated me. I knew that she despised Frank, but I would have never assumed that she was so ornery that she would react this way to her only child getting married. It broke my heart that the day that I got engaged to the love of my life was tainted by my mother's negative reaction. However, Frank and my father had been making up for where she was lacking.

With Jah and Shauka in tow, I struggled through the door of my parents' home. Shauka was nestled in my arms while Jah darted ahead of me out of the foyer.

The sounds of his excited chatter flowed from the dining room. "Hey, Grandpa! Look at my cars!"

As I made my way through the foyer, the door clicked softly behind me. My eyes carefully scanned the house in an attempt to avoid my mother. The tension between us was new. We'd never had beef, so it was so thick that it drained me. As I entered the dining room, I saw her sitting Jah down. We locked eyes. Instead of the warmth of my mother's embrace or her usual, sweet greeting, she coldly approached me wearing a disgusted snarl. I wondered why she was coming so close. We had been so distant that I hadn't felt her embrace since before the engagement. For a brief moment, I wished for it and looked forward to it. But she only took Shauka from my arms and walked out. Her silence broke me down even more, building the cold wall between us even higher. Behind her, my father caught my eye. He waved a dismissive hand, encouraging me to ignore my mother.

In the midst of the chilly reception from my mother, a warm smile etched my face as I realized that my father was seated amongst various colors of linen samples. I couldn't help but grin proudly, and it made everything better. My father's sincere enthusiasm helped fill the space that my mom had left vacant.

As I sat at the table, Jah's laughter and sounds flooded the dining room as he played with the toys scattered across the floor. He had as many toys and clothes at my parents' house as he did at mine and Frank's.

"You decided on a color combination yet?" my father asked, looking at me above his glasses.

My eyes flickered between the color swatches in front of us. "I like magenta and sage."

He gave me an impressed smirk as he slowly nodded. "Classic. Elegant. *Nice.*"

I chuckled. "You are so involved in this, Dad. I thought you were just going to give me the money and leave the planning to me. You're acting like you're the one getting married."

My father's brow raised mischievously. "You remember who decorated this house, right?"

Recalling, I giggled. My father had decorated and redecorated our family home. He had also managed the renovations a few years ago. He had an eye for it.

"I could really do my thing if I had more time," he boasted. "What's the hurry?"

Though most of the years I'd spent with Frank had been rocky, I already loved him like a husband, like family. He felt the same about me. We already felt married to one another. The ceremony would only be a public declaration that we wanted to get done and over with.

I was about to tell my father that before my mother's cold quip flowed into the room. "Because Frank wants to trap her, fill her up with babies, and make it harder for her to leave when he starts acting a fool again."

I inhaled sharply as her figure passed the dining room entryway on her way to the living room, holding Shauka and a bottle. Yet, before I could say anything, my attention was brought to my father as he jumped out of his chair.

"Now, that's enough, Linda!" His roar was so loud that Jah jumped out of his skin and dropped the toy in his hand.

Even my mother stopped in her tracks. She spun around, glaring at my father.

Because I knew defending me was useless, I tried to stop him. "Daddy—"

"No!" he barked, lifting a hand to stop my resistance. "What the hell is wrong with you? Why are you ruining this moment for her?!"

"Because she shouldn't be marrying that thug, Richard!"

My heart broke as Jah's inquisitive and confused eyes bounced back and forth between my parents.

"I'm so sick of you walking around with your ass on your shoulders like you're perfect!" my father barked.

My mother gasped. "Excuse me?!"

Fear caused Jah to run towards me and climb onto my lap.

"Get your shit together because you're not about to ruin this for her or me!" my father shouted. "You want to be an asshole, *do it quietly* while me and my daughter plan her wedding!"

Seething, my mother tore her eyes away, stomping on her bare feet into the living room. My father's nostrils flared as he returned to his seat. Finally, his anger subsided enough for him to notice the tears in my eyes.

Sighing, his shoulders slumped. "I'm sorry, baby. You and Jah shouldn't have had to see that. But that's your mother's problem; too used to us being imperfect in the dark."

———

Walking into Frank's house, my heart was heavy. My father had made an effort to push past the tension so we could choose the colors and linen for the ceremony. But I couldn't bear the thought of my mother allowing her disdain for Frank to drive a wedge between, not only me and her, but her and my father as well. So, I had quickly made my choices so the boys and I could get out of there.

As I entered, Jah sprinted towards his room. I gently placed Shauka in his swing, catching a whiff of savory Italian aromas.

Curiosity led me to the kitchen, knowing the nanny wasn't on duty that day. The sight that greeted me brought tears of gratefulness and confirmation to my eyes. Frank stood at the stove, stirring a pot of what smelled like spaghetti sauce. A tender smile pulled at the corners of my lips. I felt the warmth of love envelop me once again. Tears welled in my eyes as I marveled at this man who was old to me but new in so many ways.

"Hey, beautiful," Frank greeted, his eyes meeting mine.

My heart lovingly skipped many beats.

The sight of tears glistening in my eyes made him abandon the spoon and rush toward me, concern engraved across his face.

"What's wrong, baby?" The concern and comfort in his tone was like a soothing balm.

I took a shuddering breath as his arms slipped around my waist. Crying, I begged, "Please prove my mother wrong."

QUEEN ARIA BENSON

As me and Buck entered his place, I was relieved at how quiet it was. We hadn't spent much time here. He had basically moved into my house. I knew that was Buck's way of keeping his hoes away from our relationship. Although April and Peaches were cool, if I didn't have to be around them, I was cool with that.

"Let me grab this cash real quick. I'll be right back. Then we out," he assured me.

I nodded. "Cool. I need to go to the bathroom."

"Is your stomach still bothering you? I told you, you had to use the bathroom," he teased.

I laughed. "Yes, but it's not that kind of pain. I'm having cramps. My period is probably about to come on."

Buck nodded as we went our separate ways. Entering his bedroom, I cringed at the constant cramps I had been feeling all day. It wasn't my time of month, but I assumed that my cycle was coming early. I went into his bedroom to use the master bath. His usual scent assaulted my senses. I looked around at all of his things, admiring them as if they were memories of a man that was just a few feet away. I was falling hard and fast for Buck.

Exiting the bathroom, I heard hushed voices drifting from the kitchen. My instincts kicked in, and I tiptoed down the hall, inching closer to the source of the whispers.

As I lingered by the kitchen entrance, I strained to catch snippets of the conversation. Buck's low voice mixed with Diamond's. My heartbeat angrily quickened as irritation instantly filled me.

"What I tell you? You gotta respect my girl or move the fuck around."

"Move around?!" Diamond quipped with hurt. "I've been loyal to you for years, and now all of a sudden she comes around and you're this cold towards me?"

"Because you aren't hearing me."

"She disrespected you every chance she got! She didn't even like you!"

"That ain't yo' business! Like I said, keep her name out of your mouth before you be on the streets. I'm out."

I took off towards his room. I ran inside into the bathroom and softly closed the door. I leaned against the smooth finished wood, breathing heavily as rage built in my chest.

"Baby?" I soon heard him calling me.

I gulped, trying to smother my anger. "Yeah?"

"I'm ready to roll."

"Here I come."

I collected myself in an attempt to slow my breathing down. I then eased out of the bathroom. Buck was cool and aloof as he looked at me. I followed him to the door.

As he opened it, I told him, "Go ahead to the car. I want a bottle of water. It's hot as hell outside. I'm right behind you."

Despite him trying to act cool, frustration lines were still in his brow. "Ah'ight."

Once he turned his back to me, an evil grin spread on my face from ear to ear. I backed into the house and tiptoed through it, searching for Diamond.

I found her in her room. The door was slightly ajar, so I silently crept in without her hearing or seeing me. With her back turned to me, she was unaware of my presence. Just looking at her made frustration and anger boil over.

With my footsteps silent on the carpeted floor, I quickly approached her. Lurching towards her, I grabbed her by the back of the neck.

"Argh!" she yelped as she struggled against my tight grip, attempting to free herself.

Diamond winced in pain as my grip tightened on her neck, forcing her to keep her back to me. She couldn't break away. Sounds of our struggle filled the room.

I pulled back, bringing her ear close to my mouth. "Bitch, I have taken down bigger monsters than you. Stop playing with me. That is *my nigga*. And I didn't have to sell my pussy or beg in order to get him. He *chose* me. So, it's nothing you can say to change that shit. Keep my name out of your mouth, bitch." Then I tightened my grip, causing her to wince. "And if you tell Buck anything about this, I'm beatin' yo' ass."

With a forceful shove, I sent her flying forward. Her hands slammed onto the dresser, steadying her body just before a fall. Wild, fearful eyes met mine as she glanced back, confusion and fear written across her brow. My gaze filled with rage locked with hers, daring her to utter a word or make a move in retaliation.

Beneath her obsession with Buck was real fear because the only part of her that was street was the corners she'd stood on. So, I turned on the heels of my Jordans and stormed out.

A FEW WEEKS LATER

27

CYNTHIA "CECE" DEBOIS

I stood in front of the decorative mirror staring at the ivory lace of the wedding dress.

Queen beamed at me from the side, her eyes gleaming with unshed tears. "CeCe, you look absolutely beautiful, girl," she said a bit above a whisper.

I managed to smile, trying to push away the conflicting emotions that I was feeling. This moment was surreal, a dream I never dared to think would come true. I never imagined that things would improve between Frank and me to the point that we'd be weeks away from getting married. Yet, here I was, surrounded by tulle and silk, preparing to say "I do" to the man who had stolen my heart.

But, despite the joy and excitement bubbling in my heart, there was a heavy sadness weighing me down. My mother wasn't there, and her absence cut deep.

"And this veil is so... so... majestic," Queen chirped, struggling to find words as she stared at the chapel-length veil.

As she adjusted the veil on my head, thoughts of my mother consumed me. I wished she wasn't so stubborn so she could put aside her feelings and be there with me. But her disapproval had driven a wedge between us, and I wasn't sure if it would ever be mended.

Since the argument between her and my dad some weeks ago, things had grown more intense between us. I had stopped going to my parents' home so much. The boys were seeing less and less of her, only visiting if my father picked them up from me.

The ache in my chest threatened to overwhelm me, but I blinked back the tears, refusing to let them spill over and mar this moment more. I took a deep breath, trying to push aside the pang of longing for my mother.

Studying my reflection in the mirror, Queen tilted her head dramatically. "Stop thinking about that," she warned softly.

I sighed, blushing in shame. "I can't help it."

She wrapped her arms around me in a comforting embrace, understanding shining in her eyes. "I wish she could put her pride aside to see how happy you are, how much Frank really loves you."

"I do too," I murmured, my voice barely above a whisper.

"I can't believe your mom is letting things go this far. I mean I know she prefers you to be with a different kind of man, but I didn't think she'd let it come to this."

I let out a dreadful sigh. "I'm surprised too. But I can't let her ruin this moment for me."

Queen gave me reluctant gaze before asking, "Do you think she'll be at the wedding?"

Looking at my regal reflection in the mirror, I answered, "I don't know. At first, she was still at least present, though she was being stubborn and was not hiding her disapproval *at all*. But now, I haven't seen her in weeks since she and my father got into that argument. I haven't talked to her. It's weird. But the longer she allows her hatred for Frank to cause her to mistreat her only child, I can't bring myself to speak to her."

Frustration and sadness swelled inside me. My mother's condemnation had cast a dark, gloomy shadow over what should have been a joyous time in my life. I desperately wanted her to be there, to set aside her animosity and support me as any mother should. But the reality of our strained relationship was so large that it cast a dark cloud over the anticipation and excitement of my upcoming wedding.

Despite the uncertainty, I had a smidgen of hope that maybe my mother would find a way to set aside her feelings and be there for me eventually.

Just then, Queen winced, holding her stomach.

"Is your stomach still bothering you?"

She frowned, rubbing it. "Yeah."

"You need to go to the doctor about that. You shouldn't be having pain like that when you're not on your cycle."

"I made an appointment. It's in a few weeks." Blowing out a heavy breath, Queen forced a smile. "Let's not worry about that or your mother right now. Today is about finding the *perfect* dress. Today is all about you, boo. We're going to make it absolutely perfect no matter what, even if we gotta get drunk as hell when we leave here."

I smiled. "Cool."

"Is Tiffany going to make it to the wedding?"

I shook my head, slightly pouting. "She's going to be due any day around the wedding, so it's best she stays home."

Queen smiled. "Oh, she's having a baby. I remember you mentioning that."

As I gazed at my reflection, I finally smiled, making a silent promise to embrace this day with all the joy it deserved. I would savor every moment and hold on to the love that had brought me here, even if my mother didn't believe in it.

ANTHONY "BUCK" PATTERSON

I sat at the pub table taking a swig of my drink as Frank and CeCe danced in their own little world of pre-marital bliss. Though it had always been in his character, it was strange to see Frank so settled. But watching them, I wondered if I could ever do the same.

I glanced at Queen as she sat next to me watching Frank and CeCe with admiration. She had turned my world upside down, completely changed how I saw relationships. Monogamy was a foreign concept to me, but she had a way of making me consider things I never thought I would.

As I gazed at Frank and CeCe, doubt crept into my mind. I wondered if I could really give up my polyamorous ways. Though I had been a one-woman nigga ever since Queen had staked her claim on me, the idea of being tied down to just one person made me uneasy. Yet, Queen had a hold on me that I couldn't quite understand. She made the need for multiple women obsolete.

Glancing around the bar, my eyes landed on a woman with

milky skin and curves that could make any man weak. She sauntered into the bar, oozing beauty, sensuality, ass, and titties. Suddenly, my doubts about monogamy seemed to fade into the background as my primal instincts took over.

I clenched my jaw, feeling the tug of attraction as I watched her move through the room. Queen's influence on me was strong, but this woman had power of her own. For a moment, I felt torn between the unfamiliar pull of exclusivity and the raw desire that this woman lit in me. I took another swig of my drink, trying to shake off the sudden confusion inside me. I fucked with Queen. But as I looked back at her, I couldn't deny the challenge she presented. If anyone could convince me to change, it was her, and I was actually looking forward to it.

As I tried to refocus on Queen, I felt her piercing gaze on me. She had noticed my distraction, and I braced myself for her attitude.

Sure enough, she leaned in, her eyes searching mine. "Do you like her?"

Queen's expression was unreadable. So, I tried to play it off, shrugging casually. "Nah, I'm just scanning the room. That's all."

But Queen wasn't stupid. She knew me too well. She raised an eyebrow, a small knowing smile on her lips. "Stop lying. Your dick is probably hard."

She was smiling and there was a devilish glare in her eyes, so I relaxed. "All right, you got me. But it's not like that. Just admiring the scenery, baby."

She slid down from her seat. Closing the space between us, she slipped her arms around my neck. Instinctively, I slipped my hands around her waist.

"Do you want her?" she asked.

Her candor caught me off guard, but I couldn't help but feel touched by her acknowledgment of my unconventional ways. "Nah, sweetheart. I'm good right here with you." I gently grabbed her chin, saying, "You know how to keep me and this dick happy."

And that was true. Sitting there, I realized that had I been with any other woman, I would have abandoned her for the curvy, light-skinned new option by now. But Queen was enough. Her loyalty and devotion were enough.

Queen chuckled softly, her fingers intertwining with mine. "I do, don't I?" she teased. "But..." She slipped her hand into my jeans. Her warm, tiny hand squeezing my dick made my eyes close a bit. "Your dick is saying otherwise."

As our eyes locked in a silent understanding, I was captivated by the devilish glint in Queen's gaze. But before I could react, she suddenly spun around, tearing out of my arms and bolting towards the woman who had caught my eye, leaving me speechless and unsure of what to do.

I watched in stunned silence as Queen approached the woman with a confident smirk. She greeted the woman with a warm smile, and they began conversing as if they were old friends. I couldn't hear their words over the noise of the bar, but the sight left me bewildered. Part of me wanted to go after her, to at least understand what was happening. I had always been the one in control, but Queen was effortlessly finding ways to take the lead when necessary.

As I watched Queen and the woman engage in animated conversation, I couldn't shake the feeling that I was falling in love.

FRANK "CAPO" DISCIPLE

As we returned home from the bar, I was covered with a sense of contentment. Finally, I had my girl, and I was loving her the way she deserved. It felt like I was finally getting things right, finally understanding what it meant to love CeCe correctly. I'd found peace and purpose that I had never known before. She was my anchor, my guiding light in a world that had often felt dark and uncertain. She was the embodiment of everything I had ever dreamed of and being with her was living out that fantasy.

As soon as I stepped through the door, I made my way to check on Shauka and Jah, ensuring they were peacefully asleep in their rooms. I crept past the nanny's room, mindful not to disturb her, before making my way to the kitchen where I knew CeCe would be, since she had mentioned she was hungry on the way home. Watching her ass and thick thighs jiggle in tight colorful palazzo pants, I couldn't help but playfully follow her.

She giggled as I annoyingly held onto her waist as she

moved about the kitchen, with my dick pressed firmly against her ass.

"Why are you following me, Frank?"

I grinned. "I was told to always follow my dreams, baby," I replied, both playful and sincere.

She continued to softly giggle as I followed her to the refrigerator. I stood behind her with my chin on her shoulder as she retrieved a pot from inside.

As she closed the fridge, CeCe turned to face me. I caught a glimpse of that familiar sad flash in her eyes, the same one that had lingered since her mother had expressed her disapproval of our marriage. But that night, the sadness seemed to run deeper, casting a dark shadow over her usual finesse.

I stopped being annoying. I let her go, leaving her to roam freely in the kitchen as I leaned on the island. "Baby, what's wrong?"

She sighed softly with her gaze fixed on the pot of leftover spaghetti she was reheating on the stove. "I'm just... sad," she admitted.

"Is it your mother?"

CeCe slowly nodded. "I always imagined going shopping for my wedding dress with my mother." My heart cringed at the longing in her voice. "But now, I know that's never going to happen."

It broke my heart that CeCe was sacrificing so much to be with me. I had always hoped that Linda would grow to love me. The little boy deep down inside of me still yearned for maternal love. I always admired CeCe for having that. So, the fact that I had been the one to take that from her was breaking me.

"CeCe, I appreciate your loyalty and love," I told her, hoping it would make it a little better. "Marrying me despite how you know your mother feels means everything to me."

She sighed long and hard, peering over her shoulder at me. "I love you so much, Frank. I know it won't be easy, but I'm choosing you. I don't care what my mother thinks. If she wants to miss this, it's on her. I can't care anymore, and I don't regret choosing you again."

I was drawn towards her, my steps guided by the need to make her feel better. We stood there locked in an intense stare, deep and meaningful beyond the necessity of words. It was a look full of love and promise that spoke meaning that words could never describe or explain.

QUEEN ARIA BENSON

I led the way as we returned to my home with Siena walking alongside us. It hadn't been hard to convince her to come with us. The allure of Buck's reputation and his legendary status in The Disciple Family, not to mention his wealth, was enough to convince her to leave with us. She hadn't even told me if she was bisexual, but she seemed drawn to the promise of excitement and luxury that surrounded Buck. So, we'd left. CeCe and Frank were so wrapped in pre-marital bliss that they didn't realize we were leaving with a third.

I was surprised by my own impulsiveness in approaching Siena, but I couldn't deny the strong desire that I wanted and needed to give Buck what I knew he wanted, though I had never experienced it myself.

As we walked inside, Siena looked around, taking in the details of my home with curiosity. I couldn't blame her. My home was now a reflection of Buck's influence. Since I'd become his, he'd begun to renovate the house. I hated to see the memories of my grandmother fade, but it was refreshing to watch the horror of my grandfather, of starvation, of abandonment, and Reggie be covered up with paint, new floors, and new furniture.

Buck was adorable as his eyes bounced towards me, still confused and unsure of what to do. It was flattering to finally see him so vulnerable and humble.

"You want a drink?" I asked her.

"Yeah, that's cool."

Though she was standing, she was slightly bent over, looking at pictures on the shelves. I watched Buck, waiting to feel drunk with jealousy of the way he admired her ass spreading in her maxi dress. But I only felt pride in being the one to give him what I knew his heart desired.

I left the living room and went to the small bar cart in the corner of the dining room. She had been drinking tequila at the bar, so I poured her a straight drink into a red plastic cup. I was busy wrestling with my own thoughts as I made the drink. I wondered why I was so willing to do this. I had never been with a woman, nor did I have an attraction to them. But I was wildly attracted to the idea of making Buck happy.

I had been so deep in my thoughts that I didn't realize that Buck and Siena had gotten started until I entered the living room. Buck was seated on the couch, and she was kneeling in front of him. He looked hesitantly at me, but I smiled to ease any reservations he had. Then he relaxed, allowing Siena to venture into his pants. I waited to be filled with rage when I saw her hands wrapped around what was mine. But as she put his dick in her mouth and I saw the satisfaction cover him, I became aroused.

I kicked off my shoes before padding towards them. I sat close to Buck, tapping her on the shoulder. She looked up and took his dick from her mouth when I handed her the drink.

She gulped it down and then sat the cup on the carpet near her.

She was eager to get back to work. When she put him back inside of her mouth, though, I stopped her.

"Wait." I stood up, getting her attention and Buck's. As I got on my knees next to her, Buck's eyes lowered in lust. He licked his lips slowly as I softly took his dick from her.

"This is how he likes it," I instructed before wetting him generously. I then used both hands to massage him as I tongue kissed his head.

"Shit, baby," Buck panted.

It was then that I realized that I truly loved him. There was no envy or anger. I felt truly proud that I had been the one to fulfill his fantasy.

I took him from my mouth and returned him to her. She mimicked what I had done, drawing grunts and deep groans from Buck. Standing, I stripped, gaining Buck's undivided attention.

Once completely naked, I sat next to him, leaning into him as our lips met in a sloppy kiss. He wrapped his hand around my throat, eyes boring into mine as they narrowed with animalistic passion.

"Come sit on it," he demanded.

Sitting up, he helped my short legs straddle his massive lap backward. I rested on my tiptoes as I watched her full lips assault his large head. Looking at me, she took him from her mouth and aimed it at my center. I hovered over it and allowed her to guide it all the way to the tip of my center.

I hissed, my body still getting used to his size. No matter how many times we'd had sex, his mass still stretched me open.

With my hands planted behind me on his belly, I started to

ride him. Her mouth went to his balls, making him howl out loud, "Ooooh, shit."

Then his hand went to my waist, guiding me slowly to the base of his length all the way up to the tip again and again until I was leaking all over him.

"Ooo, you're so wet," Sieana said, making my eyes open and remember that she was even there.

Longingly, she watched his dick slide in and out of me. She left his balls and planted her palms inside of my thighs, one on each side of my center, which spread my legs open further. When she started to bring her mouth to my clit, I tensed. Buck felt my body go rigid. He sat up, bringing his mouth to my ears. His hand soothingly wrapped around me just as she began to suck my clit.

"Relax," he encouraged me. "Pretend it's me."

I listened to him. I closed my eyes and forced my body to relax into the sensation of him stroking me while she softly lapped at me with her silky tongue.

ANTHONY "BUCK" PATTERSON

I woke up with a sense of peace and calm covering me. It was unlike anything I'd ever experienced before. As I slowly opened my eyes, a smile pulled at the corners of my lips as I recalled the incredible night I had spent with two beautiful women. The memories of watching Siena please Queen was making my dick rock up. But the reminder of Queen's unwavering support made my grin grow further into my beard.

I rolled over, my eyes landing on Queen as she lie next to me, her beautiful, peaceful form illuminated by the soft morning light filtering through the curtains. I reached out and gently brushed her hair out of her face, admiring her serene beauty. The covers shifted as I searched for the comforting curve of her waist, pulling her close to me. She stirred, nestling against me as I spooned her, our bodies fitting together like they were made for each other.

With her in my arms, I felt contentment that I hadn't known was possible. Queen's presence brought tranquility to my reality, a feeling of completeness that I had previously only imagined. As I held her close, I knew that this was where I belonged, in this perfect, peaceful moment, wrapped up in the embrace of the woman who was changing me.

I closed my eyes, savoring the sensation of her breathing in sync with mine. As I kissed her nape, she began to stir in her sleep, slowly waking up.

"Good morning," she murmured.

"Good morning." As I spoke, my lips brushed against the warmth of her skin. I felt her shiver slightly at my touch. "I ain't never letting you go," I proudly declared.

She giggled, causing her body to shake against mine, stirring the beast. "Why? Because I let you fuck other women?"

I pulled her in closer, tighter, wanting to submerge myself in her. "No. Because you care about me so much that you would give me such a gift only because you know it's what I need. That's truly unconditional. And because you were that selfless with me, you'll always have my heart."

I could see her cheek slowly grow into a warm smile. As we lay with our limbs intertwined, I knew that my words weren't just a passing sentiment. They were a vow, a promise to hold on to this feeling, this connection with everything I had.

I felt like I had finally found my home and I was determined to cherish and protect it with all that I was.

A FEW WEEKS LATER

28

CYNTHIA "CECE" DEBOIS

S tanding in front of the mirror in the dressing room, I felt overcome with emotion as I took in my reflection. The elegant up-do that framed my face gave me a timeless sophistication while my flawless makeup enhanced my natural beauty. I felt so beautiful and confident.

But it was my wedding dress that truly took my breath away. The regal, long-sleeved gown draped over my figure with grace and magnificence. The fabric, a luxurious combination of rich satin and delicate lace, shimmered in the soft light. The bodice was adorned with intricate lace detailing that trailed down the sleeves, creating a stunning illusion effect against my brown skin. The high neckline added a touch of modesty along with the sheer sleeves that I had always envisioned for my wedding day.

As my gaze traveled down the length of the gown, I marveled at the way the fabric cascaded and hugged my curves in a mermaid fit that pooled elegantly around my feet. The train, adorned with delicate lace appliqués, trailed behind me, creating a breathtaking silhouette of romance and grace.

Before getting dressed, I had gone into the ceremony space to take it all in without distractions. As I walked into it, I was immediately surrounded by the most exquisite decorations. The color palette of magenta and sage created a feeling of timeless elegance that took my breath away.

The aisle was lined with lush sage greenery, accented with vibrant magenta blooms that added a pop of color against the rich green backdrop. Each pew was decorated with delicate magenta and sage ribbons.

At the front of the space, a stunning archway stood decked with cascading magenta flowers and lush greenery. The combination of the bold magenta blooms against the deep green foliage was simply enchanting, and I couldn't help but imagine how beautiful our photos would look against it.

As I stood before the mirror, taking in my breathtaking reflection, overwhelming joy and gratitude filled my heart. Everything had turned out so beautifully that day, from the decorations to the loving presence of my family and friends. However, as I glanced through the mirror, I was forced to notice the disdain on my mother's face. She seemed to be going over and beyond to look like she'd rather be anywhere else despite the loving support and encouraging words from our family members.

My grandmother, Aunt Dot, my cousin Tammy, and Queen were all in the room, surrounding me with heartfelt compliments and words of admiration.

"CeCe, you look absolutely stunning. That dress was made for you," Aunt Dot exclaimed as her eyes sparkled.

"Girl, you are glowing! Your body looks so good in that dress!" my cousin Tammy chimed in.

"Stunning, CeCe," my grandmother added with tears pooling in her eyes.

Amidst the chorus of admiration and love, the silence of my mother was deafening. Her lack of enthusiasm was dramatically evident as she sat in a chair with her arms folded and lips curled up in disgust.

Fed up, I took a deep breath and turned to face her. "Mama, why don't you just leave?"

Her rigid expression deepened with offense. "Excuse me?"

"You're going out of your way to show everyone that you don't want to be here, so leave." It surprised me how easily I had told her that. And it saddened me that she had brought me to the point that I no longer even cared if she was at my wedding.

Tammy clutched her pearls as the tension in the room became smothering.

Carefully stepping forward, my grandmother raised a hand. "CeCe—"

"Grandma, don't stop me. Stop *her*," I growled. "I've allowed her to get away with mistreating me for long enough! She's been trying to ruin this day for me since Frank proposed!"

My mother sucked her teeth while rolling her eyes with disgust. "It's already ruined, chile."

I scoffed angrily. "Please climb down off of your high horse. You act so high and mighty, but you're trying to make me live a perfect life that you couldn't even achieve yourself! You've had to forgive daddy for some shit. He's not perfect either. You just want me to think that he is so I will live the life and marry the man that *you* want me to!" My mother's head reared back as eyebrows rose around the room. "Frank may not be perfect, but nobody is, not even you, your husband, or your marriage!"

As tears came to my eyes, Queen gently grabbed my arm.

"She ain't lying," Tammy muttered as my mother and I locked eyes with glares of fury on one another.

"I love Frank," I professed as my eyes bore into my mother's haughty disposition. "And he loves the hell out of me and my kids. I've forgiven him for what he's done. Every day he's been showing me that he has changed. He's supporting me. He loves me unconditionally. And that's more than I can say for you!" As my mother's eyes bulged, I gritted. "You think he's not good enough for me when he's been loving me better than you have lately. And you better hope that I can forgive you more easily than it took me to forgive him." I took a deep breath, trying to keep the tears teetering in my eyes from falling. "You need to leave or put a fucking smile on your face."

"CeCe!" my grandmother warned in a whisper.

Tearing my eyes away from my mother, I dabbed at the corners of my eyes with the back of my hand.

"C'mon, boo," Queen softly said. "Let's get out of here and get some air."

As Queen assisted me out of the room, delicately holding the cathedral veil, I forced calm to wash over me. I reached for the door handle, preparing to step into the next chapter of my life, and nearly collided with my father as I opened it.

His warm, deep voice broke the silent tension. "CeCe, it's time for the ceremony to start." As he observed my troubled expression, his concern grew. "What's wrong, sweetheart?"

I hesitated, not wanting to give my mother more energy, not on a day that was meant to be filled with joy and love. As my father's brows furrowed together, he glanced past me. His gaze fixed on my mother. Without a word, he excused himself and stepped into the room, closing the door behind him.

On the other side, I could hear his usually calm voice rising in anger. His protective instinct had been ignited, and I knew he was confronting my mother. Despite the muffled sounds of their conversation, I couldn't make out the words.

———

"CeCe, from the moment I met you, I knew that you were the missing piece of my soul. You have shown me a love so pure and unwavering, even in the face of my mistakes. I am humbled by your forgiveness and grateful for the second chance you have given me."

As I stood at the altar, gazing into Frank's eyes. I was so full of love and excitement when he started reciting his vows. His words, coming right from his heart, felt like a sweet song that just wrapped me up in a warm hug of love.

"And as for the mother you are to my children," Frank continued, his eyes shimmering with unshed tears, "I am in awe of the love and compassion you have shown them. You have embraced them with an open heart, guiding them with wisdom and tenderness, and I am endlessly grateful for the beautiful, nurturing presence you bring into their lives." His voice grew even tenderer as he continued, "I love you more deeply than words can express. Your presence in my life has brought light to the darkest corners of my soul. I've found a home in you. Your strength, your grace, and your unwavering love have been my guiding stars in this dark world, leading me back to you time and time again."

I blinked back tears. His vows were healing any lingering doubts and fears and reaffirming the unbreakable bond we had.

"I promise to cherish you, to stand by you through every trial and triumph, and to love you with every beat of my heart," Frank declared, his eyes never leaving mine. "You are my rock, my confidante, and my soul mate, and I vow to spend every day of our lives proving the depth of my love for you."

As he finished, his words lingered, touching me like one of his tender kisses.

Gentle sniffles, swoons, and sighs came from the audience. Among the affectionate sounds, I heard my daddy's unmistakable sniffles, and when I stole a glance at him, tears were streaming down his face, as he gave me a smile of pride and joy. Even my mother seemed to have softened. Her facade of perfection had always been meticulously maintained, though.

As Frank's vows came to an end, the preacher turned his attention to me.

Taking a deep breath, I returned my gaze to Frank. As I looked into his eyes, I still felt an outpouring of disbelief that we had really made it to this moment.

"Frank..." As I began, my voice was quivering with an explosion of emotion. "From the moment our paths intertwined, you have been my greatest love. In you I have found a sanctuary of love and understanding, a place where I am cherished and treasured for exactly who I am. I promise to walk by your side, to support and honor you, and to create a life filled with love, laughter, and joy. You are my partner, my best friend, and my soul's true mate, and I vow to love you with every fiber of my being, for all the days that lie ahead, until death do us part."

FRANK "CAPO" DISCIPLE

"That was a beautiful ceremony, baby." Eleanor smiled into my proud expression as I leaned against the bar.

"Thank you. I'm glad you could make it."

She smirked as if I were being ridiculous. "I wouldn't have missed it for nothing in this world. You know that." Then she looked around the room, smiling with admiration. "Stanley would have loved this."

My eyes watched her closely, waiting for sadness to cover her. Yet, she smiled, so I did too. "Yeah, he would have although I think he would have talked shit about me settling down."

She cracked up. "Yeah, maybe so. But he couldn't talk too much shit. He settled down eventually too. He just had to meet the right one just like you did."

I smiled at the cocky expression in her eyes as she thought of how she'd managed to get a pimp to settle down with her. Thankfully, Eleanor's grief had lifted over the years. Now, she actually seemed more carefree. But I assumed that was because she no longer had to worry about the men she loved the most being in the streets.

"Well, let me go get a picture with CeCe while there aren't too many people around her."

"Okay." Before she walked away, I wrapped my arms around her. "I love you."

"I love you too, baby."

She left me leaning against the bar, surveying the wedding reception. The hall was filled with the sounds of laughter, clinking glasses, and the thumping beats of Chicago's finest deejays. The wedding ceremony had been intimate and invite-only. But we'd opened the reception to everyone. So, the Disciple crew and other familiar faces from the game had been added to the audience of people who were celebrating me and CeCe's nuptials.

As I sipped on my drink, Saint, a fellow hustler, crept up to me with a congratulatory smile. "Yo', Cap, you finally tied the knot, huh?" he said, clapping me on the back.

I nodded, returning his grin. "Yeah, man. Can't believe it myself. But CeCe is one of a kind, so I had to make it official."

Saint chuckled, raising his glass in salute. "I hear you, brother. She's a real one, no doubt."

Just then, I caught a glimpse of her across the room. CeCe was surrounded by family, her radiant smile lighting up the space. She was like a walking work of art, turning heads with every step she took. Beauty came from every pore. I felt so much pride knowing she was mine.

She moved with the grace of a queen, effortlessly capturing the attention of everyone around her. I watched as she posed for pictures, her beauty drawing all eyes to her. She was a human look book, a conversation piece, and in that moment, she stole my breath away.

I turned back to Saint. "Damn, man," I managed to say, truly mesmerized that a woman of such grace and beauty had my last name. "Look at her. She's something else, ain't she?"

Saint followed my gaze, nodding in agreement. "Yeah, she's a dime, Cap. You're a lucky man."

Lucky didn't even begin to cover it. I felt so grateful having her by my side. My eyes couldn't stop undressing her. I had been fantasizing about losing myself in that pussy all day. My dick was painfully pressing against my slacks.

Sitting my glass down on the bar, I told Saint, "Aye, I'll holla at you in a minute."

He waved me off. "Go ahead and do your thing. I know you got rounds to make."

I excused myself from Saint and maneuvered through the crowded room, making my way to where CeCe stood. As I approached her, people tried to get my attention for pictures, but I smoothly deflected them, promising I'd be right back, all while keeping my focus on CeCe. Once I reached her, I gently grabbed her by the elbow, and with an elusive nod, I led her out of the busy reception hall. She looked at me with surprise and curiosity as we made our way through the crowd.

"Frank, where are we going?" she asked. There was a flirtatious sparkle in her eyes as she allowed me to guide her through the mass of well-wishers and partygoers.

I didn't say a word as I led her out of the main area and into the corridor. The pulse of the music faded behind us as we moved farther away from the reception. Finally, we reached the nearest bathroom. Without a word, I guided her inside and locked the door behind us.

CeCe's eyes reflected curiosity and suspense as she looked at me. I took a step closer to her, immersing myself in the passion that had been bouncing between us all day.

"I need to be inside of you, baby," I murmured with my gaze locked with hers. "I can't wait anymore."

A small, knowing smile danced at the corners of her lips as she leaned in closer. The energy between us was explosive with lust.

Her voice was low and seductive as she swore, "You can have me whenever you want me."

My breath hitched. This was the only woman who could make me weak. "Say that shit again," I replied, my finger tracing a line along her jaw. "Tell me that again, Mrs. Disciple."

CeCe's eyes sparkled as she leaned in, her breath mingling with mine. "My husband can have me whenever he wants me."

A growl escaped as our lips crashed together in a breathy kiss. With my hands on her waist, I guided her to the sink, our lips never disconnecting. Once at the sink, I was able to lift her tiny frame, resting her on top of it. I hungrily gathered her dress around her waist. Finding her center, my fingers were literally drenched as I pulled her thong to the side. My dick hardened painfully as her dainty hand went to the waistband of my suit pants. She tore at the belt and buttons and quickly unzipped them, exposing my dick that was leaking with precum in hungry anticipation. She scooted further, bringing my head to her opening. I crashed inside, causing her to gasp and end our kiss.

"Oh, Frank," she sang loud and unapologetically.

With one hand on the sink and the other on her ass cheek, I slammed her down over my length. My lips dragged along the length of her neck, leaving soft, wet kisses as I stroked her, causing goose bumps to sprout all over her.

Her hand went up my shirt. She clung to my back, her nails digging into me, dragging out the animalistic strokes that I began to punish her with. I began to pound that pussy with such force that her walls stretched around me.

"Shit!" she shrieked. "Yes, baby! Give me that dick!"

"Mine," I groaned as I buried my face into her neck.

The deeper I got, the more she dug into me. Feminine growls escaped the throat that my tongue softly lapped on. She held on tighter, biting my shoulder in an attempt to take how mercilessly deep I was as I lost myself in what was now officially mine.

QUEEN ARIA BENSON

As I stepped out of the reception hall, I let out a relieved sigh. The wedding had been beautiful, but I was tired of taking pictures. My mouth was sore from smiling so much. But the day had been beautiful. Being raised in the hood, I hadn't seen many sincere, pure displays of love and devotion. So, it felt like I'd watched a fairy tale in real life.

I said my goodbyes to friends and CeCe's family while weaving my way through the dwindling crowd. Thankfully, the night was winding down. Though the wedding had been private and intimate, the reception had unfolded into a nonstop celebration, hosting the city's elite with pockets deep enough to drown anyone's financial worries. Stacks of money were as common in the room as laughter had been. So much money had been rained on Frank and CeCe as they danced that it formed a green carpet on the dance floor.

The open bar flowed generously with top-shelf liquor. With all of the nonstop partying, I needed a break. As I walked towards the bathroom, the thought of me and Buck getting married played in my mind as it had throughout the day. Buck had an unconventional way of looking at relationships. But that was one of the things I loved about him. The man had a mind of his own, and he never followed the beaten path. So, I wondered if we'd ever get married. The way his mind worked, it was hard to predict anything. But he had already taken steps to show me that he was willing to do anything for me, so whether we ever got married or not, I truly didn't care.

I pushed open the bathroom door, grateful for a moment of solitude. But as I entered, I was met with Peaches, April, and Diamond primping in the mirrors over the sinks.

Peaches and April's smiles cut through the tension.

"Hey, boo, you looked so pretty today," Peaches complimented.

April nodded. "Yeah, you did."

Their genuineness momentarily eased the fatigue and irritation etched on my face. "Thank you."

As I made my way into a stall, me and Diamond exchanged a brief glare that was filled with the weight of our beef.

The stall door closed behind me, muffling the sounds of the restroom. I took a deep breath, attempting to shake off the uneasiness that lingered between Diamond and me. Buck had never mentioned the altercation between me and Diamond. But, since then, Buck had spent even less time at his home, so I hadn't seen her. But since the three of them had known CeCe and Frank for so long, I wasn't surprised when they showed up at the reception.

Inside the stall, I could hear Diamond muttering over the sound of running water, "Why the fuck do y'all have to be so nice to her?"

I gnawed on the inside of my cheeks, suppressing the urge to explode. Linda already looked at Frank and his friends as ghetto, so I desperately didn't want to turn this reception into a reality show.

"Because that's Daddy's woman," I heard April whisper.

Diamond sucked her teeth. "She's not our wife. She's not in the game with us."

Peering through an opening in the stall, I saw Peaches' guard go up as Diamond had the nerve to get louder. "Shut the fuck up before you get in trouble," Peaches whispered.

"Right. C'mon," April urged as she grabbed Diamond's forearm so hard that the bitch flinched while being dragged out of the bathroom.

I took a moment to gather myself. I needed to diffuse the storm brewing inside me. I took deep breaths, counting to ten with each inhale and exhale.

"Do not beat her ass, Queen," I told myself. "Unt uh. You can't do it. Not up in here."

I reminded myself not to prove Linda right, not to let the frustrations of the night drag me into a display that didn't belong in this elegant atmosphere.

As I left the stall, I approached the sink, letting the hot, soapy water run over my hands. I looked at myself in the mirror, giving myself a silent pep talk. I couldn't let drama mar Frank and CeCe's celebration. Linda's preconceived notions rang in my head as a reminder to rise above the bullshit. As I exited the restroom, Buck, April, Peaches, and Diamond were near the door, caught in a moment that oozed discomfort. Buck's gaze flitted between them, his expression morphing into a subtle recognition that something was wrong. And then, he noticed me.

His immediate departure from the group signaled that he knew there was some shit going on. As he approached me, concern twisted his face. "Queen, what's wrong?" he asked. His eyes scanned my face for answers.

I shrugged off the irritation, masking it with a forced smile. "Nothing, baby. Just need to find CeCe."

He narrowed his eyes, sensing something beneath the phony surface of my unbothered gaze. His voice softened as he pressed lovingly, "You sure?"

As I looked up at him, I knew that I loved this man. I hated what pimping represented and I despised the obsession that Diamond had with him. But I loved him so unconditionally that I didn't want to put him between a rock and a hard place, feeling as if he had to juggle both.

"I'm good." I hurried away, losing myself in the thick crowd that was now in the hallway as the last few stragglers began to leave.

ANTHONY "BUCK" PATTERSON

I had studied that woman's face long enough to know when there was a storm brewing behind those eyes. Since I knew my woman had the tendency to pop off, I let her continue her journey through the crowd. Instead, I made an about face and immediately realized that Diamond and April had disappeared.

Taking my naturally long strides, I was quickly back over to Peaches.

"Where did they go?"

Her guard immediately went up when she saw steeping anger causing my chest to quickly rise and fall. "They went to the car because we're leaving. I stayed back to holla at you."

I raised an eyebrow, signaling for her to talk.

"I'm hollering at you as your best friend, not one of your hoes."

I nodded quickly, urging her to go on.

"As your best friend, I've seen you with so many women. So, I know that you love Queen differently."

I shifted uncomfortably, vulnerability flashing in my eyes because she was right.

"You know I was out there before I met you, dealing with pimps who were nothing but abusive, degrading, and controlling. But you were never like that. Although you were always about your money, you loved and cared for us. You respected us as long as we respected you. We're a family." She locked eyes with me as she stepped in closer, gently holding my hand. "But with Queen, it's something else. It's like you got a different kind of passion for her. I can see it. She's bringing a different man out of you."

My brows touched as I asked, "What you trying to say, Peaches?"

Her hand released mine and rested softly on my shoulder. "I'm saying..." She sighed as her expression softened. "Queen ain't like the rest and you know it. Even if you let Diamond go, there's always gonna be some insecure hoe trying to compete with Queen. She wasn't even in agreement with this pimp shit before she started fucking with you. She's only accepting it because she loves you. I'm a hoe, but I'm a woman too, so I know Queen is only going to be able to take so much before she leaves you. You can't let that slip away. You gotta do what you gotta do to be with her. Even if that means letting go of the pimp game, letting *us* go."

I took a step back, overwhelmed by the notion and her sincerity, "Let y'all go?"

Peaches' lips tightly pressed into a regretful line. As she slowly nodded, her eyes filled with tears as she replied, "Yeah."

29

CYNTHIA "CECE" DEBOIS

The night had been a whirlwind of celebration, laughter, and love. As the last beats of music faded away and most of the guests dispersed into the night, I was eager to escape to the Godfrey Hotel with Frank. The promise of a passionate night ahead made my clitoris thump, and the anticipation hung as thick as the dick he had dropped off in the restroom a few hours earlier.

As we made our way towards the exit of the country club, my excitement heightened. I had opted to delay our honeymoon for now; the perfect romantic getaway deserved precise planning and I couldn't stand the thought of being away from our five-month-old for an extended period just yet.

Frank and I stepped outside into the warm September night air hand in hand and in pure marital bliss. But the atmosphere shifted abruptly when we unexpectedly joined my parents at the top of the stairs. My mother stood next to my father wearing the same phony smile she'd plastered on during the wedding. After leaving the dressing room earlier that day, I refused to even acknowledge her bitterness.

"Hey, Dad," I greeted, masking the uneasiness in my voice. I reached between my parents to hug my father and kiss him on the cheek.

As I released him, he extended his hand towards Frank with so much pride in his eyes that my eyes started to moisten again.

"It was a great day, son," he told Frank as he shook his hand tightly.

Frank's shoulders lowered, appreciation weighing on them as he nodded. "It was. Thank you for everything."

"No," he said as he looked at me, telling him, "Thank *you*."

Surprisingly, my mother stepped forward. "Frank," she said, her voice shockingly warm, "It was truly a beautiful ceremony."

My mother's unexpected niceness caught me and Frank off guard, causing my body to become rigid and my eyes to balloon.

Frank's eyebrows shot up, his composed demeanor momentarily altering. "Uh... um th-thank... thank you."

Frank and I didn't hide the awkwardness we felt as we exchanged curious glances between one another and even my father as if we were trying to decipher a code. It was as if we had just witnessed a sudden drastic change in the weather, a storm that had just passed, leaving behind an uneasy calm.

My mother turned to my father, speaking over the awkwardness, "I'll see you back inside."

As my father nodded, she turned and disappeared into the country club.

My eyes darted towards my father, who was holding back a laugh.

"What did you say to her?" I asked, beyond curious.

I had yet to ask him about the angry words he had barked at her in that dressing room. None of my family members that had been in the room had said anything either. But I was sure that was because of orders that my father had given to them.

"Don't worry about it," he said winking at me. "Just know that we had a long talk." As my head tilted curiously, he added, "Your mother misses you."

Before realizing it, I rolled my eyes in disgust.

My father's head leaned to the side as his glare flashed with a bit of warning. "She does," he insisted.

"She also could have ruined this experience for me from the beginning had I let her."

My father nodded. "You're right. You two need to talk, though. She knows this. These are her words, not mine."

Defiance caused me to shrug with a pout. "Well, I'm not ready to talk."

My father lifted his hands in surrender. "I can't blame you." Then he gently grabbed my shoulder. "We'll talk about this another time. Go on and enjoy your night."

When he smiled sweetly, so did I. "Okay. I love you, Dad."

He stepped forward, leaned down and kissed my cheek. "I love you too, baby." Then, I saw his eyes water as he looked at Frank. "She's all yours now."

I had to hold my breath to keep tears from falling as Frank's shoulders squared with pride. He replied, "Yes, sir. I'll take care of her. I got her."

My father's watery eyes narrowed as his hands slipped into the pockets of his slacks. "You better," he warned before turning his back to us and going back inside.

Frank and I took simultaneous deep breaths as he took my hand. He led me down the grand concrete stairs carefully as I held the hem of my dress. I felt some relief that my father had gotten through to my mother. But there was some sadness in my heart when I realized that it might have been too late.

Just as Frank and I arrived on the last step, we caught a glimpse of Buck and Queen at the curb alongside his Benz truck with its engine running. Buck was assisting Queen inside. Then I noticed Saint's sister's best friend standing nearby. After Buck secured Queen inside of the truck, he helped Fallon inside behind Queen, smacking her on the ass as she climbed in.

My eyes bucked as Frank heartedly laughed.

I shook my head, yelling, "Y'all nasty!"

ANTHONY "BUCK" PATTERSON

As I slowly woke up the next morning, the sight that greeted my groggy eyes was enough to make any man envy me. Sandwiched between the brown, silky bodies of Queen and Fallon, I smirked. This scenario was nothing new to me, but the genuine affection and care Queen displayed by orchestrating these threesomes was something I had never experienced before.

Careful not to disturb their rest, I gently slipped out of the bed, feeling a sudden urgency in my bladder. With each step, memories of Queen riding my face while Fallon bounced on my dick seduced me.

As I made my way to the bathroom, I glanced back at the two sleeping beauties. Their chocolate skin glowed softly in the morning light, highlighting their irresistible infatuation and curves. I had always verbalized my attraction to Saint's sister's best friend around the crew, so Queen was well aware of it. However, Fallon was a traditional woman who wasn't interested in being in a sexual relationship with a pimp even if it was just for fun. So, I stayed away but always admired her from afar. But her interest had been piqued at the reception when she realized that I was finally with a woman who was more than just sex to me. She was respectful to Queen, but Queen had noticed the look in Fallon's eyes. So, she convinced Fallon to come home with us so that I could finally fulfill the fantasy of spreading those ass cheeks.

As I stepped out of the bathroom, the morning sunlight streamed through the windows, casting a blinding light across the room, highlighting Fallon's figure now standing at the foot of the bed. Fallon shyly looked towards me. Her eyes then traveled the long journey from my face and down my torso. Her eyes lingered on my morning hard-on as it swayed between my legs. She then swallowed hard, pulling her eyes away as she stepped into her dress.

"I have to go," she whispered as she scrambled to finish dressing. "I need to get to work."

The dress she adorned clung to her curves. My eyes were drawn to her, captivated by the beautiful ballet of cloth and skin as she hurriedly got dressed. But as my eyes traveled behind her, my eyes lay on a different level of beauty and purity. I walked over to the dresser, opened a drawer, and pulled out a pair of basketball shorts. I slipped them on as the sound of Fallon's zipper closing signaled that she was done getting dressed.

Looking back, I saw that she was standing there, waiting patiently. My head angled towards my bedroom door. I then walked towards it, and she followed. As I led her through the house, my stomach growled so loud that it made Fallon giggle.

"Hungry?" she asked with a raised brow.

Rubbing my protruding belly, I nodded. "Hell yeah."

As we approached the front door, a flirtatious gaze found its way to her auburn eyes. "I like to eat."

My brows met together. "Okay?"

Her eyes twinkled with mischief. "We can go get something to eat." She shrugged, suggesting, "Tell her you went home."

I scoffed. Then I had to chuckle when I realized that Queen really had me wrapped around every one of her dainty little fingers. "I don't do shit without her, shorty."

She tilted her head to the side, challenging me with a glare. "Since when are you a committed man?"

"Since I've been in a committed relationship."

Shocked, her eyes grew a bit. She folded her arms across her amazing breasts. "That's never been you."

I shrugged a shoulder. "It is now."

Competition rose in her eyes. I knew women well. This wasn't about me. She felt as if she had missed out on something and felt challenged to get it back. So, I reached past her and opened the front door. I then walked around her, opening it wider, introducing her exit.

Her eyes lowered as if she was in disbelief that after years of being fascinated with her, I'd hit it and was now dismissing it.

"I felt how you reacted to this pussy last night. It was good to you. You can have it again ... *without her*. I can make you feel good again."

She tried to close the space between us, but I stopped her, grabbing her by the chin. It was a firm but gentle grasp, enough to catch her attention without causing any harm. "You could, but you could never make me feel better than she does."

She snatched her chin away with a frown. She then tore her eyes away. Her heels hit the wood floor of the foyer angrily and then the concrete outside as she marched out.

Chuckling, I closed the door.

As I walked back into the bedroom, Peaches' words echoed in my mind. The fun night with Queen and Fallon had briefly silenced these thoughts. But, now in the quiet morning, with only Queen's soft snoring, Peaches' words became impossible to ignore. They were like a loud, constant alarm in my head. There was no doubt that Queen didn't like that I had hoes. It had been the hateful wedge between us initially. It was only our chemistry after we connected that was leading her to accept it.

I couldn't help but feel the heaviness of my divided loyalty. On one hand, I was loyal to the game. I felt obligated to protect and lead my hoes. They had always been loyal to me, so I didn't want to completely abandon them. But my loyalty to Queen was pushing me to be less and less available to them. And the tension between her and Diamond had forced me to nearly abandon them altogether.

I appreciated that Queen was accepting me for me. Her tolerance and understanding were the pure, selfless acceptance from a woman that I always yearned for. I treasured Queen's selflessness and the taste of normalcy that made me feel like I had something worth fighting for beyond the game.

I couldn't keep straddling the fence, playing both sides, though. It wasn't fair to Queen for me to keep putting her in uncomfortable positions.

QUEEN ARIA BENSON

I sat on the sterile examination table, anxiously waiting for the doctor to return. My heart was beating out of my chest and thoughts of the worst-case scenario screamed in my mind. I had only come for an annual examination, but my doctor had done an ultrasound as well to investigate the pain I had been feeling. During the ultrasound, she had tried to keep a straight face, but I had seen those worry lines.

Finally, the door swung open, and the doctor entered the room. Her face was etched with somberness that made my stomach churn. She sighed, her eyes avoiding direct contact with mine as she sat in the chair in front of the small desk and computer. "Queen, I'm afraid I have to deliver some difficult news," she began.

My eyes grew owlishly as my heart started to beat out of my chest.

I held my breath as the doctor carefully continued, "Based on your examination, it seems like the pain is due to some damage to your uterus."

"Okay," I replied slowly. "What does that mean?"

Her eyes softened. "It means that you may have some infertility issues."

I was taken aback, my heart sinking further into a pit of despair. And the despair shocked me because I had never previously cared about having children. My own childhood had been wrecked with abandonment and despair. I had not even considered having kids. But just hearing that I could possibly never have children with Buck crushed me.

"Infertility? At nineteen? How is that even possible? How did this happen?"

The doctor took a deep breath before explaining, "Trauma and physical injuries can cause damage to the uterus, leading to fertility issues. Have you ever suffered any physical trauma, Queen?"

As her words sank in, my mind wandered back to a painful, all-too-familiar place. Tears welled up in my eyes, threatening to pour out uncontrollably. I clenched my fists, feeling the anger course through me.

Reggie...

The countless nights of abuse, the relentless beatings, and the pain that ran deep had all left more than just invisible marks. They had stolen something from me that I had never imagined.

A sob threatened to escape my lips, but I held my breath, holding it back.

The doctor's demeanor softened even more. She rolled her chair closer, placing a hand on my knee. "I'm truly sorry for what you've been through, Queen. But remember, there are still options available. We can explore assisted reproductive technologies or in-vitro fertilization. Don't lose hope just yet."

As the doctor finished explaining the alternatives for some

time in the future when I was ready to conceive, anger flooded me. I felt ashamed that I had so foolishly given myself to the wrong man, allowing him to ruin me so much that now I couldn't give the right man what he deserved.

Once she was done, the doctor excused herself so I could get dressed. Alone, I let out a frustrated cry. As I struggled to redress, my cell phone began to ring. Glancing at the screen, I saw that it was Buck calling. My heart sank, and I couldn't bring myself to answer. I knew if I did, he would sense that something was wrong. I couldn't find the words to explain how I had been so foolish, how I had let my ability to conceive a child be taken away from me by someone who didn't deserve me. The thought of admitting my mistake to Buck was too painful for me to bear.

So, I let the call go unanswered, allowing it to dissolve into silence.

30

CYNTHIA "CECE" DEBOIS

I groaned when my cell phone rang, interrupting the cat nap that I was trying to steal now that Frank had finally pulled out of me. My eyes squinted as they adjusted to the sunlight that assaulted me from the floor-to-ceiling windows.

I scrambled for the phone on the nightstand. Since it was Buck's name flashing on the display screen, I answered groggily, "Hello?"

"Hey, Queen."

"What's going on, Buck?" I sighed with relief as I got back comfortable.

"Y'all still at the hotel?"

I was so worn out that I spoke with my eyes closed. "Yeah. We're checking out soon. What's up? Something wrong?"

"Have you talked to Queen?"

The concern in his voice made my eyes pop open. "Not since we left the reception last night."

"Oh."

My eyes narrowed, hearing the desperation in his tone. "Is everything okay?"

"Yeah, I'm sure it is. I just haven't talked to her since she went to her doctor's appointment this morning."

"Oh. I'm sure she is okay. But I'll try to get in touch with her for you."

"Thank you."

Hanging up, the sound of running water in the bathroom enticed me. I quickly called Queen and impatiently waited for her to answer.

"What's up? You've reached—" I hung up on her voicemail and sent her a quick text, telling her to call Buck.

"C'mon, baby," I heard my husband call for me. "It's ready."

A smile pirouetted across my lips as I basked in the pure love and comfort that resonated in his tender voice. The overwhelming wave of affection that had washed over me since marrying him was still all over me, filling my heart with warmth that surpassed the steamy passion that had projected from us all night and morning.

I returned the phone to the nightstand and climbed out of bed. The aching in my core yearned for the hot water that was running into the tub nearby. My naked frame padded towards it, legs still quaking from an unimaginable hours of lovemaking.

As I stepped into the bathroom, my eyes fell upon the remarkable sight of my husband's naked frame perched gracefully on the edge of the tub. His beautiful dick hung between his legs. The soft lighting caressed his chiseled features, emphasizing every contour and curve and every curl on his head, leaving my breath hitched in my throat. His captivating presence filled the room, as his confident demeanor exuded raw sensuality that sent shivers of anticipation down my spine.

I pulled my eyes away before he could see the longing in them and think that I could take more dick.

As I sank into the deep tub, the warm water swallowed me, soothing my aching body. Frank had taken no mercy on me when we got to the hotel. He had been fucking me at length, not even giving me a chance to sleep. He'd made me cum on every surface of the suite. We had even poured all the money that had been rained on us at the reception on top of the bed and fucked for hours on top of it until we made the bills sticky with our sweat and sex juices.

The afternoon sunlight filtered through the bathroom window, forming gentle rays that danced on the surface of the bubbles. The scent of lavender filled the air, providing the tranquility that I desperately needed.

Frank climbed in behind me, and I leaned back against his broad, hard chest. He wrapped his arms around me, allowing me to search for even more comfort in his shadow. The touch of his body against mine sent a jolt of warmth through my veins, reminding me once again that he was mine to love forever. I nestled closer to him, grateful for him despite the chaos that had threatened to separate us.

My eyes wandered over his brightly adorned skin, a vibrant canvas of colors and stories. Each tattoo on his body was like a chapter waiting to be explored, a visual representation of his journey through life. I traced my finger lightly over one of the intricate designs, marveling at the artistry and the tales they toldMuffled sounds from outside of the windows and in the hotel's hallway blended with the soft rhythm of our breathing.

Suddenly, Franks deep, sexy voice filled the bathroom, "Thank you, baby."

I looked up, slightly tilting my body so that I could look into his cognac eyes. "For what?"

His gaze was intense yet gentle as he replied, "I'm so grateful that you gave me another chance."

The sincerity in his voice and gaze made boulders crowd in my throat, leaving me unable to speak.

"I can't imagine not being in this moment with you," he went on. "I wouldn't want to be anywhere else."

He grabbed my hand, bringing it up to his soft lips to kiss the back of it. "I love you so much that every moment without you feels like an eternity."

My lips slowly met my ears. Though my eyes were weak from exhaustion, they sparkled. "I love you more than I did yesterday."

Smoothly, he gave me a small smile. "And less than I will tomorrow."

Frank was a gangster. He'd had to be hard all of his life. He hadn't had an example of how a man should love a woman like this, which was much of the reason why he'd had to learn how to love me. So, when he stripped himself of that persona and allowed it to momentarily to take a back seat, I was always so moved. Every time he revealed his true emotions, a wave of warmth washed over me that I was addicted to.

Repositioning my back against his chest, I was so glad that I had given Frank a second chance. My heart swelled with happiness, knowing that I hadn't allowed my mother's doubts to cloud my judgment. I had trusted my intuition, and it had led me to this beautiful life with Frank.

I believed that no man was perfect, but in Frank, I had found the perfect man for me. He had flaws just like everyone else, but those imperfections only made him more endearing. He had shown me his vulnerability, his sincerity, and his unwavering support. And I had fallen deeply in love with every aspect of his being.

There was a perfect match for everyone, and I was blessed to have found mine. True love wasn't about finding someone who was flawless but about finding someone who embraced you with all your imperfections, and vice versa. Frank was my imperfectly perfect man, and I couldn't have been happier to have found him. He was my kindred spirit, the one who completed me in ways I hadn't thought possible. Our connection felt like destiny, like two puzzle pieces finally figuring out how to fit flawlessly together.

My eyes brightened as I made a realization. I looked up and back at him.

"What?" he inquired.

"We have to add something to it now?"

"We have to add more to how we say, 'I love you'."

He grinned. "What do you want to add, baby?"

"I love you more than I did yesterday and less than I will tomorrow until death do us part."

Grabbing the back of my head, he leaned forward, tenderly kissing my forehead. "You're right," he replied, his lips gracing my skin. "Until death do us part, baby."

FRANK "CAPO" DISCIPLE

A few hours later, Richard, Linda, CeCe and I were in the foyer of her parents' home surrounding the front door. We'd finally checked out of the hotel and had come to pick up the kids. I was holding Jah in my arms. CeCe was holding Shauka, who was screaming so loud that he was causing her to cringe. CeCe's exhaustion was making her easily irritated. I could see it all over her face. I felt bad that she'd had only one day of relaxation. But she had insisted on waiting to go on a real honeymoon.

The look that CeCe gave me let me know that she was ready to make a quick exit. Considering that her mother had oddly followed us to the front door, I knew CeCe was ready to dip. They hadn't even spoken to one another.

Looking at Richard, I told him, "We're going to head on out. Thanks for watching the kids."

"No problem, son." He handed me the baby bag that he had carried to the front door for us. I held Jah with one arm while swinging the bag over the shoulder of the other.

"Frank, can I talk to you for a moment?" Linda suddenly asked.

CeCe shot me a bewildered stare. I felt like a deer caught in headlights.

"It won't take long," she promised.

CeCe blew out an irritated breath. "I'll be in the car."

Though Linda had been unapologetically rude to me since I'd met her and recently, obscene to her daughter, she couldn't take the same treatment. She flinched as CeCe turned her back, leaving out of the house.

"Give him to me," Richard told me, reaching for Jah. "I'll take him to the car."

"Thank you."

Richard gave me an encouraging smile as he followed CeCe out of the house.

I followed Linda into the living room. When she sat next to me on the couch and placed a comforting hand on my knee, I was visibly caught off guard.

"Frank, I owe you an apology," she began, and I raised an eyebrow in surprise. "I've been treating you unfairly. At first, I assumed you were some thug who would ruin my daughter's life. And when things got tough in you all's relationship, I thought my assumptions had been right."

I looked at her, a bit taken aback by her honesty. But I was man enough to know that Linda had been right in some ways. "I get it. I ain't exactly the poster boy for the ideal son-in-law."

Linda laughed weakly. It was evident that the strain in her and CeCe's relationship was taking a toll on her. "But I misjudged you and I let that cloud my view of your relationship with CeCe once you all gave it another try. I thought you were breaking her heart all over again and I didn't think you were capable of loving her the way she deserves."

I shifted uncomfortably in my seat. I hated that it had been my mere presence that had caused a rift in her relationship with her daughter. "I'll be honest with you. When I got with CeCe, I wanted to be with her, but I had no clue how to treat her right. I was a twenty-one-year-old kid with new responsibilities that no one had taught me how to manage. I knew that I wanted her, that she made me feel something different, but I had no idea how to earn that. I didn't have parents that showed me how to love a woman properly. I didn't grow up in a loving home environment and I didn't know how to love CeCe the way she deserved. I had to learn."

Linda looked at me, her expression softening. "I see. So, you weren't intentionally hurting her."

"No, Linda, never. I just didn't know any better. But I love CeCe, and I've been learning how to be the man she needs," I admitted, allowing vulnerability to creep into my voice.

She nodded slowly. "Honestly, I can see that. I see the change in you. I just didn't want to believe that it was real. That's my daughter, and I'm going to want the best for her. But I should have never mistreated you or made you feel uncomfortable. I definitely should have supported your proposal and the wedding. That is something I will never get back or never be able to give CeCe..." Her words lodged in her throat as tears came to her eyes. "I allowed my anger to get the best of me, but I will have to deal with the consequences."

"She'll come around eventually. She loves you too much."

Linda shrugged meekly. "I hope so." She dabbed at her eyes, sighing deeply. "In the meantime, can we start over?"

Massive relief caused me to smile from ear to ear. "Sure."

She smiled tearfully. "Thank you."

I then leaned in, taking her into my arms. "And I'm going to do right this time. I promise. If for no other reason, I have to

prove you wrong." I then started cracking up, which encouraged her to laugh as well.

Pushing back, I looked into her eyes, promising her, "You
may have been right about me at first. But CeCe brings out a
side of me I didn't know existed. She makes me want to be a
better person, to strive for greatness for her and the boys. I've
never felt so connected to someone before, like we are two
souls meant to find each other in this world exactly in the way
that we did. Everything feels so right when I'm with her that I
refuse to ruin that again."

Those tears returned to Linda's eyes as she smiled in
approval.

Her approval was relief that I wasn't the villain she'd
thought I was. But whether this apology was sincere or an
effort to get her daughter back into her good graces, I knew
that I would never break CeCe's heart again. I was as sure of my
purpose in being her husband as I was sure of my purpose of
being a boss. It was a purpose that I now embraced with unwavering determination.

The love I felt for CeCe encompassed every aspect of my
life. It was an anchor that grounded me and gave purpose to
every move I made. I was humbled by Linda's forgiveness, and
it fueled my determination to always prioritize her happiness
and well-being. It was a privilege to be her husband. Her smile
was now my guiding light that led me through even the darkest
days, reminding me of the importance of love, forgiveness, and
the power of redemption.

CYNTHIA "CECE" DEBOIS

"What can they be in there talking about all of this time?"

My father smiled at the irritable frown on my face. "It must be going well if they are still in there."

When my scowl deepened, my father reached through the passenger's window and pinched my cheek. "Fix your face."

I sucked my teeth, rolling my eyes. "What did you say to her in that dressing room?"

"That's between me and my wife," he boasted cockily, making me want to gag.

"Yeah, that's the problem. She always wants to keep things between y'all."

"Well, your smart ass can guess what I said if she's in there talking to Frank."

I pouted. "I don't want her talking to him because you made her."

"I didn't make her do anything, but I did make her see what the hell she was creating. I've been with that woman for over twenty-three years. I can make her realize things that you can't."

Disgusted, I winced.

As my father laughed, the screen door of their home creaked loudly as it opened. My eyes darted towards it, hoping to see Frank. But I was confused to see my mother instead, descending the porch steps. As I rolled my eyes, my father gave me a warning glare. Sinking into the passenger's seat, I folded my arms tightly across my chest. As my mother's footsteps grew nearer, I refused to look that way.

"Can I talk to her for a minute?" I heard her ask my father.

My eyes darted towards my dad, begging him not to leave me alone with her. But he smiled, walking away with that smooth, unhurried gait with his hands in his pocket.

I refused to look at her, causing her to blow out a long, steady breath.

"CeCe..." It made my heart melt to hear her call my name in the tender tone she used to. "I'm so sorry, baby–"

"Don't apologize because Daddy is making you," I cut in, staring out of the windshield.

"Your father did help me see how stubborn and ornery I was acting. Unfortunately, I wanted what was best for you so much that I didn't care how I was acting, so much that I didn't realize that I was missing out what would be the best days of your life, of... of my life..." As her voice started to crack, I finally looked out of the window towards her. "So much that I refused to admit that even with his flaws, Frank is what's best for you." A tear fell as her eyes nervously scanned the neighborhood. "You were right. My marriage isn't as perfect as I wanted it to seem. But I hid that from you because I didn't want to be the same wife my elders were. I wanted to be better, not take the same shit that they did. And when I ended up being just the same, I was too ashamed to admit that my man was like every-body else's man."

My heart softened as she stared at nothing in particular, allowing the tears to fall. "I wanted more for you than struggle love. I wanted you to be better than me, than your grand-mother, to not take excessive bullshit from a man just to say you had one, for it to take until your children are in high school before he finally gets it right." Wiping her face, she took a calming breath and dried her hands on her housedress. "But I guess all of these niggas need time to get it right." We both scoffed simultaneously. "But lucky for you yours didn't take as long." Finally, she looked at me. "I'm sorry, baby. I'm not perfect either, I guess."

Gulping, I nodded. "I appreciate that, Mama. But what you tried to ruin, how you treated me, can't be fixed just like that. It's going to take a long time for me to forgive you."

Her eyelids met together for a few seconds before she took a disappointed breath and nodded curtly. "I understand." With her eyes still closed, she turned towards the house. It broke my heart to see her sadly walk away with her head down, but I reminded myself that she had brazenly made me feel that much worse for months.

But my refusal to immediately forgive her hadn't been about revenge. I had to show her how to love me just as I'd had to show Frank.

QUEEN ARIA BENSON

I had avoided the house until I saw through the surveillance cameras that Buck had left. I couldn't fathom talking to him, so I couldn't bring myself to return his calls and text messages all day. To keep him from coming inside, I had put the deadbolt on.

"So, you gon' tell me what's wrong with you?" CeCe pushed a cup into my face. The strong smell coming from it let me know it was some sort of alcohol. She knew what I liked to drink, so I took it, trusting whatever it was.

I folded my legs Indian-style as I sat at the foot of my bed. With her own cup in her hand, she leaned against my dresser. "And would you hurry up? Because I'm still in marital bliss, bitch. I wanna go be with my husband."

I sucked my teeth. "That's why I told yo' ass not to come over here."

"Well, you sounded like you were in distress. Excuse me for giving a fuck."

I had answered CeCe's call because, though I felt too

ashamed to say anything, I still needed to talk and wanted the company. So, I blew out my shame, before explaining, "The doctor told me today that the pain that I've been having is because I have a bruised uterus."

Confusion drew deep lines on CeCe's forehead. "What does that mean? How does that happen?"

My gaze dropped to the floor. "Trauma and physical injuries."

CeCe let out an audible sigh. "*Shiiiit.*"

Her reaction heightened the ache in my chest, and a renewed wave of tears threatened to spill. "I will have infertility issues."

"Oh, Queen," CeCe breathed with empathy and sorrow. She moved towards me, taking a seat beside me. Gently, she wrapped an arm around me, and I leaned my head on her shoulder.

"Did the doctor say that you have options when you are ready?"

"Yeah, she said invitro was an option."

"Well, that's good," CeCe replied with some relief. "Buck can afford to get you as much treatment as you need."

"But invitro doesn't work for everybody."

CeCe chuckled, a sound that felt out of place considering how I felt. "You don't even know if it won't work for you or not yet. You're investing hurt and worry into something that might not even happen, girl."

I sat up, wiping my face. "It's more so about the fact that I gave so much of myself to Reggie that I might not be able to give everything to Buck." Tears welled, overflowing from my eyes as I stared helplessly at nothing in particular. "I feel so stupid having to tell the man who deserves everything from me that I let a bum take this from us."

CeCe's eyes washed with sympathy. "Girl, he will understand. That man loves you."

I immediately shook my head. "He's never told me that."

CeCe's head dramatically tilted to the side. "He let you take him away from three bitches in one house that was sucking and fucking *and* making him money and you think he don't love you? Really?"

Her dramatics forced me to weakly laugh through my misery.

"Girl, he will understand, and he won't judge you," she reassured me. "Stop pushing that man away. Let him continue to be there for you as he's always been."

ANTHONY "BUCK" PATTERSON

I stood in the middle of my living room, my eyes burning into Diamond, April, and Peaches. They shuffled nervously, avoiding my gaze like roaches scattering when the lights came on. I still hadn't spoken to Queen since that morning. That was unlike her. Rarely did a few hours go by that she didn't check in and she answered every call and text message, if not immediately, right away.

Something had gone down at that reception, and I needed answers.

"What the hell happened at the reception last night?" my voice rumbled through the room.

April glanced at Diamond who looked like a deer caught in headlights. I didn't need to know who the culprit was, but Peaches dramatically pinned her eyes on Diamond, bucking them.

"*Diamond, talk!*" My thunderous bark made them all jump out of their skin as the walls shook.

"Daddy, it ain't even like you think," Diamond started to hurriedly ramble. "I didn't say anything to her. I swear."

"But you was talking shit," Peaches spewed, making Diamond's eyes buck.

"Talking shit about what?" I gritted.

She meekly lowered her eyes. "I just asked them why they had to be so nice to her. She's not putting in work like us. She's not one of..." That last word caught in her throat as the sight of me taking long strides towards her made her mute.

In seconds, her tiny neck was in my grasp as I stood her up from the couch.

April and Peaches jumped out of the way with owlish eyes as I tossed Diamond on the floor. She hit the solid hardwood, hollering, "Daddy, no! I'm sorry!"

"Didn't I tell you not to say shit else to her?!" I roared, standing over her.

She answered in sobs.

"Go pack your shit and get the fuck out of my house!"

"*Noooo!*" she cried, crawling towards me on her hands and knees. "Don't do this to me!" She was sobbing as she clung to my pants leg. "Please, Daddy. I'll do better, I promise."

"I don't negotiate with hoes, you know that," I seethed. "Get the fuck off me, Diamond."

She continued to hold on.

"Don't make me stomp yo' ass out!"

Peaches' eyes expanded. I had never truly put my hands on them. Beyond not being one of those types of pimps, that wasn't the type of relationship I had with my hoes. I controlled them with my guidance and their love and respect for me, not my hands. I had rarely had to be physically aggressive with them. Peaches and April were in disbelief of the rage I was displaying.

Shaking her head, April jumped up from the couch and pried Diamond's arms from around me. "C'mon on, girl," she said as she pulled Diamond away by both of her arms.

"No!" Diamond screamed at the top of her lungs. But she knew better than to fight with April. Though I never put my hands on them, they had no issues fighting each other. And it had been proven long ago that Diamond was a lover, not a fighter.

"He said you gotta go, so you gotta go," April's voice strained as she struggled to pull Diamond's dead weight out of the living room.

Diamond let out another scream that made Peaches cringe. "Shut the fuck up!" she snapped. "You did this to yourself. He gave yo' ass a chance. Now, get the fuck out before *I* put you out."

Diamond continued to sob as April dragged her out of the living room and down the hall.

As Diamond's cries faded, I plopped down on the couch. I frustratingly held my face with both hands. I felt Peaches' body weight come close and then I felt her hand on my back.

"You right, Peaches." Sighing, I lowered my hands and looked at her. "I gotta let this shit go."

Peaches pouted sympathetically.

"I can't have her and this too and surprisingly, I want her more."

Tears came to her eyes. The glance behind them was both admiration and sadness. I understood the sadness. We had been in the trenches together forever. She was my first ride or die.

"You know I would never leave you hanging. You and April can have the house. But ya'll don't need me to lead you in this game no more. Niggas like to make hoes feel like they need a pimp to survive, but that's not true in every case. I've groomed y'all. I've taught y'all everything. Y'all can get out there and get this money without me. And if you ever need me, I got you."

Watching her tears fall made my eyes sting with oncoming emotions that I had never felt before. I hadn't felt this torn and sorrowful since I'd watched my mother love drugs more than she loved me.

I extended my large arm, bringing Peaches into my shadow. She clung to me, sobbing. This shit hurt. I knew that April didn't have enough feelings to be as upset as Diamond and Peaches. Thankfully, Diamond had made it easier by digging her own grave. But to hurt Peaches like that had pulled at regretful heartstrings that hadn't been touched since I was a boy.

Yet, even as I sat there fighting to keep my own emotions from surfacing, I knew that I'd rather leave this game, hoping that it would get Queen back than to stay in it, ruining my chances of ever having her in my life again.

———

Peaches, April, and I said our goodbyes. Diamond had barricaded herself in her room, but Peaches and April had assured me that she was gone before morning by any means necessary. I trusted them to handle the situation for me so I left and sped off to Queen's house.

Arriving at her place, my eyes immediately caught sight of her car parked out front. Anticipation and dread gripped my chest. I never liked dealing with emotions because they were the kind of trouble I'd avoided my entire life. This was why I had never truly opened my heart to a woman, why I had only fucked them and made them my property.

After exiting my car, I practically sprinted towards the house. Neighbors watched my haste curiously. As I reached the porch, the uneasiness in my stomach intensified. Fumbling with my keys, I attempted to unlock the door, only to realize they weren't working.

She had put the deadbolt on.

Frustration boiled over. I started pounding on the door with force that sent aftershocks through the neighborhood. Barks escaped my lips with a raw urgency, each thud against the door mirroring the pounding of my heart. "Open the fucking door, Queen!"

In the midst of my pounding, I heard the locks quickly disengaging. I stopped, breathing heavily in anticipation. But when the door opened, I saw CeCe, which only heightened my worry.

"Where she at?" I asked, taking large, forceful steps past her.

"In her bedroom. I'm gone."

I didn't bother to say another word to her. I marched through the house towards the bedroom. As I heard the front door close, I entered the bedroom. Queen was at the foot of the bed, sheepishly watching me as I stalked towards her.

"Baby, I'm sorry," I insisted, sitting close to her.

Her brows furrowed as her posture straightened. "Sorry for what?"

"For that shit Diamond said at the reception. She's gone, and I'm done with the game."

Her eyes bucked. "Wait. What?"

"I kicked her out. But I told Peaches and April I'm done with the game. I know you only deal with it because you fuck with me, but—"

"Because I love you," she corrected me, making my breath hitch and my chest rise.

She was finally smiling genuinely watching such a hard, massive exterior melt into butter.

I swallowed hard, taking a deep breath. "I know that you deal with it—"

"Because I love you," she interrupted, putting a hand on my thigh near my dick. "You can say it."

I smiled sheepishly, barely able to keep my dark skin from blushing. "Because you love me," I forced myself to say without grinning like a little boy. "All I knew was the game. That's all I ever wanted. But I don't need it if it's going to bring drama in something that's normally perfect as fuck."

She pouted a bit, with longing and appreciation in her gaze. "But I didn't need you to give it up. I'm happy you kicked Diamond out, but you didn't have to give it up."

"I wanted to. It makes me feel better."

"But it's not why I was upset all day."

"Then what was wrong?"

She sighed, rolling her neck. "I found out at the doctor that the years of abuse I suffered with Reggie bruised my uterus, giving me infertility issues."

My eyes closed, hating that I had already killed this motherfucker. I wanted to be able to do it again and again and again. He'd had no right to put his hands on her before. But I despised that he was affecting what was mine now. But instead of exemplifying my rage, I wanted to comfort Queen. So, I buried the fury and opened my eyes. I took her waist into my hands and brought her to her favorite place. She straddled my lap and nestled against my chest, resting her head on my shoulder.

"That shit don't matter. Can't we have like a test-tube baby or some shit like that?"

She chuckled, her chest bouncing against mine. "Not exactly, but yes, there are some alternative ways of getting pregnant when I want to."

"Then we're good then."

She pushed back, staring into my eyes. "You want me to have your babies?"

"I want you to have my everything."

Touched, Queen's shoulders drooped, and her head tilted. The vulnerability in her eyes clung to mine.

The emotions she brought out of me were new to me. They scared me because they were changing me into a man I didn't recognize. So, I avoided them. I took her face into my hands. My gaze was reassuring and possessive. I kissed away the turmoil that clouded her beautiful eyes. I took my time. It was a pledge to make all of her hurt go away, sealed with the softness of her lips against mine. The taste of salt lingered on her lips as I traced away the remnants of tears with a slow, deliberate sweep of my tongue.

In that kiss was a promise of years and the essence of forevers.

QUEEN ARIA BENSON

Waking up in the morning, I expected to feel Buck's strong arms wrapped around me. Lately, we'd been sleeping connected, always touching. It had become more intimate and passionate than having his dick deep inside of me caressing my walls. But as I scanned the room, he wasn't there. Instead, present in the room with me was a scent of sausage and something sweet. Cooking wasn't Buck's thing. His women had always taken care of that. So, I figured he must've ordered some takeout.

Climbing out of bed, I wandered over to the dresser we now shared. My home was now ours with traces of him scattered everywhere. His scent lingered on the sheets, and his clothes had found a permanent place in the drawers. It was a living space that reflected how our lives had merged in such a short time.

As I opened the dresser, I couldn't help but smile at the sight of his things mingling with mine. His cologne lingered on the clothes, a masculine scent that now felt like an integral part of my daily routine. The half-empty bag of chips he'd left on top of the dresser, a small yet touching reminder of his presence.

I grabbed one of Buck's shirts from the drawer, drawn to the warmth and familiarity of his scent. As I slipped into it, the fabric practically engulfed my frame. His shirt, designed for his massive build and baggy fashion, nearly fell past my knees, leaving me swimming in a sea of cotton. I looked comical in it, but the feeling of his essence wrapped around me was so comforting.

Leaving the bedroom, I padded silently toward the kitchen. At the entrance, the sight that greeted me stopped me dead in my tracks and made me grin.

Buck was shirtless, standing at the stove with frustration etched all over his face as he flipped the sausages. He never even microwaved his own food, let alone cooked it. He looked so overwhelmed. His pot belly almost bumped against the pots on the stove as he moved about, attempting a task that was very foreign to him.

I stood in the shadows, silently admiring the continuous ways he showed me that he cared. Buck was usually emotionless with a demeanor that matched the harshness of the streets he'd come from. He hadn't wooed me with romance and words. He'd captivated me with acts of devotion. Each act of service he'd done for me told a story of a man who loved me in the best way he knew how. He might not have uttered the words yet, but his actions painted a picture of commitment and devotion.

So, cooking me breakfast was as loving as a marriage proposal and as valuable as a Birkin bag. The fact that he had taken on the task at all spoke volumes.

There is nothing like Mister Nonchalant suddenly *chalanting*.

EPILOGUE
THREE YEARS LATER

31
FRANK "CAPO" DISCIPLE

Shauka's bedroom was filled with the normal disarray that came with having four kids, three under the age of five. Jah, Shauka, Messiah, and Najia filled every corner of the room with their energy. Our six-week-old twins, Messiah and Najia, lay squirming in their car seats on the floor next to Shauka's bed. Messiah was wailing. Surprisingly, Najia was sleeping through her twin's rage. I was on a mission, trying to get Shauka dressed, but Messiah was having a fit.

"Jah, grab me a bottle for Lil' Man," I called out, trying to keep Shauka still.

Jah shot up from his spot on the floor near the twins where he'd been playing with his Spider-Man action figure. "Okay, Dad." He darted out of the room with the kind of urgency only a hungry baby's cries could encourage.

That boy had been my right hand when it came to taking care of the little ones. He was just seven, but I'd taught him how to make bottles, change diapers, and handle the chaos that came with two infants and a toddler. Being the big brother came with responsibilities, and I made sure Jah understood that.

Shauka lay on his bed, quiet per usual. I crouched down, wrestling to get the neckline of his shirt over all of his wild, curly hair. Shauka had always been mild mannered and easy to handle. Meanwhile, Messiah was wailing at a pitch that could compete with a fire alarm. He was only six weeks old, but I could already tell he would be a future troublemaker.

"Come on, Shauka, hold still," I grumbled, trying to mask my irritation. Dressing one kid while the other one screamed his head off wasn't my idea of a good time. But Shauka just gave me that innocent look of his, making it hard to stay mad.

As I struggled with Shauka's shirt, I heard the bottle warmer finally ding down the hall in the nursery. I sighed with relief.

Within seconds, Jah re-entered the room at high speed. He beelined over to Messiah. Soon the baby's cries began to wind down, replaced by the sounds of a hungry baby slurping on a bottle.

"Good lookin' out, Jah," I told him, smiling as I watched him hold a now content Messiah. Jah had a knack for looking out for his siblings just like I'd taught him. "All right, squad, we gotta get it together. We roll out in thirty minutes."

As I struggled with Shauka's shirt, feeling the presence of the other three kids surrounding me, the usual disbelief washed over me. Having four kids and a wife was a reality I had never seen coming before meeting CeCe. Back in the day, when Stanley had molded me into the man I became, I never pictured myself as a family man. I always saw myself as a boss. But a father of four? That was something beyond my wildest expectations.

Stanley had raised me with the idea that I'd be a boss, call the shots, run the streets, and be the man. Family life hadn't even been on that man's radar. But life had a way of throwing curveballs, and CeCe walked into my world, turning it upside down. I often wondered if Stanley was looking down on me proudly or laughing in mockery.

Before meeting CeCe, I had never thought I'd be this settled down. I had always respected women and courted them differently than what I'd seen growing up. However, I had never envisioned becoming such a devoted family man.

Meeting CeCe changed everything, though. Suddenly, being a boss wasn't the only thing on my mind. Family became a real thing, a priority I never knew I needed. My father had been a ghost, and I swore I'd be different. I was intent that my children would know who their old man was. They'd feel his presence and they would be my number-one priority. It wasn't easy juggling the streets and being a father, but I made it work. It became a delicate balance between being the boss of my crew and being there for my kids.

As I looked at Jah, Shauka, Messiah, and Najia, I was overwhelmed by the joy they brought me. They were my legacy. I was still the boss, but now, my heart was divided. I was a husband and a father, roles I never knew I'd play but found myself embracing with every passing day.

As I started to put on Shauka's jeans, CeCe entered the room, cradling a clear glass jar decorated with a beautiful bow. Her sweet brown eyes were curious as she directed her gaze at me. "What is this?"

"You tell me," I teased with a smirk.

A smile spread across her chocolate cheeks. "I don't know. I found it on my vanity."

"Open it," I replied as I pulled up Shauka's pants.

CeCe settled on Shauka's bed with the jar secured in her

hands. She carefully untied the bow. She opened it and turned it over. A cascade of folded sticky notes spilled onto her lap. Her curiosity grew, and she began to read. The sweet smile on her face transformed into a waterfall of emotions as she read each one. The notes contained handwritten memories of her that I never wanted to forget, reasons why I loved her, and positive affirmations about her.

Tears streamed down her cheeks as each sentiment sunk in.

Jah watched her tears protectively as he continued to feed Messiah, sitting Indian -style on the floor. But he eased when he realized that they were happy tears.

Hearing her cries, Shauka looked at her with concern causing his brows to furrow.

"You okay, Mommy?" he asked. His innocent voice made her emotions overflow into a small whimper.

CeCe nodded, unable to speak as she continued to read the heartfelt messages.

No matter how deep I waded into the turbulent waters of the game or the challenging currents of being a husband and father, I never forgot CeCe's need for me to court her. The streets were ruthless, and being a parent came with its own set of difficulties, but I now knew that the love I had for CeCe was a safe space for me that needed to be nurtured regularly. I had to balance taking care of the ruthless world I controlled and the haven I had created for her.

That's why I made it a point to weave thoughtful gestures into the fabric of our daily lives, like the jar of sweet notes she now clutched in her hands. The game was demanding, and being a parent wasn't easy, but I refused to let the essence of our connection slip away again. It was the little things like the notes, random surprises, and the moments of vulnerability that kept the flames burning. I wanted CeCe to always feel cherished, to relax into her femininity and know that she was my queen in a world full of turmoil.

"These are so sweet." She sniffled, picking another one up from her lap. "Why did you do this?"

"We've been caught up in a lot since you had the twins. I just wanted you to know you're still my priority. You're still the woman I want to court, to love, and continue to build a future with."

Her lip poked out with admiration as she picked up another one.

"You can't read them all right now, baby. There are too many, and we have to hit the road."

CeCe sighed long and hard, looking around at all the kids. "Do you think we should go?"

I chuckled as I sat back on my knees, finally finished dressing Shauka. "It's too late to reconsider, isn't it? What's wrong?"

"All these kids?!" she shrieked with a giggle as she waved her hand around the room. "Do you want to be stuck in a van with two crying infants?"

"We can make it work like we make everything else work, but it's up to you, baby."

She released a heavy breath, staring at the twins. "It's too late to change our minds. My parents are already prepared for you to do most of the driving."

We both chuckled in agreement as I said, "Exactly."

As we did every February, CeCe and I were packing up for the long drive to Mississippi for Bernadette's birthday.

"Besides," CeCe sighed sadly. "Grandma is eighty-three. I don't know how many more birthdays she'll have left, so we should go."

"Right," I agreed with a nod. Then I tilted my head, knowing her. "You worried about leaving Queen?"

She pouted. "Yeah. I want to be here for her."

"You can't be there for everyone at the same time. This weekend is about being there for your parents and grandmother. She'll understand."

Though her lips pressed into a regretful line, she nodded. "You're right." She then smiled down at the jar. "Thank you so much for this, baby."

She bent down with her lips puckered. I leaned forward, meeting her in a sweet, soft peck.

"I love you more than I did yesterday," she said against my lips.

"And less than I will tomorrow."

Then we said in unison, "'Till death do us part."

CYNTHIA "CECE" DISCIPLE

Standing at the sink in our master bathroom, I dried my face, appreciating the remnants of happy tears that had traced down my cheeks. The last three years of my life had been a fantasy. I had been experiencing a whirlwind of luxury, love, and dreams I never thought I'd touch. I was a ghetto princess, a far cry from the life I had known. The shopping sprees, the mansion that was now our family home, and the foreign cars were all symbols of the fairy tale Frank had painted for us.

More than the material blessings, what truly left me breathless was the way Frank loved me. He didn't just love me. He loved me with willful intent. Loving me was a deliberate and thoughtful choice he made every day. He hadn't stopped dating me, hadn't ceased to make me feel like the most special woman in the world.

After cleaning my face, I moisturized again. I ran my fingers through the hip-length box braids I'd had installed for this trip. As I stared at my reflection, I felt so much gratitude for the man who had turned my life into this enchanted fairy tale. The jar of sweet notes was just a small glimpse into the depth of his love. I was living a life I never thought possible all because I had given Frank that second chance.

As I admired and perfected my Adidas tracksuit, I noticed Frank slipping into the bathroom with a mischievous gleam in his eyes. My brows furrowed as he closed the door behind himself. I caught his playful expression through the mirror as he approached me from behind. After seven years, his presence still made my heart race.

My body was covered with goose bumps and was engulfed with heated flames as he pressed his pelvis against me, his mouth finding the crevices of my neck.

His touch was intimate and mischievous. The love and desire in his touch never failed to leave me breathless. I watched his reflection flirtatiously, a smirk playing on his lips as his hands traced patterns on my waist.

"What are you doing?" I gushed as he began to pull my pants down.

"I want to feel it before we hit the road."

My core pouted in fear. We had only waited five weeks before having sex after giving birth. Since then, he hadn't been able to keep his dick out of me.

"Where are the kids?" I asked while he positioned my knee on the sink.

"Messiah fell asleep. I turned on a movie in Jah's room. I told Shauka and Jah don't move until I get back."

I knew that Jah and Shauka would be obedient, so I allowed Frank to part my ass cheeks and slide inside of me.

After seven years, I still struggled to take all of him. It was definitely a labor of love when Frank was rock-hard, super horny, and in a hurry. I knew that I was in for a battle when he planted a firm grip on my waist and secured a foot on the toilet.

He was about to show his ass in this pussy.

He began to drive every inch deep into my core until I felt him in my stomach. Using his weight, he pushed my ass forward, forcing it to slide back and meet each rhythmic thrust.

"*Ssssss*," I hissed. "Mmuph!"

I reached back, placing a hand between my ass and his strokes, trying to slow him down.

He softly slapped my hand away. "Unt uh. Take this pipe."

QUEEN ARIA BENSON

🎵 *He breaks, me down, he builds, me up*
He fills, my cup, I like it rough
We fuss, we brawl, we rise, we fall
He comes, in late, but it's, ok 🎵

When "Addictive" came through the speakers of Buck's Bugatti, I looked over at him, weakly smiling at his effort. When he glanced over at me, his eyes reflected concern and love. But he forced a grin to shine through his full, luscious beard.

"*Yeeeah*, you know this your song!" he coaxed me with a grin. He leaned over, planting a grip on the inside of my thigh with his large hand. He softly squeezed, saying, "Gon' 'head and sing for me, baby."

I chuckled, forcing back the sadness, the grief. I was tired of being a dark shadow that Buck had to nurture.

"'*I'm on, his knee, he keeps, me clean. And gives, me things, he makes, me screeeam. He's so contagious, he turns my pages. He's got me anxious, he's what I waited for'.*"

I tried to lose myself in the lyrics. The bass thumped, causing the seat to vibrate against me, but I felt a sadness crawling under my skin. I sang my heart out, trying to fill the air with my voice because I knew Buck loved it, but the grief weighed on my vocal cords like an anchor.

With the streetlights blurring by as we sped through the city, failure clawed at me. A few days ago, I had found out that another round of in-vitro was unsuccessful. My heart ached. Three miscarriages from natural conceptions, and now, two rounds of in-vitro had left me and Buck with empty arms.

He never pressured me about kids. He never asked, never made it a requirement for our love. Though he never cared if he had kids, a part of me felt like he didn't ask because he knew that it was too daunting of a task for my body. I wanted to give him everything because he had given me the world. We didn't have a biological family, so I yearned to create our own. I yearned for the pitter-patter of little feet, for bedtime stories and long, tiring nights. Yet, I was unable to give him the one thing I yearned to.

I glanced over at Buck, his dark, captivating eyes focused on the road, his strong hand gripping the wheel. He had never blamed me, never questioned my worth as a woman or a partner. But inside, I felt like I was letting him down.

The Bugatti sped through the city as I sang for my man, but my mind was in a different place, haunted by the reminders of my losses. I gazed out of the window, watching large snowflakes fall gracefully on the city. Despite Buck blasting the heat in the interior, the cold February air seeped through the window, chilling my skin.

I swallowed the lump in my throat and continued singing, each note carrying a piece of my heartache.

My cell phone rang, interrupting my lyrics. I looked down at the phone as it lay in my lap. Seeing CeCe's name flash on the screen, I answered, "Hey, girl."

"Hey. We're on our way," she announced, "We've actually been gone for a few hours."

"Okay, cool. You guys be careful. It's snowing like crazy today."

"I know, but thankfully we're used to taking this drive in this weather." She paused before asking, "How are you feeling?"

I smiled weakly at her concern. Besides Buck, CeCe had been my backbone during every loss. Sometimes, I thought she felt guilty for being so fertile in my face while I was struggling.

"I'm okay, boo," I tried to convince her.

"You sure?"

I chuckled sadly. "No, but I will be."

CeCe sighed. "I wish you would have come with us. There is room in the van."

"I know. I just wasn't in the mood."

"I understand." She then blew out a heavy breath. "Well, even though we're out of town, you call me if you need to talk. As a matter of fact, call me later."

"I will."

"Promise me," she insisted annoyingly.

I smiled, appreciating her. "We will talk later. I promise."

———

The atmosphere of Gibson's was warm in comparison to the snowfall outside. The low hum of conversation filled the air as

Buck and I sat at the bar. The remnants of our dinner lingered on the plates sitting in front of us. We held on to glasses of amber liquid. Buck's gaze held mine, soft and caring, as he spoke words that wrapped around my heart.

"You know I don't need kids, right? As long as I have you, that's all that matters to me."

I briefly closed my eyes, enjoying the soothing balm to my insecurities that his words were. I gazed at my king who never saw my flaws. "Thank you, baby. I love you, Buck."

Buck leaned in, anchoring his loving eyes on me. "I love you too, but I want you to really hear me. I'm not saying this just to make you feel better. I'm saying it because it's real. If we have kids, great, but if not, I'm good, as long as I have you."

"I know." I pouted. "I just want us to finally have a family."

"And we can. We can adopt. But kids or no kids, it doesn't matter to me. What matters is *us*, right here, right now. I don't need anything else as long as I have you by my side. You're everything to me. I've never met someone who understands my soul like you do. Kids or no kids, you're my forever."

My heart swelled. "And you're my forever, baby," I replied, our eyes locking.

As we lost ourselves in the intimacy of our exchange, a tap on Buck's shoulder jolted us back to the present.

An older black man with wise, twinkling eyes peered around Buck's large frame.

"I'm sorry to interrupt. I didn't mean to eavesdrop, but I couldn't help overhearing your conversation. I just wanted to tell you all how lovely of a couple you are. It's great to see real black love."

I blushed as Buck nodded in appreciation. "Appreciate that," he told him.

"Thank you," I gushed.

"I'm an ordained minister," the older man revealed with a warm smile. "I'd be honored to marry you two when the time comes. You're meant to be married."

I glanced at Buck, and our eyes met with a shared sense of awe. Then his gaze shifted to a hint of mischief as he turned to the older man.

"Hey, how 'bout marrying us right now?" Buck asked.

I burst into laughter, knowing he was joking.

However, Buck's expression remained serious, his gaze locked on me.

The older man, sensing his sincerity, leaned in with excitement. "I'd love to! Right here? Right now? At Gibson's?"

My laughter stuttered as I focused on Buck's sincerity. "Wait! Are you serious?" I asked, searching his face for any sign of amusement.

Buck's response was a firm nod.

As my mouth fell open, the older man beamed with enthusiasm. "Absolutely! I've married folks in all sorts of places, but randomly at a restaurant? That's a first!"

Still in disbelief, my eyes welled up. "Are you really serious about this?"

Buck took my hands in his, his eyes reflecting sincerity that went beyond my wildest dreams. "I've never been more serious about anything in my life. I want to make you my wife right here, right now."

I sat there in disbelief, my heart pounding as Buck's words replayed in my mind, words I never thought I'd hear. The thought of marrying Buck had always been foreign, especially considering his non-traditional past. Yet, here he was, gazing at me with sincerity that made my heart beat solely for him.

I recalled the times when he wasn't a traditionally monogamous man. I had convinced myself that marriage wasn't in the cards for us. But Buck, through his actions and commitment, had proved me wrong. He was willing to leave his old ways behind for me.

His eyes pleaded with mine, and I found myself on the brink of a decision I never thought possible. "Yes," I whispered, the word escaping my lips like a prayer. "Let's do it."

The older man grinned widely. "All right then! Stand up, both of you," he instructed. The excitement in his voice was contagious, making me giggle.

As Buck and I rose from our seats, the other patrons in the bar turned their attention toward us. My cheeks flushed with embarrassment and joy. The older man, now standing beside us, became the impromptu officiant in our unexpected love story.

I couldn't hold back the flood of happy tears that streamed down my face. Buck took my hand, his touch grounding me as we stood there, ready to embark on a journey we hadn't planned for that night.

The patrons at Gibson's had now curiously shifted their focus to us.

The older man leaned in, telling us, "My name is Reverend Johnson."

Grinning, I told him, "Nice to meet you. I'm Queen."

"I'm Bu- Anthony," Buck corrected. "I'm Anthony Peterson."

Reverend Johnson beamed, completely unfazed by randomly officiating a wedding. He looked overjoyed as if we were the highlight of his night.

"Ladies and gentlemen, we're gathered here today to witness a special moment between this beautiful couple," he declared, his voice causing a curious hush over the bar. "Love is a powerful force, and it has a way of surprising us when we least expect it. Now, Anthony and Queen, do you both promise to stand by each other through thick and thin, for better or worse, in sickness and in health, until death do you part?"

Buck squeezed my hand, his eyes never leaving mine. "I do," he affirmed in a steady voice filled with conviction.

A lump formed in my throat as I uttered words I never thought I'd say. "I do," I whispered in disbelief and overwhelming joy.

Reverend Johnson continued, "By the power vested in me, I now pronounce you husband and wife. You may kiss the bride!"

Buck's lips met mine in a kiss as the bar erupted in cheers and shouts. As we embraced, I glanced at the patrons around us, some gushing, others taking out their phones to capture the moment.

With an adoring twinkle in his eye, Reverend Johnson declared, "Ladies and gentlemen, let me introduce you to Mr. and Mrs. Anthony Peterson!"

32

CYNTHIA "CECE" DISCIPLE

♫ *Lovin' you*
Has made my life much sweeter, baby
Baby, since I've got you
Everything is alright ♫

"Ooo, this is my song! Turn this up, Frank!" Using my elbow, I softly nudged him on the side. Then I began to snap my fingers along to the beat of "Lovin' You."

Frank eyed me flirtatiously. Yet, a stern expression deepened his beautiful dark orbs. "Not if you keep calling me Frank."

I smiled sexily, gushing at him in the driver's seat. "I'm sorry, *Daddy*."

"Oh my God," my mother groaned with repulsion from the

second row of the van. Her disgust made Jah giggle uncontrollably behind her.

Thankfully, by now, her disgust was playful versus a few years ago when she was *truly* disgusted by Frank being in my life.

Apologizing for her behavior when Frank proposed marked a turning point in my relationship with my mother, but it took time for things to truly normalize. Forgiving her wasn't easy because her behavior back then had left lasting bitterness. Despite her genuine effort to show that she accepted Frank, our connection never fully recovered. But we were on the road to completely healing.

"Stop all that shit and let that man pay attention to the road nie, gull," my father warned me. "All this snow falling and shit. Let that man focus."

Always giving me what I wanted, Frank turned up the volume. The song started to flow through the speakers, a bit louder, allowing my off-key singing to accompany the O'Jays. "*'You know you make me feeeeel. You make me feel so good. From my head down to my toes. And sometimes I wanna shout! I wanna scream!'*"

"What you know about this?" my father teased me.

I sucked my teeth, looking back at him. "Daddy, stop playin'. You know Mama loves her some Eddie LeVert. She said that was my real daddy."

My father playfully scoffed as he narrowed his eyes at my mother, who was smirking with guilt. "You shoulda got some of that nigga's money then."

Everyone started laughing, even Jah, catching my attention as he sat in the third row with Shauka and the twins.

Suddenly, a curdling scream erupted from my mother's throat, snatching my attention. "Oh, Lord! Watch out for—"

I spun around, my heart pounding, instinctively following my mother's terrified gaze out of the windshield. My breath caught in my throat as I gasped. My eyes widened at the sight of a car hurtling towards us head-on in the southbound lane. Before my mother could fully articulate a warning, ghastly screams erupted from my father, Frank, and me.

In a frantic attempt to avoid the car, Frank wrestled with the steering wheel, desperately trying to change lanes. He, however, lurched the van in the opposite direction to prevent colliding with other vehicles traveling in adjacent lanes. The highway became chaotic as our vehicle started weaving uncontrollably in violent jerks.

"Hold on!" Frank barked as he lost control of the van.

"Oh, God!" my mother cried out.

I could only hold on to the door handle, my other hand desperately gripping Frank's leg as I prayed. The van took on a life of its own as it brutally careened through the snow-covered highway. The closed windows couldn't muffle the deafening screech of tires or the blaring horns, intensifying the racket of chaos in the van.

The fear of being in a van full of people, hurtling out of control on a snowy road, amplified the dread that gripped us. Each passing moment felt like an eternity. The collective gasps and silent prayers in the van echoed our terror.

I had never heard Frank so scared and frantic. "Fuck, fuck, fuck, fuck, fuck!"

The sudden chaos engulfed us as the van careened out of control. I could feel the terror tightening its grip on my heart, the fearful screams of my parents filling the air. In the midst of the pandemonium, I was paralyzed, unable to let out a scream of my own. My mind was consumed by the silent prayers I fervently sent for my kids.

Suddenly, the van brutally collided with an unseen force. The impact unleashed a violent crash that resonated throughout the entire vehicle. The collective scream of terror from everyone in the car shook me. The world blurred causing a disorienting whirlwind of panic and confusion as the van started to roll.

Amidst the commotion, my head collided with something unforgiving causing searing pain. The pain was unbearable, and for a moment, everything went dark. The relentless crash continued, but my senses were overwhelmed by the throbbing agony. As I struggled to maintain consciousness, the world spun around me, and then, mercifully, darkness consumed me.

ANTHONY "BUCK" PETERSON

After our spontaneous ceremony at Gibson's, I wasn't about to let the night slip away without sealing the deal properly. I paid the tab faster than I said, "I do," and practically bolted out the door, leaving the cheers and clinks of glasses behind. I was in a hurry to catch the jewelry store before it closed.

Once at the store, we had to hurriedly go through those glass cases, picking out rings quickly like we were on a heist. Queen insisted on buying my ring. She was still grinding as Frank's assistant. She had her own bag, so she wasn't about to let me foot the bill for my own ring. We found two rings that were like us, flashy, unapologetic, and expensive.

Exiting the jewelry store, I fumbled for my phone. "We have to go get marriage licenses in the morning to make it official."

Queen nodded, while staring at her ring. "Okay, baby."

I can't wait to tell Cap and CeCe this shit," I said, grinning.

Queen giggled, eyes still glued to the diamonds on her finger. "They are going to freak the hell out!"

As I dialed Cap's number, Queen asked, "You think they'll be mad that they weren't there?"

"Hell yeah," I chuckled deeply. "But they will understand that it was spontaneous."

Frank never answered. So, I hung up and called CeCe.

When I hung up, Queen pulled out her phone. "Let me try."

She dialed Frank and CeCe's numbers as well, but she didn't get an answer either.

"Maybe they are taking a nap while Richard drives," I suggested.

"Probably," I agreed.

Queen gasped as her eyes widened. "Maybe we should wait until CeCe and Frank get back to go get the marriage license. That way they can come with us."

I nodded quickly. "That's a good idea. Then they can still be a part of a ceremony." Smiling in agreement, Queen nodded frantically with relief. "Right."

I watched her, giving her a sneaky smirk. "So, you ready for your honeymoon?"

Her eyes darted towards me, beaming through the snow falling on us. "Honeymoon?!"

I nodded, grinning. "I can book a private jet and we can be in Jamaica in a few hours."

She gasped before her mouth fell open. "Jamaica, baby?!" she shrieked, jumping up and down. "What about clothes?"

I shrugged nonchalantly. "We can shop when we get there."

Watching me, her smile faded, and she took my hand. "Baby, are you doing all of this just because I'm sad?"

"I could have bought you a car or taken you on a shopping spree if I just wanted to put a smile on your face. Hell, I could have got you some Harold's. You love a good four-piece with salt, pepper, lemon pepper, mild sauce, and a hot pepper."

Her head fell back as she laughed.

I took her hand and planted a sincere gaze on her. "I'm doing this because I love you, and I want you to be happy. Reverend Johnson being there tonight was destiny. Today, I wasn't even thinking about getting married. The thought hadn't crossed my mind. But when I saw the look in his eyes when he said he wanted to marry us, I felt like the time was right then."

Her eyes softened as she looked up at me. "Okay, baby."

"Now, let me take you on this honeymoon."

She grinned as she shrieked, "Okay!"

As I led her away from the restaurant, my cell rang. I stopped abruptly, assuming that it was CeCe or Cap returning my call. Though the number calling wasn't saved in my contacts, I answered anyway. "Hello."

"Hello? Is this Buck?" I heard an elderly voice struggling to ask through tears.

My brow furrowed deep as I stopped in my tracks. "Who is this?"

"This is Bernadette," the voice answered as Queen looked up at me strangely.

"CeCe's grandmother?" I asked, causing Queen to grip my arm.

"Yes, baby. You.... You need to come to Indiana, honey."

"Wh-why? What's wrong?"

I heard Queen gasp. "What's wrong? Did something happen?"

"CeCe and Frank were in a terrible accident," Bernadette revealed over sobs.

My heart hammered in my chest as I took off marching towards my ride with Queen struggling to keep up with me. "Are they okay?!" I blurted into the phone.

Heartbroken, uncontrollable moans answered, "N-no, baby. No, they aren't okay."

————

Instead of the anticipated excitement of hopping on a jet to Jamaica, the reality was a somber flight to Indianapolis. The quick flight felt unbearably long. Queen was a shattered reflection of herself, inconsolable in her grief.

As I sat beside her, the heaviness of loss settled over me like a suffocating blanket. The sudden, profound absence of people that had become an inseparable part of our lives was debilitating. My brother, more than just a partner, was a best friend— the kind you don't replace, that could never be replaced.

The pain was indescribable. A rush of emotions flowed through me like a hurricane of sorrow and regret that threatened to drown out any sign of hope. I would glance over at Queen, watching the uncontrollable flow of tears of the shared agony that gripped us.

Desperation clawed at me as I tried to be the strength Queen needed, but this weight of grief threatened to crush even the strongest, hardest men. I excused myself, slipping into the bathroom, shutting the door behind me.

In the confined space, with the hum of the engines as my only company, I let the tears flow. I allowed my composure to shatter into hopeless pieces. It was a kind of sobbing I'd never experienced before—raw, unfiltered, and born out of the depths of pain that words couldn't describe.

The loss could be heard in each sob, echoing through the small bathroom. It was a desperate, failed attempt to shed the grief that threatened to consume me. I gripped the edge of the sink, my knuckles white, trying to cling to any control I had left.

As we deplaned, I made a desperate wish that Bernadette's old age had twisted reality, that this was all some cruel fiction. The ground beneath me wavered as I took hesitant steps toward a truth I wasn't prepared to confront.

Arriving at the hospital, a knot tightened in my stomach as I approached the medical staff.

One of the nurses spoke gently, as if trying to soften the blow that would inevitably shatter my world. "I'm sorry, Mr. Peterson, but Linda, Frank, and Richard did in fact, pass away. CeCe passed away in the ambulance."

For a moment, I couldn't find my voice. But Queen did, collapsing on the tile floor in tears.

The hope that clung to me like a tattered lifeline shattered, leaving behind an emptiness that nothing would ever be able to fill.

As if denying reality would rewrite the tragic fate life had penned, I murmured, "Nah... This ain't true. It can't be."

33

ANTHONY "BUCK" PETERSON

But it was devastatingly true. Our grim reality sunk in when custody of the kids was given over to us temporarily. Staring at them as they slept in the bed in the hotel suite, it became painfully evident that CeCe and Frank and Linda and Richard were gone.

"I spoke to the Department of Children and Family Services in Indiana and assured them that you all are the next of kin. I wish that I could take them, baby, but I'm too old to handle them." Bernadette was still in tears the next morning as she spoke to me over the phone.

I groaned, pressing the cell phone against my forehead. Animosity boiled over. Part of me blamed her. Had she moved to Chicago like Linda had been asking her to, none of them would have been on the road when that drunk driver hit them head-on as he attempted to run from the police.

With a deep, tired breath, I told her, "All right, Bernadette. I'll let you know about the services once the arrangements are made when we get back to Chicago."

"Thank you, sweetie," she said, sobbing.

"Call me, if you need me."

"Okay."

I hung up with a heavy heart. I looked over at Queen, assuring that she was still sound asleep. She hadn't been able to close her eyes until I purchased some Tylenol PM from the hotel's gift shop.

The responsibility weighed on me heavily as I stared at the kids. A twisted irony settled over me. I had joked with Queen about having kids no matter what. She had been crying for days about not being able to give me a family. Now, we found ourselves with custody of four kids. The reality of the situation hit me like a ton of bricks, and as I gazed at the infants, overwhelming waves of uncertainty washed over me. I didn't know the first thing about taking care of babies.

Thanking God that Najia had emerged unharmed from the accident, my eyes fell on Messiah's tiny face. A scratch across his cheek blemished his innocence. Small cuts and scrapes had been bandaged up on Jah and Shauka. Rage boiled in me at the thought of the drunk driver. I wished that he hadn't met his end in that crash so that I could personally make him pay for the pain he'd inflicted on all of us.

I wasn't prepared for fatherhood to slam into me so suddenly. The reality of caring for these kids overwhelmed me, and doubt crept in. But in my heart, I knew there was no other option. I loved CeCe and Frank more than anything, and I couldn't fathom anyone else raising their legacy. As uncharted as this territory was, my determination to give these kids the life they deserved burned hotter than my grief.

QUEEN ARIA BENSON

I sat on Jah's bed, surrounded by his clothes. My sister, May, was folding a stack of shirts nearby. Her expression mirrored the sorrow drawn into my own.

May was helping me pack up the kids' things. Buck was in CeCe and Frank's room collecting their valuables. Nicole, the nanny, was down the hall tending to the kids. She had been thankfully so supportive. Nicole had been on deck, helping me with kids. Jah had been mute since his parents' death. But he had been unnecessarily strong, trying to help with his sister and brothers. Shauka was confused, not understanding why his parents and grandparents weren't coming back.

Being in their home without CeCe and Frank was a painful reminder of the reality I couldn't accept. The tears flowed down my cheeks as they had been since Buck received that terrifying call. It had been three days since Frank and CeCe were taken from us, and the ache in my heart felt fresh, raw, and relentless.

Frank had been more than a friend to me. He had been a mentor and a guardian angel. He had given me my first real opportunity to make real money, to survive and thrive in a world that offered little to people like us. His absence was a void in my life that no amount of tears or prayers could fill.

Every time I thought of CeCe, my heart ached painfully. She had been more than a friend. I had considered her my sister in every sense of the word. We had shared our hopes, dreams, and struggles, and now she was gone, leaving behind a painful wound on my heart that I knew would never fully heal. I felt lost without her.

I didn't understand how we were supposed to just go on without them.

May sighed heavily as she settled down next to me. She had moved back to Chicago a few months ago, and I thanked God for her presence in these dark times. She had been my rock, never leaving my side since my world fell apart. Oddly, CeCe and Frank's death was bringing me and my sister closer.

"I can't believe they're gone," I mumbled, tasting my salty tears. "It just doesn't feel real."

"I know," May said, regretfully shaking her head. "It's like a nightmare that we can't wake up from." She put a supportive arm around me. "You'll get through this. It's going to get better."

My pleading gaze darted towards her. "When? Because I can't live with this pain. I miss them so much, it hurts. It literally hurts."

Just then, one of the twins' cries traveled from their nursery.

May blew out a heavy breath. "It's terrible that these kids are going to have to grow up without their parents. Poor babies."

My eyes cut at her. "So, poor me?"

May's eyes bulged. "No, I wasn't—"

"I grew up without parents. You think I'm fucked up?!" I turned towards her, locking my rage on her.

"I didn't say that, Queen!" she insisted.

"You think I can't raise them?!"

She gasped. "I never said—"

"You know what? Just get out!" I shouted.

Confused, May slowly stood. Buck appeared in the doorway with the same worry he'd had in his brow for days.

"What's going on?" he asked carefully.

May lifted her hands in surrender, slowly shaking her head with confusion as she inched out of the room. Heaving, I darted up and began to pace.

The closer Buck came to me, the worse my sobs became.

"What's wrong, baby?" He grabbed my waist, forcing my pacing to cease. He turned me around, and as soon as I looked into his eyes, I broke.

"How am I going to raise them when no one raised me?" Sobbing, I buried my face into his chest, submerging my tears in the cotton that smelled of him. I gripped his shirt, holding on for the life I felt like I was losing.

He lovingly wrapped his arms around me, allowing me to lose myself in his mass. "Neither of us had good upbringings, but we're going to figure it out. We had good examples because we watched Frank and CeCe do it."

"I can never be as good of a mother as CeCe," I wept. "I've lost every baby I was supposed to protect. I don't know what I'm doing. I'm not fit for this."

"Yes, you are, baby. You're a mother."

Thinking of the babies I had lost, my sobs became uncontrollable. "No, I'm not."

He gently grabbed my chin and lifted my eyes to his. There

were so many tears that my vision blurred. I could hardly see the sympathy in his eyes.

Yet, I was able to see the lone tear that fell from the corner of his eye. "Yes, you are. You're a mother now. I'm a father of four kids. We don't have a choice. And we're going to honor CeCe and Frank by being great parents to those kids and we're going to keep Cap's legacy going by continuing to run these streets."

A YEAR LATER

34

ANTHONY "BUCK" PETERSON

I stood in the courtroom next to my lawyer. The cuffs bit into my wrists, reminding me of the bullshit I'd gotten myself in. The orange V-neck shirt and pants branded me as a prisoner in the eyes of everyone in the courtroom.

"Mr. Peterson." The judge's voice was so devoid of sympathy, "After careful consideration, I am denying your bail. You will remain in custody until the date of your trial."

The words hit me like a physical blow. A bitter taste filled my mouth. The weight of the shackles on my wrists felt heavier all of a sudden. I could faintly hear the judge and lawyers exchanging legal jargon, but all I could truly hear was the relentless echo of my own self-pity.

Since Frank and CeCe's deaths, my head hadn't been in the game. Their loss had torn a hole in my world, leaving me floating helplessly in a sea of grief and rage. I blamed myself for not being by his side that night where I was supposed to have been. I should have died next to him. With Frank gone, I felt like I was drowning in a storm of emotions, never able to find solid ground.

It wasn't like when I lost Stanley. Back then, I had Frank by my side, guiding me through the darkness, giving me purpose and direction. But now, with Frank gone, the grief and rage were blinding me, clouding my judgment, and leading me to make mistakes.

I hadn't kept my eyes open. An informant I thought was a homie had betrayed us, leading the police straight to our head-quarters. Queen and I had been inside, completely caught off guard. The police arrested us, charging us with multiple gun and drug offenses.

As I listened to the legal jargon being tossed around, failure swallowed me. I had let Frank and CeCe down.

In the last year, the only thing I had managed to do right was raise the kids. It hadn't been easy for Queen and me to fall into the role of parents, but we had learned quickly. I fell in love with watching Queen mother those kids. We had proudly showered them with stability and love amidst the chaos that had engulfed our lives. It had been the one thing I'd done right in the midst of all the darkness.

But now, as a result of my arrest and Queen's, the kids were wards of the state. There was no one else willing or able to take care of them. Eleanor wanted to, but she was fighting stage-three breast cancer and old age. I had even reached out to Tiffany, who just couldn't bring herself to ask her husband to take care of four children, in addition to the three she already had. The thought of the kids being lost in the system, separated and lost, filled me with failure that broke me.

I prayed that Queen would be released on bond, not just for her sake, but for the sake of our kids.

As the bailiffs led me away, I glanced back at her. My heart clenched at the sight of her. Her once vibrant spirit had dimmed. Her eyes glistened with tears that threatened to spill over at any moment. It had only been a day since our arrest, but the toll it had taken on her was already painfully evident. Her usually immaculate appearance was now disheveled, her hair unkempt, and her eyes haunted by loss and despair.

I knew that the tears she shed were not just for herself, but for the kids. Queen had fallen in love with being a mother, pouring her heart and soul into caring for them, and now the wrenching separation from them was tearing her apart.

As our eyes met, I held her gaze, wanting to convey all the love and strength I could muster in that short moment. I mouthed the words "I love you," silently hoping that she would find some comfort, even in the midst of this shit storm.

Then I was led out of the courtroom, leaving Queen behind, and the heavy doors closed behind me with a finality that reflected the uncertainty of the road ahead.

Sitting in the small holding cell, unexpected relief washed over me. For so long, I had carried the weight of a burden that wasn't mine to bear. My head hadn't been in the game. The role I had been thrust into felt like an ill-fitting mask, a facade that I had worn out of duty rather than desire.

I had never wanted to be the boss. That was Frank's calling, his destiny, and his passion. I had only played the role to keep the legacy going, to ensure that the empire he had built would be there for Jah to take over in ten years, when he turned eighteen. I had done it for the sake of the family, for the sake of the future, but it had never been my true ambition.

If I couldn't be Frank's right hand, I didn't want any other position. I didn't crave the power, the influence, or the notoriety.

A short time later, I heard my lawyer's voice echoing

through the corridor. My heart started to race with anticipation, praying for good news. But since we were already fighting previous gun and possession charges, it was hard to hold on to hope. I leaped to my feet and gripped the bars of the cell, my chest tightening with worry.

Soon, Robert appeared, and my heart sank at the sight of Queen's defeated tears as she stood next to him, shackled. The prison issued garments swallowed her.

"I'll give you two some privacy," Robert said solemnly. "But it has to be quick."

Queen rushed to the bars as Robert stepped a few feet away. I mirrored her movements, and our hands reached through the cold metal to touch each other. As our fingers intertwined, I could feel her trembling.

"It's gonna be okay, baby," I tried to reassure her.

"I love you so much," Queen whispered, tears streaming down her cheeks.

Our lips met through the bars desperately. I held her as close as I could, not wanting to let go.

"I love you too more than anything," I said.

"What about the kids?" she cried as she looked desperately into my eyes. "What's going to happen to them?"

Thinking of them caused a sinking feeling to flow violently through my stomach. My shoulders sank under the heaviness of my failures as I admitted, "I don't know."

THE END

Please note: The end of this book was previously written in the story of the Disciple children, Property of a Rich Nigga. So, the deaths of CeCe and Frank and Buck and Queen's arrest was inevitable. Don't be mad at me! :-)

Read the Disciple children's story here:
PROPERTY OF A RICH NIGGA (COMPLETE SERIES)
Property of a Rich Nigga
Property of a Rich Nigga 2
Property of a Rich Nigga 3

Don't miss a release from Jessica N. Watkins! To receive a text message announcing future releases from this author, using your phone, text the keyword "Jessica" to 872-282-0790.

Other Books by Jessica N. Watkins

THE GIRL FROM ENGLEWOOD (STANDALONE)
PROPERTY OF A SAVAGE (STANDALONE)
WHEN MY SOUL MET A THUG (STANDALONE)
SAY MY FUCKING NAME (STANDALONE)
I'LL KISS ALL YOUR WOUNDS (STANDALONE)

A RICH MAN'S WIFE (COMPLETE SERIES)
A Rich Man's Wife
A Rich Man's Wife 2

EVERY LOVE STORY IS BEAUTIFUL, BUT OURS IS HOOD
SERIES (COMPLETE SERIES)

Every Love Story Is Beautiful, But Ours Is Hood
Every Love Story Is Beautiful, But Ours Is Hood 2
Every Love Story Is Beautiful, But Ours Is Hood 3

WHEN THE SIDE NIGGA CATCH FEELINGS SERIES
(COMPLETE SERIES)
When The Side Nigga Catch Feelings
When the Side Nigga Catch Feelings 2

IN TRUE THUG FASHION (COMPLETE SERIES)
In True Thug Fashion 1
In True Thug Fashion 2
In True Thug Fashion 3

SECRETS OF A SIDE BITCH SERIES (COMPLETE SERIES)
Secrets of a Side Bitch
Secrets of a Side Bitch 2
Secrets of a Side Bitch 3
Secrets of a Side Bitch – The Simone Story
Secrets of a Side Bitch 4

A SOUTH SIDE LOVE STORY (COMPLETED SERIES)
A South Side Love Story
A South Side Love Story 2
A South Side Love Story 3
A South Side Love Story 4

CAPONE AND CAPRI SERIES (COMPLETE SERIES)
Capone and Capri
Capone and Capri 2

A THUG'S LOVE SERIES (COMPLETE SERIES)

A Thug's Love
A Thug's Love 2
A Thug's Love 3
A Thug's Love 4
A Thug's Love 5

NIGGAS AIN'T SHIT (COMPLETE SERIES)
Niggas Ain't Shit
Niggas Ain't Shit 2

THE CAUSE AND CURE IS YOU SERIES (PARANORMAL
COMPLETE SERIES)
The Cause and Cure Is You
The Cause and Cure Is You 2

HOUSE IN VIRGINIA (COMPLETE SERIES)
House In Virginia 1
House in Virginia 2

SNOW (COMPLETE SERIES)
SNOW 1
SNOW 2

GET NOTIFIED

Want to be notified when the new, hot Urban Fiction and Interracial Romance books are released? Text the keyword "JWP" to 22828 to receive an email notifying you of new releases, giveaways, announcements, and more!

JESSICA WATKINS PRESENTS IS ACCEPTING SUBMISSIONS

Jessica Watkins Presents is the home of many well-known, best-selling authors in Urban, Interracial, and IR and AA Paranormal Romance. We provide editing services, promotion and marketing, one-on-one consulting with a renowned, national best-selling author, assistance in branding, and more, FREE of charge to you, the author.

We are currently accepting submissions for the following genres: Urban, Interracial, and IR and AA Paranormal Romance. If you are interested in becoming a published author and have a FINISHED manuscript, please send the synopsis, genre and the first three CHAPTERs in a PDF or Word file to jwp.submissions@gmail.com. Complete manuscripts must be at least 45,000 words.

Made in the USA
Columbia, SC
07 February 2025

52755747R00261